Happiness Sold Separately

Please return on or before the latest date above.
You can renew online at *www.kent.gov.uk/libs*
or by telephone 08458 247 200

_____

_____

CUSTOMER SERVICE EXCELLENCE   **Libraries & Archives**

00884\DTP\RN\07.07   LIB 7

Happiness Sold Separately

Lolly Winston

LARGE PRINT

Oxford

First published in Great Britain 2006
by
Hutchinson, one of the publishers in
The Random House Group Ltd.

Published in Large Print 2007 by ISIS Publishing Ltd.,
7 Centremead, Osney Mead, Oxford OX2 0ES
by arrangement with
The Random House Group Ltd.

British Library Cataloguing in Publication Data
Winston, Lolly
    Happiness sold separately. – Large print ed.
    1. Childlessness – Fiction
    2. Adultery – Fiction
    3. Love stories
    4. Large type books
    I. Title
    813.6 [F]

ISBN 978–0–7531–7808–9 (hb)
ISBN 978–0–7531–7809–6 (pb)

Printed and bound in Great Britain by
T. J. International Ltd., Padstow, Cornwall

In memory of Lindy Winston

There is no point in witnessing the destruction of a man who is thoroughly virtuous or who is thoroughly corrupt.

— ARISTOTLE

Love don't make things nice, it ruins everything. It breaks your heart. It makes things a mess. We're not here to make things perfect. Snowflakes are perfect. The stars are perfect. Not us.

— RONNY CAMMARERI, *Moonstruck*
(John Patrick Shanley, screenwriter)

CHAPTER
ONE

Elinor Mackey is cleaning out her purse, trying to lighten her load, wondering how a broken sprinkler head wound up among the contents, when she first learns that her husband, Ted, is having an affair.

As she putters in the warmth of her dimly lit laundry room, she tries to gather the energy to sort more than a hundred work e-mails on her laptop. (*Russian Teens with Tiny Tits!* are stuck in her spam filter. Should she let them out? Do men consider this a *good* thing?) Maybe she'll make spanakopita for her book-club potluck. Yes, everyone should make Greek dishes, since they're reading *The Iliad*. Lately, Elinor's brain wanders like this — like the hand of a child who can't color within the lines, jerking across the page, making the trees blue and the sky brown. She squeezes the sprinkler head, remembering that she had planned on taking it to the hardware store to buy a replacement. This is a trick her father taught her: Take the broken part along, and usually a clerk will help you find a new one and explain how to fix the thing. Elinor picks up the phone to call her friend Kat to tell her about the Greek dinner. Then she hears Ted's voice on the line.

"Gina, *Gina*," Ted whispers.

Elinor holds her breath. She looks up at the boxes of Bold and Cheer on a shelf above the washer.

"I miss you," whoever this Gina is says softly.

Elinor drops the sprinkler head on the floor, stands up, turns off the dryer. *Ted? An affair?*

"What's that noise?" Ted asks.

"I don't hear anything," Gina says.

Or maybe someone's borrowing the phone? It could be that weird phenomenon where you accidentally break in on a stranger's phone conversation. This happened to Elinor once. She started dialing, and the next thing she knew she was listening in on what sounded like a student bargaining with his teacher for a better grade.

"We can't see each other so often," Ted says. It is definitely Ted, talking to a sniffly Gina. Ted, who hates parties and meeting new people! Ted, who sleeps in torn flannel pajama bottoms that have cowboys and Indians on them.

Elinor exhales, tilting her mouth away from the phone, as though blowing out smoke.

"We should talk about this in person, tonight," Gina says. "I get off at six. I want to *cook* for you." She moans the word *cook* as though it's a lascivious act.

"Okay," Ted concedes. Elinor swears she hears dread in his voice.

An *affair*. Elinor waits for jealousy to enrage her. Instead she feels pity. For Ted, for their marriage. And fatigue. It creeps up her spine, pushing her head forward.

2

She hugs her empty purse to her chest. The contents are spread across the dryer. In college, she carried a bag large enough to smuggle a six-pack into a rock concert. Now her big purse holds an expensive leather wallet bulging with charge cards and receipts, a Palm Pilot, reading glasses, a cellular phone, migraine medication, a tube of under-eye concealer touted as "forgiveness in a bottle," and a huge ring of keys, some of them mysterious.

Ted and Gina hang up. Elinor presses the phone to her sternum. Ted, an affair. Their marriage, unraveling.

Run and tell him you need to talk, she tells herself. *Then schedule a session with the marriage counselor.* This is the calm, take-care-of-business sensibility that carried Elinor through college, law school, and fifteen years as an employee relations attorney at various high-tech companies in Silicon Valley. But lately this competence has been replaced by an overwhelming urge to lie down. By an exhaustion that lingers in her bones like a flu.

The malaise seemed to come on after she and Ted stopped trying to have children. They tried for a year on their own with no luck, then succumbed to two years of tests and treatments, including three intrauterine inseminations and two in-vitro fertilizations. Elinor got pregnant once, but she miscarried early on. Still, this gave them the hope to continue. She longed for two boys — she loves boys. Instead she wound up with a diagnosis of "unexplained infertility" — probably due to her age, the doctor explained — twenty extra pounds, and hormone insanity. By the time her fortieth

3

birthday rolled around, she felt like a malfunctioning farm animal that needed to be put down.

"Mind if I go to a testosterone flick?" Ted shouts down the hall, startling Elinor. She realizes she's just standing there, dumbfounded, holding up a stray sock.

"Uh," she says. Sometimes she and Ted go to the movies separately. She likes art-house movies and period films, while Ted prefers shoot-'em-ups. *Confront him about the affair!* The sock trembles in her hand.

"You there?" There's worry in Ted's voice.

"A movie!" Elinor shouts back to him. "Sure. Have fun!" She sounds too enthusiastic, overly cheerful. "Wait," she says more softly. She hears Ted's footsteps as he ambles down the hall and through the kitchen. The garage door rumbles and creaks. *Do something!* She drops the sock and runs down the hallway. *Follow him.* Heading for the garage, she remembers that her car is in the shop. She turns and crashes through the back patio doors and between the bushes to her neighbor friend Kat's house to borrow her minivan.

"I'll explain later," she pants, grabbing the keys from Kat.

"You're barefoot." Kat peers out from under a baseball cap pulled over her short black hair and points to Elinor's feet. Elinor appreciates the lack of judgment in her voice as she states this simple fact. Kat is the least judgmental person she knows.

Elinor catches up with Ted at the stop sign at the end of their street. She snatches Kat's sunglasses from the visor and ducks behind the steering wheel. The car is stuffy with August heat, and she punches on the

4

air-conditioning. *The Lion King* plays on a little TV screen in the back of the van. Elinor can't figure out how to shut the damn thing off. "It's gonna be King Simba's finest fling!" the animals cheer as she jabs at the buttons.

Ted surprises her, turning into the parking lot of their gym. Elinor makes the turn too suddenly, thumping over the curb. A woman waiting on the sidewalk out front waves to Ted. Elinor recognizes her from her own infrequent trips to the club. The woman works there, as a trainer. She's in her early thirties, slim and fit, with long, light brown hair down to her ass — an ass that Elinor envies, small, hard, and round, like an apple. Sometimes the girl wears a coaster-size pin on her tight black T-shirt that says ASK ME ABOUT THE ZONE! Elinor pulls to the back of the lot and watches the trainer climb into Ted's car, tossing her gym bag in back.

Elinor follows them onto the freeway ramp heading south. They turn off a few exits down, then wind through an unfamiliar neighborhood. Ted pulls into a Healthy Oats grocery store and parks. The woman — Gina, this must be Gina — jumps out and does a little leap, as though she's been taken to Tiffany's. As she squeezes Ted's hand in hers, he looks around furtively. *Ted! Holding hands with your fling in broad daylight?* Ted pulls his hand away, but Gina doesn't seem to notice. She bumps up against him as they head into the store. Elinor turns off the minivan and waits. There's a Healthy Oats in her neighborhood, too, but Elinor's only been there a few times, buying chalky protein shakes and balking at the produce prices.

Maybe *this* would explain the flax. About a week ago, when she was fishing for an umbrella, Elinor found a one-pound bag of pungent grain in the backseat of Ted's car. It was from the health food store where they rarely shopped. Upon closer examination, Elinor saw that the mixture was tiny, honey-colored seeds, shiny and slippery through the plastic. Another bag was filled with a fine golden powder. WHOLE GROUND FLAXSEED MEAL.

"What're these for?" she asked Ted, setting the bags on the kitchen counter.

When Ted turned from the sink and saw the bags, he flinched with surprise. His face flushed red.

"It's flax," he stuttered.

"Okay." Elinor laughed. "Didn't mean to pry." Sheesh. He'd reacted as though the bags were porn or cigarettes.

Ted launched into an unnecessarily long explanation of how flaxseeds and flaxseed meal were the healthiest way to get your grains. Flax was rich in fiber, omega-3 fats, and lignans, whatever those were. That's what Dr. Edmunds had said. If you were going to eat carbohydrates, they needed to be complex.

"That sounds good," Elinor replied. "When did you see Dr. E?" Again, she didn't mean to launch a flax inquisition; she was just trying to talk to her husband. They talked so little lately.

"Last week," Ted said.

"While you were at the conference in Monterey?" A podiatrist, Ted had spent all of the previous week at a conference with his podiatry colleagues. But Dr. Edmunds was a GP.

"On the golf course."

Ted hated golf. Usually he managed to get out of it at conferences. Still, maybe he'd started playing again — and eating flax.

"I'll make you some flax pancakes," Ted offered, finally turning off the water and drying his hands.

"Okay," Elinor said. "Flax jacks." Her head hurt.

Now the relentless honking of a car alarm makes Elinor want to drive Kat's minivan through the serene pyramid of apples and strawberries just outside the store. *Call the marriage counselor*, she thinks, *and schedule an appointment for tomorrow*. But her cell phone's at home, with her wallet and shoes. She likes the cocoon of the counselor's sunny office, the Oriental carpets, the shelves of books, the dust motes floating lazily through the air. When she and Ted discussed how infertility had ruined their sex life, the counselor — Dr. Brewster — nodded sympathetically and insisted this was common. When Ted lamented how the treatments made Elinor angry and distant, Dr. Brewster explained that the hormones caused these mood changes. Elinor couldn't help it.

During those early months of procedures and doctor's appointments, Elinor had managed to fight off the hormone horrors. She practiced yoga and visualization, took watercolor classes. She imagined OshKosh overalls and tiny cowboy boots. The lab evaluated the quality of their two embryos during the first in vitro and gave them a grade A, the best you can hope for. Elinor wanted a bumper sticker: MY EMBRYOS ARE GRADE A AT STANFORD HOSPITAL! But that cycle didn't work.

"Something's wrong with me," Elinor insisted.

"It's not *your* fault," Ted replied, taking her into his arms. "I love you. Let's take a break from all this. Let's go to Paris."

Elinor pushed him away. "*Non, merci,*" she said glumly.

During the second in vitro, somewhere around the twentieth injection Ted gave Elinor, the hormones engulfed her. She slammed doors and snapped at him. Everything was his fault. Raining? Flat tire? Tedious meeting at work? Chalk it up to Ted.

One morning Elinor tried to smash a home pregnancy test stick with a hammer, a task that's impossible, it turns out. She whispered to the stick, *Just give me the second. Pink. Line.* Setting the stick on a paper towel, she washed her hands, then closed her eyes. She opened them. Nothing. Then she flew to the utility room, yanked the hammer out of the toolbox, returned to the bathroom, and smashed the stick. Or tried to. One swift hit did nothing. The second blow chipped the sink, but barely dented the stick. She became a whirling storm of rage and sobs and repeated strikes with the hammer. Her face burned, and she saw a silvery strand of drool hanging from her mouth. Finally, she collapsed on the floor cross-legged, cradling the hammer. Ted pushed open the door. He gaped at

Elinor on the floor as though she were a stranger on the street you'd definitely want to steer clear of. She'd never felt so unattractive. It was then that the fatigue draped her, as heavy as an X-ray smock.

The marriage counselor encouraged Ted and Elinor to take a break from the treatments: go on vacation, go out to dinner, get massages. They were supposed to take a break *together*, but Elinor has really been taking a break on her own, recoiling from Ted, retreating from the fury, into the laundry room. It's comforting to wash and fold clothes — a task that's easy to complete. She runs small, unnecessary loads, just to be lulled by the sound of the dryer. She especially likes the clinking of buttons and zippers — a metal-against-metal metronome that brings calm as she stares into the blue screen of her laptop, never actually doing any work. As her energy has waned, she's quit separating loads by color. Now all of their clothes are a purplish gray reminiscent of bad weather. Ted doesn't seem to notice. He's always grateful, never picky. "Let me help you," he'll insist whenever he finds Elinor in the laundry room. "You shouldn't be doing this."

"Why *not?*" Elinor will ask defensively. How did she get to a place where it's weird to wash her own underwear?

Ted brings flowers, fixes pots of homemade soup. Elinor doesn't thank him enough. Their sex life has faded to nil. Sex only leads to disappointment. Elinor obsessively does the laundry and reads novels, burrowing back into the comforting familiarity of the classics she read in college — *Anna Karenina, The Age*

9

of Innocence. Meanwhile Ted obsessively works out at the gym. Or so Elinor has thought.

What's taking Ted and Gina-from-the-Gym so long? Are they in there kissing by the bulgur bin? SUVs clog the store parking lot, everyone shopping for dinner. Elinor's not sure what she'll do when they come out of the store. She tries to muster rage. *Anorexic juicehead bitch!*

Finally, Ted and Gina emerge, each hugging a bag of groceries. Paper, not plastic. For the first time, Elinor sees how much weight Ted has lost. He mentioned the fifteen pounds before, but now she notices how his pants hang at his waist. Her husband is aging-high-school-football-star handsome — stocky, with a broad chest, sloped shoulders, boyish face, endearing crow's-feet. Gina smiles up at Ted and blows a strand of light brown hair from her face. Elinor realizes that she has not let go of the steering wheel the whole time these two were in the store. She grips it as though turning into a sharp curve. Gina's black leggings outline firm calves and a circle of tanned skin above her white ankle socks. Elinor reaches in for the anger, tries to coax it. *Hey, Sandy Duncan! Put some fucking pants on!* For a moment she imagines a public scene, Ted's worst nightmare. Anything to avoid a scene. *Ted, you jackass!* she could scream across the parking lot. But that would only bring them both humiliation.

Elinor follows Ted and Gina through the winding streets of a strange neighborhood. Ted seems familiar with the route. He and Gina don't appear to talk on the way. She gazes out her window and Ted looks straight ahead, never checking his rearview mirror. Elinor manages to mute *The Lion King*, but the animals flicker on the back windows of the minivan. "Did I mention that I'm mortified by this car?" Kat, a stay-at-home mom, asks Elinor on a daily basis. The two became fast friends when they discovered that they share a dry sense of humor, and they're both former English majors who partied a little too much in college. Elinor thinks of Kat as her road not taken — the mother of three boys who love to play touch football with her in the front yard. Kat says Elinor is *her* road not taken — a successful lawyer whose husband beams when he talks about how good Elinor is at her job. Of course, most of their friends pull off both the well-paying career *and* the terrific kids. But Kat and Elinor have confessed to each other that they've never felt capable of both.

Finally, Ted pulls into a town-house complex. Elinor wonders what to do next. Until recently, she's been an ace problem solver — settling compensation disputes, fending off litigation, handling difficult employees. One employee who hadn't been taking his meds insisted that the CFO was talking to him through his car radio. Another woman tried to claim her wedding cake in her expense report. Now Elinor wants an easy solution to the Gina Problem. She imagines busting out a whiteboard in their living room at home, Ted sitting before her on the sofa. *Gina,* she'd write on the whiteboard, breathing in the chemical smell of the erasable marker. Then she'd draw an X through the name.

She drives past Ted and Gina as they park, observes which unit they hurry into, then pulls into visitor parking. The gravel walkway is cold and sharp under her bare feet. The whips of a sprinkler sting her calves as she makes her way between buildings to Gina's backyard.

Hunkering behind a low row of newly planted poplars, she peers out over the deck and through the sliding-glass doors, hoping Gina won't draw the curtains. The condo is a split-level deal with a combination kitchen/living room/dining room on the first floor. Ted sits at the kitchen table, drumming his fingers. Gina bounces down the stairs in a short kimono robe, wet hair slicked back. No makeup, no blow dryer necessary. Long sleek legs. Elinor runs a hand over the pooch of her belly.

Gina gets to work chopping vegetables. As she tosses them into a wok, a huge cloud of steam billows toward the ceiling. She speaks as she cooks, nodding her head with determination, then shaking it with uncertainty, then wiping her cheeks and nose with the sleeves of her robe. An argument? Ted looks glum. Elinor can tell by his posture. Shoulders curling toward his chest. *He doesn't love you, Gina!* Elinor tells the poplars. Surely they are about to break up. But then Ted gets up from the table and ambles up behind Gina. He pulls her away from the stove, his arms circling her waist, his hands sliding up under the V of her robe and across her breasts. Gina closes her eyes and tips her head back against his chest. Ted kisses her neck, kisses her shoulders, and the robe falls away. Then *they* fall away, onto the kitchen floor, where Elinor can't see them anymore. Making love on the kitchen floor while the wok blows steam at the ceiling. The special effects affairs are made of.

Elinor covers her face with her hands and falls to her knees. The mud beneath the grass seeps through her jeans with a disturbing sucking noise. She wants to go back, to erase the past two years. It seems that the spam filter for their *life* has broken, and all kinds of junk is pouring through: painful medical procedures, negative test results, sleepless nights, and now this bimbo in leotards.

The next day, Elinor finds a book tucked under layers of under-shirts in Ted's drawer while putting away the laundry. *Live Healthy in the Zone*. Inside the paperback, there's a date and an inscription: *Dear Ted, Congratulations on reaching your goal! I knew you could do it. Here's a reminder of some of your favorite dishes. Love, Gina.*

Elinor flips through the pages, which are smudged with ingredients. Corners are turned over and hearts are drawn beside some recipes. The hearts seem to be a grading system, like stars for rating movies. "Soybean Croquettes" gets only one heart, while "Rainbow Vegetable Sauté" is worthy of three. "Creamed Tomato Soup with Cognac" gets four and a half.

The night she finds the cookbook, Elinor fixes Lean Cuisines for dinner. Rushed and tired, she and Ted often resort to frozen foods, grilled cheese, or scrambled eggs.

"These things are mostly carbs," Ted says, poking his fork at the too-bright green beans. He pushes away the dinner. "I'm trying to cut carbs. Stick to complex carbs, anyway."

"Oh? Since when?" Elinor asks. *Why don't you cook us a Zone dinner!* she wants to holler. "Since *when?*" she repeats. The anger hisses and clanks, like the radiators in an old house when you turn on the heat on the first cool day in the fall. A slight burning smell. The house trembling and creaking all over.

Ted shrugs at his little black tray of pasta and beans. "Dunno."

"I think you *know.*" The inscription in the cookbook was dated June 1. He and Gina have been having their low-carb trysts for at least two months.

Ted cocks his head and frowns.

"I know . . ." She wants to say *I know about Gina. I know about the affair*, but suddenly she has the uncontrollable urge to flip the table over on Ted. She presses her palms against her thighs to stop her legs from shaking; she pictures herself becoming less and less attractive in Ted's eyes as she rants and raves and threatens and forbids. She cannot find the means to confront her husband with the firmness, grace, and composure she had hoped for.

Finally, she gets up from the table, carries her unfinished dinner to the sink, and stuffs it down the disposal. "Sometimes," she says, unable to look at her husband, "I find complex carbohydrates a little *too* complex."

★ ★ ★

14

Elinor awakens the next morning to the shrill whine of a table saw. It's Saturday, but Ted is up already, out in the garage working on the cherry hutch he's building from a kit. Save for the hours he's fled to the gym, he's been holed up in the garage working on this project for weeks. They do not need a cherry hutch. But the buzz of the power tools and the pages of detailed directions seem to soothe his nerves. "Perhaps this makes Ted feel as though he's able to fix something," Dr. Brewster gently suggested during their last session. Elinor kvetched about Ted only caring about the hutch. She knew this was an odd complaint, since all *she* seemed to care about was the laundry. But when Ted quit trying to make Elinor feel better and retreated to the hutch and the gym, she began to miss him — to realize that she'd been taking him for granted. She wondered what kind of madness would make her irritated by her husband when he was attentive, and then resentful when he stepped back to give her room.

Now she lies in bed, clammy from a restless night's sleep. Her reading glasses and her heavy copy of *The Iliad* are tangled in the covers. She fell asleep reading again. While she found *The Iliad* impenetrably boring in college, now she likes escaping into the bloody tragic mess. She's rooting for handsome Hector, who's stuck in a war simply because his cocky brother fell for a beautiful girl who wasn't his.

Elinor composes a Saturday-morning to-do list in her head. *1. Get rid of husband's lover.* She will deal with Gina herself. Forget the counselor, forget confronting Ted. She'll go straight to the source of the problem. This is what she does at work. Call in the perpetrator and lay the cards on the table. She doesn't want this Gina problem to be overly complicated, to be dramatic. She's had enough drama in the past two years. She rehearses what she might say to the girl: *I know you're sleeping with my husband. Please stop. He and I have had our troubles but we're going be fine . . .* No — Elinor certainly doesn't owe Gina any explanation of her marriage.

She gets up, brushes her teeth, then sits on the edge of the bed, squeezing the cordless phone. Finally, she dials information and is connected to the gym. A woman's voice breaks into the Muzak on the line. Elinor asks to make an appointment for a fitness consultation with Gina. The woman cheerfully announces that Gina has a cancellation in an hour, which is *really lucky*, because Gina's very popular.

"Oh, I *know*." Elinor has the urge to smoke, something she hasn't done since college. "Sign me up!" She tries to sound cheerful. She looks anxiously into her closet. What should she *wear* for this encounter? She's never mastered the breezy casualness of gym attire. Most women in her suburban town dash from their workouts to the grocery store in stylish velour sweats with matching hooded tops, somehow looking trim without ever seeming to perspire. But Elinor always feels dumpy.

She showers and chooses jeans, a white V-neck sweater that shows off her tan from working in the yard, and red high-tops, which she hopes convey that she has the self-confidence not to care about trends. She wore

16

Converse high-tops all through high school. Petite and funny, Elinor was voted "cutest" in her yearbook, a title she secretly loathed. She didn't want to be cute. She wanted to be beautiful. But her blond hair, upturned nose, little Chiclet teeth, and apple cheeks would never be deemed movie-star sexy. In the 1980s, she tried to shed any hint of cuteness by spiking her hair and donning rubber bracelets and torn sweatshirts. Now when she sees photos of herself during this era, she has to laugh. It looks like she's wearing a Halloween costume. By the time she entered the corporate world, she succumbed to slacks and flats and a tidy French braid.

Hurrying through the kitchen, Elinor spies Ted's bag of flaxseeds on the counter. He's been spooning out two level tablespoons every morning and sprinkling them on his fruit and plain yogurt. She slides the bag off the counter into her purse. Maybe she'll return it to Gina. *You left your damn flax in my husband's car.*

Elinor glances at her day planner as she picks up her keys. Twelve noon is circled with pink highlighter. In an *hour* she's due to have lunch with Phil, the CEO at her company, to discuss the details of a merger. Phil wants to outsource the employee relations part of the merger to an outside law firm, a blow to Elinor's impeccable track record of keeping everything in house, thereby saving the company money. But Phil has grown wary of Elinor's absences and missteps, which got worse as her infertility appointments wore on. Elinor's afraid she's about to be demoted or let go or God knows what. This

17

luncheon is Step 1 of her Corporate Comeback. The venue for the *I'm-your-man* speech.

For what? Who cares? She's tired of always working nights and weekends because she doesn't have children. She grabs the phone and dials the CEO's admin, who's always strapped to her desk on weekends.

"Food poisoning," Elinor says.

"He canceled his *golf* game to meet you," the admin admonishes. Being sick is never an excuse for missing meetings at Elinor's company. You're supposed to show up in a medicated haze and breathe germs on your colleagues.

"I'm vomiting." She wishes this were the case, rather than *my husband's having an affair*.

"Dry toast," the admin replies coolly.

"Right." Elinor clutches her car keys, snaps her bag shut. The heft of it tugs at her shoulder as she heads out the door.

She waves to Ted as she backs out of the driveway. He looks up from his table saw and waves back, smiles — a flash of white teeth and faint dimples. Elinor closes her eyes for a moment and imagines his smell — sawdust and Mountain Spring deodorant — and wishes they could lie side by side on their comforter for the rest of the day. Stripped of passion. Down to just love.

More than anything, Elinor loves her husband's face. A big, handsome Irish face. Boyish, yet slightly jowly with age. Pools of brown chocolate for eyes. Thick lustrous hair she'd clutch and hang on to when they made love. She hates her husband and loves his face

18

and hates herself and . . . thump, *thump*, she backs over the curb at the end of the driveway. Ted looks up, waves his hand for her to steer to the left, smiles. She waves back, pausing under the shade of the big oak tree in their front yard.

After the second in vitro, Elinor would lie under the tree, trying to calm herself. It was hot that spring. In the evenings after work she'd drag an old sleeping bag outside and take refuge on the cool grass, reading and dozing. Ted would join her, grabbing a beach chair from the garage. "Can I get you anything?" he kept asking Elinor. He'd nervously tap his palm against the arm of the aluminum chair, his wedding ring making a little clinking noise that made Elinor want to scream. She felt bad for being so irritated. What was *wrong* with her?

Now, as she heads for the gym, Elinor flips down the visor to look in the mirror. She runs her fingers through her shoulder-length hair, which she's decided to wear down for once. As soon as she gets rid of her husband's girlfriend she's going to get a new haircut. Maybe whiten her teeth. She snaps the visor back into place. Today Gina's going to evaluate Elinor's health and fitness needs and develop a workout plan for her, the receptionist who scheduled the appointment explained. Gina and Elinor will work together to accomplish these goals. Except that Gina's goal is to sleep with Ted, and Elinor's goal is to make Gina go away.

Gina meets Elinor in the lobby at the club. She doesn't seem to know who Elinor is. A blank-yet-pleased expression passes over Gina's face as they shake

19

hands. Is Elinor as unrecognizable as all of the other drooping, middle-aged women at the gym? Gina's fingers are long and thin. She's wearing black warm-up pants and a collared shirt. Her long, light brown hair is pulled into a high ponytail, with bangs that fall into her eyes. She's lithe, buff, but not exactly beautiful. Her face is a bit flat and her eyes set far apart, reminding Elinor of a flounder. These cheekbones certainly wouldn't break a man's heart.

They sit at a table in the snack bar. Gina asks a list of questions, filling in the answers in small, square handwriting. She is all energy and spunk. Nimble fingers, spry ovaries. Beautiful eggs. A group of retired men share a pitcher of beer at a table next to theirs, even though it's not even noon. This is the quirky thing Elinor loves about their gym: The snack bar serves brownies and beer alongside the smoothies and salads. Elinor would like to join the gentlemen. Give in to gravity and Father Time.

"Age?" Gina asks. Her lips shimmer with rosy gloss.

"Thirty-nine," Elinor lies. While she had no problem *turning* forty, she does have a problem *saying* forty, especially in the company of Gen-X fitness Nazis who are romancing her husband. "The real problem may be your age," the doctor had gently explained when Elinor first couldn't conceive. While she hadn't looked forward to turning forty, she never thought her birthday would constitute a medical emergency.

"Really? You look *great*," Gina says without looking up.

I lost my ass, Elinor wants to say, as though it might actually be here at the gym's lost-and-found. She wishes for a moment she were consulting a fitness expert for real. It's a shallow, vain thing to fret about, but what she hates most about aging is the southern migration of her buttocks after two decades of sitting on her duff for corporate America. Somewhere along the way she lost her figure — the small-framed size 4 build she'd had all her life. Then the infertility treatments made her belly bloat, like an overripe melon. Elinor doesn't mind the two coppery age spots forming on her hands, or the crow's-feet crinkling at the corners of her eyes, but she wants her body back.

Gina says she's going to weigh Elinor and give her a stress test and body fat analysis after they finish the paperwork. Then she'll recommend classes, such as spinning *and yoga!*

The flax in Elinor's purse on her lap is heavy in a comforting way, like a cat curled up there. She'd been all riled up driving here, but now she can't think of a single thing to say to Gina. She's too tired. She figures she hasn't had a good night's sleep in about two years. While she can barely keep her eyes open during office meetings and conference calls, she lies awake at two AM cataloging a dizzying inventory of worries: donor eggs, adoption (foreign or domestic?), mounting medical bills and insurance forms.

"What would you say your overall fitness goal is?" Gina asks.

Once, while walking on the beach in Hawaii, Elinor saw a woman fishing. At first she thought the woman was a man. But when she reached the fisherman, she realized he was a woman, with beautiful white hair cropped short and blown back in the wind. The woman wore khaki shorts and a black T-shirt, and her legs were muscular and tan. She was solid and as beautiful as the scenery. Yet she was sort of genderless — not really feminine or masculine, just a person, smiling up into the sun, the ocean a sparkling carpet before her. Just fishing. She looked at peace. Not worrying anymore about crow's-feet or how her rump would look in a tankini. Elinor wants to tell Gina that this is her fitness goal.

Gina leans across the table and looks at Elinor intently. Her wide-set eyes are green and almond-shaped and her skin is flawless. The bangs-falling-into-the-eyelashes look is definitely sexy.

"To lose fifteen pounds," Elinor says. "And firm up my . . ." *everything*, Elinor wants to say. But she doesn't want to admit this to her husband's lover. She clears her throat. "To firm up my butt. I don't get to the gym much. I'm too busy." *I am successful*, she wants to tell Gina. *Okay, maybe not at the things that matter now. But at the things that mattered before. Did you know, if you live in Holland and your pipes freeze, you legally get the day off with pay?* Elinor is a fountain of knowledge when it comes to international employee relations law.

"First thing?" Gina says. "If you'll let me? I'm going to come to your house and clean out your cupboards."

Elinor laughs. "And mop the floors?"

"I'm going to purge your *carbs*," she says firmly. "Your pastas, breads, and cereals?"

"Cereal?" Elinor asks.

"Cereal is the worst!"

"Uh . . ." *You're taking my husband and my Frosted Mini-Wheats?* Elinor considers this unlikely scenario: Gina, at Elinor and Ted's house, cleaning out the cupboards. Gina and Ted sweating under the bright lights in the kitchen. The whole thing out in the open. Remorse. An apology. More important: an agreement. Gina will never come near them again. "Okay," Elinor finally tells Gina. "But it'll have to be in the evening. I work during the day."

"Sure," Gina says.

"My husband will be there. Is that okay? He wants to cut carbs, too. Well, he *already* is. He started without me." Elinor hates the bitterness in her voice. Maybe after they give Gina the boot, Elinor and Ted can take a trip to a tropical resort. Eat steamed fish and brown rice and soak in a tub for two. Run on the beach and have sex on the marble bathroom floor of a luxury hotel room. Elinor will catch up with Ted. Lust and exercise. They don't sound bad at all.

"Great," Gina says. "I can fuck both of you." But Elinor is sure she said help. I can *help* both of you.

As Elinor sprinkles tarragon over three chicken breasts, she feels the need to prove to her husband and his lover that she *can* cook. Gina is due to arrive at their house in forty-five minutes. Elinor's fixing a low-fat, low-carb dinner — broiled seasoned chicken breasts, zucchini

23

split and stuffed with ricotta cheese and chopped mushrooms and onions, butter lettuce salad sprinkled with the ubiquitous flaxseeds, and fresh berries for dessert with just a dollop of whipping cream. She begins setting the kitchen table for three.

Ted turns the channel on the little TV in the kitchen to a *Nova* show about coal. "Too fine to use in the steel-smelting process, the coke is sold for heating and cooking on small stoves," the narrator says.

"What do you know?" Ted says. He's mostly interested in factual things. Details that don't require you to form an opinion.

"How come three?" he asks, looking at the place mats.

"A gal who might join my book club is coming over." Elinor sets out the napkins and silverware. Soon this will be a part of the past. They'll get their lives back.

Ted regards the TV.

Elinor sprinkles more thyme and tarragon on the chicken breasts, worrying that they're going to taste bland — as bland as sex became with Ted before they quit making love altogether. She wonders if Jerry Hall's mother ever really uttered those infamous words: "In order to keep a man you must be a maid in the living room, a cook in the kitchen, and a whore in the bedroom." Gina's a whore in the kitchen. Innovative, Elinor will give her that. Meanwhile, Elinor's become a lump in every room: in the bedroom, in the kitchen. Maybe because she had to become a numb lump on the doctor's examining table to ward off the pain of all those procedures. "Just a little pressure," the doctor would say. Why couldn't they use the *real* P-word? *Pain. This might hurt.* Instead there were euphemisms: pressure, a pinch. Once, when Elinor had an outpatient procedure to remove cysts on her ovaries from the drugs, they let Ted accompany her. "Squeeze my hand," he whispered sweetly. Elinor grimaced, a flame of pain shooting toward her hip. Ted's hand was solid and warm, the only comforting thing on the planet.

The doorbell rings. Elinor drops a tin of white pepper clanging to the floor. She wipes her hands and heads into the hallway. Before opening the door, she pulls her apron over her head. Too suburban and matronly.

Gina stands on the porch wearing a long tie-dyed skirt, a tiny white T-shirt, and leather thong sandals. A strip of her flat tan belly peeks out above the skirt's low-cut waistline. Elinor would like to slam the door.

"Come in," she tells Gina.

Ted turns off the TV and saunters into the hall, being the polite husband. His head jerks back when he sees Gina. Gina's eyes pop open, but then she narrows them, redirecting her alarm into a smile, her expression making a U-turn.

"Gina, this is my husband, Ted," Elinor tells her.

Ted limply shakes Gina's hand. "Nice to meet you." He opens the coat closet door. "May I take your coat?"

Suddenly Elinor's embarrassed by the coat closet. It's jammed full of junk, much of it a testament to her athletic failures. The tangled jump rope, the dusty hiking boots, the too-small ski suit.

"She doesn't *have* a coat," Elinor tells Ted. Still, Ted lingers with his head in the closet, as though he'd like to dive in.

"Can I get you a drink?" Elinor asks Gina.

"Do you have tomato juice?" Gina asks. Bracelets tinkle on her wrists.

Ted closes the closet door. He and Gina are busy not making eye contact. So far, Elinor would give them an A-minus on this not-knowing-each-other thing.

"No tomato juice," she tells Gina. "Diet Coke?"

"Oh, artificial sweeteners," she says. "That's one of the things we're going to have to purge." Clearly she's trying to be firm, but nervousness bubbles under her sentences.

You're one of the things we're going to have to purge, Elinor thinks as she motions Gina into the kitchen.

"Hey, I recognize you," Ted finally says to Gina. "From the club." Perspiration darkens his armpits.

"Yeah." Gina cocks her head and squints her eyes. "You work out a lot."

Gina places a little food scale and a spiral notebook on the kitchen counter. Elinor hands her a glass of orange juice. If orange juice has any evils, she doesn't want to hear about them.

"You get to have artificial sweeteners on Weight Watchers," she tells Gina while looking at Ted accusingly. "What's the deal with *that*?" Her jaw hurts. Now that she's found anger again, she wishes she could reel it in. Her hatred for the fickle diet gurus. Her loathing of the world.

26

"Well, ladies," Ted says. "I have some work —"

"I was hoping the three of us could eat dinner together," Elinor tells him. "Talk about things."

Ted freezes in the doorway.

"Oh, I can't stay for dinner." Gina places her untouched juice on the counter.

"Really? But you two *like* to eat together," Elinor says. Suddenly she's dizzy from the intensity of this encounter. She wants to sit on the floor. Call this crazy intervention off.

Ted rests a hand on the doorjamb, turns halfway toward Elinor and Gina.

Gina giggles nervously. "*What?*"

"Sleep together? Eat together? All that good stuff." Elinor pulls the Zone cookbook from its hiding place in the bread drawer (Ted would never look there!) and waves it at them.

"Elinor," Ted says. He faces Elinor with his back to Gina, his eyes pleading. Suddenly he looks old — slim from his newfound athleticism, but in a gray, gaunt way, not in a rosy, happy way.

"Ted," Elinor says.

Please, his eyes say. *I'm sorry*, and *please*.

"I better go." Gina picks up her food scale and notebook.

Elinor looks at Gina's impossibly small waist, remembers how easily Ted crossed the room in Gina's condo, how quickly his hands slipped up under her flimsy robe to touch her breasts. *He* made the first move. Suddenly she can't stand being in the kitchen with these two. She can't stand being in her own house.

27

For the past few days Elinor fantasized about going away with Ted to Hawaii — skinny-dipping and stargazing and oversleeping. She even surfed the Web and chose a resort on the Big Island, sighing at the thought of the last time they visited the Kona Coast and left blissfully worn out from too much sun, sex, and rum. Yet now she wants to go away by herself. Leave these two with the carbohydrate charts and bland chicken breasts. Maybe before you can fix something, you have to let it break completely.

"I have to go," she tells Gina. She opens the cupboard, yanks out the bags of flaxseed and flax meal, and shoves them into Gina's arms. Gina flinches as though Elinor's going to deck her, then looks curiously at the bags.

"Flax at it!" Elinor races up the stairs to pack. Just like in the movies. There is something liberating about being the first one to leave in a situation like this — sort of like being the first one up in the morning or the first one to dive into a cold swimming pool. What does she need? A few work outfits, hose, shoes, comfy pajamas, slippers, toilet articles, bubble bath, magazines, *The Iliad*. She folds the things into her little black suitcase. She's a pro at packing quickly for emergency business trips. She'll drive to the Fairmont downtown. Order room service. Pancakes with real maple syrup.

Elinor nearly crashes into Ted on her way down the stairs. She lunges past him for the front door, her legs and knees suddenly rubbery at the sight of him.

Ted reaches for her bag, trying to stop her. "Don't leave," he says. Gina appears to be gone.

Elinor turns to look at her husband. He's as tired as she is. She can see that. Many nights when she thought he was sleeping and he thought she was sleeping, neither one of them was. They'd discover this in the morning as they tripped over each other in the kitchen. Instead of watching the indifferent blue numbers on her clock radio click toward dawn, Elinor wanted to roll over and hold Ted, talk to him. But despite her inability to sleep, or maybe because of it, she was too exhausted to move.

"She's gone," Ted says now. "Listen, I *know* we can work this out."

Elinor squeezes the handle on her suitcase and tugs it past Ted.

"I love you," Ted says, his voice rising with desperation.

I love you, too, Elinor thinks. *I did. I do. But that's beside the point! Isn't it?*

"What are you going to do?" Ted asks as Elinor opens the door.

"What am I going to *do*, Ted?" She pictures him unbuckling his pants and sinking to Gina's kitchen floor. "What am I going to *do*? I'm going to call the Dalai Lama. Do you think he's listed under *D* or *L*? I'm going to lie on my yoga mat and rub soy milk in my third eye, and weave baskets out of turkey bacon. I'm going to spend a week in the *Zone*."

Ted steps toward Elinor. Elinor backs away from him out onto the front porch. Maybe she'll finally get a good night's sleep at the Fairmont. She looks away from her husband toward her car in the driveway. She closes her eyes for a moment and imagines sliding between crisp white hotel sheets. What do they use to make them so *clean*? That crisp white cleanness of starting over. Starch? Whatever it is, it seems less pedestrian than starch. More otherworldly.

She opens her eyes. Ted hovers in the hall, not wanting to step over the threshold. He doesn't like to leave the house in his bare feet. Not even to retrieve the newspaper from the driveway.

"Excuse me." Elinor reaches around Ted for the door handle. She wants the satisfaction of closing the door behind her. As she pulls it shut with a *thump* and a *click*, the image of Ted's drawn face disappears. Good-bye, then. She steps off the porch. But then she stops halfway down the driveway to her car. Life is never like it is in the movies. Not her life anyway, because she has left her car keys inside, on the kitchen counter. She takes a deep breath of cool, moist air and tries to gather the gumption to walk back in. Then she remembers her hide-a-key. A few years ago, when she slid the thin, magnetic box under the driver's side of her new car, she wondered if she'd ever lock herself out. She tried to picture such a scenario: rushing in the parking lot at work, or spacing out while loading groceries. She never would have imagined this night.

She continues down the dark driveway, halting again when a shooting star streaks across the horizon, just above the trees. It's big and bright, followed by a greenish tail. The Perseids. The meteor shower is marked on Elinor's calendar so that she and Ted can make their annual trek to the backyard, with lawn chairs and blankets. "I saw one!" they usually shout to each other, almost competitively. Last summer she wished on every meteor for a baby. Although she's not a superstitious person, Elinor has always taken wishes seriously. As a kid she would hover over her birthday cake candles until islands of wax pooled in the frosting. While trying to get pregnant, she wished on everything from found pennies to stray eyelashes. Now Elinor tips her head to look up at the sky. According to the newspaper, tonight there will be up to 150 meteors per minute. The next neon green streak makes Elinor gasp. She squeezes her eyes shut. For the first time, she's not sure what to wish for.

CHAPTER
TWO

The affair is *over*. As Ted drives to work on a hot August morning — a thirty-minute, second-to-third-gear rush-hour crawl to his podiatry practice in Menlo Park — he exhales, letting out breath it seems he's been holding for weeks.

Last night, after Elinor ran upstairs, Ted told Gina they could never see each other again. Gina nodded and headed for the door. There was pride in her posture — shoulders pulled back, chin pointed forward, cookbooks tucked firmly under one arm. As she brushed past Ted in the hall, he caught the earthy-sweet smell of her China Rain perfume. But then, when Elinor came downstairs, *she* left, too, the door shutting with a gentle yet final click for the second time that evening. Standing alone in the empty house, Ted felt a surge of self-loathing. He couldn't blame his wife for leaving, and felt certain that now his lover would be better off.

He waited an hour, then called Elinor on her cell phone. She had checked into the Fairmont downtown. "El," he pleaded. "It's over with her. Please come home. I love you. I'm so sorry. Let's start over. Let's go back to the counselor — to Dr.

Brewster." Maybe he's a snob, but Ted resents calling these PhDs *doctor*, especially since they seem to have so little to offer in the way of a remedy.

"I took a bath," Elinor said. "The water here is *really* hot." She sounded like a kid. "And the tub is huge." She bit into something crunchy. While doing the infertility treatments, El hadn't been allowed to take baths. She said she was forbidden to have the two things that comforted her most — a hot bath and a big glass of wine. Ted was hurt that he wasn't one of the two things. "I love this robe," Elinor continued. "Everything is so *clean* in hotels." There was a manic calmness in her voice that made Ted nervous. *Yell at me!* he thought.

"I could get the house professionally cleaned," he offered. "One of those deep cleaning deals." He pounded his fist into the counter. For the past six months he'd been at a total loss for what to say to his wife. They used to finish each other's sentences and laugh at each other's jokes. Now every word Ted uttered seemed to make Elinor flinch or frown.

Elinor explained that she needed time to herself. A break from her life. Of course this meant a break from Ted, the philanderer, the *adulterer*.

"You don't have to come home, then," he said. "We can go away together. How 'bout to Bermuda?" Elinor had loved it there. She said the sand was pink. Color-blind, Ted struggled to imagine this.

"Maybe," El said. Her indifference was eerie.

Now Ted queues up to go through the metering lights onto the freeway. It's a stifling yet cloudy day, the sky the dull gray color of car primer. He pops the lid off his yogurt and eats with a plastic spoon. This is one of the few carbs he allows himself a day. The affair is over, but he's going to stick to Gina's healthy regimen. She helped him get onto the Zone Diet and actually do that triathlon, which made him feel healthier than he had in years. Now he's determined to keep off the fifteen pounds. For the past two months, he's experienced an odd paradox of feeling fit and healthy and like hell at the same time. The result of a steady diet of turkey bacon, and sex with the wrong person. He will have to find another gym.

During the three months that the affair went on, Ted broke up with Gina several times in his head. He practiced his breakup speech in the shower and on his way to work: *You're a wonderful woman*, he would tell her, imagining a safe distance across a restaurant table, *but I love my wife. I know you'll meet somebody else. Not an old fart like me.* Ted was forty-five and working on a breakup speech. What an asshole. A fool and a liar and a cheat. How hard could it be to say, *No, I'm married?*

Yet Gina seemed drawn to Ted *because* he was married. "You're a grown-up," she'd murmur wistfully. This was in contrast to her former boyfriends, the "bad boys" who got DUIs or lost their jobs. Even though Gina rolled her eyes when she mentioned these guys, the thought of them made a flare of jealousy burn in Ted's chest.

Ted shifts into third gear, which is liberating, if only for a moment. Although she was a health nut, Gina said you needed *some* fat in your diet. Once, she fixed Ted fried eggs and thick slabs of nitrate-free bacon in a cast-iron skillet. The smell made Ted wish for snow and a remote cabin, for sticky sex under flannel sheets. Gina occasionally smoked pot, too, an activity that was accompanied by a mini-diatribe about how alcohol is actually *much* worse for you.

They'd had sex in crazy places — in their cars, at the park, buried under blankets from Gina's trunk. Gina carried a wad of bedding in her car that she referred to as a *bed-in-a-bag*. She had assembled it the last time the country went on Orange Alert, and the newspaper listed items you were supposed to stockpile, including water, batteries, and flashlights, plus snacks and blankets in your car, in case you had to relocate instantaneously or got stranded while on the road. Or in case you needed to screw in the park under an old sleeping bag that smelled like a campfire. That time under the tree, fear and excitement had surged through Ted's brain until he was sure he'd have an aneurysm. Even when they wound up back at Gina's condo, they never seemed to make it to her bed. Gina alleviated a pain that Ted wasn't fully aware of until he met her. Everything happened so fast and felt so good and then so horribly wrong and awful. It was as though Ted had started sniffing glue or robbing banks.

As Ted creeps along two car-lengths behind a BMW, he takes an inventory of how things got so screwed up between him and Elinor. It all seemed to start with the infertility treatments. First their sex life was downgraded to a clinical failure. Even their kissing seemed obligatory, Elinor presenting her cheek to him like a handshake or a clean napkin to go with a sandwich. It wasn't that she was cold, but she was always fretting now — obsessing and talking about the latest study she'd read or acupuncture data or donor eggs. Then they lost their ability to communicate. Elinor thought that Ted's quiet bewilderment meant that he wasn't listening to anything she said. He just couldn't think of anything to say that was the *right* thing to say. Finally, they lost their dignity. For Ted, there was a defining moment when he lost his: the day he dropped his semen sample in a corridor at the hospital, and it rolled under a giant refrigerator.

Ted hated doing in vitro. For the first time in his professional life, he was overwhelmed by medical information. He had never considered himself a control freak, but the complexity and uncertainty of all the hoops they had to jump through — shots, ultrasounds, egg retrievals, embryo transfers — left him feeling unglued. He liked being able to fix things. In college, he'd spent hours in the driveway tuning up his old Plymouth Scamp. You could open the hood of that car and identify everything under there. Ted misses that V-8 engine the same way he misses Johnny Carson and the house he grew up in. Now, when he looks under the hood of his Audi, he is mocked by a gleaming electronic mass.

Ted was nervous as hell the morning of that first egg-retrieval surgery. How much higher could the stakes be? Christ. When they got to the clinic at the hospital, he sat with Elinor while the nurse started a

Valium IV. El smiled at the ceiling as if it were an old friend. It was a relief to see her relax. Ted kissed her forehead and each of her cool cheeks. Then he headed to the nurse's station, as instructed, to get the key for The Room. Ha-ha: The key chain was a white plastic *sperm*. He lumbered down the hall, clutching the plastic sperm.

Later, Elinor wanted to know about The Room. Ted told her how it was just a bathroom with a stall and a big black chair like the ones you sit in to give blood. There were lots of magazines. No, not *Newsweek!* The magazines were worn and smudged and covered with white stickers that said PROPERTY OF REI CLINIC: DO NOT REMOVE. Elinor thought that was pretty damn funny. At first she had managed to find humor and irony in the treatments. One of the things Ted loves about his wife is her dark sense of humor. She is so smart and funny and beautiful.

"How was your date with the cup?" she'd tease.

"Oh, the romance!" Ted would reply.

While he laughed, Ted was terrified he'd mess up the sample somehow, after Elinor had gone through all that agony: four shots of hormones a day for ten days so she'd produce more eggs. Thighs bruised from the shots, and a belly so swollen with follicles and fluid that she walked on her toes, grimacing. And now this surgery. As Ted carried his sample to the lab, he worried about Elinor's anesthesiologist. The guy looked about twelve! What if he screwed up and gave El too much Versed? Ted lost his bearings in the confusion of corridors on his way to the lab. *You're a doctor*, he told himself. *Get ahold of yourself.* Still, his hands shook. The cup sprang out of his fingers like a live fish. He was supposed to carry it in the little brown paper bag they'd given him, but he'd sort of ruined the bag in The Room and thrown it away. That was *another* story. In a flash, his specimen rolled under this giant refrigerator thing that had a padlock on the front. Ted fell to his hands and knees and peered under the machine, which rattled and hummed. He could see the cup all the way toward the wall, pinned under a loop of metal that hung down. He pressed his cheek to the floor and slid his hand under.

He was on his knees, ass in the air, up to his elbow in dust and grime under the giant refrigerator, when a man's voice said, "Can I help you?" White Nikes, blue scrubs. A bearded face hovering above.

"My specimen cup rolled under there." Ted could hear the panic in his voice.

The guy kneeled, peered under the refrigerator. "Man," he said.

They couldn't reach the cup or budge the refrigerator. The guy — a nurse, his badge said — could call someone from facilities to move the machine, but for some reason that would take more than the allotted forty-five minutes for delivery of the specimen. Ted had to return to the nurse's station. Back to the key, back to *The Room.* He wasn't sure if it would all work out again. It did, but he had to believe that the second sample wasn't as good as the first, even though Dr. Weston assured him it would be fine.

But it wasn't fine, or something wasn't fine, because the in vitro didn't work.

"Let's adopt," Elinor said after the negative pregnancy test. When they got the news, Elinor canceled her meetings at work, drove home, and curled up in a ball on the sofa for twenty-four hours. But soon she was back on the Web, doing research and enthusiastically laying out Plan B for meeting with an adoption agency. Meanwhile Ted feared the process would be too hard on them. Close friends of theirs had had their newly adopted baby taken back by a fickle birth mother. Another couple's foreign adoption fell through at the last minute, after they'd already traveled to Russia. "It's not like a trip to Sears, where you show up and plunk down the Visa," Ted argued. Ted wasn't sure he was up for this kind of letdown. Besides, a foreign adoption might involve medical problems that could break their hearts. "Can't we just take a break for now?" he asked, embarrassed by the simple fact that he wasn't as strong as Elinor when it came to this stuff. What if they did another cycle and it worked, but Elinor miscarried a second time? He couldn't bear to go through that again.

Elinor insisted there was no time for a break, so they tried another cycle of in vitro, even though the odds were low. Ted felt the impossibly narrow slice on Dr. Weston's statistical pie chart closing in on them. It seemed best to quit. But saying that made him unsupportive.

Finally, Ted merges onto Highway 280, shifting up to fifth gear. Air rushes across the open sunroof. He looks up at the hills above the freeway, which are still bone-dry from the summer heat.

After they quit going to the doctor, Ted was sure they'd get their lives back. Take hikes, travel. Instead of regaining a zest for life, though, Elinor seemed to *quit* life. She retreated into the laundry room. Disdain crept into her voice.

"I don't *care*," she'd reply when Ted asked if she'd like to go for a walk or if he could fix her dinner or rent a movie. *I'm going through this, too!* he wanted to shout. Instead he, too, receded. Out for long walks, down to the gym, and eventually under Gina's old sleeping bag.

He had signed up for a diet and exercise training program at the gym during the treatments. He figured it might even help his sperm count, which varied from month to month. ("Hmm, quite viscous," the Gen-X doctor had said, frowning at the report from the lab on his clipboard. The next cycle he said, "Unusually low motility this time around." You *jack off into a cup!* Ted wanted to say.) Eventually everything seemed futile except for those trips to the gym. The more Ted went, the better he felt. It was purely Pavlovian. At some point, he realizes now, he did start looking forward to seeing Gina. Not really in a romantic or sexual way. Just to get a hit of her optimism.

"You're doing *great*, Dr. Mackey," she'd say, smiling over her clipboard, light brown bangs falling into her eyes. "You've made the most progress of *all* my clients. You should do a triathlon! I can help you train on the bike and in the pool." Ted was touched by her confidence in him.

Still, the initial seduction took him by surprise. It happened during a fitness test ten weeks into his exercise program. He and Gina were in an upstairs office in the club. Gina took Ted's blood pressure, checked his resting pulse. She chattered on about baseball, talked about the players as though they were movie stars. She was a Red Sox fan, and she was certain her team would make it to the play-offs this year. Ted ran on the treadmill, then Gina took his pulse again.

"Perfect, Dr. Mackey," she said. For the hundredth time, he insisted she call him Ted. But Gina seemed enthralled by Ted's profession.

"I'm only a podiatrist," he told her. "It's not like I'm a brain surgeon."

"The feet are *so* important," Gina insisted. Then she ran her fingers lightly up the inside of his arm as she wrote something on his chart. Ted shuddered. Her hand circled and squeezed his wrist. She lifted his index finger and slid it into her mouth. Slowly.

"I'm married, Gina," Ted told her.

"I know," she said sadly. Then she joked halfheartedly, "Marriage is terrible for the waistline." She let go of Ted's hand and bounced out of the room, leaving him wanting more. Hating himself for wanting more. More of the cheerfulness, more of the optimism and attention, more of the warm inside of her mouth.

Now the thought of the warm inside of Gina's mouth, the memory of the time at the park under the sleeping bag when she managed to get his pants off (he must have helped!) and started licking the insides of his legs and then everything else as it started to get dark and — Jesus, they could have gotten *arrested* — sends a shudder through Ted. He shakes his head hard, once, like a dog shaking itself off after bounding out of a pond. He closes his eyes for a second. When he opens them, he's crested a hill, and a sea of brake lights fills the road before him. He's going fast now, faster than he realized. There is a nauseating surge of adrenaline, and then he brakes, downshifts, swerves, brakes, and *thunk*, hits an old pickup teeming with rakes and mowers and blowers and shovels. The truck, just barely creeping along a few inches behind a BMW, smacks the Beemer, which *thump*, hits a green Passat, which *bump*, hits some other car that Ted can't see. All of a sudden a rake from the truck crashes onto his windshield. He is in the far-right lane now. His dress shirt sticks to his back. He pulls into the breakdown lane, peering through the tines of the rake, and turns off his engine.

To avoid the oncoming traffic, Ted climbs out the passenger's door of his car. He scrambles along the steep hillside, peering into the window of the truck and apologizing to the three men wedged shoulder-to-shoulder across the bench seat. "Telephone?" one of the men asks. He smiles. Two of his teeth are capped with silver. Ted reaches for his phone in his pocket, then sees that two other people are already making the call.

Dry grass and brambles nip at Ted's pants as he makes his way along the edge of the hill to apologize to the woman. "I'm so sorry," he says through her closed window. "I've probably ruined your day."

"What?" the woman says, rolling down the passenger's-side window.

"Just . . ." Ted mops his brow with the back of his sleeve. "Sorry."

"Uh, okay," the woman says, punching at the keys of a Palm Pilot now.

"It's my fault," Ted tells the officer when he arrives. "I wasn't paying attention."

Back in his car, he buckles his seat belt, even though he's clearly not going anywhere for a while. The cop nods, reviews Ted's license and registration. He says that these things happen all the time. This rush-hour stop-and-go traffic is a nightmare. Ted wishes the cop weren't so understanding. He deserves to be punished. Admonished at least.

After the cop takes down everyone's information, the cars start up one by one and pull away. Ted tries to slide his registration back into the glove box, but there's a bunch of crap in there — plastic forks, dental floss, napkins, straws. *Jesus, El,* he thinks. Elinor is like a squirrel, always hoarding little stuff. Elinor! Ted has forgotten for a full half hour that his wife has left home, left *him*, possibly. He crumples the stuff from the glove box into a wad and throws it into the backseat. He can't drive now.

He climbs over the passenger's seat and out of his car again. With a scrabble of stones and dry earth under his loafers, he scales the edge of the hill to sit down. Sharp grass pokes at his legs. He looks at his watch: eight fifty.

His first patient has been sitting in the waiting room for twenty minutes. He pulls his cellular phone out of his pocket. Three missed calls. He doesn't want to drive. He phones the office and asks for his partner, Larry, who agrees to cover for him.

"You okay, buddy?" Larry asks.

"Elinor moved out."

"Jesus. I'm sorry."

"Yeah . . ." The entire past two years seem to catch in Ted's throat. "Well," he says. He wants to tell Larry about Gina and what a screwup he is. But Larry has to run so he can get to all the backed-up patients. They hang up.

Ted clutches his knees to his chest, balancing a bit precariously on the dry hill beside the freeway. The traffic speeds up. Cars roar past him, hot air tugging at his pants like an undertow.

Every Thursday afternoon, between one and four, Ted visits his mortality. This is when he makes rounds at the Shady Glen rest home to "chip and clip," as he and Larry say. To cut old people's toenails.

As Ted steps into the home, the double sliding-glass doors whoosh shut behind him. He pauses on the rubber mat, smooths his hands over his white lab coat. He takes a deep breath, immediately wishing he hadn't. The smells of urine and canned peas and body odor make his eyes tear. He continues down a corridor and is buzzed into the big common room. The whiteboard on the wall is filled with block letters:

44

Today is: **August 12**
The weather is: **Warm**
For lunch we're having: **Spaghetti and meatballs**
You are in: **San Jose, California**

A woman slumped in a wheelchair chews on a greeting card.

What Ted likes about podiatry is that he's usually able to help people — to alleviate their pain — whether it means trimming a callus or operating on a metatarsal fracture. Yet working at Shady Glen overwhelms him with a sense of futility. Old people's toenails — impossibly thick and ridged — have a stubborn way of burrowing right back under the flesh to pinch and stab. Instead of helping these patients, Ted senses that he's barely maintaining their grim status quo. He had this same sense of uselessness during the in-vitro treatments, when there wasn't anything he could do to improve the situation or make Elinor feel better.

Ted's first patient, Mrs. O'Leary, isn't as old as the other residents. She's incapacitated by a brain tumor. Her white stubbly hair is as short as a marine's, and her most recent surgery has left a golf-ball-size dent above one temple. One of her eyes has sunken shut. Her face is swollen from steroids, and all but one of her teeth has fallen out from radiation. She looks like a jack-o'-lantern.

Mrs. O'Leary is relieved to see Ted. She sits straight up in bed, her one good eye wide and imploring. "Curtis!" she whispers loudly.

"No, Mrs. O'Leary," Ted says, "it's Dr. Mackey. I've come to have a look at your feet." As Ted peels back the covers to examine her dry, pink toes, she lists the rest home's imprecations in an anxious whisper: The nurses have stolen her checkbook, and someone has built a covered bridge in her room. Could he please issue a press release?

Ted used to think he should help the patients get a better handle on reality by correcting their senile fantasies. He's learned, though, that people find it more comforting when you humor them a bit.

Really? Can you imagine? The nerve! The patients seem relieved that someone's at least listening and responding.

Mrs. O'Leary's nails aren't so bad, since she's only in her sixties. When he's finished clipping, Ted presses on the cushiony pads at the edges of her toes.

"Any pain?" he asks, to make sure the ingrown nails are gone.

"Much better," she sighs.

Ted rubs cream into her feet, then tucks the covers back over them. Exhausted, he sits down for a moment in the chair beside the bed.

"How *are* you, dear?" Mrs. O'Leary asks. Although she's off her nut, she is one of the sweeter residents. Other patients have screeched at Ted, thrown water on him, cackled and flashed their withered genitalia.

"My wife left me." Ted's words tumble out.

"That Margaret is *no good*," Mrs. O'Leary says conspiratorially, lifting her head from the pillow, her good eye bulging at him.

46

Ted shakes his head. "I love her."

He never should have put that cookbook in his dresser drawer. That was painful for Elinor to find. But he wasn't good at hiding things. He never had to create elaborate lies during the affair. Elinor wasn't interested in spending any time with him, so he could come and go as he pleased. When he returned from a visit with Gina, she never asked where he'd been. It was hard to coax her out of her laundry room/office. He fixed her dinner every night, and she'd come out long enough to eat. Then Ted would clean up while she went back to whatever it was she did in there. "Can't you just sit at the counter and talk with me while I cook?" he'd asked her. But it was painful when she did. She'd cross her arms against her chest, as though cold, and fidget at the pages of the newspaper without reading it. They'd confirm that their days were fine. They rarely even argued anymore.

Ted reaches to unclench Mrs. O's hand from the sheet. "Everything's going to be all right," he says, smoothing over her fingers. Ted's learned that the secret to good bedside manner can be as simple as touching a patient on the hand or arm. Any gentle touch other than an exploratory prod. He stands. "You try not to worry so much," he tells her.

He pulls the table with her lunch tray closer. "Vanilla ice cream," he says, peeling back the cardboard on the little cup. "Have some. The calcium's good for you." But Mrs. O has already fallen asleep. Ted looks at the photo on her nightstand. Mrs. O is in her wedding dress, a mass of inky black curls surrounding her rosy face. Her husband, a little bucktoothed, smiles into the camera. They are dancing, nearly airborne.

"Listen," an agent from Ted's insurance company says over the phone later that day, "you don't need to be so honest."

Ted's laughter comes out sudden and hard, like a bark.

"You're not supposed to say *anything* to the other drivers," the agent continues. "You're just supposed to wait for the police." He sighs. "Tell me your side of the story."

My side of the story? Let's see. I was speeding and thinking about the time I got a blow job at the park from the nutritionist at my gym, then I rear-ended a truck and caused a major pileup on the freeway. "I was going too fast," Ted tells the agent. "Suddenly I came over a hill and the traffic had slowed way down. I wasn't paying attention. Was I supposed to lie?"

Of course not, the agent insists. But now Ted's rates will go up. He'll lose his Good Driver discount . . .

Ted doesn't care. He's already lost his Good Husband status. "Is there a point to this phone call?" he asks the agent. "Other than to ride my ass?"

"Calm down. I just need to hear from you what happened."

"And I told you. I was entirely at fault."

But is he entirely at fault for his crumbling marriage? The more determined Elinor became about having a baby, the more peripheral Ted felt. Over the months, she turned inward and became angry with him — as

48

though it was his fault they couldn't conceive. When he touched her, she'd flinch or withdraw. Sometimes when he came into a room, she'd jump, startled by his presence. Ted began to feel unnecessary, then downright repulsive.

When he suggested a break from the treatments, she accused him of not wanting children. He couldn't seem to convince her that he *did*. He'd always hoped for three girls. Little girls killed him. The miscarriage was one of the few times in his life when he'd had a stiff drink before noon.

And yet he didn't want to sacrifice their marriage anymore for these crazy shots and trips to the doctor. He used to have this fantasy that he'd come home one day (truly a fantasy, since Elinor always got home from work after him), and El would be in the kitchen, at the stove, and surprise him with the news of her pregnancy. The announcement would knock the wind out of him. He'd lift Elinor off the floor, carry her to the couch, and coat her face with kisses.

The agent rattles on about how one woman says she hurt her neck. Ted knows for a fact that pain from whiplash doesn't set in until the day *after* the injury, but he doesn't say anything.

"Just send me the paperwork," he tells the agent and finally hangs up. He realizes he's been clutching his shoe in his hand the entire time he's been on the phone. He had just walked in the door and was changing to go out for a run. He squeezes the Boston Common oxford with its heel pad for shock absorption, suddenly hating its practicality. He snaps open the sliding-glass door from their bedroom, then chucks the shoe overhead into the yard as hard as he can, as though it's a football. It clears the entire lawn, piercing the juniper trees. He misses football, which he hasn't played since high school. He tugs off his other shoe. *Lead with the elbow, back foot to front, belly facing the receiver.* Bingo. The shoe disappears into the neighbors' yard.

He turns to their bed — a California king. It's too big when he and Elinor sleep together. There's no way he's crawling in there alone. For the past two months, they've gone through the nights barely touching. Elinor would utter the requisite "I love you" and drift off almost before Ted could reply. He'd lie there wishing they would talk before falling asleep, the way they used to. Wishing they'd make love. "How was your *day?*" he'd ask loudly, angrily, startling Elinor awake. "What?" she'd gasp. "Fine! I was sleeping!"

Now he's depressed by the fact that when he thinks about sex, he thinks about Gina. He has to strain to recall intimacy with his own wife. He whips off his tie and throws it toward the closet, where it lands draped across Elinor's sneaker. He lunges into the closet, scooping up shoes and hurling them out into the backyard. Sneakers, clogs, hiking boots. His, hers, whatever he can get his hands on. Screw this. What happened to the woman he married? He needs to get his wife back. Get her back into their house and then to the marriage counselor. Figure out what the hell happened to them.

He slams the sliding-glass door shut, then heads for the bathroom to take a long shower.

After changing into jeans, a T-shirt, and sneakers — one of which he has to retrieve from the lawn — Ted feels calmer. He grabs the phone book and calls the Hyatt downtown. He'll check in down the street from Elinor. She'll think that's funny. He'll call and invite her over for room service at his place. Neutral territory. The therapist always crows about this.

At the Hyatt, Ted peels the stiff bedspread off the bed and looks out the fourth-floor window up the street to the Fairmont. His hands are cold and sweaty at the same time. Finally, he picks up the phone to call El.

"We have room service over here, too, you know." He laughs nervously.

Elinor's tone is calm, distracted, yet all-business. She's not charmed. She can't have dinner with him because she's about to check out and leave for the airport. She's going for two weeks to stay with her mother, who's just gotten home from rehab after having a knee replacement. Elinor's got the vacation time, God knows.

"Let me drive you," Ted says.

"No thanks, sweetie," El says. "Kat's going to take me."

The calmer her tone, the more panicked Ted becomes. She sounds as though she's got everything figured out. What if *everything* includes leaving Ted forever? There's a burning in his trachea that feels like a pill stuck there.

"Call me when you get there?" Ted crumples onto the bed. Elinor's like a departing train. Doors hissing and closing, speed gathering. Ted's running on the platform.

Elinor says she'll phone to let him know that she's arrived, but then she'll need a real break, and doesn't want to talk during the two weeks she'll be away. She'll call him when she gets back.

"Then we'll go to the counselor?" Ted asks. "I'll make the appointment."

"Okay." Elinor pauses. "How are you?"

"Great," Ted says, immediately regretting the sarcasm in his voice. He wants to keep things civil. "I sort of had an —"

"Do you think this knee surgery will alleviate my mom's pain?" El's breathing is labored as she gathers her things. "She says it hurts *more* now."

"— accident. Oh, the prognosis is usually very good. Even in the elderly. It should relieve a lot of her pain once she makes it through a few more weeks of physical therapy."

"Wait, what kind of accident?" Ted can hear that Elinor has stopped moving around the room.

"In the car. It was minor. Everything's okay." He decides not to go into the details. "Hey, depending on how your mom's doing, maybe she could come and stay with us." Right. Like *that's* going to save their marriage. He clenches his fists, trying to wring out the feeling of helplessness.

"Ha, she'd never budge. Hey!" Elinor's voice brightens. Ted thinks maybe she's got some good news

— an idea for how they can work things out. "I swam fifty laps in the hotel pool today."

"Oh. That's great." *Yeah, it's great that your wife's at the Fairmont!* "Don't you think . . . Don't you want to *talk?*" He stands. "El, I want you to know how sorry I am."

Elinor sighs. "That's the problem. I don't think I'm *capable* of talking, Ted. I can scream, I can break things, but I don't think I can talk."

"So scream."

"I don't . . ." She pauses, starts to cry, then catches her breath. ". . . want to."

Great. He's managed to make her feel even worse. "Come in!" she calls out to someone at the door. "I've got to run," she tells Ted. "We'll talk. Of course we'll talk. I just need some time. Jesus *Christ*, Ted."

"I know," Ted says. "I'm . . . Travel safe."

"Always do," El says. "Bye."

"I love you." Dial tone. Too late.

Ted hangs up and looks at the expansive California king bed in his hotel room. He opens his suitcase, takes out his toothbrush, brushes his teeth, shakes off the toothbrush, then puts it back in his bag and zips it shut. The Hyatt is just as lonely as their house. He envies Elinor's break — the change of scenery. The distraction of a flight to catch. Her mother's grocery list waiting on the kitchen counter. The fulfillment of being able to care for someone. Ted picks up his suitcase, shaking his head. He has checked into a hotel room to phone his wife and brush his teeth.

Dizzy, hands shaking, Ted realizes on his way home from the Hyatt that he hasn't eaten anything since breakfast. He stops off at the Country Kitchen Café, where the food is healthy and comforting. He orders black bean soup, grilled chicken, brown rice, and a fruit plate.

After the waitress leaves, he covers his face with his hands. This day has seemed as long as a week. He doesn't want to go home. Hell, he should sleep in his car. He rubs his face and forehead until his eyes squeak. When he opens them he sees a swirl of spots, then an attractive foot sticking out from the booth up ahead. Ted's always a bit myopic when he's out in public, homing in on feet and shoes.

He looks at the straight, longish tanned toes painted with pink polish. They're remarkably well shaped. No weird knobby middle toe. Silver toe ring. Purple Reef flip-flops. A good choice if you're going to wear thongs. The flare of a long skirt falls softly around the ankle. Gina. *Gina's* flowing paisley skirt. Gina's perfectly formed pink foot. Ted looks up and sees the back of her head. Long, light brown hair, smooth and soft. The individual strands are thin, but there's so much of it that it forms a thick curtain that is lovely to burrow through, to hide behind. Gina. Well, she *is* the one who turned him on to this restaurant.

Ted slides down in his booth, his chin resting on his chest.

"Tired?" the waitress asks, setting the fruit plate before him.

"Whipped." Ted peers around the edge of his booth. There are two places set at Gina's table. Her dining partner is in the bathroom or somewhere. Gina tips her head back, drinking her white wine too quickly. She does this when she's nervous. As self-confident and firm as she is, there's always an undercurrent of nervousness, of wanting to please. Once, Ted took her cheeks in his hands, held her gaze, and said, "Relax."

Maybe she's nervous because she's on a date. Ted leans farther out of his booth, slipping on the Naugahyde and nearly tumbling onto the floor. He grabs the table, knocking his glass, water sloshing out. Gina's dining partner seems to be having soda instead of wine. Maybe it's one of her DUI boyfriends. Suddenly Ted can't stand the thought of this Pepsi drinker kissing Gina. Someone else having her lips, pouty and always slightly sweet and shiny with that pink lip stuff. Gina is a good kisser. This is what got to Ted first. The way she would trace the outline of his mouth with her tongue, nibble his lower lip, and sink her teeth in just enough to make his scalp tingle. Then she'd draw his lip into her mouth and slowly suck on it, mimicking something even better to come. Ted bangs the heel of his palm on the table. Jealous of an empty place setting! Jesus. While trying to *reconcile* with his wife. He ducks back into his booth and stabs a crescent of honeydew with his fork.

A thin boy stumbles around the corner from the restroom and ambles up to Gina's table. A thick tangle of honey-colored curls falls into his eyes. He's probably around eight. He collapses heavily into the booth across from Gina as though defeated by something.

Who's the kid? Ted wonders, holding the chunk of honeydew up on his fork like a flag.

Just then the boy points to something behind Ted. Gina turns to look, squinting, her chin tipped up, her mouth slightly open. The restaurant has all kinds of wacky stuff on the walls — everything from moose heads to C-list celebrity photos.

Gina's eyes widen and her mouth drops open. "*Ted.*" She smiles, then seems to catch herself, suppressing her usual cheer. "Ted?"

"Hi." Ted waves his honeydew feebly.

The waitress appears, Ted's salad resting on her hip. "Wanna join them?" She takes a step toward Gina's booth with the salad.

"I . . ." Ted lowers his fork.

"Sure." Gina laughs nervously. "Join us." She moves over in her booth to make room.

The kid wrinkles his nose, stuffs a french fry into his mouth.

Ted swallows and spreads his hands across the table, bracing himself.

CHAPTER
THREE

You probably shouldn't cut your own hair a week after you discover your husband has slept with another woman. Yet Elinor has used common sense all her life and where has it gotten her?

She leans over the sink in the bathroom at her mother's house in Ohio and studies herself in the mirror. Her straight blond hair is cut evenly at the ends, falling just below her shoulders. Too sensible. Sensible haircut pulled into a French braid, low-heeled shoes, successful career. Egg-quality issues. She wants something sexier. One of those shaggy cuts she's seen on movie stars in magazines. A crazy mop of varying lengths, with bangs that fall mischievously into the eyes. She bunches her hair up over her forehead to get an idea of how it should be. When she lets it drop, it falls neatly back into place, too thick and stubborn to look tousled.

Elinor pads out to the living room, where her mother is stretched on the couch, one leg elevated on a pillow, a black zipper of stitches running down her knee. A cigarette burns in an ashtray on the end table beside her. Somewhere along the way, Beatrice shrank. Now she's a corn husk floating in a blue terry-cloth robe.

"Ma? You have any sharp scissors?" Elinor raises her voice over the blare of the TV.

"Stupid!" her mother whoops, engaged in her morning ritual of chiding the contestants on *The Price Is Right*. Beatrice points without taking her eyes off Bob Barker. "Laundry room."

"Awwww," the audience laments when a woman is far from guessing the price of a microwave.

The drapes are drawn. Bob Barker's dentures are the only flash of light in the dark living room. He's thin and weathered and tanning-booth brown. Elinor pulls open the curtains. She feels guilty that she's depressed by her mother — by the dim, musty condo and the sight of her parked in front of the TV all day. The house smells like cigarette smoke and Lysol and the Jones pork sausage that her mother burns in a skillet every morning. She tugs open the sliding-glass door to let in some air.

Beatrice points to the TV. "Oh, now there's glare." She sighs. "Why do I watch this crap anyway?"

"You don't read anymore?" Elinor hopes this doesn't sound critical. Her mother used to plow through a library book a week.

"I just read the same paragraph over and over. My concentration has gone the way of my bone density. Can't read, can't open jars, can't dance."

Beatrice's exasperation with aging troubles Elinor. "With any luck I won't wake up," she'd grumbled over the phone before the surgery.

"You never even *liked* to dance," she reminds her mother.

"I didn't? See. I can't remember."

"Yes, you can." This comes out sounding like an accusation.

Her mother points at Bob Barker. "That man looks like human beef jerky."

"Can I get you anything?" Elinor tries to sound more cheerful. "Maybe I could rent us some movies." She stubs out her mother's cigarette when she isn't looking.

"You could take me out back and shoot me."

Elinor feels her chin quiver and her eyes burn. "Don't *say* that."

Beatrice struggles among the cushions to sit up and look at Elinor. Her face darkens when their eyes meet. "Sweetheart, I'm *joking*." She mutes the TV. "Lighten up, for your old ma."

Elinor recalls the voice of her father, who died of a heart attack during her first year in law school. "Smile, Ellie," her dad would often say, punching her lightly on the shoulder. She was a serious child, always reading. "I'm okay," she'd insist. People thought she was frowning when, really, she was just concentrating. Concentrating on the wrong things, apparently. When Elinor was paying attention to her career, she should have been paying attention to her biological clock. When she was paying attention to her biological clock, she should have been paying attention to her husband.

"Why do you think you put off having children?" the marriage counselor asked at their first meeting. Elinor explained that she hadn't meant to: She met Ted when she was thirty-five; they married seven months later, when she was thirty-six. Shortly after her thirty-seventh birthday, she went off the pill and started prenatal vitamins, and they tried for a year to get pregnant. At thirty-eight, her OB handed her a list of infertility clinics. By the time Elinor and Ted found the right doctor, made their way up the waiting list, had all the tests, went through three intrauterine inseminations, the miscarriage and its recovery period, a hysteroscopy, and two failed in vitros, her fortieth birthday had arrived. Suddenly she was forty and childless. But how could she have been any more proactive?

"I'm sorry to be glum, honey," Beatrice says. "I just don't feel well."

"I know." Elinor unmutes the TV. Her mother just wants to watch her show. She should stop futzing with her environment. She realizes how helpless Ted must have felt when trying to comfort her during the IVF treatments. "Can I get you anything?" he'd ask sweetly. When Elinor shook her head, Ted would look disappointed, pained.

"Honey, you know, you can go home now." Beatrice smiles, tilts her head, and looks at Elinor with a puzzled expression. "I'm okay on my own. Really. Go see that sweet hubby of yours."

Elinor hasn't bothered her mother with the news of Ted's affair, with the fact that her marriage is falling apart.

"I can't change my ticket," Elinor says, even though she probably could, for a fee. Besides, she likes helping her mother — doling out prescriptions, fixing meals on trays, refreshing ice packs, holding on to her brittle arm as they wobble up the stairs together at night. She needs her mother to need her. This is part of what she

60

looked forward to about having a child: having someone to care for. Coats to button, noses to wipe, nerves to soothe. Meanwhile, she over-looked the fact that *Ted* needed her all along — for love, sex, attention, companionship. All the elements of a good marriage.

The only scissors in the laundry room are pinking shears. Maybe they're just the thing for a shaggy look. Elinor spreads newspaper across the sink. Pulling a strand above her head, she makes a quick chop. The hair comes away in her hand, silky and soft. She immediately misses it. Unlike most of her friends, she hasn't had to color her hair. Her custard-yellow shade isn't prone to graying. Maybe it would have been better to let it grow long. Long blond hair down to her waist. *That* would have been sexy.

She studies herself in the mirror. Ted says Elinor's face is heart-shaped, an observation that secretly thrills her. She finds her face too long, her chin too pointed. What she considers a pug nose, Ted claims is a button nose. He always makes her feel prettier than she thinks she is.

"You look great for your *age*," Gina chirped at the club. As she tugged out her ponytail to refasten it, her light brown hair fanned around her waist — thin and wispy and ethereal. Collegiate.

Elinor doesn't know how to be the right kind of mad about the affair. She wants to either fly home, crash into the gym, and shove her fist through Gina's charming overbite, or curl into a catatonic ball at the foot of her mother's bed. She doesn't know how to be taking-care-of-business mad. Dignified.

The shorter, jagged piece of hair does have a nicely unkempt look. Elinor lifts another chunk and makes a quick angled snip. The hair falls with a flicking noise onto the newspaper, hitting the Dear Abby column.

Dear Abby: My husband had an affair. Elinor works her way around the crown of her head, trying to remember hairdressers' techniques. The scissors creak and snip. Soon a small haystack of hair covers the crossword and horoscopes.

Creak, snip. *Abby, I could have been nicer to Ted.* Elinor resented Ted's resistance to adoption, and his relief when they quit the infertility treatments. That annoying spring in his step. She snapped at him for insignificant mistakes, such as forgetting to pick up the dry cleaning. Anger poured from her before she could stop it, like throwing up before you can make it to the bathroom. But bitterness proved to be a useless defense mechanism, like an insect that dies after it stings.

"This is hard on me, too," Ted insisted. There was a twinge of guilt in his voice, as though he wasn't allowed to say this.

"I know, sweetie," Elinor would reply. *All you have to do is land sperm in a cup!* Still, she knew it must have been difficult for him. Strangers critiquing his sperm, the dwindling hope of ever becoming a father. Maybe Ted needed to feel sexy, too. Elinor smacks the scissors on the bathroom counter, thinking of Gina's bare, flat belly above the waist of her low-slung workout pants.

62

Of how Ted's hand lightly cupped the small of Gina's back as they headed into Healthy Oats.

Ted can shove his flax up his ass. Creak, snip, creak, snip, creak, snip. She hates that she misses him. Misses his smell, which is like pine trees, and the warmth of his stocky body in bed. Strong thighs, muscular arms, sloped shoulders. Bear hugs that shut out the rest of the world. She misses those few minutes they spend in bed every morning after the alarm goes off, looking out the windows at their garden. Ted always wakes up in a good mood. Even if they've argued the night before, everything has rolled off his back by morning. And he always laughs at Elinor's jokes, no matter how dark. After their first date, Elinor called her mother to say, "He *gets* me."

Elinor has insisted that Ted not call her in Ohio. They'll talk when she gets home. By then she will have figured things out. So far she hasn't figured anything out. She and Kat talk every night. Elinor feels a mixture of gratefulness and guilt for rattling on about the affair. She doesn't want to be a drama queen. "It's so cliché," she says. "It's *okay* to feel like crap," Kat tells her. "Cut yourself a break." Elinor loves Kat because she's never one to dole out silver linings. (*You can sleep in when you don't have kids! You can fly to Paris!*)

Many couples are able to put an affair behind them, Abby would probably advise. Creak, snip.

Maybe Elinor can forgive Ted for the affair. She's pretty sure she can. Snip, snip, *chop*, snip. But not while anger boils so close to the surface of her skin. Frightening anger. Yesterday, when she went to the store for her mother's yogurt, she had a panicky thought when she saw an attractive woman in yoga pants by the sorbet. *What if the affair isn't over? What if Ted's shacked up with Gina and her flax?* She wanted to ram her shopping cart into the glass freezer case.

Snip, snip, snip. Just a teeny bit more off the bangs. When she gets back from Ohio, she and Ted will go see Dr. Brewster. Snip. Arguments in that office are somehow productive. Snip, snip. Snip. Shorten up the sides.

She steps back from the sink, contemplating her shaggy haircut. The raggedy style is a little longer than she'd like in the back. No more cutting, though. She'll go to a hairdresser when she gets home to get it cleaned up. To make it the right kind of messy.

She bends forward and blows off the back of her neck with a hair dryer she finds under the sink. The heat warms her scalp. When she lifts her head, her hair is tousled in a million different directions, reflecting her emotions.

"Oh!" her mother says when she sees Elinor's hair. She smiles. "You did that? It's darling."

"You think?" Elinor stammers, pulling at the ends of her hair. "You think Ted would like it?" She wants her hair back. Her waistline. Her ovarian function. Her sex life. Her bikini. Her *husband*.

"Oh, honey." Beatrice clicks off the TV and hoists her lame leg off the couch, patting the cushions for Elinor to sit. Elinor sinks into the sofa and rests her head on the soft shoulder of her mother's frayed robe. Beatrice rubs Elinor's back, but doesn't say anything.

64

She's never one to pry. For once, Elinor wishes she would.

"Ted and I are having troubles," she says softly.

"Oh, *honey*." Elinor burrows her forehead into the warm, dry crook of her mother's neck, breathing in the comforting smell of A&D ointment.

"Is it the infertility? That was so much for you two to go through."

As Elinor clutches her mother's back, she's alarmed by the sharp frailty of her vertebrae. "That, and other things."

Beatrice nods. "The miscarriage must have been so hard on you two." Her tone brightens. "But at least you know you can conceive."

Many people said this after the miscarriage. But Elinor is ashamed to admit that she already *knew* she could conceive. She'd had an abortion in college. Her boyfriend, Caleb, a poet and fellow prelaw student, had been killed in a car accident over Thanksgiving break. Elinor returned to school in a daze. One night she drank too many Kamikazes and slept with James Slandler, a Tom Cruise look-alike who was sweet and tender and had had a crush on her since they'd been debate partners. Since her heart was broken, she had the melodramatic notion that she'd lost the will to live. So she went to James's room, and she didn't worry about not having birth control. That was the *only* time she hadn't used contraceptives, and *boom*, she'd gotten pregnant. From then on she mistakenly thought she was "fertile as a henhouse."

James was sweet. He drove her to the abortion clinic and brought her chocolate milk shakes and cut daisies. At the time, Elinor was sure she'd made the right choice — college first, baby later. By contrast, her mother, a straight-A college student, had gotten pregnant in her freshman year at Ohio State when she and her father had had too much beer after a football game. Beatrice dropped out of college, trading Yeats and Keats for Dr. Spock and the diaper service. She'd had Elinor and never returned to school.

"I already knew that I could conceive," Elinor confesses, studying the black spidery threads of stitches in her mother's knee. "I had an abortion. A long time ago. In college?" She looks up at Beatrice, whose expression is so accepting and nonjudgmental, Elinor could cry. "I thought it was the right thing to do at the *time*."

"Oh, honey, it was." Beatrice gently rearranges pieces of Elinor's newly shorn hair.

"Maybe I was supposed to have my baby back then." When she and Ted couldn't conceive, Elinor began fantasizing about her "college baby," who would be a teenager already, probably arguing to pierce her navel or go to rock concerts on school nights.

"No, no." Beatrice shakes her head. "That's just what we did back then. We women didn't have choices the way you gals do." She adds this last part a bit wistfully, then stops herself. "Oh! Not that I didn't enjoy every minute of having you. You were *such* a sweet baby."

"God, I hope so." Elinor has always felt a little guilty that she's the reason her mother couldn't finish college.

They sit quietly staring at the blank gray TV screen, and Elinor actually misses Bob Barker.

"Choices." Elinor finally says, repeating her mother. "That's kind of a fairy tale, you know?" She leans her head on Beatrice's bony shoulder. Elinor has always been pro-choice, but it never occurred to her that one day she'd have *no* choice. There are many things you can do later in life, but having a baby isn't necessarily one of them.

Ted sits down a little too heavily in the booth beside Gina at the Country Kitchen Café, making her bounce in her seat. They both laugh nervously. Gina gives him a light, friendly hug. He touches her shoulder, which is tanned beneath the thin straps of her white yoga leotard. The round outline of her breasts shows just beneath the thin fabric. Ted glances away.

"This is my son, Toby," Gina says. She looks at the boy, smiling, almost bursting.

"Your . . . son?" Gina never told Ted she had a son. Were there even any *pictures* of him in Gina's house?

The boy peeks out from his moppy snarl of curls.

"Toby has been living with his dad."

"Oh." Ted blows on his soup even though it isn't hot anymore.

Gina's trying to be cheerful, but he can tell she's stressed. She finishes her wine and orders an iced tea, stirring it until the ice cubes begin to melt.

Toby sighs, raps the table with his spoon. "Now I gotta live *here*." The disdain in his voice makes Ted feel bad for Gina.

"That's great," Ted tells Toby.

"Toby's father is going back to school," Gina says. "So he won't be home much."

Toby kicks the table leg, and their glasses wobble.

"How old are you, Toby?" Ted takes a spoonful of the black bean soup. It has a mushy cardboard consistency.

"Ten."

"Eat your salad, honey." Gina points to a pile of greens beside Toby's french fries.

Toby wrinkles his nose. The weight of his curls seems to pull his forehead toward the table. His elbows, which are too big for the rest of his body, are covered with splotchy brown scabs. He scratches them.

"Don't, honey." Gina reaches for Toby's hands. He recoils, shoving his arms under the table. "Somebody's accident-prone and has eczema," Gina tells Ted.

Ted orders a half-bottle of Chardonnay, which the waitress brings with two fresh glasses. Ted tries not to drink too quickly.

Gina nods at Toby. "Somebody needs to lay off the McDonald's. I'm trying to get him to eat just one small salad a day." Her silver bracelets tinkle as she dips into her own salad.

It annoys Ted the way Gina refers to Toby in the third person — as though he's not really there. He can't remember Gina ever annoying him. Of course not, if all you ever do together is climb the Precor, eat home-cooked meals, and have sex.

Toby furrows his brow at Ted, crossing his arms so he can scratch both elbows at once. "Did you know that a decapitated person can remain conscious for up to four minutes, because there's still blood in their brain?" Toby's back straightens with enthusiasm as he asks Ted this.

"Really?" Ted sets down his fork, refilling Gina's wineglass, then his own.

"Yeah, but probably you wouldn't feel any pain."

"Somebody's got a penchant for grisly stories," Gina tells Ted. "Ted's a doctor," she tells Toby.

"They're not *stories*," Toby says. "They're anecdotes. They're true." Blood runs from one of the scabs. "What kinda doctor?" he asks Ted hopefully. "A surgeon?"

Gina hands Toby a napkin and he blots at his elbow.

"A podiatrist. I do some minor surgeries."

"Cool!"

"Say, what's your favorite subject at school?"

"History. Only we don't really have it yet. We have stupid social studies. Junk about Plymouth Rock. I like *real* history. You know, Greece and Rome. I watch the History Channel and my grandfather has these Time-Life books."

Normally, Ted worries about coming up with something to say to kids that will pique their interest. Questions that will solicit more than one-word answers. But this kid talks nonstop.

"We can't get Toby to read his schoolbooks," Gina tells Ted, a little exasperated, "because he's always reading those Time-Life books."

"Wow," Ted says.

"She doesn't read *anything*," Toby tells Ted.

"I *read*." Gina stops eating, aligns her place mat with the edge of the table.

"Yeah, those stupid nutrition books. Buncha baloney."

Ted finds it odd how Gina and her son talk to him rather than to each other. "Well, that baloney helped me lose fifteen pounds," he tells Toby.

"Yeah," Toby says. "Hey, you know Cicero? You know how he died? He wanted Rome to be a republic only Marc Antony didn't, so Marc Antony murdered him and then you know what?"

"*Breathe*, Toby." Irritation creeps into Gina's voice.

"Cicero was murdered?" Ted says. He knew Caesar was murdered, but frankly, he didn't remember what the hell Cicero wrote or did. He was just another Roman C-guy. Elinor would like this kid. This stuff's right up her alley.

"Yeah, they *chopped* off his head and hands and nailed them to the Forum walls." When he says the word *chopped*, Toby karate-chops the table. Gina's wine tips over and splashes onto her leotard. She jerks backward, then presses her napkin to her chest.

"Sorry," Toby says. But he keeps his eyes on Ted, his captive audience. "Yeah, and that was when the republic started going down the tubes."

Ted wants to help Gina, but he doesn't want to look at the yoga leotard, let alone touch it. He hands her his napkin.

"Wasn't our republic based on theirs?" he asks Toby.

"Yeah!" Toby says, giving Ted a verbal high five.

"Jeez, I hardly remember any of this stuff," Ted says to Gina. "You okay?"

Gina nods, shrugs, puts down the napkin. There's a South America-shaped splotch of wine across her chest.

"Toby was in the GATE program last year in Maine, where his dad lives," she tells Ted. "But he stopped doing his homework and his grades went down. So now he can't be in GATE here." She raises her eyebrows at her son.

"Gate?" Ted asks, feeling his face flush. He's embarrassed by the fact that he knows the details of Gina's outfit by heart. The Indian skirt is a wraparound deal, and you take it off by unknotting the bow and then with one tug you can whip it off, like a bullfighter snapping his cape. The white yoga leotard is also one piece. There are three tiny snaps at the crotch that come undone with a gentle tug. Sometimes Gina wears underwear underneath and sometimes not. If there's underwear, Ted would quickly push it aside and slide his fingers inside her, always surprised by the warm wetness. She would arch her back and bite into his earlobe. Soon she'd be straddled on top of him and he'd be pulling the yoga top up over her head and tossing it onto the floor.

"It's the advanced program —" Gina explains. She's clearly proud of Toby. Proud and exasperated at the same time.

Ted pushes his soup away. Clears his throat.

"I don't care." Toby sulks. "I don't even want to *go* to school here." He starts with the kicking again.

"Toby's used to living with his dad," Gina explains. She tries to run her hand through Toby's curls, but her fingers get stuck. Toby turns his head to release himself from her touch.

Ted spears a banana on his fruit plate.

"That's the carbiest fruit," Gina says, smiling.

"*Carby?*" Ted pops the banana into his mouth.

"Worse than ice cream." She raises her eyebrows. "And sooooo good." Her skin is golden and somehow glistens with tiny sparkles.

"It takes an hour and a half to reduce the average adult corpse to ashes," Toby announces. "You know, like when they cremate a body."

"Sprinkle me in a redwood forest," Gina says.

Toby pulls a paperback out of his backpack and buries his face in it: *A Macabre Miscellany*. A THOUSAND GRUESOME AND GORY FACTS! the cover boasts.

"I joined the Y," Ted tells Gina. He wants to declare his separation from her gym.

Gina agrees that the Y is pretty good, but recommends other gyms. Of course, hers is the best, considering the outdoor pool, and the yoga studio with all the windows. She looks around the restaurant as she talks.

Ted has the urge to remove her yoga leotard with his teeth. It is a sudden and alarming compulsion — what he imagines Tourette's must be like. He should have gone home and grilled himself a burger for dinner. Watched the ball game. Gina wants to know if he's training for a second triathlon. No. He shakes his head. It's probably too late now. But he's found a bunch of guys to play soccer with two nights a week. Gina insists

72

it's not too late to train. She seems to think Ted can achieve anything he'll put his mind to. The waitress says she has to go home, and another waiter is taking over.

The waiter, Derrick, arrives to ask if they'd like dessert. He doesn't take his eyes off Gina. She doesn't seem to notice. She touches Ted's arm, suggesting a lemon sorbet for him. He feels like an ass for being proud of her attention. *See, Derrick*, his self-esteem says. *She prefers me*. He declines dessert. While he hasn't eaten much of his dinner, he's no longer hungry.

"Didn't like the soup?" Gina asks as the waiter clears it away.

Ted shrugs.

"It's better to eat at home," she says. "Listen to me, the food Nazi." She sips her wine. "I'm taking this job *way* too seriously."

"No, you're good at it," Ted says.

"Yeah, well, you should cook," she says sadly. "You should cook dinner for Elinor."

"She left," Ted says. "I mean, she went to stay with her mom for a few weeks."

"I'm sor —"

"So she could help her after her knee replacement. She's coming back." Ted wishes he hadn't shared this information. "She's —"

"Somebody's got homework to do," Gina says.

Gina's car is across the parking lot in a lone corner. Ted remembers that she parks far from places so she can fit in extra exercise. As they part ways in front of the restaurant, she gives Ted a little kiss on the cheek. It's dry but soft, and causes a spark of static electricity.

"Nice to see you." She absently pats Toby's curls. Distracted by his book, Toby leans into his mother, resting against her hip.

"Great seeing you," Ted says. Too enthusiastic. He coughs. "Good," he adds.

Gina nods, smiles. Her eyes scan his face as though reading something.

"Toby," Ted says, extending his hand for a shake, immediately feeling like a geek. "Keep on top of those battles."

"I should show you my battle of Salamis book," Toby says, squinting up at Ted. "This one guy —"

"Good luck with the triathlon." Gina steers Toby toward her car, moving ahead of the boy at a fast clip. She never lingers over good-byes; her departures are sudden and quick, leaving Ted wanting more. Cursing himself for always wanting a little more.

When Elinor opens the front door to retrieve her mother's morning newspaper, she finds a huge bouquet of coral-colored roses on the porch. Her favorite.

"Oh!" Her breath puffs up in a cloud. She doesn't like red roses, which are almost artificially perfect. Red roses usually mean somebody got laid or somebody's in the doghouse. Ted knows she likes messier, more natural-looking flowers.

Maybe the roses are for her mother. Elinor reaches for the card.

Come home now. Bring your mom. She can fly. Call me. I love you. I need you to come home. A long, detailed message for flowers. Elinor imagines the clerk at the florist trying to get it all down, reading it back to Ted. She's sorry she made him resort to this method of communication. She knows it's illogical not to talk to her husband on the phone. But she wants to say just the right thing. The words to make him love her again. She realizes this now, standing on the porch, cradling the flowers to her chest, breathing in their hopeful fragrance. She knows her husband still loves her. But maybe he'll never love her the way he once did.

Ted decides to finish the damn cherry hutch before Elinor returns home. Get the mess out of the garage. If he stays up all night, maybe he can finish it. El clearly doesn't care about the thing. He thought she would like to store their china, silver and candleholders and crap they never even use. But he could tell she struggled to muster enthusiasm for his project, trying not to hurt his feelings. She's not domestic, not a nester. She's too cerebral to be picky about that stuff. Except for the yard. She's very particular about plants and flowers.

He has the overwhelming fear that Elinor's not coming back. Rather, that she *is* coming back, but not to him. Why won't she talk to him? What's the point of doing nothing? Is she reaching some sort of decision? Is he on trial in Ohio for infidelity? Shouldn't he at least be *present* at his own trial?

Thankfully, the screech of the table saw is louder than his anxiety. The clean smell of sawdust is comforting, reminiscent of a fresh start. He holds up the directions to read about the fluted corner he needs to make before the bottom apron goes on. He is in over his head. He should have chosen something Shaker-style, instead of this complicated Queen Anne deal, with all its curves and inlays. He decides to work on the drawers instead.

He is upset by the fact that it was good to see Gina at the restaurant. Why didn't she ever tell him she had a kid? He's a strange boy. Cute little guy. Elinor needs to come *home*, damn it, before Ted loses his mind. He draws two *X*'s where the brass handles will go on the drawers, pressing the pencil so hard that the lead snaps off. He reaches for the electric screwdriver.

During the affair, Ted liked seeing Gina outside the context of the gym — in long skirts and sandals, with her hair down. He remembers the time he and Gina smoked pot and had sex in the backseat of her car. He left his car at the gym after work and they went for a drive in hers under the pretense that she was going to show him a local track where he could run. As they drove away from the gym, she pressed in the lighter, lit a joint. Despite his better instincts, Ted took a hit. He held the smoke in, coughed, exhaled, and felt the stress of the day float away from him. He imagined it running alongside the car, like a dog trying to catch up. He laughed. Gina smiled. "Better not smoke and drive," she said, pulling into a darkening cul-de-sac. Ted handed her the joint. She took a hit, exhaled, tipped back her head, closing her eyes.

"My one vice," she said. She rolled her shoulders a few times and sighed with satisfaction, as though someone had reached an itch on her back.

What about sleeping with a married man? Ted wanted to ask. Yet he didn't want to know anything more about her love life, past or present.

Gina smiled, opened her door, got out, opened the back door. "Come on," she said to Ted, giggling. "Let's ride in the back for a while." He climbed into the backseat after her. They ate grapes out of Gina's grocery bag. She carefully rinsed them, bottled water running down her arms. In the distance, streetlights came on. They ate and stared at the backs of the headrests.

"Are we there yet?" Gina giggled. She kicked off her sandals and leaned over to kiss Ted, her mouth warm and sweet from the grapes. Then she pulled off her underwear and threw it into the back. She reached for Ted's pants and got his zipper and belt undone.

Ted said no, but it came out *ner*. What if people saw them? But there was no house in front of the car, just bushes. The street behind them was empty and dark. Then Ted didn't care. Gina straddled his lap, one knee on either side of his legs. She lifted her skirt and it fell around them so that nothing showed. The soft fabric tickled Ted's arms. In one swift movement Gina arched her back and plunged down on top of Ted. Then she rose up onto her knees again, pulling away from him completely, bowing her head so it wouldn't hit the roof of the car. Ted squeezed her thighs, which were remarkably strong. Gina froze. Ted thought they were stopping. Okay. This was crazy. But then Gina plunged all the way down again, and he was gone.

"I'm an adult, goddamn it," Ted tells the cherry hutch now. *I have control over my life, over my desires. I do!* Crack! He drives his fist through the front door of the hutch for emphasis. His arm catches in the jagged wood and he can't move it. His hand throbs and burns. He's standing there in his garage, up to his elbow in splinters, when he hears the voice of his neighbor, Carl, from the driveway.

"There's no end to the frustration, eh?" Carl waves and laughs.

Ted turns, waves with his free hand. "Damn hinges." Next time he should close the garage door.

Carl, a retired civil engineer who recently gave up cigars, takes two walks a day in lieu of his post-lunch and post-dinner stogies. He shakes his head, laughs. "Elinor away on business?" he asks. The retired neighbors notice everything. When the sprinklers are busted, when your car hasn't been in the driveway for a few days. Ted and El used to think of this as lucky. What a great, safe neighborhood. But now Ted wishes he were anonymous.

"Yeah," he lies, tugging his arm through the door of the hutch. Blood and splinters streak his work shirt, which he hasn't bothered to change out of. The sleeve is torn.

"Hey, buddy, can I help you?" Carl steps toward the garage. "Maybe you need stitches."

"Nah, I'm fine." Blood soaks Ted's tie. "Better run in and wash up." He heads for the kitchen door. "I'm okay!" He calls over his shoulder, pressing the button to close the garage door, leaving Carl standing there, hands in his pockets, mouth agape.

Elinor is nervous as she dials. One phone call isn't going to make or break an entire marriage, she tells herself. Just thank him and tell him you'll be home soon.

There's a commotion as Ted answers the phone, dropping it, then picking it up again.

"Hello?" Elinor says tentatively.

"Elinor!" Ted's surprised, out of breath.

"How are you? What's going on?" She's childishly nervous, as though he's a boy she likes in school.

"I'm . . . Nothing. I cut myself."

"Are you okay?" She sits down on her mother's bed, rubs the nubby chenille bedspread under her fingers. Its frayed familiarity relaxes her.

"I think so. Oh, it's so stupid."

"What?"

"I put my fist through the door."

"In the house?" Despite Ted's sweetness, his compassion, he has a short fuse. He loses his patience easily, often pounding his fists or breaking things. The outbursts are almost always directed at himself, and he recovers from them quickly.

"Through the hutch."

The hutch. Elinor feels guilty for not caring about that thing, for resenting Ted's attention to its every detail. But why? She hasn't wanted him to pay attention to her. Maybe because he found solace in the project, while no activity comforted her. Unless you counted folding the laundry. She could have helped Ted with the hutch. Read the directions aloud. Instead she shunned every idea that Ted came up with for their recovery together. "Are you okay?" she repeats.

"Sure."

"Ted. Thank you so much for the flowers. They're beautiful. And for the note. Just . . ." Elinor stands up. "Thank you."

"In-the-doghouse flowers."

"No, you're not in the doghouse. We're in the shitter. Together."

"Yeah?" Ted says sadly.

"I'm coming home. I'm sorry I wouldn't talk to you. I was afraid I'd make things worse."

"Leave that to me."

"I love you," Elinor says. "I'll see you soon."

Ted stands bare-chested before the smashed hutch, his throbbing arm swaddled in a dish towel. He jumps when his cell phone rings in the kitchen. He stumbles back inside. Hopefully it'll be El calling back. Or maybe God calling to say there's been a mistake: The past three years didn't happen. He and Elinor aren't infertile, Ted didn't have an affair, his wife isn't in Ohio. He hasn't just trashed a woodworking project he wasted two months on.

"Ted?" It's Gina's slightly gravelly voice.

"Gina?"

"Hi. I'd like to talk to you about something. I need to see you, if that's okay." She sounds nervous, rattled. Not her usual cheerful self. "It's a logistical thing."

"Well," Ted says. He's an idiot. He shouldn't have drooled over her, told her that his wife left town.

"I have to go right now," Gina says. Ted hears something crashing in the background. "Can you stop by my house tomorrow night? Around seven?"

"I . . ." Ted is taken aback by her tone, which is fraught with worry.

"See you then?"

"But —"

Gina hangs up.

Ted starts doing math in his head, counting backward to the last time he slept with Gina. Could she be *pregnant*? Wouldn't that be the hellish irony Ted deserves? She's on the pill, but crazier things have happened. Jesus! Ted's losing his mind. It's as though he's impregnated Gina with his outrageous fantasies of her. He tries to calm himself with the argument that Gina certainly would have told him at dinner. But how could she have, with Toby there? What else could she possibly want?

Exhausted, he stumbles into the living room and collapses onto the couch, elevating his injured arm on a pillow. He should get up and fetch a drink — straight vodka from the freezer, the biggest bang for the carbs. He tries to gather the energy to stand.

Here's the bottom line: Gina is a vibrant young woman and Ted's an unavailable geezer. After this favor, or whatever it is, she'll likely want nothing to do with him. Ted waits for the sense of relief that should follow this conclusion, but it doesn't come.

CHAPTER
FOUR

Quit staring, Elinor wants to tell the baby curled on the woman's lap beside her on the plane home. The baby's blue marble eyes — which seem too big for his head — lock onto Elinor. *Blink, why don't you!* Elinor looks out the window at the tarmac, tears burning the edges of her eyes. Babies under a year old are still so generically soft and doughy and underbaked looking. They could be anybody's, really. The baby screeches and Elinor turns and forces a smile. The mother blows her bangs off her forehead and smiles back apologetically. Elinor worries she's exuding a bitchy vibe. In Ohio, bitterness gave way to forgiveness and optimism. But now she feels bitterness wafting off her body again, like heat emanating from pavement.

She wants to tell the woman that her baby is sweet, and she's sad because she can't have children of her own. But that's far too much information. Besides, is it even *relevant?* When will this fact stop defining every *moment* of Elinor's life?

The baby lurches and throws his pacifier, bubbled with spit, at Elinor's feet.

"Sorry," his mom says.

"Please, don't worry." Elinor bends to pluck up the pacifier with a tissue and hands it to the mother, mustering another sympathetic smile. Then she turns to rest her forehead against the cool Plexiglas plane window. You're supposed to *love* babies, not recoil from them. It doesn't bother Elinor anymore that she can't have her *own* baby. She's not wild about her DNA anyway — an alcoholic gene from her grandfather, her proclivity for the blues. She's more disappointed that she can't have *Ted's* baby. That they can't have a child with Ted's smarts and boyish good looks. Whenever Ted held a baby at a party, Elinor's throat swelled.

Elinor sits up and cracks open *The Iliad*. The goddess Athena has created a blazing light around Achilles' head to intimidate the Trojans. Achilles has lost his armor, but his mother arranged for him to get a special shield made by the gods. Elinor doesn't like Achilles, who is driven by revenge and always gets saved by the gods. What kind of hero needs his *mom* to commission him a special shield?

A flight attendant bangs an overhead bin shut, and Elinor jumps. She pokes a finger through the hole in the knee of her jeans. At her mother's house, she found her old 501 Levi's and her cowboy boots. She'd left them behind on an earlier visit — shedding the clothes she preferred to wear, but rarely got to, given her corporate schedule. Somewhere along the way to becoming a successful businesswoman, it seems Elinor left her identity at the coat check. She tugs at the ends of her short hair. Before leaving Ohio, she drove into town and got highlights — bright strands that make her look and feel younger. She wishes she could get her *psyche* highlighted, brighten it up, too.

The plane rattles and rumbles and takes off. Achilles thunders after Hector, spears flashing. The baby screeches. Achilles drives his sword through Hector's throat. Why can't Elinor travel with magazines, like a *normal* person? As the plane reaches cruising altitude, Hector's body is dragged through the streets, his muscular limbs torn apart.

Below, the neighborhoods and swimming pools blur into a patchwork of brown earth and white clouds. As much as Elinor wanted to get away from home — from Ted and his gym bimbo and his turkey bacon and their troubled marriage and her demanding job — she realizes now what she really wants to get away from: *herself*. She'd like to escape to the tropics and leave her churning inner monologue behind.

For the first time that she can remember, Elinor doesn't look forward to going back to work. Suddenly employee relations seems so petty. She thinks of the one file on her computer that's labeled COMPLAINTS, SMELLS. By law, workplace rights prohibit "offensive conduct of any type." Sexual harassment and outright hostility are easy enough to identify and address. But Elinor's come to dread the more obscure, trivial grievances, many of which seem to fall into the "odors" category lately. There's the woman who microwaves fish for lunch every day, the guy with the caustic BO, the admin with the suffocating Chanel No. 5. Their managers want Elinor's legal advice on how to approach these people. The corporate world has become so formal and paranoid and litigious, that you can't just sit someone down and tell them to get a clue. Instead of firing off her typical diplomatic e-mails, Elinor has let her inbox overflow while she hides in the laundry room at home.

Wispy clouds skitter by below the airplane. Maybe Elinor should take her sabbatical from work. She's been eligible for it for over a year now. Ted wanted her to take the time off while they were doing in vitro, so she could really relax. But Elinor was certain she'd lose her mind if she didn't work. Sitting at home between appointments, crossing days off the calendar, waiting for test results. She needed her job, which at least she could control. But she's tired of trying to control things. She can't even control her own *biology* or her husband's sex life.

What will she do during her sabbatical? Maybe soon she, too, will be guessing the prices of Bob Barker's appliances. She had hoped to take the time off after the baby was born. Dizzy with sleep deprivation, she'd make her own baby food. She butts her head against the plane window, wishing she could burst through and fly away.

As Ted steps through the door into Gina's condo, the smells of hot sesame oil and ginger from the wok, and the spice of her China Rain perfume, make his head swim.

"Hi." Gina lightly touches his arm. She looks worn out. Her eyes are sunken with bluish circles. Baggy sweats and an old men's T-shirt hang from her limbs, looking as defeated as she does.

"Toby?" Gina calls toward the spare bedroom.

"Minute!" Toby hollers.

"Turn it *off*, please." Ted's surprised to see Gina agitated. At the gym, she uses praise and encouragement to motivate her clients. Yet she doesn't seem to have this finesse with her son.

The computer game emits a great rumbling crash.

"Ten more minutes," Gina concedes. "Glass of iced tea?" she asks Ted.

"Sure." He follows her to the kitchen. She fills two glasses with ice, pours the tea, and cuts slices of lemon.

"You okay?" Ted asks. Gina cooked dinner for him twice in this small, narrow kitchen while Elinor burrowed in the laundry room, refusing to eat. What's he doing here now? He should have flown to Ohio and surprised Elinor.

Gina nods dismissively and puts down her tea without drinking any. "Listen, may I ask you for a favor?"

Ted's shirt sticks to the perspiration gathering between his shoulder blades. "Shoot."

"Toby needs a tutor. He's so smart, but he can't focus. He needs help with his math and science. I can't help him. The two of us sitting down together turns into a disaster. I hired this high school kid, but Toby gave him a rough time and now the guy won't come back." She looks at the floor. "I explained to Toby that if he doesn't work with a tutor once a week, he'll have to go to summer school, which means staying here,

God forbid, instead of going to Maine for the summer. *That* caught his attention. He asked if you would tutor him." She turns away from Ted to fuss with a dish in the sink. "I explained to him that you and I are just acquaintances." She laughs, shakes her head. "But you're the only thing he likes about California so far." She turns to Ted, raises her eyebrows. "See what you can do to a person in half an hour?"

Ever since Ted met Gina, she's had this unwavering admiration for him that he's never understood. *You're mistaken*, he always wants to tell her. Is that why he slept with her? Because she made him feel worthwhile? How narcissistic.

"*Die!*" Toby shouts from his room.

"I want Toby to *like* it here." Gina wipes the counters, even though they're already clean.

"How come you never told me about Toby?" Ted asks, trying not to sound critical.

"Too complicated." Gina's tone flattens, and she bows her head. The topic is obviously painful for her to discuss. "And embarrassing. What kind of mother doesn't have custody of her own kid? I mean, I *have* joint custody, but then Toby decided he didn't want to live with me during the school year." Gina's persistent cheer and optimism seem even more remarkable to Ted now, given that her life clearly hasn't been easy. He wants to comfort her, without hugging her. He takes a step toward her, jams his hands in his pockets.

"Were you married to him?"

Gina shakes her head. "No. We only dated for a few months. He's a lobster fisherman." She examines her cuticles indifferently. Ted can't read how she feels about Toby's father. "Toby always lived with *me* and spent summers with his dad. Then when he turned eight, he said he would rather live in Maine with his father. Now Rod's going back to school to study landscape design. His new wife doesn't want Toby living with them, since Rod will be gone most evenings. Toby *loves* her, even though she doesn't even want him there. She doesn't have kids." She squeezes her palms together, visibly trying to maintain her composure. "My son prefers to live with a woman who doesn't *like* kids."

Ted takes another step toward Gina, clenching his fists in his pockets. "Oh, Gina. I'm sure it's just a preteen thing. He's a 'tweener." Ted has read articles about this rocky stage.

"Sure, he loves me. But he doesn't *like* me." She pours her tea down the drain. "Anyway, that's beside the point. The point is that he makes it through the school year. So —" She pauses. "— I know it's a weird request, but I wondered if you could help him with his homework." She starts wiping the counters again.

Ted can tell from the hesitation in her voice that Gina didn't want to ask him this.

She looks up at him — a little sheepish, a little shy, mostly tired. "You guys could meet at the library. Of course, I wouldn't be there."

"Uh," Ted says. *You're reactive*, Ted hears Elinor's voice say. *You let life happen to you. Be more proactive.* Ted sits on a bar stool at the counter.

88

"Toby's father is so inconsistent. He doesn't call when he says he will; sometimes he won't call for weeks. Then he overcompensates with big presents. I told Rod, kids need dependable, day-to-day love more than they need big presents." Gina seems to realize she's been mindlessly scrubbing the counter, and tosses the sponge into the sink. "Anyway, Toby's talked about you pretty much nonstop since the other night." She crosses her arms and squeezes them against her stomach.

Ted feels silly for being flattered by this. But Toby probably just needs a guy in his life. Maybe he could introduce Gina to that young athletic patient who had the metatarsal fracture surgery last week. What was that guy's name? He was single, wasn't he? The thought of that handsome kid with Gina creates a spark of jealousy that surprises Ted. He wedges his hands between his knees.

"I don't think it's a good idea," he finally says. "I'm sorry." He clears his throat. "Elinor's coming home. We're reconciling. I called the counselor and made an appointment."

"That's good," Gina says.

"So I worry about —"

"I mean it. That's good." She turns toward the sink, her back to him. "I like Elinor. I really liked her when I met her." She quickly folds a dish towel.

"I mean, Toby's a great kid, but I —"

"You know, I never slept with a married man before."

"Oh." Ted is even more uncertain about the trajectory of this conversation.

"I just wanted you to know that. It was a terrible mistake and I'm sorry." She turns toward him. He's never seen her look so distracted or tired.

"I just worry about making a commitment to Toby." Ted stands, pushes in the bar stool. "I'm sure you can find a tutor through the community college. Besides, you're a natural teacher. You taught me how to use every one of those contraptions at the gym."

Gina nods resolutely. "It's a crazy idea. I'm getting a little desperate." She massages her temples. "I've got to get my *act* together."

"Gina." Ted tips his head to catch her gaze. "You're so complimentary of everyone else — so supportive and thoughtful. Try to be that way with yourself." He sounds stupid and new agey.

"Really? Yeah, you're right. Okay," she says halfheartedly, gliding out of the room.

"Toby?" she calls out. "Ted's here. You want to come and say good-bye to him?"

Toby appears in the living room. "Hey! Did you have any surgeries today?" His tanned, thin limbs poke out of baggy swim trunks and a black T-shirt with a picture of a big white mosquito and the words CAMP ITCHALOT.

"Nah, just checkups. How was school today?"

Toby rolls his eyes, scratches at his knee.

"Some kids played a prank on him," Gina tells Ted.

"Yeah." Toby sulks. "They filled my locker with Ping-Pong balls and when I opened it they all rolled down the hall and *I'm the one* who got in trouble."

"I'm sure there's a way to get those mean kids back," Ted says.

Toby's face lights up with so much hope that Ted flinches and coughs, sucking in saliva or air the wrong way. He coughs until he's gasping, looking around the room for relief. He sees the door, the window — emergency exits — then Toby. Gina pats him on the back, gives him water. Finally, he catches his breath.

"Wanna play Risk?" Toby asks.

Ted pants, gulps at the water.

"Ted has to get going, honey," Gina says.

"Why?" Toby kicks the carpet.

"We can play for a little while," Ted says, mopping his brow. After all, he may never see these two again. And he dreads the thought of his empty house — of eating dinner with Larry King again, going to sleep with the too-perky weather lady.

"Yay." Toby reaches for the box under the coffee table. "We can start now and finish next time. I'll keep everything right here." He pats the coffee table.

"Just for half an hour." Gina shoots Ted a worried look.

Ted sits across from Toby on the leather couch, which is cool and supple and comfortable. He blushes, recalling how he and Gina lay here side by side, Ted tracing each of her vertebrae. Ted always wanted a leather couch. "Too disco," Elinor said. "Leather couches make me feel like I should be snorting coke in LA with ponytailed people."

Toby looks up at his mother. Gina is smiling now, her hands on her hips. "*You're* not gonna play, right?" he asks her hopefully.

Gina turns and heads for the kitchen, mustering a weak laugh. "Don't worry."

"You know, your mother is good at every sport on the planet," Ted tells Toby. "Tennis, basketball, you name it." To mix up his cardio workout, sometimes Gina would shoot hoops and hit tennis balls with Ted at the club.

"Yeah, well, I don't like sports." Toby sets neutral army pieces out across the game board, tiny infantrymen pointing their rifles at Ted.

Ted reaches across Scandinavia and grabs Toby's hand, surprised by his own boldness. He squeezes the small, gummy fingers. "Tobe?"

"What?" The boy dips his chin to his chest. He looks up at Ted through his curls.

"Go easy on your mom, okay? She's a good person and you need to cut her some slack."

Toby's mouth drops open. He nods.

"You wanna be red?" Ted finally asks.

Toby nods. He uncurls his fist under Ted's palm, but he doesn't take his hand away. His skin is warm. Finally, Ted lets go. He pats Toby's forearm, then his shoulder.

"'Kay." Toby nods vaguely and counts out his artillery pieces.

"One day," Ted tells Toby, pointing to Italy's boot shape on the board, "maybe you'll get to go to Rome and visit the Forum. You know, I heard there are still

92

coins melted into the stone floors from the time of the invasion of the barbarians."

Toby says, "Yeah, right. Like anybody's ever gonna take *me* anywhere."

Gina reappears, setting a glass of ice on a coaster for Toby, with a bottle of root beer beside it. "I'm making you frozen cheese pizza," she tells him. "Your favorite."

"Thanks." Toby makes eye contact with her, which Ted has noticed he rarely does. "Hey," he says to Ted. "I asked my mom if you could tutor me and she said maybe —"

"Sweetie," Gina says. "Ted's got a lot going on right now. He's just too busy."

"Tell you what," Ted says. "I'll tutor you until we find a student who can take over. Maybe just once or twice." The word *we* hangs in the air. Ted wants to take it back. He realizes that during their tryst he did nothing for Gina. She helped him with his diet and exercise, provided motivation, bought him books, brought him homemade soup. What did he do for her? Nothing. He never even gave her a gift.

"Flight attendants, please prepare for landing." Elinor wakes up. Her eyes sting from the dry airplane air. Her mouth feels glued shut. She dreamed she was holding Hector's dismembered head in her lap, stroking his gnarled hair. The FASTEN SEAT BELT light is on, and now she can't get up and wash her face and brush her teeth. She must look like hell. She reaches for her purse, burrows for gum. Next come eyedrops, ChapStick, lipstick, blush and powder. Will Ted be in the airport or out at the curb? Did they decide? She wishes she could take a shower. She looks through the dusty mirror of her compact at her bleary reflection. Years of reading legal briefs into the evening hours have left two deep lines between her brows that make her look cranky. She rubs off some of the blush and blots the lipstick, both of which seem to be trying too hard.

Anticipation burns in Ted's stomach as he stands waiting in the swarm of people outside security at the airport. He liked it better when you could walk out to the gate.

"Hey, wow!" he blurts when he sees Elinor step onto the escalator with the other passengers making their way down to baggage claim. Her hair is cut short and shaggy, and it's blonder. Her eyes scan the crowd. Ted ducks behind a taller man, relishing this moment of watching his wife as though she's a stranger. *His* stranger. She's wearing jeans and her cowboy boots, which she wore all the time when they first met. Back then she looked disheveled in a sexy way — jeans, boots, and one of Ted's baggy old sweaters or sweatshirts with a camisole underneath. The incongruity of the feminine lace and bows always excited Ted.

Elinor's eyes stop scanning the crowd. She hugs a down parka to her chest and frowns, as though she's given up on Ted.

"El!" He waves his arms overhead.

She sees him, smiles shyly, waves once, and steps off the escalator.

For a moment the shortness of her hair makes Ted nervous. When they got married, her hair was nearly down to her waist. He liked to lift it off her shoulders and press his lips to the back of her neck, finding that warm, moist spot that smelled like apples. But then she was promoted at work, and the longer her hours grew, the shorter her haircuts became. What if the sweet apple spot isn't there anymore?

Ted elbows his way through the crowd, reaching for Elinor's hand. "You look *great*."

"Really?" Elinor laughs, bunches a clump of hair in her fist. Ted brushes strands of bright bangs from her eyes, tries to tuck them behind her ears.

"Yeah, really." He pulls her away from the crowd and into his arms, closing his eyes and inhaling her perfume. Ted used to find the smell of his wife's perfume sexy. Now he finds it comforting, reassuring — something he can count on, like the newspaper in the driveway every morning. Welcome, but not exactly thrilling. But now, this *hair*. He kisses Elinor hard on the mouth. Her back stiffens. She clears her throat in his ear, then finally relaxes in his arms.

He steps back from her. "I thought you might never come home." He jingles the keys in his pocket and runs his fingers over the bumps in each key. This usually soothes his nerves.

Elinor shrugs, works up a smile. "I'm here."

They stop for lunch, choosing a booth at the back of a nearly deserted restaurant. Ted slides in beside El, so they're both facing the wall. He curls his fingers through the hole in her jeans and tickles her knee. She laughs nervously. He laughs, too, not sure what they're laughing at. When the waitress comes, he orders two pale ales.

As Elinor reaches for her beer, Ted sees that she's not wearing her wedding ring.

"Where's your ring?"

"I took it off."

"But we're still married." This comes out somewhere between a statement and a question.

Elinor wipes beer from her upper lip with the back of her hand. "I feel in between right now."

"In between," Ted repeats.

"Maybe I should move out. While we're going to Dr. Brewster. I don't know if I want to live with you when I'm still so mad."

"What? You just *got* here. You can't move. How is *that* reconciling?" The best part about Elinor coming home was that he wouldn't have to spend another minute alone in that empty house. "El, you can be mad. You're *supposed* to be mad." Ted is talking too fast and raising his voice. He can't help it and he doesn't care. He pulls Elinor closer to him. The first few sips of ale make a headache collect between his eyes. "I just want things to go back to the way they were."

Elinor's bangs fall into her eyelashes. Ted wants to kiss her forehead, her nose, her mouth. He just wants to *kiss his wife.*

"But we can't," she says. "That's the problem." She picks at the label on her beer bottle. "Besides, I think that's called denial."

Ted lowers his voice. "Just because I don't want to analyze everything to death doesn't mean I'm in denial. Why can't we just start over?" He squeezes his glass. Slippery with condensation, it slides out of his hand, beer sloshing on the table and drizzling into his lap. "Dang." He mops at the table and his pants with paper napkins.

"We need to see Dr. Brewster. This is going to take work."

"I know," Ted says. The operative word being *work*. He tosses down the wad of wet napkins. It's not that he's lazy or unwilling, but why does everything have to be so much work for them? He'd been hoping they'd cruise up to wine country for the weekend. Make love in one of those ridiculous canopied beds at a B&B, worrying about their neighbors hearing them. Of course, he can't expect Elinor to quickly get over the affair. He brushes his fingertips through her hair, tucks little pieces behind her ears. "Listen, El. I know my behavior was absolutely unacceptable. I'll do anything to make this better."

"Then go with me to see Dr. Brewster."

"We're going. *I* made the appointment." Ted swallows, suppressing his aggravation.

They are both quiet for a long moment. "Do you think we can do this?" Ted finally asks, immediately terrified by the question. "Work things out?" He realizes he's nearly whispering.

The waitress, who's wearing black slacks, a stiff white shirt, and a little black bow tie, arrives with their lunches. "Careful, plates are hot," she warns.

Elinor reaches for a french fry. "Maybe. I want to." She takes one bite, then pushes her plate away. "I'm going to take my sabbatical."

"Great." Ted stops chewing his salad. "Wait, you're not leaving town again, are you?"

Elinor peels the last bit of label off her beer bottle. "No. I'm just going to take some time off." She sounds anxious, as though she's not entirely certain about this. "I really want to focus on my marriage."

My marriage. Sometimes it seems like *Elinor's* marriage and *Elinor's* infertility, as though Ted is merely a variable in the algebraic equation of her life. Job, house, husband, baby.

"If you're taking time off, maybe we can go on a trip," Ted suggests. "Drive up to Yosemite, then over to Tahoe."

"We'll see. Let's see how we do at the counselor."

"Right. No fun allowed." Ted feels like a kid lobbying for a better summer vacation. He opens his mouth, decides to shut up.

"We'll do some fun stuff," Elinor protests wearily.

Ted squeezes Elinor's small hand in his. He thinks of Gina's long fingers — languid and flexible, like the rest of her body — compared with Elinor's small, chapped hand, her bitten nails. He's maddened by the way Gina pops into his head like this — like a crazy tic, like a seizure. He closes his eyes and concentrates on the warmth of Elinor's fingers as he massages them. He loves their smallness, their imperfection. He wants to protect her. From what, he's not sure.

★　★　★

"*Eight weeks?*" Phil, Elinor's CEO boss, isn't happy to learn that she's finally decided to take her sabbatical and the rest of her overdue vacation time. He leans back in his towering black leather chair, which is almost as big as the recliner at the dentist's office.

"You've been encouraging me to do this for *months*," Elinor reminds him.

"Yeah." Phil laughs with resignation. "I just never thought you'd actually do it." He cups his palms behind his head and gazes morosely out the window.

Of course, he probably wishes that Elinor had taken her sabbatical while she was doing IVF — while she was scatterbrained and working a measly forty-five hours a week. Now that she's stopped the treatments, he must hope that she'll amp back up to sixty-hour workweeks. Give up on having a family.

"I need time to get my life organized," she tells him.

"I don't know what we'll do without you."

"I'm sure the joint will shut down," Elinor jokes. "Don't worry. I'll get everybody up to speed before I go." She wants to reassure Phil, but frankly she's getting annoyed by how these Silicon Valley companies operate. Always making you believe that you're indispensable. Once, when Elinor was slaving over one of their few cases that went to trial, Phil told her, "You're Steve Young, and we're about to go to the Super Bowl!" She laughed out loud at this ridiculous analogy. "Okay, Coach," she'd said, lugging another stack of files and her dinner of burned microwave popcorn back to her desk.

"Don't worry," she repeats now. *There's life beyond this place*, she thinks. That is, if you don't let it fall apart while you're here.

The week before her sabbatical begins, Elinor works late to catch up and leave her office in order. When she finally gets home in the evenings, Ted has eaten and is already in bed, often asleep. Elinor showers, slides into a silk nightgown, and climbs in beside her husband, sighing at the warmth his body has created. He rolls over sleepily to kiss her. She tickles his face with her damp hair or kisses the firm center of his belly and finally, on her third night home, they make love.

Elinor has forgotten what it's like to be touched for anything other than medical purposes. During the infertility treatments, it got to the point where any human contact felt invasive. Ted would merely brush against her and she'd recoil. It hurt his feelings, she knew it, but she no longer liked being touched. Even clothing hurt, fabric tugging mercilessly at her tender belly and bruised thighs. The only sensation that felt good was swimming. She'd fly through her laps in the neighborhood pool, weightless, the water kissing her skin. But the adult swim always ended too soon, the neighborhood kids screaming and jumping into the water with their foam noodles. Elinor would flee, racing in her towel to the heat of her car.

Now, as her husband runs his fingers up the insides of her thighs, she feels caresses instead of jabs. Still, it's hard to fully relax, with the jittery tape loop running in her head: *She's so pretty and fit and young! That silky hair. Those long legs. Is she a better lover?* Elinor wants to drill Ted on the details of his affair. What kind of birth control did they use, for one thing? But Ted is so sweet and gentle, kissing and touching her as though nothing had ever happened. Elinor fights to imagine that THE AFFAIR is not in the room with them, looming in the dark.

The first morning of her sabbatical, Elinor tries to unwind with coffee and the crossword, but the blank canvas of the unstructured day makes her pulse race. There's nothing to do between now and her upcoming appointment with Ted and Dr. Brewster. She's depressed by the fact that she has to consult a PhD to connect with her husband. It seems they've had to outsource their entire marriage — first the sex part, and now the love part.

Earlier in the morning, Elinor got up with Ted and scrambled egg whites for him as he showered. Deciding they looked anemic and unappetizing, she shoved the eggs into the garbage and covered them with junk mail, hating Gina. When Ted burst into the kitchen, Elinor was overwhelmed by how handsome he looked — freshly shaven face, flushed from the shower, a forest-green shirt that emphasized his deep brown eyes and soft brown hair, festive yellow tie, sturdy sloped shoulders, narrow waist, firm jaw. Suddenly she didn't want to visit the counselor and dredge up all the ugly stuff. First she wanted to nurse this renewed appreciation for her husband — to let it sink in, the way you'd let a coat of paint dry before adding another one.

Ted had to run; he had a surgery. His mouth tasted of Crest as he kissed Elinor good-bye. She stood on the front porch and watched him back out of the driveway, feeling left behind. While Ted's been shaping up, she's been spacing out. Yet he obviously doesn't want to embark on a midlife crisis *without* her. He wants her to go along — biking or camping, scuba diving to Australia. His enthusiasm for these activities makes Elinor nervous. She's afraid she doesn't know how to be fun anymore. She's afraid she'll disappoint him.

Three-letter word for a small scrap of food. Elinor looks back to the crossword. She fills in *ort*. Then she gazes out the kitchen window at the roses, which are still blooming. After fifteen years of working under fluorescent lights, absorbing LED rays from her computer monitor, and breathing sick-building air, she just wants to be outdoors. She gathers her coffee, newspaper, and *The Iliad*, grabs an old quilt from the linen closet, and heads for her front yard.

She spreads the quilt under the big oak tree and leans back against its bumpy trunk, which is firm and certain against her back. She pushes aside her puzzle and book and sips her coffee, watching the neighborhood women drive by in their SUVs and minivans. Some of them see her, slowing down to do a double take, then waving tentatively. Except for Kat, Elinor doesn't know the other wives in her neighborhood very well; children are the common denominator among them. Neighborhood swim meets, Halloween parties. It seems pointless for her and Ted to show up at these gatherings without kids.

When people ask if Elinor has children, she used to say, "We're trying," or "No luck in that department so far," but that brought unsolicited advice ranging from acupuncture to Robitussin. Now she just says no.

After finishing her coffee, Elinor lies on her back and gazes up through the tree's canopy of branches. The oak is arthritic yet glorious, probably older than she or any of the houses in the neighborhood.

A car idles in the street. "Miss? You all right?" an elderly gentleman calls out. "Did you fall?"

"I'm fine." Elinor sits up. "Just weeding!" She yanks up a clump of grass and tosses it in the air.

CHAPTER
FIVE

"My teacher says I talk too much." Toby fidgets and kicks the table at the Barnes & Noble café, making the foam on Ted's skim milk latte slosh out of his cup. "My mom says so, too. Too much and too fast. I'm supposed to sit still and listen more. To what? It's not like anybody's saying anything that interesting."

"Try not to kick the table, okay, champ?" If Ted can just get Toby to focus on these fractions, maybe he'll pass his quiz tomorrow.

"Sorry." Whipped cream and caramel rim Toby's upper lip. His large front teeth are crooked and ridged on the ends and just into his lower lip, leaving two raw indents. He's at that clumsy stage where parts of his body are too big for the rest — those knobby elbows and knees always whacking into things. He pushes out his lower lip, stops kicking, and starts drumming the tabletop with his stubby fingers. As Ted frowns, Toby wedges his hands under his thighs. But one leg jerks in a spasm, knocking the table and spilling more of their drinks. "*Sorry!*" Toby pleads. "If I can't kick, I have to tap."

Ted sops up the coffee and milk with a handful of napkins. "It's okay, buddy."

"At school I have to sit on my hands and count."

Ted wonders if maybe Gina should take Toby to a pediatrician for this.

"I only count to five, but really fast, like this: onetwothreefourfive, fivefourthreetwoone. There's ceiling tiles in my classroom, which are good for counting. They have all these little holes in them, so I can count those, too. I can't help it, but my lips move when I count. So Todd Francis says, 'Who are you talking to, fuck face?' He swears more than anyone at school. I told my dad about him. My dad said Todd's going to work at Burger King and I'm going to be a CEO of a Fortune Five Hundred company." Toby licks his chapped lips. "Do you think I could be a CEO?"

"Not if we don't work on these fractions. You'll need them for your board presentations."

"Yeah, okay. I'm glad you're gonna help me." Toby's earnestness kills Ted. "This is *way* better than the gym," he adds. "My mom thinks I should be so happy because they have a swimming pool. But there are always screaming kids in there, and the grown-ups yell at you if you put, like, *one toe* in their lap lane. I like to hang out at the snack bar, where there's A/C, and play my Game Boy, but she always wants me to go outside." Toby slurps from his drink and looks around the café, nodding in time to the thrumming bass of a jazz CD. "We should study here all the time."

Ted leans across the table. "Listen, sport, I'm going to help you today, and maybe next week, but then —"

"I know you dumped my mom."

"Well, I . . ." Ted doesn't know what information Gina shared with Toby.

"It's a bummer because you were her best boyfriend."

"I really wasn't —"

"Her other boyfriends are total dorks. Her boyfriend Shane? He can't even drive. He got a DIU."

"DUI." Was Gina seeing these guys while she was seeing Ted? It's arrogant to think that he alone could make her happy. *Sleeping* with these other guys, though?

"Yeah, that's Shane. He shows up in a taxi. What a derelict. You're the only guy she's dated who's not a total loser. Then there's Barry, who's some kinda concert promoter. He knows *Eminem*, like that's such a big deal. I could care less. He's pretty nice to me, though. It's weird — he treats me like everybody treats the popular kids at school. Trying to get them to like you and kind of afraid of them at the same time?"

"Trying to win you over." Ted pushes the sheet of fractions toward Toby.

"Right. He's got lots of money. His backseat is pretty cool. There are seat heaters and speakers and there's a shade I can pull down. But, seriously? I think my mom likes you the most. Still."

"You know I'm married, Toby." Ted can't think fast enough to keep up with this kid. His tongue is burned from his drink and feels raw on the end.

"I mean, the other guys are probably better *looking* than you, but I know she likes you the most. And I don't think it's just because you're a doctor. I mean she

106

talks about how you're a doctor, but I think she just likes you the most."

"Your mother's a very nice woman . . ." Ted's not sure how to find his way back to the fractions.

"Shane? He's just plain *crazy*. He has to work days installing skylights with this other guy, 'cause he can't make enough money playing in that *stupid* band. He's always got insulation and junk all over his clothes. He drinks alcohol and he's so crazy for my mom. When he calls, my mom says not to answer it anymore. We can see his loser name on the caller ID."

The blender whirs and the espresso maker hisses angrily. Ted raises his voice over the noise. "Okay, well we've got to think about this quiz tomorrow." He flips to Toby's test material. *Wc know that 5/10 is equivalent to ½ since ½ times 5/5 is 5/10. Therefore, the decimal 0.5 is equivalent to ½ or 2/4 . . .* He takes a deep breath.

"Hey, how come you dated my mom if you're married?" Toby narrows his eyes at Ted.

"I made a mistake, Toby. My wife and I were having troubles. It was my fault. Your mother had nothing to do with it. Marriage is very difficult sometimes."

"Well, I wouldn't know, since my parents never *got* married."

"I know, sport, but both your parents love you."

"Yeah? My mom said I'm a one-night-stand baby."

Ted doesn't know how to put a positive spin on this bit of information. "She said that to you?"

"No. But I heard her say it one time, to her girlfriend. What does that even *mean*?"

"It just means that your mother and father only dated for a short time. Even though they don't live together, they care about you very much."

"Yeah? Her whole *life* is a mistake." Toby slams his math book shut and crosses his arms over his chest. "I want to live with my dad. You should help me write him a letter."

"Toby, we have to study right now. And *you* have to give your mother more of a chance. She's trying hard to make you happy."

"Hey, bean sprout!" a voice calls out from across the café.

Toby looks up, shudders, then slides down in his chair.

Ted turns to see a hefty kid wearing a backward baseball cap lunging toward their table. "Whatcha doin', Fruity Tofutti?"

"That's Jamie." Toby lowers his voice, keeping his eyes on Ted. "He makes fun of my lunch."

Ted shoots Jamie-the-bully a scowl. The boy retreats into the gardening aisle. For a startling moment, Ted thinks he sees Kat perusing a large hardback with flowers on the front, but it's another woman with similar short dark hair. The anxiety thrumming in Ted's chest confirms that he shouldn't be here without telling Elinor.

"Try having a *nutritionist* pack your lunch," Toby complains. "Whole wheat tortillas wrapped with tofu and junk. One time a bean sprout fell on the floor and now that's what everybody *calls* me. And those protein bars? They *look* good, like candy, but they taste like

108

piss. And the sad thing?" Toby starts with the kicking again. "She spends like an *hour* the night before making my lunch. Now I just throw it in the trash and use the money my dad sends me to buy lunch. But I'm out of money for this week." Toby looks away, shrugging.

"Have you explained this to your mom?"

Toby shakes his head. "I can't talk to her!"

"Yes, you can." Ted pulls his wallet out of his pocket. "Your mom's a good listener, Toby. Just tell her what happened and I'm sure she'll make you a different lunch or give you lunch money." He hands Toby fifteen dollars. "For now, try not to worry so much." Ted has forgotten how stressful being a kid can be. He feels sorry for Toby, having to transfer into Silicon Valley schools. They're supposed to be among the best in the country, but they're also freakishly competitive. High-tech, high-achiever parents pushing their kids to work like little CEOs.

"This is *just* for lunch, okay, champ?" Toby pauses, then takes the money, folds it, and puts it in his wallet, which is blue nylon with Velcro. The inside flaps hold Toby's school ID and a card that Gina has filled out with parent identification. ALLERGIC TO BEES, it says in her neat writing. Something about the flimsiness of the wallet tugs at Ted's heart. It seems so precarious to send a kid out into the world every day to fend for himself.

Ted buys a packet of index cards to make flash cards, and finally the two of them work their way through the fractions. On their way out of the store, he tells Toby to choose a book he'd like to buy. Toby picks a tome on medieval knights and armor. "Even the horses have armor," he says with awe, running his fingers over a stallion on the cover.

Ted picks up a newly published book on antioxidants. "Let's get this for your mom." Gina is big on antioxidants. "It can be from you." He's desperate to fill the gap between Gina and Toby, a gap he worries he's falling into.

Toby rocks from foot to foot. "I don't want to get her anything."

Ted leans closer to the boy, inhaling his smell of sweat and erasers. "You have to be careful not to hurt your mother's feelings. It makes her sad."

"I make her sad?" Toby kicks a table stacked high with cook-books. "*I* make her sad?" He kicks the table again and the books topple over onto the floor. Clenching his fists at his sides, he scowls at Ted. "*I make her sad!*"

"Sir!" a clerk scolds from behind the information desk. "Please ask your son to pick up those books."

The marriage counselor's waiting room is a dark place Ted thought he'd never have to return to. It's so calm and soothing, so *empathetic*. The Oriental carpet and flowery couches seem to say, *We know you're screwed. It's okay. So long as you brought your checkbook.* Suddenly he resents Dr. Brewster's empathy. Ted and Elinor tell her how bad they feel, how screwed up things are, and she nods knowingly. These things happen. It's okay that everything's a mess!

Ted and Elinor sit side by side on a rattan couch, as shy and nervous as two junior high students at a dance. Ted reaches for the tassels of frayed cotton fringing the holes in Elinor's jeans. He rolls one between his fingers, finding it remarkably soft.

"Your legs are tan," he says.

"From reading under the tree."

"Good." In the hours leading up to this appointment they've been choosing their words carefully, as though looking for the least slippery rock to step on while crossing a stream.

"You okay?" Ted asks her. "I mean, you *look* great."

Elinor's wearing an old Talking Heads T-shirt and no bra. She looks rested — no circles under her eyes or lines creasing her brow.

"Fine," she says. She is not fine. *They* are not fine. Ted should stop asking stupid questions.

Elinor stretches her legs out before her and bends her head down until her forehead reaches her knees. A dance student in college, she is still remarkably flexible. The room is quiet except for the tinkling of classical piano music coming from a boom box in the corner. A big potted plant sprawls behind it. Some kind of pointed thing with flowers. Ted can't tell if it's real. Elinor hates silk plants and Ted hates the fact that he can't tell the difference. How are you supposed to know? He has the urge to hurl this one against the wall. Instead he cracks his knuckles.

Once inside Dr. Brewster's office, Ted watches El pull Kleenex after Kleenex — *whoosh, whoosh, whoosh* — out of the box on the table beside her.

Although she rarely cries at home, once she's behind this door, the dam breaks. She's always been one to do the right thing in the right place — a talent for compartmentalizing that makes her good at her job.

"It's like it doesn't affect you," Elinor says, referring to the fact that they can't have a baby. Ted can't believe they haven't even *gotten* to the affair yet.

"Not true." Maybe it's time for him to finally speak up on this topic. "It didn't affect me in the same way that it affected you, therefore you conclude that it didn't affect me at all. That's faulty reasoning."

"You should have been the lawyer." Elinor looks away. "Anyway, I guess you fucked your way through the pain." Elinor claims that swearing with abandon is one of the only things she likes about not having children.

"I wanted a daughter!" Ted leans toward her, catching her gaze. "I *wanted* a little girl." He'd always been afraid to say this — as if being hopeful would bring bad karma.

Elinor looks surprised. She lowers her voice. "See, I never *knew* that, because you don't *talk* about it. You just want to turn back the clock or jump ahead without discussing anything."

"That's because everything I say belittles *your* pain. The *physical* pain, which I'll never experience. I'm not allowed to experience it in my own way, because I never put my feet in the stirrups."

The therapist nods. Ted feels as though he's made a point in a tennis match. *Deuce!*

112

A car splashes by on the street. It's one of the few rainy days of summer. The air conditioner ticks and hums.

"Oh," Elinor finally says softly. "I see what you mean." She is a compassionate listener. It's another trait that makes her a good lawyer. In a way, this makes it hard being married to her. Because she listens carefully and looks for meaning in people's words, Ted wishes he were more profound.

"The thing to understand," Dr. Brewster says in her hushed voice, "is that big events, such as an illness or the loss of a baby, or infertility, touch people in very different ways. A man and a woman may react and cope entirely differently. You become angry with your partner for not seeming to be as sad as you are, even though this is rarely the case. Ironically, this causes a rift between people when they need each other most."

Elinor is weeping again, balling up Kleenex in her hands.

"Infertility and infidelity are two huge topics to address in a marriage," the therapist adds.

Elinor nods. The therapist nods. Their consensus hangs heavy in the air. Ted wishes they could open a window.

"I know the affair must seem unforgivable," Ted says. "I wish I could undo —"

"You *can't* —"

"I *know*, Elinor. I know!" Ted hears his voice getting louder, but he can't stop it. He wants to chop off his arm and give it to these two women! "Which is why you *should* be angry. Maybe we *should* yell. Yell at me!" he hollers.

Dr. Brewster leans toward them as though she's watching a program that just got interesting. She always wears the same muted beige and brown tones as her office wallpaper and carpet and furniture — a tweedy neutrality that bugs Ted.

"Oh, we're not supposed to yell." Ted throws his arm in the therapist's direction. "No. We're supposed to listen to classical music and shred Kleenex and calmly talk about our *feelings*."

"What *are* you feeling?" Dr. Brewster asks Elinor. She frowns at Ted, signaling for him to hush for a minute.

Ted sighs heavily, then tries to reroute the impatient rush of air it into a cough.

"Maybe it's a good thing Suzie NoRisotto came along," Elinor grumbles, "to force us apart. I mean, maybe we had to break up before we could get together."

Ted's back seizes up at the mention of Gina.

"Sorry," Elinor says facetiously. "I can't say her name."

"Why are you sorry?" Dr. Brewster asks.

"I don't *like* being bitter," Elinor says defensively. "It's like having the flu, only worse, like it might never go away. I hate it." She laughs weakly. "I'm bitter that I'm bitter."

"But you seemed angry with me *before* the affair," Ted points out.

114

There is a silence and Elinor nods. Her face is puffy with red splotches. Ted tries to reach for her, but his weight seems to pull him away from her and into the center of the leather chair, which is slippery and scooped like a baseball mitt. Finally, he leans out and catches El's hand. He squeezes it, maybe a little too hard.

"What are you feeling now?" Dr. Brewster asks Elinor.

"Terrible," Elinor says through sobs. "We've established that! I feel terrible, Ted feels terrible. What else have we established?"

Dr. Brewster gets up to open her desk drawer. She pulls out two yellow pads and hands one each to Ted and Elinor, followed by pens. "I want each of you to make a list of ten things you love about the other. Just list anything that comes to mind, and then we'll talk some more."

Ted is amazed by how quickly Elinor's pen hits the paper and the scurrying, scratching pace as she writes. He's intimidated by his own blank pad. He loves a million things about his wife, but it always takes him a moment to gather his thoughts on any topic.

Elinor freezes. Ted senses her looking sideways at him.

He writes: *Sense of humor, intelligence, beautiful, smooth knees, perfect teeth.* Ted thinks of how Elinor's teeth flash across the room at a party, of how she always makes everyone laugh. *Work ethic, humor.* Oops, he already wrote humor. He scratches it out, realizing this probably looks to Elinor and the therapist as though he's changed his mind about something. He quickly adds to the list: *Everything she knows about chairs*. He thinks it's great that Elinor can tell a Louis XIV from a Louis XV from a Louis XVI chair. Something to do with the stretchers and the legs. She honestly thinks *furniture* is what caused the French Revolution. She has smart, funny theories like this. "Think about it," she'll say. "The royalty taxed the hell out of the people so they could dip their chairs in gold. Wouldn't you be pissed?" Then there's her theory that caffeine caused the Industrial Revolution. "How come it didn't happen in China, then, where tea *came* from?" Ted had asked. "Hmm, good question," Elinor pondered, reconsidering. They used to talk about random stuff like this all the time. Not about their problems, about their *issues*. Jesus, all they did was try to start a family!

Ted realizes he's staring into space while Elinor and Dr. Brewster watch him, waiting. He turns to El. She looks hurt, probably because Ted isn't working on his list. She hugs her pad to her chest.

"Would you like to read your list?" Dr. Brewster gently asks Elinor.

"Handsome," Elinor begins. "Strong and athletic. Thick, perfect hair. Gorgeous biceps. I mean, c'mon."

Ted feels himself blush. He's never thought of himself as handsome. He's stocky and goofy, isn't he?

"Shy in a sweet way. Kind, nice to his patients. Okay, sometimes maybe a little *too* nice. He'll listen to a patient's *entire* life story while the waiting room is backing up." Elinor frowns at her pad. "Doesn't stay mad for long, but gets frustrated too easily and

116

sometimes has a temper. Sorry, that's a negative." She skips over something on the paper.

Ted wants to hear it, wants to know what the other negatives are.

". . . hard worker, nice to old people," Elinor continues, "gives good shots — better than the nurse, *that's* for sure — great laugh, strong hands, good teacher." She looks up at Dr. Brewster, a little embarrassed. "He taught me how to throw a softball."

"That's great," Dr. Brewster says. "When you live with someone, it's easy to forget these things. Ted?"

Ted doesn't have to refer to his pad to name all the things he loves about his wife. The list comes tumbling out: smart, funny, beautiful, sharp-dark-quick wit, great lawyer, kicks ass at Scrabble, doesn't care what people think, yet she's thoughtful about others — nice to her employees at work — knows all about chairs, loves the outdoors, makes their garden beautiful, supportive of him. *At least until recently*, he thinks. It wasn't that El stopped being supportive; it's just that somehow they aren't in things together anymore. They're each in their own orbits, somehow incapable of holding each other up. Gina does this, though. Gina lifts Ted's spirits and holds him up. He shudders at this thought, relieved that Dr. Brewster is talking now, proposing a plan: Ted and Elinor should meet with her once a week, and go on a date twice a week. One date should be a fun outing and the other should be something they do together at home.

"It can be a project you've been meaning to work on, or you can cook dinner together, or take a walk in your neighborhood," she suggests. "Or you can just sit and read. Try not to plan too many high-expectations events. You don't need fancy restaurants and candlelight all the time."

Ted rubs his face. Two months ago his sperm and Elinor's eggs were shacked up in a petri dish. Now they're *dating*.

"And Ted, do you have an idea?" Dr. Brewster asks.

"Idea?" He'd stopped listening for a few minutes.

"Of a neutral territory place for a date," Dr. Brewster says.

"Bowling?" Ted ventures. El likes bowling. The cheap beer, greasy french fries, the way the bowling shoes make you float across the floor. *Like the floor's a Ouija board*, El always says. "At Camp David," he adds.

Elinor laughs at his joke, wiping her cheeks.

Ted feels himself smile. "Good. It's a date." *Bowling*. It's as though he's said the right thing for the first time in a year.

Ted wakes up in the middle of that night and knows immediately that Elinor isn't in bed with him. He looks at the clock radio. It's two in the morning, and she's gone. His arm flies out to explore the cold covers beside him. She's in Ohio. No, she's home. They went to sleep together. Read, kissed good night, tried to spoon, decided they weren't comfortable, and each rolled to their side of the bed.

"El?" The lights aren't on in the bathroom or hallway. Ted stumbles out of bed, cursing. He pulls on sweats and pads down the hall. "El?" He peers into the laundry room. She always finds *something* to wash — even if it's beach towels or holiday place mats. But the laundry room is dark. He blinks and squints as he turns on the kitchen light, then opens the garage door. Both cars are there. Elinor's office, the dining room, living room. Dark, dark, dark. He reaches for the front door, surprised to find it unlocked. He slides on his flip-flops and steps onto the porch. The evening air is moist and cool. The streetlights glow amber. The sky is tinged with pink from the city lights downtown. Ted scans the yard, spotting a lump under the oak tree in the yard.

"El!" he calls out in a loud whisper. He hurries across the lawn to find Elinor curled in a sleeping bag on top of an old quilt. Her pillow is bunched under her head. She sleeps soundly in a fetal position, shadowed by the broad trunk of the tree. Jesus; any kook could drive by and find her here. Ted kneels beside her, brushes her cheek.

"Elinor?"

She jumps and gasps, squinting up at him. "Time to go to the marriage counselor?" She frowns, closes her eyes again.

"Time to go to *bed*. Honey, what on earth are you doing out here?"

"I turned off the sprinklers," she says, as though this explains everything. She tucks her chin to her chest, licks her lips.

Ted sits beside her, damp grass poking at his legs through the blanket.

"Couldn't sleep," she mumbles.

"But you can't sleep out *here*."

"Why not?"

"It isn't safe, for starters." He kisses her forehead. "Let's go inside."

"Lie with me." Elinor scoots over on the blanket. She unzips the sleeping bag and tries to drape it over Ted, managing to cover one of his thighs. Then she's asleep again. Ted looks around, making sure no one's lurking on the street, then scoots onto his side and wraps his arm around her waist, burying his face in her hair.

Elinor's skin is warm and damp. As he runs his fingers over the soft silk of her camisole, he closes his eyes. He cups her breast, massages her rib cage. She is so tiny. It is the first thing he noticed about his wife when he met her. It was the summer his buddy Duncan worked at the same law firm as El, and invited Ted to their company picnic. As the softball game started, Elinor sat alone at a picnic table, drinking beer. Ted asked if she'd join the game.

"Okay, confession," she said. "I've never told anyone this."

Ted laughed.

"I don't know *how*." She said no one had ever taught her how to throw or hit a softball. She was a bookworm geek as a kid, and must have been absent the day they learned at school. So she secretly dreaded summer picnics and their ubiquitous softball games. Ted decided not to play that day, either, and he and Elinor sat and talked and drank beer until everyone left the picnic and it started to get dark. Over the next few weeks they met after work, and he taught her how to throw and hit a ball. Seven months later, they were married.

What if the cops drive by? Ted thinks now as he drifts off to sleep under the tree. He opens his eyes. Can you get a ticket for sleeping in your front yard? He breathes in the smell of wet grass. While everyone else in the neighborhood has gardeners, Ted prefers to do the yard work himself. Hell, he's the only one he knows who owns a lawn mower. He likes the mindlessness of mowing, raking, and pruning, even the familiar dull throb in his back that comes afterward.

Elinor stirs and coughs, rolling to face Ted. She opens her eyes. They're bright and almost feverish. She reaches to touch Ted's cheek, then pulls her hand back as though his skin is hot. Her hair sticks out in a halo of points around her head. Ted traces the outline of her jaw with his finger.

"I love our house," she says.

"You do?" Elinor bought the place before she and Ted met, but she hated it then, because it had so many ranch-house money-pit problems that she didn't have the time, skill, or cash to fix. Once they were married, she and Ted worked on the place together, tearing up linoleum, replacing cabinets, even buying a beater pickup truck for their trips to Home Depot.

"If you love it, then let's go inside," Ted teases.

"I love all of it," Elinor says, throwing an arm out of the sleeping bag. "I love this *tree.*"

Ted tickles the inside of Elinor's arm with his fingertips, something she used to always ask him to do.

121

"I loved our almost-baby," Elinor murmurs. "Our zygote."

"I know." Ted bends to kiss her forehead. Then he slides his arms underneath her waist, scoops her up off the ground, and carries her into their house.

In bed, Ted laughs as he pulls leaves from her hair, collecting them on the nightstand. He tugs at the top button of her 501 jeans. "I remember doing this in the old days," he says, undoing the row of buttons with one yank. Elinor's breath is warm in his ear. She lifts her hips so he can slip off her jeans and underwear. And then they are making love. For no reason. Not to have a baby or to keep up with the statistical average in some dumb women's magazine article or to make up after a fight or because one of them wants to and the other doesn't. They are making love because Elinor couldn't sleep inside and Ted couldn't sleep outside, and because it feels good.

Elinor giggles.

Ted flinches and pauses in a low push-up over her. "*What?*" he says, embarrassed.

"All those years when I worried about contraceptives."

The bowling alley is jammed with people out on a Friday night. Led Zeppelin blasts on the classic rock station, and colored lights flash overhead. Ted watches Elinor swoop across the floor, one leg curling up behind her, and toss out her ball. It lands perfectly in the middle of the lane. She stands poised like a statue as it spins and crashes through the pins. A strike. She turns, shaking her fists over her head, the lace of her camisole showing under Ted's baggy old cable-knit sweater.

"You're kicking my butt," Ted says as she approaches, a little out of breath. She sits on his lap as he marks their score sheet. The beer is cold, the grilled cheese is warm and greasy in a good way, and the back of his wife's neck has that sweet apple smell. He feels an erection swelling in his jeans. Elinor must feel it, too. She wiggles her ass, gently grinding into him.

"Bet you didn't know this bowling alley had lap dances." Elinor turns to kiss him, her lips cold and fizzy with beer.

"This bowling alley has everything I need right now." Ted lifts her hair and licks the back of her neck.

"Look at us, Mr. and Mrs. Getaroom."

"Don't sound so surprised." He squeezes her thigh as he slides out from under her to take his turn.

Ted scoops up a bowling ball and stands poised to throw it, closing his eyes first and listening to the cacophony of clattering pins and laughter. He breathes in the smells of mildew, stale beer, and old cigarette smoke, finding their sourness oddly comforting. The bowling alley is like a time machine. This could be any year in his life. He opens his eyes and tosses out his ball. It hits the lane a little too hard, veers right, and only hits three pins.

"Good." Elinor marks down his score.

"I stink." Ted wipes his palms on his jeans.

"Hey, Dr. Mackey!" a voice calls out.

Ted turns to see Toby bouncing through the crowd, a toothy grin on his face. Ted's chest tightens as he peers past Toby to see if Gina's with him.

"Toby, hi, what are *you* doing here?" Ted asks.

"Birthday party." Toby shrugs shyly when he sees Elinor. He points a shoulder in the direction of a gang of raucous boys a few lanes over.

"Well, great to see you." Ted says this with finality. *Good-bye, then!* Toby looks hurt. He takes a few steps backward, crossing his arms to reach for the scabs on his elbows.

"Aren't you going to introduce me?" Elinor asks.

"You *Mrs.* Mackey?" Toby folds the soft toe of his shoe, which is about two sizes too big, into the floor.

"I am." Elinor laughs. "What's your name?"

"Toby."

"Nice to meet you, Toby." She shakes his freckled hand and holds out a bag of peanut M&M's.

"I'm allergic to peanuts," Toby grumbles, as though the candy has offended him. He kicks an empty chair and it rattles across the floor.

"Patient's kid?" Elinor smiles at Ted.

Ted clears his throat.

"Is your mom the new nurse at the office?" Elinor asks Toby.

"Yeah, right." Toby looks at Ted. "My mom's a *nurse*. She can't even do her times tables."

"This is Gina Ellison's son. You know." Ted coughs again — a dry, nonproductive cough that feels like leaves in his throat. "Gina, the trainer at the gym?"

124

Elinor smiles stiffly at Toby. "We don't *go* to that gym anymore."

"Yeah, it's crap," Toby says. He's pitched forward and he's got that look on his face like he's about to launch into a ten-minute talking streak. "That's why it's better when Dr. Mackey takes me to the bookstore."

"Oh? The bookstore?" Elinor turns to Ted. "You didn't tell me she had a kid," she says through clenched teeth.

"I didn't *know* she had a kid until recently." Ted lowers his voice, hoping Toby can't hear him.

"Recently? How recently?"

"While you were in Ohio."

"And you've been taking him to the bookstore?" Elinor turns toward Toby, a helpless look on her face. "He seems to be a big fan of yours."

"I ran into them. Then Toby and I went to the mall and I helped him with his homework. Once." It's best to tell the truth. Ted at least owes his wife the truth.

"Study? Once?" Elinor looks to Toby.

"He helped me with my fractions," Toby says proudly. "Hey, I got an eighty-two on the test!"

"Homework," Elinor says with disbelief.

"Yes, but I've told him that I can't help him again. Right, Toby?" Ted reaches for Toby's shoulder, squeezes it.

Toby kicks the chair again. "Whatever. Yeah. Maybe you could tutor me at your house?" He looks at Elinor, asking *her*, speaking with desperation more than chutzpah.

"What?" Ted says. "No, Toby." He clasps the boy's shoulder and steers him away from Elinor.

"Excuse me." Elinor stands, throws her purse over her arm, and rushes past them toward the back door of the bowling alley. She breaks into a jog as she passes the pinball machines.

"Toby, you need to go back to your party." Ted places his palm over Toby's small, sharp shoulder blades and gives him a push.

"Bean sprout butt, you're up!" one of the boys from the party hollers. Toby turns away from Ted and heads in the opposite direction of the party, toward the locker rooms.

Ted reels around and heads after Elinor down the dark, narrow hallway. Tacky red-and-black carpet with a crazy pattern of pins and balls spins under his feet.

"*Shoes!*" a voice shouts at him over the PA system. "*No shoes outside.*" Ted crashes through the back exit doors, smashing his hip in the process. He finds Elinor climbing into the car.

"What are you going to do," he calls after her, "leave me here?"

Elinor rolls down the car window. "You can get a ride home with the birthday party."

Ted reaches the car, out of breath.

She turns to him, a deep red high in her cheeks. "You didn't tell me she had a kid."

"El, he *knows* I'm married." Ted pants and spreads his hands against the car door, as though trying to hold the car in place. It's still light out. The air is cooling, but the asphalt emanates heat.

126

"So you're not really cheating on me with an eight-year-old?" Elinor starts the engine.

"He's ten. He's small for his age." Without intending to, Ted says this defensively.

"Jesus, Ted." Elinor sounds more vexed than angry. "Okay. So you broke up with him. You broke up with your former mistress's ten-year-old kid."

Ted nods.

"What the hell is the matter with us?" Elinor shouts into the parking lot. Two veins emerge like cords in her neck. "Why do we make life so damn hard!"

"El, please . . ."

"Please what?"

"Please let's not fight. I've told you everything there is to know. That's it, I promise you. I ran into her while you were in Ohio, and I helped her kid once with his homework because he's struggling and they haven't found a tutor for him yet. That's it. It's over."

"How many times is it going to be over, Ted?" She frowns at the windshield, as though concentrating on heavy traffic.

"Okay. I know," Ted says.

"He's a cute kid." Elinor sounds calm. She grips the steering wheel, narrowing her eyes. "Doesn't look anything like his mother."

She bends down and her head disappears as she fumbles under the dashboard. Then she reappears, handing her bowling shoes through the window to Ted.

"Wait, I have to go inside and pay." As Ted turns toward the bowling alley, he hears the car clunk into drive.

"Yeah. Take a taxi, would you?" Elinor's a little apologetic as she says this. She starts driving away from him. "I'm going to move out of the house," she calls over her shoulder.

"*What?* You can't . . . How are we married if you move out of the house and you're not even wearing your wedding ring?"

Elinor slows down, turns her head, and gives him a *you-can't-be-serious* look.

"Listen, I won't tutor Toby anymore. I wasn't going to anyway. I mean, I —" He picks up a stone, throws it at the back wall of the bowling alley.

Elinor steps on the gas, gravel whipping up behind the rear wheels.

"See you at the counselor?" Ted shouts.

Elinor brakes suddenly, lurching forward against the seat belt. She leans out the window, shaking her head. "I don't think so. I need a break from dating you." She motions at the bowling alley. "Or whatever the hell this is." The car jerks forward again. She speeds out of the parking lot, not even looking in the rearview mirror.

"Let *me* move out!" Ted hollers after her, cradling the dusty bowling shoes to his chest. The tastes of ketchup and beer burn in his throat. Dusk closes in on him. "*Let me!*"

CHAPTER
SIX

There is always something wrong with the men Gina loves: They drink too much or break things or bounce checks or can't hold down jobs. Ted is a new kind of wrong. Married. Add that to the list of unsuitable attributes.

Why can't she fall for any of the men she *should* love? Bob, for example. After the first time they slept together, he told her he loved her and wanted to take her to Paris. He wanted her to move in with him. Gina continued to go to dinner and movies with him, but there was no chemistry. When he picked her up for dates, his nervous enthusiasm made her want to jump out of the car. It didn't help that he was the worst kisser on the planet. As a clump of spongy tongue that didn't seem to have a tip shoved its way into her mouth, all she could think of was how she wanted a drink of water.

"To hell with chemistry," her friend Donna said. "Bob's a partner at one of the top law firms in the Valley! Chemistry will come later." Gina hoped this would happen. But in her experience, chemistry never comes later; it fades.

She wants to travel to Paris. She wants to make out under the Eiffel Tower. With Ted.

Is she one of those dysfunctional women who can only love men who don't love her? But Shane loves her, and she loved him at first. There was certainly chemistry *there*. She fell in love with him at a bar — not the best venue, admittedly — where he played in a band. While the lead singer leapt around the stage like an MTV wannabe, Shane closed his eyes and strummed his bass with somber concentration that touched Gina. His hair, black and shaggy and down to his shoulders, made a frame around his pale face. He looked lean and fit in his simple jeans and T-shirt. When she finally met him — a week later, between sets — she couldn't believe the startling contrast of his blue eyes with that jet-black hair and fair complexion. Sex with Shane was sweet and intense at the same time. He's probably the best lover Gina's ever had. While he's almost forty, he has the body of a college boy — thin but muscular and sinewy, with a smooth chest and ribbed abs that he doesn't have to work to maintain. He lacks the vanity to work out or obsess over his diet. His shaggy haircut and his clothes — jeans, T-shirts, and flannel shirts — are sort of 1970s, which Gina found endearing at first — as though he could take her back to an easier time.

In the mornings, Shane always cooked Gina breakfast, singing silly songs as he flipped cheese omelets and smeared toast with preserves. Even though he's a guy's guy — with the Marlboros and small tattoo of a snake on the inside of his ankle — he's remarkably domestic. His mother was killed in a car accident when he was sixteen, and his father worked nights, so he had to take care of his four younger sisters. As a teenager, he taught himself how to cook and do laundry and even iron. So he doesn't think anything of vacuuming Gina's condo, or being silly just to make her laugh.

Gina soon learned that the problem with Shane is booze. He drinks too much and keeps insane hours and drives too fast and smokes and swears. When he drinks, his mood evolves from affectionate to playful to sarcastic to sullen to angry. Once the rage sets in, he's in constant motion, pacing and ranting. The tirades aren't directed at Gina; usually they're abstract screeds about the music industry or the inattentive patrons at the bar. Still, the intensity of his anger rages like an out-of-control fire, its randomness suggesting that it could easily turn on her.

Then there's the jealousy. One night Gina made the mistake of talking about Ted. It was before she'd become involved with him. Shane asked how her job was going — who her favorite client was. Having grown up with sisters, he was good at making conversation like this. She said she couldn't get over how grateful this one guy Ted was for her ideas, how starved he seemed for a little praise and encouragement. His wife was this high-powered attorney who didn't seem to pay attention to him. This wife sounded fiercely independent and not the least bit needy — two characteristics Gina secretly admired.

"I'll bet this guy loves you!" Shane said accusingly, slamming his hand on the table. He was four beers into the evening, each bottle making his voice louder. Gina quickly rerouted the conversation into an overexaggeration of how out of shape and heavy and *old* Ted was, then she asked Shane questions about the band.

Two shots of tequila later, Shane hit her. It wasn't a hit, so much as a shove. Still, it hurt and left a bruise on Gina's arm. She had made the mistake of saying that she couldn't blame people at the bar for talking while the band was playing. She'd even chatted with a guy during the last set. Then Shane pushed her against the kitchen wall. In the instant in which she was pinned there, trapped with his red-eyed rage and hot beer breath bearing down on her, she fell out of love with him. In a flash, she saw the potential for Shane to hurt her, to hurt her son, and *boom* it was over. She'd like to think it was that rational, that noble, but really it wasn't. Gina simply fell in and out of love instantaneously. It didn't happen often, but when it did, it was sudden, like a thunderclap.

This is how it happened with Ted. He sat across her desk at the club one morning, telling her how he'd spent the day before helping his neighbor find a lost dog. The dog had run off up the hill behind their houses and Ted tromped through the woods and brambles with the guy for two hours, until they finally found the dog in another neighbor's backyard, eating the cat's food. The dog was coated with burs and Ted performed minor paw surgery, using nail clippers to yank one out from between *the poor fella's* toes. Gina bent down to retie her sneaker, listening, laughing, admiring Ted's kindness. When she lifted her head,

132

Ted's handsomeness overwhelmed her. She felt heat emanate from her chest up into her face. *Damn, I love this guy. Shoot, shoot, shoot. This married guy!* For weeks after that, Gina tried not to look Ted in the eye. It was his face that got to her. A big Irish face with full lips that broke easily into a broad smile. Deep brown eyes and gumdrop earlobes that demanded nibbling.

She tried to put Ted out of her mind. Even though she'd broken up with Shane, she called and encouraged him to attend AA. She offered to go with him. Shane said you weren't supposed to go with your *mother*. Gina knew this sarcasm was the Jack-and-Coke talking. But then Shane did quit drinking and started calling Gina every night. He missed her. He loved her. He wanted her. He needed her. They spent hours talking on the phone. She said everything she could think of to be supportive and helpful. They slept together again and it was passionate and slow and perfect and she didn't love him anymore. (Would her heart *ever* consult her in these matters?)

Meanwhile, Gina learned that Ted was having problems with his wife. One day during his workout, Gina suggested that he and his wife hike together on the weekends, because exercising with a partner is more fun. "On a hike, you're outside and talking, and you don't even *notice* that you're getting a great workout," she said.

"You're making the assumption that she would do *anything* with me," Ted said.

The sadness and frustration in his voice surprised Gina. She tried to hide her alarm, turning away to crank up the elevation on his treadmill. "Isn't it always that way?" she said cheerfully. "You start out thinking you have so much in common then before you know it . . . There was this one guy I dated who said he loved swap meets, then as soon as we got serious he wouldn't go with me." What the heck was she *saying*? Pure babble. She wasn't sure how she always managed to be so cheerful. It was something she'd pulled off since elementary school. She was the pretty girl who was always cheerful. Not prissy, but buoyant. Optimistic. Never for herself, mind you, but always for others. That's why she became a personal trainer.

Ted broke into a run on the treadmill, smiling down at her. His wife didn't want to *do* anything with him? What the heck? She'd be all *over* that man. She shuddered and faked a headache and cut their session short, letting Ted finish up and stretch on his own.

The first time they slept together, at her house, Ted kissed her so much (light, warm, moist kisses all over her body), and hugged her so tightly, and came so hard, that she couldn't help but love him more.

Then Barry, a successful concert promoter, asked her out by a mountain of shrimp at Healthy Oats. Gina immediately said yes, any stranger anxiety being quelled by the fact that she'd do almost anything to unglue her heart from married Ted. She willed every bone in her body to be attracted to Barry. But he was . . . slick. The way he called her "babe" made her feel like a showgirl — like an accessory along the lines of his Rolex or Jaguar. Still, it was better than dating Bob, whom she broke up with because he always lavished her with gifts and fancy dinners, and she knew she couldn't reciprocate.

She had never been attracted to anyone more than Ted, and yet Ted wasn't even as good looking as Shane. While Ted's face was handsome, his body was banged up and lopsided from years of playing football and soccer. One ankle was swollen like an orange, from the time he'd broken it playing basketball. His knees and shins were dinged with reddish scars that almost looked like burns. Gina liked to kiss every one of these imperfections. Then she'd run her tongue up the insides of Ted's thighs until he shuddered. She had never loved anyone so fiercely, and she hated that it was out of her control.

Her clients had no willpower when it came to eating and working out. Gina had no resolve when it came to controlling her heart. Dove Bars? Who cares? She didn't get it. Why were people so insane over food? One client, who wasn't even heavy, tortured herself over chocolate pudding cups. "I had one," she'd say desperately to Gina, as though she'd set a building on fire. "Okay," Gina would encourage. "Let's move past that and get on the bike and get those endorphins going!" *Eat a salad*, she wanted to say, *eat a bowl of strawberries, eat whatever. Who cares? It's just food. Get a grip!* Yet when it came to Ted, Gina could *not* get a grip.

She was blissfully happy in the twenty-four hours before she saw him and while she was with him, then overwhelmingly sad when they were apart. She knew this wasn't healthy. You couldn't diet or exercise *this* toxin out of your bloodstream.

Gina fought the urge to tell Ted that she loved him. She was too proud to be the first one to say it. Potentially the *only* one. No, that wasn't it. She was afraid that as soon as she told him, he would run. To men, the words *I love you* seemed to mean: "I want something from you." As though you wanted to harvest a dang kidney from them. Gina didn't want anything from Ted. She didn't want anything and she wanted everything. She didn't want to break up his marriage. She just wanted to sleep with him every day. No, every *other* day would suffice. Yes, every other day would do. Some days they'd do it twice or even three times. Then Ted would trudge home to his wife.

I love you I love you I love you! she wanted to holler over their Cobb salads at lunch.

Two months passed and Ted never said that he loved her and probably he didn't. He was married. He loved his *wife*. He was a good man. Being a good man meant he felt awful about sleeping with Gina. She could tell by his huge sighs of desperation as he sat on the edge of the bed before showering and dressing to go home. Yet he continued to invite her to lunch, to cover her face with kisses, to moan the words "beautiful girl" as he came inside her. Once, she turned her head so he wouldn't see her cry.

How could Ted's wife reject him? "She won't even look at me," he told Gina as he climbed onto the StairMaster. He was sad about this. Sad, and guilty for sleeping with Gina. Which was why Gina knew she had to break it off. She had never slept with a married man before. What kind of morally bankrupt tart sleeps with married men? Besides, she didn't like being someone's frigging chocolate pudding cup.

So it was a blessing when Toby's father called to say that Toby needed to move back in with Gina. It was a blessing when Elinor Mackey confronted Gina and Ted, and they broke up. She would forget Ted and fall in love with the right man, sooner or later. (*Soon*, please!) Meanwhile, she'd devote her attention solely to her son.

It had broken her heart two years earlier when Toby announced he wanted to live in Maine with his dad full-time and attend school there. Maybe Gina should have seen this coming. Toby had reached a stage where he was retreating from her. He didn't want to cuddle anymore. He no longer crept to her room in the middle of the night, frightened, wanting to sing songs. Although he was becoming a big boy, she still loved to hug her son — to pick him up and swing him in the air and tickle him until he begged for mercy. "There is *not* honey behind my ears!" he'd shriek as she wrestled him to the ground and pushed back his big ears to kiss the soft pink skin behind them. "There *is*, right *there!*" she'd insist.

Touch establishes the conduit through which our children feel safety, Gina had read in an article. But shortly after his eighth birthday, Toby announced in the car one morning on the way to school that he didn't want to be hugged anymore.

137

"Oh, of course!" Gina said, trying not to show her hurt feelings. "You mean when I drop you off at school."

Toby fidgeted and scratched. "At home, either," he said, looking out the window.

"Okay, sweetie," Gina said. "Have a good day!" she cheered after him as he climbed out of the car. She clenched her jaw so she wouldn't cry, a sore ache starting in her ears.

"Thank you," he said, in an unusually polite, grown-up tone. Then he closed the door and lumbered toward the school without waving good-bye.

This had to be normal. Especially with boys. Gina made a point of subduing her physical affection, particularly in public. She felt she understood what her son must be going through; it couldn't be easy having divorced parents. (Actually, she was never even *married* to Toby's father.) Yet when Toby moved back in to live with Gina, she was in no way prepared for his disdain. She had looked forward to his return — getting out and laundering the Spider-Man sheets, arranging his little desk with school supplies, buying granola bars and apples for his lunch box. When Toby stepped off the plane, he seemed more gorgeous than ever to her. Those eyelashes were to *die* for. In contrast with his sandy hair, Toby's lashes were impossibly dark, long, and curled at the ends — like false eyelashes! His tanned arms were covered with blond hairs, freckles, and scabs. She loved his scruffiness. He was still a little boy! She resisted the urge to hug him and instead teasingly ran her fingers through his hair.

"*Mom!*" Toby said with irritation.

"*What!*" she replied, pretending that he wasn't killing her.

From that day on, she couldn't do anything to please her son. Meanwhile, she and Ted were broken up, and not seeing him felt like someone had died. No one she'd ever dated seriously had disappeared from her life so suddenly. Somehow she'd remained friendly with her exes. Life's too short for grudges. Missing Ted made Gina ill. She got migraines, threw up.

It was a crazy idea to ask Ted to tutor Toby. But Toby had been on the phone to his father every night, begging to go "home." *Home* to freezing-cold Maine to live with his even colder step-mother. The first night Toby didn't call his father was the night they ran into Ted at dinner. Toby seemed to fall in love with Ted as suddenly as Gina had.

"Really? You helped him do a triathlon?" Toby pressed in the car on the way home. "You know what? I think he likes you. Mom, he totally likes you! Why don't you date him?" This was the first time Toby ever seemed remotely proud of her. She realized that's what she wanted as much as her son's love — for him to be proud of her. Or at least not ashamed.

"He's married," Gina had to admit. Not exactly something to be proud of.

"What?" Toby said incredulously. He looked out the window for a long time. "Well, he might be getting divorced."

What on earth? Toby was so grown up in some ways.

"Why do you date dork loser Shane and dork loser Barry? How come you can't find a *nice* guy, like Dr. Mackey?"

"Barry's not a loser," Gina said feebly.

Toby rolled his eyes, kicked the dashboard. "You should date Dr. Mackey."

"*I did!*" Gina shouted, losing her control, finally, after ten days of her son's unrelenting disdain. "I found him. I dated him. We broke up. He's married!" *Don't ever talk to or argue with your child as though he's your peer*, Gina heard the words from her parenting book scold. She pulled off the road to regain her composure.

"I'm sorry, sweetie," she said, her voice wavering as she smoothed over her skirt. "I know that's more information than you need. It's just that's why we won't ever see Dr. Mackey again."

Toby nodded. Then his tongue clicked in his mouth the way it did when he was figuring something out.

Over the next week, Toby went on and on about how Ted would be the *best* tutor. Finally, like an idiot, Gina gave in and asked Ted.

Now, for some reason, God only knows *why*, since he's gotten back together with his wife, Ted has decided he will tutor Toby every week, instead of the once or twice he originally agreed to. He's told Gina to take down the signs at the community college; there's no need to hire a tutor. Even though they're not sleeping together, seeing Ted a little bit is better than not seeing him at all. Criminy, she's pathetic. The worst part is that the two men she loves most — Toby and Ted —

seem to have no use for her. She hates the reactions she garners from them. From Toby: disdain. From Ted: pity. There's nothing worse than someone feeling sorry for you. She sees it in Ted's eyes. *Poor Gina, with the out-of-control kid and crappy math skills.* Okay, so she doesn't remember how to do fractions. She's not a corporate lawyer.

Gina would almost rather be hated than pitied. She'd rather be a bitchy force-to-be-reckoned-with. She could never master bitchiness, though. She certainly wanted to back in high school. She was captain of the drill team, and voted the student with Best School Spirit. Kids made fun of her enthusiasm. "You know what the guys call the drill team?" Amanda Cranson asked Gina in the girls' room one day, raising an eyebrow at the short skirt of Gina's uniform. "The *Screw* Crew."

Gina tried to muster a callous comeback. But she just stood there, at a loss, hating being the perky girl.

"You don't know anything about me," she finally said, her hands trembling as she reached for a paper towel. But Amanda was out the door already, out the door and into the raucous sea of screaming kids in the hall, a sea that made Gina's stomach churn.

CHAPTER
SEVEN

Ted can't stand the thought of living in the house without Elinor, so he convinces her that he's the one who should move out. He signs a month-to-month lease for a furnished condo, wishing it could be week-to-week. Breath-to-breath. He wants to tell the realtor to wake him up when his wife has forgiven him and he can move back in with her. When he can stop thinking about having sex with Gina *all the time*, even when he's examining bunions.

At home, he packs a medium-size suitcase, the biography of Ulysses S. Grant he's been meaning to read, and a pound of bacon from the meat drawer in the refrigerator. Elinor raises an eyebrow at the bacon. They don't speak.

The living room upholstery at Ted's rental unit has an oily sheen that makes him want to stand in the middle of the room to watch TV. Until recently, the place has been used as temporary housing for workers relocating to the Valley during the boom. Now that the economy has slowed, schleps like Ted can move in at a reduced rate. *We want this to feel like your home away from home*, a rental brochure by the telephone says. Your hell away from hell. The TV is bolted to the wall.

Ted puts his pound of bacon in the fridge and the bottle of vodka in the freezer. Nice diet. And he's a doctor.

The apartment is painted dark, oppressive colors, which seem to be the latest trend. In the bedroom, the burgundy walls close in on Ted as he opens his suitcase. The blood-red shade seems to suck not only the light from the room, but the air, too, and Ted feels a twinge of claustrophobia. He drags his suitcase out to the slightly lighter mushroom-colored living room. He wrestles open the fold-out couch and sinks into the soft center. The thin mattress bends around him like a taco. The sheets smell slightly moldy. He remembers when he and Elinor painted their kitchen and family room. She chose a pale yellow — pineapple ice — that she said would "draw in the natural light." As he watched her pop open and stir the first can of creamy paint, he felt grateful to be married.

He clicks on the TV and mutes a guy who's shouting about trucks. Flipping through his stack of mail, he finds a letter from the insurance company:

Dear Mr. Mackey,
    We have made a decision based upon our investigation of the facts regarding responsibility for the automobile accident on August 12. According to California law, a driver may be considered principally at fault in an accident if the driver's actions or omissions were at least 51% of the cause of the accident. The results of our investigation reveal that Theodore Mackey was

100% responsible for this accident for failure to maintain a proper lookout . . .

Elinor has insisted that regardless of what the insurance company or cops decide, Ted should schedule a court date and plead not guilty. "Bank on a bureaucratic snafu," she told him. "Chances are the cop won't show and you'll get off. Then our insurance won't go up."

"But I'm *guilty*." It irked Ted that bureaucracy could absorb this fact.

"Doesn't matter," she insisted. "You don't perjure yourself by pleading not guilty."

Loopholes. Ted sighs, closes his eyes. When he opens them, he spots a bug scurrying across the kitchen floor. A cockroach? That lazy-ass realtor could have found him something better than this squalid shoe box. His pulse pounds in his ears as he lunges into the kitchen. A brown insect freezes under his gaze. It's some kind of beetle. Still, he grabs the phone book from the kitchen counter and annihilates the vermin with one smash. "Fucking squalor!" Pounding the floor with the phone book feels good — right, somehow. Squatting on his haunches, Ted beats at the flattened beetle or whatever the hell it is until it is just a brown smudge.

"Hey!" A muffled shout comes from the apartment below. "Shut up!"

"*You* shut up!" Ted hollers back. He raises the phone book high above his head and slams the floor again and again. "*Shut. The. Fuck. Up!*" He pounds and shouts until his throat burns and his head throbs and his hands ache — experiencing one of those rare moments where pain feels good.

The only thing Ted looks forward to all week is seeing Toby and Gina. While Gina seems glad that he's tutoring Toby, she keeps a careful distance from Ted. She's dating the concert promoter now — a guy who's clearly loaded. The last time Ted picked up Toby to study, he watched the two of them pull out of the parking lot in a Jag. Gina waved to Ted, laughing at something Richie Rich said. Ted hasn't told Gina that he's separated from Elinor. He worries this will just make him a troublesome complication in her life. Instead, he'd rather be helpful, bringing Toby's math grade up to at least a C-plus.

On his way to Gina's one Saturday, Ted spots a Toys "R" Us and swerves off the road to buy a present for Toby.

"What kind of games do ten-year-old boys like these days?" Ted asks the teenage clerk behind the glass case where the computer games are locked up. The kid seems to have been waiting all day for someone to ask this.

"For what kind of player?" he wants to know. "Does he have the Xbox 360?" The boy, who has two silver hoops in his ears like a pirate, rubs his palms together, savoring this possibility.

Ted has no idea.

"PS2?"

Ted shrugs. "He has a Game Boy. What's the coolest game for that?" Ted winces as he hears himself use the word *cool*. What a geezer dumb-ass. "Is there something with lots of battles?"

This sparks an enthusiastic list of pros and cons from the clerk, and finally Ted chooses a game that he thinks will be gory enough for Toby without horrifying Gina.

At the checkout he peruses a collection of unfamiliar action figures (where are Superman and Batman?), then buys a big box of Matchbox cars as a backup gift.

"Ow. *Owwwwwww!*" Toby's voice rings in the air as Ted heads up the walk to Gina's condo. He squeezes the toy store package under his arm and breaks into a jog. Toby appears from around the hedges, hopping down the sidewalk on one foot. "Bees!" he screams, his face contorted and red, tears streaming down his freckled cheeks. "Beeeeeeees!"

"It's okay, sport," Ted says, even though he's not sure.

Gina appears, chasing after Toby with an EpiPen syringe. When she sees Ted, she throws back her head. "Thank *God!*" She thrusts the needle toward him. "He needs this." Her hand shakes. "He's allergic."

Toby stops, closes his eyes, and waits for the shot. As Ted takes the EpiPen, he sees that Toby hasn't been stung just on the foot; there are red spots all over his leg, too. Ted's heart races at the thought of Toby going into anaphylactic shock.

"Okay, sport," he says. "Okay." He pops the green cap off the syringe and quickly gives Toby the shot in his thigh. "It's easy," Ted tells Gina. "You can even do it through his clothing." Elinor always complimented Ted for giving painless shots. Ironically, the trick is to insert the needle with a quick jab — like ripping off a Band-Aid all at once.

"*Dad* knows how to do it." Toby scowls at Gina.

Toby's body goes limp. He leaps forward as soon as the epinephrine hits him, bouncing on his toes. "It *hurth!*" he yells. His tongue is obviously swollen, and he isn't breathing as easily as he should be.

"Oh, honey," Gina says, reaching for Toby. "He hit a nest under the deck," she tells Ted.

"Stay away from me!" Toby screams at her. "Thee why I hate to *play outhide!*"

Gina retreats a few steps toward the house and doubles over, hugging her waist.

"*You* okay?" Ted asks her.

She nods. "Stomach cramps."

"Listen, let's go to the emergency room." Ted tries to sound calm as he prods Toby toward the car. "You might need another shot, Tobe, since you were stung so many times." Toby hesitates, so Ted stoops and lifts him into his arms, grabbing the computer game from the grass. He's surprised by how light and leggy Toby is — like a spider. The scabs on his arms are rough against Ted's skin.

"Ow, ow, *ow.*" Toby rhythmically knocks his head against Ted's chest.

Gina hurries behind them.

"I know, champ," Ted says. "I know."

At the hospital, everyone assumes Ted is the husband, the father.

"Squeeze your dad's hand," the young emergency room doctor says as he gives Toby another shot of epinephrine. Your *dad*. The assumption fills Ted with remorse. But he doesn't correct the doctor. Neither does Toby or Gina. Toby's fingernails dig into Ted's palm as the adrenaline surges through his limbs.

Gina watches from a chair beside Toby's gurney, a pink bucket cradled between her legs. When they arrived at the ER, an Indian woman who had cut her hand with hedge trimmers dripped blood across the floor through a makeshift dish towel bandage. Somebody said, "You can see the tendon," and Gina almost fainted. Somehow Ted managed to catch her and still hold Toby until a nurse came from behind with a wheelchair for Gina.

Now panic flashes in Toby's eyes. "My *thung!*"

"I want you to breathe through your nose for me," the doctor says. He can't be more than thirty. Ted puts his face in front of Toby's, seals his lips, and inhales deeply through his nose to illustrate. Toby's eyes lock on Ted's. They breathe together. As tears slide past Toby's quivering jaw, Ted has the primal urge to carry the boy away from here, although he knows this is the safest place to be.

The additional shot makes Toby's heels hammer the gurney. A nurse layers another blanket over him. His head rolls back and forth, and his lips move as he begins to count. "Through your nose," Ted reminds him. He steps behind Toby as the doctor bends over the patient to peer in his eyes with a penlight. Gina leans over her bucket.

148

"Don't worry, honey," the nurse tells her.

"No more shots," the doctor says, patting Toby's leg. "We'll just keep an eye on you now."

You're a trouper, Ted is about to say when he remembers that this was Elinor's pet peeve. "If one more Gen-X intern says I'm a *trouper* I'm going to strangle him with his stethoscope," she'd fume. "You should *ask* a patient how they're doing, not tell them."

"How you doing, buddy?" Ted asks Toby.

Toby's legs slow to a jerky shake. "I hate bees."

Ted nods.

"You're a brave fella." The doctor pats Toby's shoulder. "What's your favorite sport?"

"History," Toby says distractedly, looking over at his mother.

"He's a history nut," Ted tells the doctor.

"Wow," the doctor says. "Well, I think you'll be back to the books in no time." He gives Ted a *you-must-be-proud* smile on his way out of the room. Ted bends to kiss Toby's gnarled curls, surprised by their softness. Toby's looking away, and Gina doesn't see it, so the kiss seems like a stolen pleasure.

In the car on the way home, Gina says to Toby, "Baby, you were brave. I'm proud of you."

"See, that's why I don't want to *go* outside," Toby says gloomily. "That's why I want to stay *inside*. Why can't you let me stay *inside* and read?"

Gina closes her eyes.

"Oh, now," Ted tells Toby, "those stupid old bees could get you while you're walking to the car to drive to the mall."

"Whatever," he says. "I could have *died*." His eyes dart back and forth, watching the passing scenery.

"We'd never let that happen," Ted tells him. He wants to take back the words *we* and *never*, both of which suggest permanence on his part.

They ride in silence. Finally, Toby unbuckles his seat belt and leans between the front seats to talk to Ted. "Hey. Did you know Guillotine was a guy?"

"You're pulling my hair, sweetie." Gina tugs her head forward to loosen her long hair from his grip.

"Sorry." Toby moves his small hands to Ted's headrest. "Did you know that he was a doctor who invented the guillotine? He figured out that decapitation is the quickest way to die."

"Ouch," Ted says.

"Yeah. The blade weighed eighty-eight pounds. That's more than me!" He flops back against the seat.

"Toby, honey, we just came from the *hospital*." Gina grasps her forehead. "Buckle your seat belt now."

"Okay, but did you know that the guillotine was on wheels and they rolled it around Paris during the revolution and that's how they killed Louis the Sixteenth? And you know that lady, Marie Antoinette? You know what my book says?"

"What's it say, sport?" Ted asks.

"It says that she never said, *Let them eat cake*. She never *said* that." Toby is miffed by this misconception. He buckles his seat belt.

150

"Really?" Ted asks. "See, it's good to question history."

Gina shakes her head. "How'd I get this genius kid?" She pushes the button to roll down her window partway. The wind blows her hair off her cheeks. She closes her eyes, arches her back, and tips her face up. Her body forms a long arc from her chin, down over her throat, between her breasts, and across her belly to the dark red waistline of her batik skirt. Ted swallows, looks back to the road. At the ER, he took care of everything: Toby, Gina, the discharge paperwork. While he couldn't ever do anything to make Elinor feel better, with Toby and Gina it seems all he has to do is *show up*. They need him. Is this a weird thing to be grateful for? Hell, that Jaguar guy could probably fix everything, too. All he'd have to do is write a check.

"Stew's Steak Shack!" Toby shouts, startling Gina. "Can we stop?"

"No." Gina frowns.

"Please?"

"*Please?*" Ted echoes in a kid's whine, trying to be funny.

Gina smiles. "Why not?" she concedes. "A steak sounds good."

The three of them slide into a circular booth, Toby in the middle. Ted and Toby choose hamburgers. Gina encourages Ted to order his burger protein-style, which means no bun. "You're doing so well," she says.

Ted straightens his back and sucks in his stomach.

"Look, you can have strawberry shortcake without the short-cake for dessert," Gina adds. She manages to make these suggestions without seeming bossy. Ted likes it when she fusses over him.

As they eat, ketchup seeps between leaves of iceberg lettuce, dripping off the ends of Ted's fingers. Clutching his wrist, he waves his hand in front of Toby's face, grimacing. "Gahhhhhh," he moans, feigning a B-movie injury, ketchup dripping like fake blood.

Toby laughs. "Ha! Gross! Like the lady who got cut by the trimmers!" He bounces in his seat, making them all bounce a little.

Gina sighs and smiles at Toby, her eyes shining.

Toby says, "Hey, we didn't study!"

"Next Saturday," Ted says. "I'll come over and help you."

"I have a quiz on Thursday." Anxiety makes Toby stand up in the booth.

"All right," Ted says, "I'll be there Wednesday, at five o'clock."

"Can you show me how to do the shot then?" Gina asks Ted.

Toby rolls his eyes. "*Mom.* It is *so* easy."

They polish off their steak, burgers, and salads and order the strawberry shortcake. As the restaurant slowly fills with families sitting down to dinner, Ted is struck by the realization that he is happy.

After Toby showers and climbs into bed, Ted busts out the Matchbox cars — a big assorted case like a giant box of chocolates — and sets them on Toby's lap.

152

Toby pouts at the cars. "Those are for, like, first-graders," he says, pushing the box down the bedspread.

"Toby!" Gina scolds.

"Sorry." Toby collapses against the pillows.

"And look." Ted pulls the Game Boy game from behind his back.

Toby sits up. "*Wow!* I *so* wanted that one!" He pounds his covers with his fists, then gives Ted a high five. "Thank you!"

Ted looks to Gina, who's leaning in Toby's doorway. Her expression is somewhere between a smile and a grimace. Ted should have asked her about the game first. Gina is forever battling with Toby to cut down on his "screen time" — all those hours spent playing computer games and watching TV.

"Now, you can only play this after you finish your homework," he tells Toby.

"Okay," Toby agrees, ripping open the shrink wrap.

Gina smiles weakly. Ted pats Toby's head and steps out of the room to give the two of them privacy.

He stands in the entryway by the front door, jingling his keys in his pocket, hoping this suggests his intention to leave soon. The truth is, he doesn't want to return to that cavernously dark condo.

"Cup of tea?" Gina asks softly as she pulls Toby's door shut.

Ted lets go of the keys in his pocket. "Sure."

They sit at opposite ends of the couch, sipping Mint Medley.

Gina stares into the empty fireplace as though there's really a fire. "Does Elinor know you're tutoring Toby?"

"No." The edge of the mug burns Ted's lip.

"Ted, you can't *lie* to her." Gina firmly sets down her cup on the glass end table, the noise startling Ted. "An omission is a lie."

"I moved out." Ted reties his sneaker to buy time. Why the hell can't he talk to women? "Of the house."

Gina studies her feet, which are propped up on the coffee table. "You guys trying to work it out? Seeing the marriage counselor?"

"No. Not now. She won't go with me."

Gina's shoulders drop. "Does Toby know?"

"Know . . . ?"

"That you're not living with Elinor."

"No."

"Good. Please don't tell him." She sighs, crosses her legs into the lotus position. "I don't want him getting his hopes up about . . . anything."

"Okay."

After a long pause, Ted says, "I'm sorry about the computer game. I should have asked you first."

Gina nods. "I'm trying to get him to cut back."

"You know, for some kids it just doesn't come naturally to be athletic and outdoorsy. When I played football in high school, I saw parents pressure their kids to be better athletes. Maybe you don't have to push Toby to play out —"

"Thanks for the parenting advice, Dr. Mackey." Ted hasn't heard this sarcasm in Gina's voice before.

154

"Maybe I don't need you to point out what a crappy parent I am. Maybe I already know."

"Gina, no. Oh, my God." Ted moves closer to her on the couch. "You're a great parent. I'm sorry. I'm being a busybody."

She scoots away, hugging her waist.

"People who don't have kids always think they'd do a better job of managing yours. If that were *my* kid, *blah, blah, blah.*"

"I didn't mean to be sanctimonious."

"Of course, you and Elinor would make *great parents*. That's the irony, isn't it? The educated people with the great jobs can't have kids, while we lousy parents are reproducing like rabbits. Why do people like me get to have the babies, anyway?" She turns to Ted, flipping her bangs out of her eyes. "Because we *had* them, *that's* why! I got pregnant, and it was an accident, but I *had* my baby. I didn't have a yuppie plan for having kids. I didn't wait until a baby fit into my life. While you were picking out your heated bathroom tiles, I had my baby. And you want to get all over my butt because I'm not perfect."

"I —" Ted stammers. He didn't mean to be a blowhard asshole, but she could cut him a *little* slack. "Gina, I'm sorry. That's not what I meant at all. I guess I was just thinking aloud, really. Realizing what it must be like for Toby not to be as athletic as you. You're a great mom."

"No, I'm not." She massages her temples.

"Maybe I'm a jerk." Ted moves closer to Gina. He takes her hand in his and massages it, rubbing each of

155

her long fingers. "But I don't have heated floor tiles." He nudges her, trying to get her to laugh.

Gina reaches for a Kleenex. "One of my clients does." She blows her nose quietly. "She did IVF, too."

"I'm sorry," Ted repeats.

Gina shrugs. She turns his arm over and runs her fingers up the inside of Ted's elbow, sending a shock of pleasure from his scalp down his spine. As he relaxes he feels like he's sinking between the couch's slick leather cushions. He reaches out and clutches Gina's forearm. It is a clumsy gesture — like grabbing onto someone when you're trying to climb out of a boat. While he's been trying to cheer *her* up, he has the distinct sensation of Gina pulling him up. That's what she's done for him for months now. Pulled him up out of his miserable state of self-loathing, his self-absorbed despair. And now all he's done is make her feel bad about herself as a parent.

Gina closes her eyes. "You're not a jerk. Life would be much easier if you were."

They end up in the walk-in closet in Gina's bedroom, which is one more closed door away from Toby's room. Ted lays Gina on her back, shoving aside her many pairs of sneakers and grabbing some kind of sweatshirt to make a pillow under her head. He pulls the tie of her wraparound skirt with the one firm tug it takes to get the thing undone. Then he slides his hands up the smooth insides of her legs. He pulls off her underwear and throws it over his shoulder, making her giggle. Then he pushes himself inside her, burying his face in her hair and breathing in her China Rain

156

perfume. Gina kneads his back — a touch that is more loving and therapeutic than the desperate throes of their earlier lovemaking. Ted lifts his head to look at her. Stripes of yellow light shine through the slats in the closet across her face. Her green eyes are half closed. As he dips his face back into her hair, his self-loathing gives way to soaking heat and ecstasy.

As Ted drives home later that night, a light rain makes the streets shine. He creeps along, dreading his dark apartment. Although he's not a religious man, he suddenly has the urge to pray. He's not sure what for. While he respects other people's faith, he's never chosen a religion of his own. Funny, he and Elinor visited churches and cathedrals almost daily while traveling through Europe. They both loved the architecture and the pageantry and the music, the organ chords rumbling through their bones. "We heathens can't get enough of these cathedrals," Elinor laughed. He misses her. How can he want Gina so much *and* miss his wife? His foot hovers between the brakes and the gas. He isn't driving or stopping or pulling over. He's drifting.

A swirl of red and blue lights appears in his rearview mirror. A police car. Of course. It probably looks like he's drunk. He pulls over. The cop shines his traffic light into the passenger's side of the window.

"Anything wrong?"

"No, Officer."

"You're drifting and hugging the bicycle lane."

"I just have a lot on my mind. I'll pay better attention." *Hugging the bicycle lane*. He'd like to do just that. Get out and curl up in the street spooning the solid white line.

"Been drinking?"

Ted shakes his head. "Nothing but tea for the past three hours."

"Would you step out of the car, please?"

Ted gets out and dutifully performs the sobriety test tricks — counting backward from one hundred, then touching each of his fingers to his thumb. As he's demonstrating that he can walk a straight line, a car pulls up and stops at the light. Through the rain-speckled window, Ted recognizes his patient Rolf Andersson, an old Swedish whip of a man who's prone to calluses. He mouths the words, *Dr. Mackey!* Then looks away.

If you're going to have a midlife crisis, you should have it in style. There should be a Dodge Viper, trips to a tanning booth. It should not involve a sobriety test in the rain in front of FedEx Kinko's, overwhelmed by the urge to pee from too much herbal tea, your patient spotting you and turning away with shame.

"Okay," the cop says sternly. "You're good to go." Ted climbs back into the car and fastens his seat belt. The officer pats the car door. "But keep your eyes on the road. You'd be surprised how many accidents result from people just not paying attention."

CHAPTER
EIGHT

Hermione hadn't planned on slitting her wrists at the baby shower. But a combination of things got to her. The crescendo of trilling flutes on the Vivaldi CD; the raspberry sherbet breaking into bubblegum globs in the punch; the quiche, with its strings of cheese that hung like rubber bands from one woman's chin; the Awwwwwws! and Cutes! echoing through the living room as the baby gifts were opened. As the circle of women fawned over the onesies and diaper bags, Hermione hovered by the buffet table, sawing at her wrist with a sterling-silver pie spatula. Of course, it wasn't sharp enough to do any damage. Perhaps she could stab herself with a dessert fork. Drown herself facedown in the punch? Or stop going to baby showers. Yes, that is what she would do. She would just send gifts and cards from now on. Even better, she'd order the gifts online, so she didn't have to go to Toys "R" Us or Baby Gap. Her women friends didn't need her at these parties, on the brink of tears, her crazy sadness wafting through the room.

"Whatcha writing?"

Elinor looks up from her spiral notebook to see Kat standing beside her on the lawn under the shade of the oak tree. She bends forward to rest her hands on her knees, panting and grimacing, out of breath from her morning run.

"I was just opening the mail from yesterday and I got this shower invitation. I'm writing a sort of reply." Elinor closes her notebook. When she goes back inside, she'll call the hostess with her regrets.

"Showers are the worst." Kat collapses on the blanket and pours herself coffee from the carafe. Her legs are long and tan from running and swimming. Elinor's always admired her athleticism and low-maintenance prettiness — her small, pointed features and black hair cut short like a boy's.

"Doesn't anyone just lie on the ground and look up at the sky anymore?" Elinor asks, stretching out on her back, resting her head on her balled-up sweatshirt. Rabbity white clouds blow by overhead as though on a conveyor belt, breaking into clumps and wisps.

"You make a lovely lawn ornament." Kat may be the kindest friend Elinor's ever had. Your neighbor goes off the deep end and camps out under a tree in her yard. Do you tell her she's off nut? No, you sit under the tree with her. They meet under the oak every morning now, after Kat's taken her kids to school. If it's raining, they talk on the phone, conducting their conversation through their dining room windows while holding up visual aids. (*Do you think I can wear this coat with this dress? Let me see, turn around.*) Kat calls it dining-room-window videoconferencing.

"All I do is lie down, and the neighborhood thinks I've had a stroke," Elinor says, admiring how the oak leaves make a lacy green pattern against the sky.

"This tree needs a name." Kat squints up at the branches. "Stella, maybe."

"I think it's a he."

"A he-tree?"

"Warren," Elinor decides, reaching out to touch the rough silvery gray bark. As she traces a splotch of lichen it crumbles into dust on her fingertips.

"Warren," Kat repeats. "Your new man?"

"He's there for me."

"My friend Elinor is dating a tree," Kat announces.

Elinor pounds her fist into the cushiony grass. "Ted's dating a ten-year-old? Fine. I'm dating a tree."

"He is a tree of few words. The strong, silent type."

"That's right. We don't have to *talk* about everything. We don't have to dissect our relationship like it's a frog in biology class."

Kat sighs. "I want to be supportive, but I'm sad that you guys are throwing in the towel. I can see how much Ted still loves you."

Elinor sits up too fast, making her dizzy. "But it's a relief to stop trying to fix everything. Like I've stopped banging my head against the wall."

Kat nods, doesn't say anything more. She's about to lean back against the tree's trunk when Elinor spots a long dribble of molasses-colored sap in the grooves of the bark. "Careful, what's that?"

They bend forward to examine the goop. A string of tiny brown beetles marches up alongside it.

Elinor grabs a rock and squashes as many of the bugs as she can. "That better be symbiotic!"

Kat tugs off her running shoe and helps smack the beetles, which scurry in all directions. "I need to bake and decorate thirty cupcakes by noon," she says, whapping her shoe harder.

"What about Safeway?"

"You're supposed to bake them yourself." She throws her sneaker in the grass.

"Says who?" Elinor throws the rock after the sneaker, turning away from the beetles.

"The Mommy Police. If you work full-time, you can buy Safeway cupcakes. If you're a stay-at-home mom, you're supposed to bake and decorate them." Kat lies on her back, balancing her mug on her sternum. "Of course, there are mothers who work full-time *and* bake. Unlike me, they probably know the difference between cake flour and flour flour."

"If you cracked their heads open you'd find wires inside," Elinor says. She can't imagine bringing a baby home from the hospital, let alone ever having a child old enough for elementary school and cupcakes. She throws another rock, this time so hard that her shoulder burns from the exertion. "Gina would definitely make *her* cupcakes from scratch." An ant approaches her on the blanket. She smashes it with her thumb. "With whole ground flaxseed flour."

"The kids would retch." Kat frowns. "Hey, now I think you're banging your head against the wall."

Elinor knocks her head against the tree trunk. *Thunk, thunk, thunk. Ouch, ouch, ouch.* Bark pierces her forehead. She rubs the spot. "Can't I just *rant* for a minute?"

162

"Of course."

During their couples therapy sessions, Elinor withheld her Gina criticisms from Ted and the counselor. She didn't want to let the jealousy boil over in front of them. It felt so unattractive. She wanted to be above all that. Composed. Classy.

"I think she's into Buddhism. She tried to get me to read this Buddhist book as part of her approach to 'walking away from food.' "

Kat wrinkles her nose.

"She's this cute tie-dyed *hippie* chick." Elinor feels her voice speed up. She's on her knees now, pointing a finger in the air. "Right. Nama-fucking-ste! You're a health nut, *but* you smoke pot —"

"She does?"

"When I asked Ted how it all started, he said that's what led them to having sex the first time. What led them to *smoke pot?* I wonder. You go to a personal trainer so you can get stoned?" Elinor pauses. "Actually, that doesn't sound bad." She sits back on her heels. "Anyway. So she's a Buddhist, but she sleeps with married men. I hate these second-generation hippie wannabes. She's not old enough to be a hippie! Buddhism and pot and infidelity. What a hypocrite! A *hippiecrit!*"

"Oh, El." Kat snorts with laughter. "See? That's what Ted adores about you."

"Maybe that's how she could rationalize screwing my husband — she doesn't have attachments. Not to Krispy Kreme *or* her married clients."

Elinor curls her chest over her knees, rolling herself into a ball and turning her head to rest her temple against the scratchy army blanket. "I'd make a terrible Buddhist. I get attached to everything. Even this tree."

Elinor feels Kat's hands knead her shoulders, her fingers a little sticky from juice boxes.

"You know what you need? A trip to the spa!"

Elinor sits up, untangling a leaf from her hair. "I hate the spa. Those whispery, drippy ladies. Lying in the dark and listening to that stupid new age music with the electronic seagulls." She gathers the coffee cups and spoons onto a tray. "Have you ever noticed that that music never *goes* anywhere? It has no beginning, middle, or end. It's the musical equivalent of an unmade bed. It drives me crazy."

"But the hot stone —"

"And they're always trying to sell you those expensive damn creams when you're on your way out. Eighty dollars an ounce for Australian kangaroo sperm facial scrub or whatever. There's always the teeniest dig at your self-esteem that goes with the sales pitch. 'Oh! You *could* be pretty, if you just bought this obscenely over-priced snake oil. A *salt* rub.' No thanks; salt in the wound."

The look on Kat's face is somewhere between frustrated and hurt.

Elinor squeezes her hand. "Oh, sorry. See what my husband *doesn't* love about me?" Elinor picks up the tray and stands. "Let's go grab a beer and shoot some pool. My treat."

"Sold."

164

"What about the cupcakes?" Typical: Elinor's so self-absorbed she forgot about Kat's challenges for the day.

Kat smashes a beetle on the blanket with her fist. "Safeway."

No matter what time of day, the inside of Ray and Eddie's Tavern is that perfect kind of dark that makes everyone look young. At night, the bar is lined with contractors who've been demolishing ranch houses to replace them with hacienda-style mini mansions. Once in a while, Elinor, Ted, Kat, and her husband, Jack, stop here for nightcaps after an outing. They're usually overdressed, in their restaurant or symphony clothes, but Elinor always feels at home, the informality of the place as comforting as big flannel pajamas.

Now only a few students from the nearby community college are hanging out — playing darts and drinking dollar beers out of jelly jars. Elinor and Kat park themselves at the bar and order shots of tequila with beer chasers. As Elinor swallows, a flame of heat expands in her belly, and the lemon burns against her lips. She tugs her sweatshirt over her head to cool off. Her silk camisole is much more comfortable. Technically, it's probably underwear. She's not sure. She's been wearing office clothes for so long, she's been having trouble cobbling together a sabbatical wardrobe. All she knows is that she'll never wear Dockers again. The bartender sneaks a sideways peek at Elinor's chest. She dips her head to see that the camisole is drooping in the middle. Her nipples are visible through the silk.

What the hell. She can't remember the last time she felt sexy.

"El," Kat whispers, shielding her mouth with the back of her hand. "Are you sure you're supposed to wear that without a shirt over it?"

Elinor takes another shot, wincing and sucking air in through her teeth. "Yeah, I don't know." The tequila burns through her anxiety and dread. She orders a third shot.

"It's a camisole, aka *underwear*."

"Who gives a rip?" Elinor sips her beer, the bubbles tickling the inside of her mouth. Drinking feels dangerously good right now. She turns to Kat. "Do you know how lucky we are that we *have* breasts — that we don't have breast cancer?" A mutual friend of Elinor and Kat's died last spring. Their neighbor, Joanna Fried, just started chemotherapy.

Kat nods, peeling the label off her beer and reassembling it on the bar. "We're lucky in a lot of ways. So, are we celebrating by drinking tequila in our underwear?"

"I guess so." Elinor tips back her head and peers through the thick bottom of her shot glass. "Tequila gets the job done. I hate cosmopolitans. Can I just say that?"

"You can say that. But are you sure you're okay? You're like Thelma and Louise wrapped into one."

Elinor burps, a harsh gurgle roiling in the back of her throat. "Back in a minute." She slides off her stool and heads barefoot across the old wood floor toward the bathroom. Peanut shells and dust stick to the bottoms of her feet. She tries to make her tequila sway look purposeful, in time to the Steppenwolf song on the jukebox.

Two college guys playing pool look up at her, smiling. Are they laughing with her or at her. *Don't be paranoid*, the tequila says. She stops, places her hands firmly on the pool table, and leans across the green felt at the boys.

"You like my haircut?" she asks them.

"Sure!"

"I cut it myself."

"Great!" Both of the guys are Levi's-and-washboard-abs-cute. They're like an ad for youth.

"You know how much a woman's haircut costs in suburbia these days?"

The boys laugh, shrug.

"A hundred and fifteen dollars. That's why I wasted my thirties in an office building. So I could get hundred-dollar haircuts."

"Bummer," one of the boys says. He is James Dean handsome — Levi's and white T-shirt and damp hair, as though he just got out of the shower.

With horror, it occurs to Elinor that she is older than both Mrs. Robinson and Blanche DuBois. *Forty is the new thirty!* the tequila counters.

"Can I buy you a drink?" James Dean asks.

"No thanks." Elinor covers her mouth, afraid she might burp again.

"Aw, c'mon," the boy insists. "Just one beer can't hurt."

"'Kay . . ."

167

But then Kat is at her side. "You challenging them to a game?"

"Sure." Elinor digs in her pockets for quarters and slides two on the table. She has dispensed with her purse. Lightened her load to cash, car keys, license, and lip gloss.

"I wanna be on your team," the beer-buying boy tells Elinor.

"Oh, yeah?" Elinor walks around the table toward him. A Stevie Ray Vaughn song comes on. The boy's arm circles Elinor's waist, pulling her into a dance. His chest is warm and hollow, as flat as his belly. He has no soft spots. He smells like Marlboros and beer. He smells like college.

Kat cues up the balls, keeping an eye on Elinor.

The boy twirls Elinor away from the pool table, gently pushing her through a doorway and into the hall by the pay phone and restrooms. She closes her eyes, a swirl of orange light buzzing like neon. She hears Kat tell the other boy, "She's going through a rough time."

"I hear ya!" the other boy says. The pool balls crack. "You're up."

The dancing boy nuzzles Elinor's neck. His cheek is remarkably soft. "You're totally fun." He said fun. Not old. Not crazy. *Fun*. The boy accidentally backs into the wall. "Whoops!" he says. A surge of strength rushes through Elinor. She throws his wrists over his head, pinning them to the wall, and slides one knee up the inside of his thigh. He reaches forward to kiss her. It is the first time she has kissed anyone other than her husband in how many years? Probably six. *You're*

168

separated, the tequila says. The inside of the boy's mouth is cool and tangy from the beer. Elinor would like to take him home. A Ray and Eddie's door prize.

"You joining the wrestling team?" Kat leans in the doorway into the hall.

"Oh, my mother's here." Elinor giggles, pulls away from the boy. "Just having some fun." Elinor licks her lips, moist from his. "Better than a hot stone massage," she adds. "Cheaper, too."

"I don't know if Warren would approve of this." Kat raises her eyebrows.

"Warren your husband?" The boy tugs at the waist of Elinor's jeans.

"*Boy*friend," Elinor says huskily. She leans forward, pointing her forehead toward the boy like a bull about to charge.

"Oh." The boy sounds indifferent. He smiles and lets go of the belt loop.

"I'd watch it if I were you." Kat steers Elinor by the shoulders toward the bathroom. "Warren's a *big* guy."

"Whoa, a big guy!" The boy laughs, stepping backward away from them.

Elinor waves to the boy as Kat ushers her toward the women's room. Arm in arm, they bumble through the door. The room won't hold still and the tequila won't stay down. Elinor lurches toward the sink and turns on the cold water. Before she can splash her face she gags and throws up into the drain. A bitter taste burns the back of her throat. She looks up. Her watery reflection in the mirror is scary — pale face and sunken eyes and damp hair stuck to her forehead.

"How attractive," she tells Kat.

"Don't worry." Kat presses a wad of cold wet paper towels to Elinor's forehead, then her cheeks. "You're the life of the party."

Elinor's hangover awakens before her, driving pilings into her head as she drifts up from the gluey clutches of sleep. How did she get *home?* Taxi, she remembers with relief. She recalls the boys — she never got their names — leaning into the window of the cab to bid her good-bye. Kat rolled up the window on the sleeve of one of their shirts. Elinor thought this was the funniest damn thing she'd ever seen. "We caught one," she howled.

"Don't worry, she already barfed," she remembered Kat telling the driver. Lovely.

The drapes are drawn and morning light seeps through. She has slept all afternoon and all night, and she's still in her jeans and camisole. She spies a large glass of water and two ibuprofen on the nightstand and a note from Kat:

Call me. XX-OO.

Elinor is debating whether toast or more sleep would be better when the doorbell rings. Her legs are numb and heavy as she slides them out of bed.

She opens her front door to discover a broad-chested man in khakis and a dress shirt standing there in the sun. He's almost completely bald, the light making the tanned top of his head shine.

"Morning," he says cheerfully.

Elinor looks at the papers in his hands. For a horrible moment she imagines that he's a lawyer serving her with divorce papers from Ted. She clutches her forehead, the urge to vomit tugging at her gut.

"You okay?"

"That depends. What do you want?"

"I'm the city arborist." He looks at his hiking boots a bit shyly.

"Okay." Elinor had no idea such a job title existed.

He hands her a business card. NOAH ORCH. CHIEF ARBORIST AND TREE SURGEON. There's an embossed tree beside his name. "Some of the trees in the neighborhood are sick." He motions toward the street. "I'm afraid your tree here has sudden oak."

Elinor steps onto the porch. She shields her face with her hand from the morning's glare to see where he's pointing. *Warren.* "That sounds awful. Is there such a thing as gradual oak?"

He laughs, tipping back his head. His thick salt-and-pepper mustache is neatly trimmed, and Elinor notices he's not completely bald; a band of salt-and-pepper hair scoops in a U-shape around the back of his head. "I'm sorry," he says. "You're going to lose the tree."

"Oh, but." Elinor's knees wobble. She needs a cracker and a shower. She sits down on the porch, the concrete alarmingly cold through her jeans. "Isn't there something you can do? A spray?"

The man, Noah Orch (what kind of name is that?), shakes his head. "I'm sorry. It *is* a beautiful tree." He

171

holds his paperwork to his chest, looks up respectfully at Warren.

Noah goes on to explain that the tree has *cankers*, which have spread into the trunk. "All those bugs? They're bark beetles. They're eating the tree."

Elinor rests her forehead on her knees, closing her eyes. This morning needs to go away.

She looks out at the empty street. "What's tree surgery, anyway? You can't operate?"

"It's just glorified pruning, really."

Elinor turns her head and rests her check on her knees, looking sideways at Noah Orch. "Sorry. My head's too heavy to hold up right now."

Noah cocks his head, smiles. "Home sick today?"

Elinor nods. "You see, I only just started to appreciate this tree."

"Oh, well, that's nice. Most people don't even really notice their trees." He winces. "The city's coming Monday."

"The whole city?"

"The city tree service. With the chipper."

"Jesus. You call that surgery?"

"I'm sorry. It's the cycle of life," he adds, trying to console her. "But we'll plant you a new tree. There's a short list of city-approved trees that you and your husband can choose from."

"My hus — He's not. We're separated," Elinor finally says. She believes she's capable of carrying the mortgage and taking care of the house without Ted, but choosing a new tree overwhelms her. That's one of the

172

things she liked best about being married: making decisions, no matter now mundane, with a partner.

"I'm sorry," Noah says, digging the toe of his hiking boot into a crack in the brick porch.

Elinor turns to rest her forehead on her knees. She will not cry in front of a man named Noah Orch. "Mother Nature is just cruel sometimes, you know?" she says to the concrete below. "Mother Nature can be a bitch sometimes." She wishes she didn't believe this.

To her surprise, Noah says, "I know."

She lifts her head, turns to him. His mustache and sideburns are surprisingly thick, given how little hair there is on his head. He's handsome — one of those attractive people who probably don't think they're very good looking. It's been a long time since Elinor's kissed a guy with a mustache. Has she ever slept with a bald man? Why is she *thinking* this? First the kids at the bar, and now the tree guy. She notices the absence of a wedding band on Noah's finger. Maybe he has to take it off for work. It might get caught up in tree-trimming equipment.

Noah points to the trees lining the other side of the yard. "That cypress over there is in a little trouble. I think maybe its roots have been damaged. Cypresses have roots that grow very close to the ground." He holds out his hand, forking his fingers to illustrate. "Trees have major roots and minor roots, sort of like arteries, that carry water and nutrients to the tree. You can cut one of their major arteries, but not two. If you cut two, they often die."

Elinor feels like her two major arteries have been cut. Her husband, her chance to have children. "Will you be there?" she asks Noah.

"Sorry?"

"When they cut down the tree, will you come, too?"

"No, I have to . . ." Noah Orch looks out at the grass, then at Elinor. He pats her arm. It's a gentle gesture, but it's not condescending. "Sure," he says. "I'll be there."

CHAPTER
NINE

Here's the thing Roger hates about cleaning houses: When women ask what he does for a living, he has to say, "Clean houses." Who's going to date a twenty-six-year-old guy with a crappy car and overdue student loans who's a maid? The only person who wants to sleep with him is Sallie Mae. Maybe he'll start saying he's a physics teacher. His friend Phil is a high school earth science teacher and girls love that. *Oh, a teacher!* Like Phil nailed himself to a fucking cross.

Roger's a kick-ass cleaner. Bathtub rings? Ammonia and baking soda. Cat hair? Two swipes with a wet rubber glove. Blood? White vinegar and hydrogen peroxide. Thank you, Internet. He could mop up after a mafia murder, if it weren't for his weak stomach.

His client Mrs. Wilcox made him clean a tent once. "Get the pine needles out," she demanded, pointing a tent pole at the floor of a green-and-yellow-striped circus monstrosity pitched in her backyard. She wanted it spotless. What's the point of camping? Roger plucked pine needles and dead spiders, scrubbed mildew. He dried the walls with a hair dryer at Mrs. W's insistence, a long orange extension cord snaking out of her house.

He imagined wrapping the cord around her ankles and felling her large body like a tree.

Roger hates it when people are home while he's cleaning. Then you can't blast the radio or check out their medicine chests. Then he has to talk to people, take their bullshit. So he's disappointed when he gets to the house of his new client, Mrs. Mackey, and clearly she's not going anywhere. When Roger rings the bell, she opens the door slowly, shielding her eyes and peering out like a hibernating animal. Roger focuses his eyes on the mailbox, because she's not really dressed. Men's pajama bottoms hang from her waist, and her nipples show through a pink tank top that says THE RAMONES. A cordless phone is cradled between her shoulder and cheek. She looks at Roger's vacuum and bucket of cleaning supplies blankly. Then she seems to remember that she called him and smiles, revealing a mouthful of perfect little teeth like baby teeth. She waves him in.

"Ted can shove the *Zone* up his ass," she says to the person on the phone. Roger takes a step backward. "I'm doing Atkins. Eggs and bacon every morning. So there." She opens the door wider. He notices that she's wearing clunky hiking boots, the laces all undone around her ankles. He drags his canister vacuum cleaner rattling over the threshold.

"Is this a bad time?" he whispers.

"I'll just be a minute," she whispers back. "Have a seat." She points to a chair in the hallway. Roger sits dutifully. He likes the implied intimacy of their whispering. Mrs. Mackey disappears through a

176

swinging door into the dining room, the laces of her hiking boots flying and snapping. Roger can still hear her on the phone.

"I've still got ten IVF pounds to drop. Tell me what's worse than being fat, tired, and *not* pregnant."

The hallway smells like wool and lemons — like grown-ups. Rubyred Oriental carpets, mahogany antiques, gold-framed mirrors — the place is like a museum. In college, Roger visited kids who lived in houses like this. *Real* houses, with entryways and art on the walls. Not like his mother's rentals, with their cheesy wood paneling and indoor/outdoor carpeting that served as a feeble barrier from the cement slab below — from the fact that they always lived in someone's converted garage or basement, in the dank shadow of a *real* house.

"Yeah, just don't eat the bun." Mrs. Mackey explodes back through the swinging dining room door. She clicks off the phone and smiles at Roger. Her short blond hair is all over the place. She looks like Meg Ryan after a hurricane. "Thanks for coming," she says. "Sorry to make you wait. Wow, I love your pants."

"What? Thanks." Roger looks down self-consciously at his plaid polyester pre-cuffed trousers, which he bought at a thrift store. If he weren't so damn skinny, they'd fit better. He likes to clean in a T-shirt and old pants from men's suits circa 1980. If they get trashed with bleach or something, he can just toss them.

Roger can't decide if Mrs. Mackey is cute or annoying. She picks up his canister vacuum and carries it into the kitchen. This is the first thing he likes about

177

her. Why is *she* carrying the vacuum? Okay, maybe her nipples and the hiking boots were the first thing.

In the kitchen, Mrs. Mackey offers Roger coffee, eggs, and bacon. He just takes the coffee, even though he's hungry, because he never manages to eat breakfast.

"Sorry, I'm not quite dressed yet." Mrs. Mackey looks at her feet in the boots. "For fifteen years, I got up at five thirty, put on panty hose, and commuted to an office. Now I'm on sabbatical and can do whatever I want." She glances around her kitchen, which smells like Denny's, but is pretty clean. "You'd think I could at least get dressed and clean my own house."

Roger notices a worn copy of *The Iliad* on the kitchen counter. "You a professor?"

Mrs. M laughs. "No. I'm on a corporate sabbatical. You give the company sixty-hour weeks for ten years and eventually they give you six weeks with pay. It's an incentive to waste ten years of your life so you can get a month and a half to do what you *really* want." As she talks, she roots through the crisper drawer in her refrigerator. Finally, she finds what she's looking for — a cigarette.

"Sweet." Roger would take a big trip or something.

"I tacked on a few weeks of overdue vacation. Only now I don't know what I'd like to do." She flips on the electric burner. "That's the thing about ten years of sixty-hour weeks. You forget what you *really* wanted to do, like have a baby or maybe go to Italy and see Brunelleschi's dome."

178

As she bends over the orange coils of the stove to light the cigarette, the sickeningly sweet smell of burning hair tinges the air.

"You're burning your hair." Roger puts down his coffee cup.

"Oh," Mrs. Mackey says without alarm. She laughs and waves a hand in front of her face. With the lit cigarette dangling from two fingers, she turns toward the kitchen window and pulls up the chunk of burned hair to examine it in the light. Then she grabs a pair of poultry scissors from the butcher block and chops off the ends. Hair sprinkles into the sink.

Mrs. Mackey is the first client to treat Roger like a real person, instead of like Cleaner Robot Guy. She asks where he lives and how the traffic was driving to her house. Her disheveled state is sexy — like she just got out of bed or she's about to go to bed. Heat prickles in Roger's cheeks as he tells her about his uneventful commute.

As they talk, she leans over the sink and blows smoke out the kitchen window. "Sorry," she says, waving at the smoke. "I don't really smoke. It's just temporary. Everything is kind of temporary right now." She runs water over the cigarette, shudders, and tosses it in the trash. "My husband just moved out."

"Oh, sorry." There's a long silence. *No kids?* Roger wants to ask. "I've been to Florence," he says instead. "It's cool. That dome took, like, twenty-eight years to build." He pulls on the soul patch on his chin, which he trimmed down from a goatee last night, out of boredom. It probably wasn't such a good call, because

179

now his skin feels raw and bumpy. Suddenly he wishes he didn't look like such a geek.

"Really? I'm going to research that trip today." Mrs. Mackey doesn't say this with much conviction. She lingers at the window. "You like cleaning?" she asks.

"Yeah." Funny, Mrs. Mackey is probably the only person Roger would admit this to. Chipping petrified toothpaste out of sinks and scrubbing burned spaghetti sauce off stoves kind of sucks, but at least these are tasks you can finish, unlike his portfolio, which he can't seem to complete. Besides, he'd rather scrub toilets than sit in a cubicle doing some shit marketing job. And he sure as hell doesn't want to have to be an assistant at wedding shoots. His friend Devon has a great-paying job doing spreads of fancy houses for an interior design magazine. He's got a sweet apartment in the city. But Roger doesn't want to shoot throw pillows and dream kitchens, either.

"I'm a photographer," he tells her. "I went to a fine arts college." He rolls his eyes. "Haven't found a real job yet." What he really wants to do is black-and-white portrait photography. To him, people's faces present the most interesting landscapes.

"A photographer? *Really?*" Mrs. Mackey makes it sound like Roger said he was a rocket scientist. "I'd *love* to see your photos."

"Yeah, well. I'm having a hard time finishing my portfolio. A little trouble with procrastination and perfectionism. Bad combo." When Roger first graduated, he got a job at a newspaper working with the police beat reporters. A hyperactive gag reflex

180

prevented him from taking very many pictures, though. He'd arrive at the scene of a major-injury traffic accident or a shooting and wind up doubled over, hurling into the gutter. "This is *nothing*," the police beat reporter would tell Roger, all annoyed. That Pall Mall — parched asshole got Roger moved to the food section. Then he had to shoot crème brûlées and heads of cauliflower. Cheese Danish glistening with shellac. Next thing, Roger was laid off. "Last hired, first fired," the assignment editor said.

"Maybe I can help you," Mrs. Mackey offers. "If you give me your résumé, I could look it over and make some suggestions."

"Okay, thanks." Roger is suddenly uneasy with this attention. He reaches for his vacuum and bucket of cleaning supplies. Some people want you to use their stuff — this one lady insists he use only vinegar and water and this bogus environmentally friendly spray that cleans jack shit — but he likes his own arsenal of products.

"Listen, Roger . . ." Mrs. M's voice drops with seriousness. "I need to show you the laundry." She says this as though the laundry is a dead body in her backyard.

"Sure." What's the big deal? He follows her down a hallway to a dark warm room at the back of the house. There are two baskets of towels and stuff. She opens the cupboards over the washer and dryer to show him an impressive array of liquid and dry detergents, stain removers, special soap to kill dust mites, fabric softener, bleach for colors, bleach for whites, spray bottles, dryer sheets, lint removers.

"Wow, great."

"I'm trying to wean myself off the laundry." She hangs on to the cupboard knobs.

"Some people don't like strangers, especially a *guy* doing their laundry. But I'm happy to do it." Roger hears his voice shake a little. Why does Mrs. Mackey make him nervous? "Either way." Shit, maybe this lady is better off working those sixty-hour weeks. Roger can't put his finger on it, but something isn't right about Mrs. Mackey. Maybe it's allergies, but she looks like she's been crying. She's got this vulnerability that's sweet and freaky at the same time.

"Anyway . . ." Mrs. Mackey looks at the baskets of laundry. Roger likes how her nose curves inward between her eyes then swoops up on the end. A ski-jump nose. If he could shoot her portrait, he'd have her stand under the soft bulb of the laundry room light, which creates shadows in her hair. "In my next life, I'm going to *have* a life." She pats Roger's arm absentmindedly and pushes past him out of the room.

Roger tosses in the laundry soap first. His girlfriend in college, Elissa, showed him this. Soap, water, clothes. After they graduated, Elissa went to law school and met another guy. Only she didn't *tell* Roger until he flew cross-country to visit her. She thought it would be better to tell him in person. Great. She could have saved him the fucking airfare. Her calmness just made him feel worse. "Don't do this to yourself," she said. He smashed her English teapot against the wall. "What are

182

you even *doing* here?" he yelled. "What about your art?" She had majored in painting. "You're selling out!" God, Roger sounded so pompous. He slept on the lawn in the quad that night, then flew home to do a three-hour shoot of a bowl of cream of pumpkin soup for the fall food spread. Roger had barely slept the night before. He felt high, he was so tired.

"Did you shoot the soup?" the art director asked him in the hall that afternoon. Like the soup needed killing! He burst into hysterical laughter. Shoot the soup! Laughing, laughing, laughing, then coughing, then choking. Tears ran into his mouth. Fucking *tears*. He fell to his knees, afraid the art director might see, afraid he might puke. "Man, it's *all right*," the art director said, pounding Roger on the back.

Usually you can get a person's whole story from cleaning their house. Mrs. Mackey's whole story is under the sink in her master bath, where Roger finds a crazy stash of medical stuff. The first thing he sees is a red sharps container, like they have at the hospital. He can see through the thin plastic that the thing is nearly full with used needles. Maybe she's diabetic. But there are vials of stuff that aren't insulin. He picks one up. GONAL-F. He turns to close and lock the bathroom door, then switches on the fan. He never takes anything from people's medicine chests, but he always likes to look — a fascination he's ashamed of, yet compelled by.

Sitting cross-legged on the floor, he peers into the cupboard. There are boxes filled with little ampules of Pergonal, *for intramuscular injection only*. Ouch. Jesus.

183

Another box has ampules of Gonal-F. Some ampules hold a white powder, and the others sterile diluent. Roger unfolds the packet insert. *Gonal-F stimulates ovarian follicle production in women* . . . Jesus. Mrs. Mackey must feel like a science experiment. That's got to suck. No wonder she's such a space case. There's a whole array of other stuff in the cupboard — progesterone capsules, syringes, alcohol swipes, Band-Aids, pregnancy test sticks. What the hell? How do you *not* get pregnant? Now that her husband moved out, what's Mrs. Mackey going to do with all these drugs?

Roger finally closes the cupboard door, feeling a little sick, as though he ate too much junk food. He cleans the sink, toilet, and shower, which are pretty much clean already. He dusts the books on the built-in bookshelves beside the toilet. The Mackeys read everything from Shakespeare to *This Old House* magazines. One stack of books is turned with the spines facing the wall. He stands on the toilet to reach them. A gray coating of dust makes him cough. *New Technologies for Treating Infertility. The Fertility Book. Resolving Infertility*. God, there's a how-to guide for everything these days. Next thing you know, somebody's gonna write a book on how to take a crap. It's sad the way the books are turned toward the wall, as though that's all Mrs. Mackey had the energy for. He finishes dusting them and hides the spines again.

Back in the bedroom, he wipes the lamp shades and the night tables. Mr. Mackey couldn't have left too long ago and he probably hasn't left for good, because his nightstand is still stacked with podiatry journals and mystery novels. A film of dust floats at the top of a glass of water on his side. Maybe their separation is only temporary. Roger hopes so, for Mrs. Mackey's sake. Or maybe not. Maybe her husband's an asshole.

He smooths the already neat comforter and fluffs the pillows, pausing to contemplate peeling back the covers. Last week Roger started putting little stuff in people's beds: an acorn, a page of junk mail, a strand of string. Trash. You could say he's putting trash in people's beds. Because they're so oblivious. If people were more observant, maybe they'd appreciate fine arts photography.

He figures it was kind of gay, but he used to do extra stuff for clients. Make that little triangle with the toilet paper. Cut flowers from their yards and leave them in a vase on the kitchen table. Clean out the fridge. But no one noticed. If they did, they didn't say anything. So maybe they'll notice *these* details. At the Rowinsons', he snuck three tiny pinecones from the yard into their bed. Those two couch-potato workaholics need to get closer to nature. The Waxmans' sheets are always so unrumpled and perfectly tucked in; you can tell there's not a lot of action in *that* bedroom. He stuck a couple of red rose petals under their pillows. The Carters' place is so dark it looks like a funeral home, so he slid a page from a magazine with an ad for a skylight between their sheets. Roger pictures that barge Mrs. Carter exploring the cold sheets with her toes. She'd be all, "What's this?" pulling out the skylight ad. "How'd *this* get here?" And her husband would shrug, all annoyed. "How the hell should I know?"

He sneaks back to Mrs. Mackey's living room and pulls a page of sheet music from the piano bench to slide between her covers. A Chopin prelude. He imagines her tiptoeing through her dark house with the sheet music, wearing the long white nightgown that hangs from the hook on the back of her bathroom door. He pictures her seated at the piano, her small square fingers slipping between the keys.

When he's finished cleaning the house, Roger finds Mrs. Mackey sprawled on a blanket under a tree in her front yard. She's surrounded by a laptop, books, pads, and pens. Instead of using any of the stuff, though, she's lying on her back staring at the sky.

"My office," she says, sitting up as Roger approaches. There's a fancy home office in the house with a big desk and a complicated-looking chair.

"Nice," Roger says. Mrs. Mackey might even be nuttier than old Mrs. Warrington, whose dining room table is piled with empty tin cans she obsessively washes and collects. But, hell, Roger figures if somebody shot *him* in the ass with all those needles, he would be whacked, too.

Mrs. M grimaces at the tree branches above her. "The city's coming to cut down this beautiful oak."

"Why?"

"It's dying."

"Really?" Roger looks up. The tree is gnarly — all bent and twisted. It's cool that Mrs. Mackey thinks it's beautiful. "It seems okay."

"On the outside. But it's all rotten on the inside."

"I can relate to that." For some reason, Roger feels comfortable telling Mrs. Mackey this.

Mrs. M turns to him, wrinkling her little nose and smiling in a sweet way that makes him want to lie under the tree with her.

"Will you want service weekly?" he asks. "You can check out the house and let me know."

"I'm sure everything's great. Go ahead and come next week. Thank you, Robert."

"It's Roger."

"Oh, God, I'm sorry. How rude!" Mrs. M smacks her forehead.

He'd like to shoot her like this, while she's backlit, the sun making her messy hair glow around her face. Roger points to *The Iliad*. "I hated that book in college."

"Oh, I *know*." Mrs. Mackey sits up on her knees. "Me, too. But this is a new translation." Her eyes widen as she stares at her house. "I've been thinking of my husband's lover as Helen of Troy, but frankly that's giving her *way* too much credit." She looks at Roger. "You know what I mean?"

Roger nods. He has no fucking idea what Mrs. Mackey means, but she looks at him so hopefully that he keeps nodding. Roger glances around the neighborhood. It's empty, except for gardeners. "Nobody's ever home in these nice neighborhoods, are they?" he asks her.

Mrs. M shrugs. "We've all got to go to work to pay the mortgages."

"Are people happy here?" Roger immediately regrets this sophomoric question.

"Ha, is that the impression you get from cleaning people's houses? You can clean up the dust bunnies and coffee rings, but you can't sweep away the unhappiness?"

"Sort of."

"Well, maybe you could invent a product. Cuts grease *and* malaise!"

Roger laughs.

"Bleach away your husband's lover!"

Ouch. Roger can't think of anything funny to say.

Mrs. M nods and looks across the street at her neighbors' place. "These houses are nice. Some of them come with swimming pools. Some have fancy kitchens and whirlpool bathtubs. None of them comes with happiness, though. None of them comes with babies."

"Those amenities are sold separately." Roger steps into the shade, then crouches beside Mrs. Mackey on her blanket.

"Ha. That's right."

"You know, my English prof said that supposedly Hemingway once wrote a six-word short story. It went, *For sale: Baby shoes. Never used.*"

Mrs. M turns to him. Her expression is somewhere between stunned and grateful. "Oh, I . . . that's . . . Sometimes you don't need many words, do you?"

"Yeah, well, nobody knows for sure if he wrote it." Maybe Roger has upset her. He should probably go. He stands up.

"Bring your portfolio and your résumé next time. I'd love to see your work." Mrs. Mackey smiles. Man, those little teeth!

"Thanks." Roger tilts back his head to study the oak. "That's a total bummer about your tree," he says, trying to make her feel better. *Dude, I'm sure.* He sounds like a fucking surfer.

"Have you finished your graduate school applications?" Roger's mother asks during her monthly phone call to him that night. She always tries not to sound pushy or judgmental. Roger's got to give her credit for that. Per usual, Roger mumbles on about how his portfolio isn't finished.

"Let me know if you need help with money, sweetie," she says. "To free up your time for those applications." But Roger won't ever ask her for money. She probably has hardly enough for retirement. He wants to get a scholarship. Make her proud and relieved.

After they hang up, he crawls into bed with Letterman and a beer. His hands are raw from cleaning. Creases and cracks are starting to bleed in places. Real sexy. *Not.* The cool beer bottle soothes his sore skin.

He imagines it's him on Letterman.

"Great stuff," Dave says, holding up Roger's portfolio of photographs.

"Hey, thanks," Roger replies. (Picture this: a planet where people gush over fine arts photographers, not just actors and models.)

189

"And you're sleeping with that doll Elinor Mackey?" Dave asks. "How's that going?"

Roger beams at the audience. "Awesome."

CHAPTER
TEN

"Choose a couple horses and bet low, babe," Gina's date Barry says in his cheerful growl, grinning and tossing a few twenties through the window to the bookie at the racetrack. "It's always just for fun when the stakes are low."

Gina studies the horses' names overhead — Proud Athena and Hang-Tough Harry — savoring the realization that this is what she likes about being with Barry: the stakes are low. She doesn't love him. It's never occurred to her that *not* loving someone could feel good. With Ted, the prospect of losing him nearly crushed her. Afraid of scaring him away, she always tried to play down her affection, to suppress the irrepressible joy at just *seeing* him. It made her feel silly, like a puppy locked in a car.

After she and Barry place their bets, they move on to the concession stand. Barry buys vats of popcorn, hot dogs, peanuts, Milk Duds, bottled water, and beer. The cashier hurries to fill the order, calling Barry "sir." Something about Barry instills this respect in people, making them scramble to wait on him. Maybe it's his combination of designer clothes and self-confidence.

Gina watches as Barry pays the young man and shoves five dollars into the tip jar. Even though it's Saturday, Barry's dressed sharply in pressed slacks and a collared knit shirt. His dark hair forms a U-shape on his forehead, a sheen of perspiration dotting the pink balding patches on either side. His nose is small and bulbous. While he's not really Gina's type, he's got a Tony Soprano sexiness that she knows many women find irresistible.

These are good carbs, she's about to comment as she digs her hand into the popcorn. Who cares? The pieces are warm and salty against her lips. She takes another mouthful as Barry leads her to two seats in the middle of an empty row. He uses a napkin to wipe off her seat. Once she's settled, he hands her a hot dog. She hasn't eaten a hot dog in years. The beer goes straight to her head and the sun warms her face. The bright yellow mustard tastes like summer.

Barry pats her knee. "You, my love, have the most beautiful legs on the planet."

Gina's wraparound skirt falls open, and she reaches to close it. She smiles at Barry and dabs mustard off his chin with her napkin. Has she ever been in a relationship where she and a man loved each other equally? How are you supposed to know? That must be a safe, happy feeling. Those would be *healthy* low stakes. Although maybe the stakes would be higher, since something could happen to your one true love. Or maybe that feeling of security would lead you to take each other for granted, as Ted and his wife seemed to. Gina crushes her hot dog wrapper in her fist. Why must everything circle back to Ted? She takes a long drink of her beer, trying to push him out of her mind.

"Here we go!" Barry jumps up as the horses explode out of the gates. Gina stands beside him. He curls an arm around her waist, pulling him toward her. He smells like something newly bought at a department store — like cologne and cotton sizing. "Give 'em hell, Harry!" he cheers.

"Attagirl, Athena!" Gina yells. Even when they do things she never imagined she would enjoy, she always has fun with Barry. If Ted was her heroin, Barry is her methadone. Does that mean she's using Barry as a crutch? She takes another long drink of beer while it's still cold. She should quit analyzing everything. Barry's the one who always calls *her*. For all she knows, he has other girlfriends. The best part is she doesn't care. Imagine! A sensation that's almost like self-confidence.

After betting on two more races, winning ninety dollars, and eating snow cones that melt and drip off their wrists, they finally leave the racetrack, climbing back into Barry's Jaguar.

"Am I the handsomest motherfucker you've ever dated?" Barry laughs and checks his hair in the rearview mirror, readjusting a toothpick in the corner of his mouth.

"Don't swear." Gina giggles. She's not a prude, but she doesn't like foul language, which always seems born out of anger. "Of course," she teases. "The toothpick does it for me." Barry doesn't mind when she pokes fun at him. While he can be gruff and stern — she's heard him chide his employees on the phone — he doesn't take himself too seriously.

"A toothpick's better than a cigar." He speeds up and pulls out of the parking lot. "It's been a year, you know. I went from cigarettes to cigars to toothpicks. Gimme another year and I'll be off these things, too. Okay, gorgeous?"

At a red light, Gina leans over and pulls the toothpick from Barry's mouth, then traces his lower lip with her tongue.

"Mmmmm." He kisses her, his large lips covering hers. Gina closes her eyes, willing the chemistry to blossom. She always closes her eyes when she and Barry kiss or make love. When Shane made love to her she would touch and admire his long black hair, which was a startling contrast with his pale skin. Shane always closed his eyes, sighing deeply and telling her he loved her, then falling into the same soulful concentration he had while playing his bass onstage. But when Ted made love to Gina, he would look *into* her eyes and hold her gaze, something no one else had ever done. As the light turns green, Gina shifts away from Barry, cracking her window to get some air.

Gina is surprised when the doorbell rings at ten thirty that night. Maybe Barry's come back for something he left behind. She peers through the peephole to see Shane swaying on the porch. She opens the door in time to watch a taxi back out of the driveway.

"Baby." Shane's hair is damp at the ends from the shower, making two dark spots on the shoulders of his

194

blue plaid flannel shirt. Under the flannel, he's wearing his typical white T-shirt and black jeans.

Gina crosses her arms over her chest, feeling like a flimsy barricade.

"Are we together or are we broken up or what are we?" Shane's voice is too loud.

"You fell off the wagon?"

"Bad day." He dips his head. "What are we?" Shane is always having a bad day.

"Friends, Shane. We're friends. As long as you're not drinking, we're friends. If you're drinking, we're not even friends."

"Well, maybe if we were more than friends, like we used to be, like we're *supposed* to be, I wouldn't *be* drinking." He spits a little as he speaks.

Right, I *ruined everything*. Gina can't reason with him when he's drunk. "I'll make you a cup of coffee." One cup of coffee, half an hour of talking, *max*, then she'll call him a taxi. She heads for the kitchen.

Shane sits slumped at the table as Gina programs the coffee-maker and puts out low-fat milk and sugar. She takes wheat bread, cheese, and turkey from the refrigerator, and fixes him a sandwich.

"You could make anyplace feel like home," Shane says. "You could make a fucking cold hole in the ground feel like home. You *are* home." This romantic intensity captivated Gina when she first started dating Shane. But now his darkness is more ugly than intriguing. There are purplish circles under his eyes, and he smells like whiskey and cigarettes. He reminds her of the bar after last call — when the bright lights are turned on to reveal the bleak dirtiness of the place.

Toby appears in the doorway. When he sees Shane, he rolls his eyes, stomps his bare foot on the floor, and turns to leave.

"Hey, slugger," Shane calls after him.

Toby grunts and slams his bedroom door.

"And he's not even a teenager yet," Shane says with disgust.

"That's right." Gina puts down a place mat and sets the sandwich before him. "He's just a *kid*, Shane. He's a kid, and he has every right to be upset when people show up drunk at our house at ten o'clock at night."

Shane looks at her with surprise. For once she's not trying to cheer him up or see things from his point of view. She is not negotiating. Not tonight.

"What happened to AA?"

"I had a setback." Shane sips the coffee, hiccups, sputters, and dribbles brown spots on his shirt. Nice. She used to be so attracted to him! She remembers the time, soon after they started dating, when he braided her hair into two perfect braids. It was after they made love. "I did it every morning for my little sister," he explained, concentrating on weaving three sections of Gina's hair. "But I won't tie your shoes. You gotta do that yourself." That's when Gina fell in love with him, as he sat behind her with his legs curled around hers, finishing the braids, then tickling her cheeks with the ends, his chest warm against her back, his voice rumbling up through her spine as though he were a part of her.

She sits across the table from him. "You should have called your sponsor tonight," she tells him. "You have to *want* to get better, Shane. You have to make it a serious goal."

"You're my goal." He reaches for Gina's hand. She pulls it away. "Babe," he says softly, sadly. He throws down his sandwich and it falls apart. Gina gets up and stands at the sink, her back to him. "If you want to see me, you have to quit drinking. You can't have everything." She reaches for the phone. "I'll call you a taxi."

"Not yet, in a minute. Wait."

She can hear that his mouth is full. She turns to see him gobbling the sandwich in big bites. "This is good!" He looks up at her, nodding maniacally and swallowing. Then he pauses in her gaze. "Let's talk. Just for a minute." He takes a gulp of the coffee. He's stalling for time. No different than a ten-year-old who wants fifteen more minutes of TV. She's tired of constantly bargaining with people. Bargaining with her son to get him to stop playing that stupid Game Boy. Bargaining with her clients to get them to do five more reps, *just five more!* Bargaining with Shane to go to AA. At one point, she thought she could marry him if he'd just quit being two people.

"You been dating?" Shane asks.

"Yes." She sighs, immediately regretting getting into *this* conversation.

"Who? Barry?"

Gina nods.

"He's a fucking concert promoter, Gina!" Shane stands, his fists hanging at his sides. "The worst whore scum of the earth." Spit flies from his mouth.

"Game over." Gina reaches for the refrigerator magnet with the taxi telephone number. Shane lunges toward her. She steps to one side and he pounds his fist on the freezer door. Then he turns to face the table as though looking for something. He picks up the sugar bowl and hurls it smashing against the wall.

"That's nice." Gina doesn't have the energy to be angry with him anymore. "It's late and you're drunk. I'm calling you a cab. We can have lunch tomorrow. Come to the club and I'll buy you lunch and we can sit outside. It's supposed to be beautiful." She has no intention of seeing Shane tomorrow. She won't be at the club. But this is all she can think of to get him to calm down and leave.

"The club," Shane sneers. "The fucking yuppie fitness club. If those people had *lives* they wouldn't need to work out on machines. Constantly running toward the TV on the treadmill. Jesus. If they were real people, like farmers, *life* would give them exercise."

"That would solve the world's problems," Gina says, surprising herself with the quickness of her reply. "If everyone was a farmer." As she taps in the number of the taxi, Shane's fist flails at her, knocking the phone onto the floor. It shoots across the Pergo, batteries spilling out.

"Okay! You want me to go, I'm going." Shane charges past Gina and out of the kitchen. Gina scrambles to collect the pieces of the phone, pressing them back together. She hits REDIAL and heads up the stairs after Shane.

"Charley's Taxi," the dispatcher says. Gina tells the woman she needs a cab immediately, wondering if maybe she should have called the police instead. She follows Shane into her room. He bounces up and across the bed, then climbs up onto her desk by the window, knocking over her photos of Toby and her mother. Before she can reach him, he pops out the window screen and disappears onto the roof.

"Shane!" Gina tosses the phone onto the bed and climbs up onto the desk, kneeling on the window ledge. "Shane, get back in here," she tries to whisper, mortified that the neighbors might hear.

"No. You want me to go home? I'm going home. I'm going aaaaaallllll the way home!" He scrambles across the roof, hovering just at the edge of Gina's sight. She sticks one leg through the window, about to climb out. Then she realizes he could easily take both of them down. She pulls herself back in, kneeling on all fours on the desk with just her head out the window. She turns on the desk lamp. The light from the bulb makes it harder to see outside, so she snaps it back off.

"All the way home," Shane repeats, shouting now. Laughing and shouting and standing on the roof with his arms extended as though he's riding a surfboard.

"Hey, jackass!" Gina hears Toby shout from his bedroom window below. "What are you doing on our roof?"

"I'm gonna jump, slugger."

"Go for it!" Toby hollers, his voice hoarse from postnasal drip and hormones.

"Shane." Gina tries to sound more empathetic. "C'mon in, baby. C'mon in now." She extends a hand toward him.

"Are you trying to *kill* yourself?" Toby shouts, disdain and disbelief in his voice.

"Bingo, slugger."

"That's a joke. You won't *die*. You'll just break your legs. Or maybe your back." Toby is a connoisseur of such information, having memorized most of the THOUSAND GRUESOME AND GORY FACTS! in his *Macabre Miscellany* book. "Loser," he adds. "Then you won't be able to drive *or* walk. What a loser!" Toby breaks into laughter, cracking himself up at this thought.

"Toby!" Gina calls out, still trying to whisper.

"You're right. I am a loser," Shane says loudly. "Shitty band. Installing skylights," he mumbles to himself.

Just then Gina sees the shadowy figures of her neighbors, the Jensens — an elderly couple who walk their golden retriever every night.

"Gina? Dear? You okay up there?"

"She's fine!" Shane shouts.

"We're okay," Gina tells them.

"Toby, son?" Mr. Jensen calls out. "Get down from there now."

Gina dials 911, whispers her address into the phone.

"I'm down here," Toby calls from his window. "That's Shane!" he adds with excitement. "He's gonna jump! Go ahead, loser, jump!"

200

Gina hears the sound of six weeks of kids being mean to Toby in her son's voice. She hears the school bully and the father who doesn't want his son living with him.

"Shane?" Mrs. Jensen asks. "Are you a friend of Gina's?"

"Not anymore," Shane says. "She doesn't want me."

"Well, let's get down off the roof now," Mr. Jensen says.

Gina is horrified. Great: She's the pathetic single-mother drama-queen neighbor with the lunatic drunk on her roof.

"I *am* a loser," Shane repeats, bending precariously over the edge of the roof to talk to Toby. "You're a smart kid."

"You're an idiot," Toby says.

"Shane!" Gina shouts this time. He turns toward her, takes a few teetering steps back up the roof in her direction. A shingle shoots out from under his feet, making a loud *splat* in the driveway. "You think there aren't days when I don't want to jump out this window?" Gina lowers her voice, hoping the Jensens can't hear her.

"What?" Shane asks.

"You think I don't want to jump off a ten-story building some nights?"

Shane sits down.

Gina swallows. While her voice is somehow steady, her legs wobble, and her stomach burns. "But I can't. Because I have a son and I love him and I have to take care of him. And you can't because you have your music."

"My music is shit."

The Jensens back out of the street onto the sidewalk. "The police," Gina hears Mrs. Jensen say.

"No, it's not shit. You're talented and the world needs your music. People need music." God, she is so tired of trying to inspire people.

"I need *you*. I love you."

"Come back inside. And we'll talk." The overhead light in her bedroom flashes on. She ducks back into the room.

Toby stands in the doorway. "Nice *boyfriend*."

Gina squints at him. "Honey, he's not — I'm sorry. Turn out the light. I can't see."

Toby flips off the light, lingering in the doorway.

"Don't leave me," Shane begs.

"Shane, everything's going to be all right. I promise. Please, come inside." Gina leans her head out the window. Shane hovers at the roof's edge again.

Just then yellow and red lights streak the night sky. A fire truck rumbles around the corner. Gina wonders why there's no siren. Maybe to avoid startling the jumper. She sighs with relief, closing her eyes for a moment. When she opens them, she sees Shane leap from the roof. It is an odd image, because first he goes up, taking a leap that carries him above the line of the roof, as though he's trying to fly. For an instant, like the camera flash for a picture, his flannel shirt forms a cape-like triangle around his skinny body, and his arms are extended like a snow angel's. Then he's gone. There

202

is no sound, and then there are three sounds: Mrs. Jensen's scream, the crackle of shrubbery, and the loud thump of Shane's body hitting the ground. What, though? Grass? Bushes? Concrete? Gina sits on the edge of her bed, stunned.

"Mom?" Toby says. The mean school-bully voice is gone. He's scowling, but his lip quivers. "Do you think he's dead?"

By the time Gina steps off the porch onto her front lawn, the paramedics have put Shane onto a stretcher. He moans incomprehensibly. Gina hovers close to the house, not wanting him to see her. The night air is cool and moist. Toby peeks out from behind the front door. The Jensens bow their heads and hurry up the street with their dog.

A policeman interviews Gina. She tells him everything about this evening, and Shane's drinking problem and angry flare-ups. Because Shane was violent and threatening, the policeman asks if Gina wants him to call a victim advocate from the local shelter.

"A . . . what?" She is *not* a battered woman. She hates that Shane has made the police and the neighbors think that she's a battered woman. "He hasn't *hurt* me," she tells the officer. Why did she ever fall in love with someone at a *bar*?

"I understand." The officer nods knowingly. "But he's violent and an alcoholic and you may want to file a restraining order at some point. Perhaps later." He hands Gina a brochure. "There's a number here you can call. You don't need a lawyer. You just go down to the family court and fill out some information on any incidents that have occurred. You'll get a temporary order that day. Then you and the gentleman will be called to court for a formal hearing on the matter. The judge will likely issue a permanent order, making it illegal for the gentleman to come within a hundred yards of you or your son or your property."

"Thank you." Gina takes the brochure. *Gentleman.* What a joke.

"It's my job."

Gina bristles at the look of pity in the policeman's eyes. Maybe she's being paranoid. Maybe it's just kindness. She nods and tells herself to smile.

After the police leave, Toby and Gina sit at the kitchen table. Gina pours out the coffee and fixes Toby chocolate milk. "You want to play your Game Boy?"

Toby shakes his head.

"Watch the Disney Channel?"

Toby sighs, disgusted. "That's for babies."

"Oh, okay, I'm sorry." She gets up to wash the coffeepot.

"Do we have to visit Shane in the hospital?" Toby asks.

"No, honey." Gina will call the hospital to make sure Shane's okay, but she won't go to see him. If he bothers them again, maybe she will file that restraining order.

"Mom?"

"Hmm?" She's wondering whether the hospital will give her information over the telephone.

204

"Could you marry Dr. Mackey?"

Gina turns off the water running into the carafe. The refrigerator clicks and sighs. "Honey, technically he's still married."

"But I think he's getting divorced."

"Honey, he would have to ask me." She puts the carafe in the drainer and turns to face her son.

"Why don't *you* ask *him*?"

"Look how late it is!" She points to the clock. "After midnight already!"

Toby furrows his brow at her.

"Well, even if Dr. Mackey is getting divorced —"

"What? You still wouldn't ask him?"

Gina shakes her head.

Toby kicks the table again and the creamer slides off and crashes to the floor. Half-and-half gurgles out in a stream.

Toby looks up at her as though he's probably in trouble.

Gina shrugs. "I know, honey," she says. "I know." She opens the bottom junk drawer by the telephone, takes out the hammer, and hands it to Toby. "You can smash the pitcher if you want to. We already lost the sugar bowl tonight." Gina had hoped to own the whole set of Viceroy china, with their purple African violets and gold-veined leaves. The dishes are expensive, so she's been buying them one at a time. Now she doesn't care.

Toby cocks his head at her. She sets the hammer on the table beside him.

"You know I love you?" she asks.

Toby nods. She squeezes his shoulder. He is too thin. Tomorrow night she'll make him a big dinner of homemade macaroni and cheese and hot dogs.

"You want to call your dad and talk with him for a while?"

Toby shakes his head. "How come *you* can't ask Dr. Mackey?"

Because I know the answer, she wants to say. Because I would be even more hurt and humiliated than I already am. Even though I don't think he loves me, I'm willing to sleep with Dr. Mackey. I love him almost as much as I love you, and I want nothing more than for you and me and him to move into a house together in a neighborhood with a school that you like and kids who appreciate you. And then I want Dr. Mackey and me to have our own baby. But only if that's what you want. Only when you're ready for that. First I just want the three of us to be together.

"Because, honey . . ." She pushes her fingers into Toby's thick curls, searching for the right words. His hair is silky, despite the snarls. For once he doesn't recoil from her touch. "It just doesn't work that way."

CHAPTER
ELEVEN

Elinor wakes to a mosquito buzzing in her ear. West Nile virus! No, a leaf blower in her backyard. No, a *chain saw* in the front yard. The tree cutters or maulers or whatever you call them — *murderers* — have arrived already. It isn't even eight o'clock. They aren't supposed to come until nine! As she throws aside the covers, a sheet of paper sails to the floor. She crouches and sees that it's a page of music. What's Chopin doing in her bed? She tosses the waltz, which she always found too complicated, into the trash, stumbles into the bathroom, splashes water on her face, and swishes her toothbrush through her mouth. Then she pulls on jeans under her nightgown and a sweatshirt over her head and heads for the yard.

Outside, the August sun already scorches the sky. The angry snarl of the chain saw echoes through the neighborhood. The tree is the property of the city (she didn't know this before Noah told her), but the guys could have at least rung the bell. A man dangles high in the branches of the oak, attached by a clip at his waist to a leather loop around the tree. Orange cones cordon off a section of the street. A big truck with a trailer blocks the driveway. Elinor doesn't see any sign of Noah.

"*Hey!*" she hollers up to the guy in the tree. All she can see are his denim-clad legs. A large branch crashes onto the driveway. A second man appears from around the truck, stoops, and shoves it into the chipper at the back. A loud grinding is followed by a whir and a shriek, like a blender loaded with too much ice.

"*Turn it off!*" Elinor charges toward the man, waving her arms. Perspiration trickles down her chest under the sweatshirt. "Turn everything off!"

The man jumps, startled when he sees her. "Ma'am?" he shouts.

Elinor plants her hands on her hips, trying to convey authority, even though her nightgown hangs around her thighs. "You're not supposed to be here until nine." She points to the oak, which now looks as though it has had a bite taken out of its leafy shape. "All I wanted was *one* cup of coffee under that tree."

The man frowns, confused. He turns off the chipper and slashes his hand in the air, signaling for the guy in the tree to cut the chain saw. The saw quiets to a low drone. "We're starting early on account of the heat," he says, pulling off his cap and wiping his forehead with the back of his hand.

"Well, I —" Normally, Elinor would offer contractors lemonade or coffee. "Can you wait? I just want to . . ." What? She just wants them to go away so she can take a shower and get her blanket and book, lie under the tree, and reclaim her morning.

208

Kat pulls into the driveway after dropping off her kids at school. When she sees Elinor, she turns off the car and jumps out.

"Already? You sure you want to watch?"

Elinor feels her head nod.

"I'm sorry, ma'am," the chipper guy says, scratching his meaty, tanned arms and squinting. "The disease can spread to other trees. You knew we were coming?"

"At *nine*."

"Listen, can we just have a minute with the tree?" Kat asks the man.

He rolls his eyes. "Hang on!" he hollers to the guy in the branches above.

Kat pulls El toward the tree and they stand together in the shade.

"No more coffee with Warren." Elinor claps the oak's trunk with her open palm, as though slapping someone on the back. The tree feels solid. It's her head that feels rotten and hollow, buzzing with bark beetles.

"We can still have coffee outside every day," Kat reminds her. "You can go through the Sunset book and pick another, heartier tree."

"That'll be expensive." Elinor wonders how much a *divorce* costs, and whether she'll even be living in her house in six months. *This* is what she should be worrying about. "Trees cost money," she says.

"Trees don't grow on tree!" Kat punches her arm lightly.

Elinor snorts with laughter. "Look at me. Who needs *tree* closure?" She turns to Kat. "Were you so patient before you had kids?"

Kat crinkles her small, pointed nose, considering this.

"I take your patience for granted," Elinor says before she can answer. Kat must feel as though Elinor's her fourth kid.

Kat shrugs. "Nah. Don't sweat it."

"*Okay?*" the man swaying above them in the tree asks with irritation. It can't be comfortable to hang like that. "Step *aside*, please? Some of us have work to do!" The chipper guy stomps out a cigarette in the driveway, as if to emphasize this fact.

Elinor leaps out from under the tree and darts to the porch, Kat following behind her. The oak is dying and threatening the health of other trees. These guys have a job to do and they're sweltering in the heat. Kat needs to get on with her day. The chain saw rips and howls, sending branches smashing into the driveway. Elinor and Kat cower on the stoop.

"Can I make you coffee?" Elinor shouts over the noise to Kat.

"No thanks," Kat shouts back.

Elinor studies the chipper's orange metal chute, with its shrieking blades and big, triangular DANGER labels. Suddenly she has the urge to throw something from the house into it. Her laptop, with all those e-mails from the office. Why did she agree to do e-mail while on sabbatical? *CC, BCC, FYI, blah, blah, blah*. Or she could toss in the Zone cookbook. Whatever happened to it, anyway? Did Ted give it back to Gina? A book would easily spin through the chipper's maw. Yes. She stands up.

"I'll be right back," she tells Kat. "One sec." Kat nods, grimacing at the noise as she reads over school information photocopied onto different-colored papers.

Elinor hurries through the screen door into the house, down the hall, through the bedroom, and into the master bath. As she reaches up to slide the infertility books off the shelf, the pages scrape her neck and chin. She holds them in her arms, flipping through the top book, shuddering. She remembers when she first bought the guides, how intimidating it was to read about the procedures, which became increasingly complicated as the chapters wore on: hysteroscopy, egg retrieval, assisted hatching, intracytoplasmic sperm injection. *Thank God we'll never have to resort to that!* she thought when she first bought the books. But gradually she and Ted worked their way through the chapters, and now pages and pages of explanations and diagrams are dog-eared and underlined with highlighter pen. She's kept the books because she'd always hoped she and Ted would gather the strength to try another cycle of in vitro one day. But strength doesn't seem to have anything to do with the outcome. She hugs the stack to her chest and bolts out of the bathroom.

"What's up?" Kat shouts as Elinor sprints past her down the driveway.

Elinor waits by the hedges for the chipper guy to turn his back and reach for a fresh branch. When he does, she lunges at the machine. There's no time to feed the books into the chute individually, so she tosses them in all at once. A blur of spines and covers and pages tumbles away, stripes of highlighter pen flashing in the sun. The thick volumes bring another kind of sound from the chipper, a dull, mournful rumble, instead of the shrieking whine. The chipper guy shifts to feed in another branch. He looks hot and ready to be through with this job. Elinor backs away from the machinery, her arms feeling pleasantly light without the books.

As Elinor settles back in beside Kat on the porch, a big green pickup pulls up the drive and Noah climbs out. He peers from under his ball cap to assess the tree situation. When he sees Elinor, he hurries up the walk.

"Morning!" he says.

"What are you so cheerful about?" Elinor asks.

"Sorry," he says sheepishly, removing his cap and fidgeting with it. Is he glad to see her? He is a large man — over six feet tall with broad shoulders and muscular arms. Where has Elinor *seen* him before? Oh! He is the Brawny Paper Towel Man. An older, balder version. But he isn't goofy. There's something inherently attractive about him — about someone who spends all of his time outdoors. Elinor considers her outfit: white nightgown hanging over ripped Levi's, husband's old sweatshirt, bare feet, pink toenail polish, bed head. She runs her tongue over her teeth, hoping for remnants of toothpaste. She introduces Noah to Kat and they wave hello to each other.

"You see a lot of sick trees these days?" Kat shouts to Noah.

"Unfortunately."

"Quite an efficient operation you've got here," Elinor grumbles.

"I'm sorry about the tree." Noah sits beside her. He has to lift his elbows to rest them on his knees. The hair on his forearms curls in graying wisps. He has a sharp, clean smell — like eucalyptus. Elinor pulls her sweatshirt over her knees in a lame attempt to cover her nightgown.

Cute, Kat mouths when Noah is concentrating on the tree. "I'll make coffee," she shouts to him a little too cheerfully — like a firstclass flight attendant. Noah says no thank you, but Kat winks at Elinor and ducks inside the house anyway.

Warren has been reduced to a twelve-foot totem pole. One thick branch remains, like a Statue of Liberty arm reaching toward the sky. The trunk is spotted with white circles where branches have been lopped off. The guy on the ground continues to feed the chipper. As the machine chokes and sputters, Elinor wonders aloud, "Is a *tree* too much to ask for?"

Noah doesn't hear her.

The chain saw slows to a moan, the man in the tree shimmying down to the last branch. Across the street, three slim birches do a flirtatious hula in the breeze, fluttering their leaves, taunting Warren with their limber beauty. Elinor turns to Noah. His salt-and-pepper mustache is thick and remarkably even at the ends. She has the urge to touch it.

Warren's remaining thick arm is stubborn. The man in the tree struggles to cut through it. Finally, the branch snaps and plunges to the ground. Elinor feels vindicated when the chipper guy has to leap out of the way as it rolls toward his feet.

The men heave the saw and their weight into the remaining pillar of tree, working to fell it. Circles of sweat stain the underarms of their T-shirts. Sawdust arcs into the air behind them. Finally, Warren tips, teeters, and hits the street with a hollow smack. The man with the saw loses control for a moment, his arms flying into the air as though he's following through on a clumsy golf swing. He falls to his knees and switches off the saw. Finally, the noise stops completely, like a headache going away. Still, Elinor's ears buzz with tinnitus. A crow caws overhead.

Kat returns with coffee. Noah nods with appreciation and the three of them sit and sip, watching the men roll the last wedge of trunk to the truck, count to three, then hoist it into the bed. Next they toss in the orange cones, sweep the street, wave to Noah, climb into the cab, and pull away, towing the chipper behind them.

The yard is too bright without the oak, like an overexposed photo. Elinor starts across the lawn, the grass moist and sticky under her bare feet. Noah and Kat follow. Warren is now a flat stump, like a table. Elinor plucks up a stray leaf. It's bumpy and eaten away in places. As she drops it, twirling, to the ground, she notices that the hair on her arms is coated with fine yellow sawdust. It *smells* healthy, like something newly built.

"Can she plant something well established that will provide shade right away?" Kat asks Noah.

"The city will only pay for seedlings," Noah explains, "but residents can pay the difference for more established trees. I have a book in my truck. I could show you some pictures if you like."

"A book!" Kat exclaims, as though Noah said he had a thousand dollars. "Well, I've got to run and make appointments with the orthodontist. Can you believe it? Already? But wow, that would be great if you'd help Elinor pick out a new tree." She shakes Noah's hand and bounds off toward her house.

"Maybe I'll see the forest for the trees now," Elinor tells Noah.

Noah cocks his head, smiles. "It's nice that you appreciate trees. Most people don't even notice them."

Suddenly Elinor feels shy. "Mammals were letting me down."

"You don't want the liquidambar," Noah says, leaning over his tree book at Elinor's kitchen table. "They have round sticker cones that are a menace when you step on them. Oh!" His eyes brighten with an idea. "You should get a *Ginkgo biloba* — a maidenhair. Look." He points to a picture of a bright green fan-shaped leaf with a scalloped edge. "In the fall, these turn yellow. When the sun hits them, they're gorgeous. And they're on the list of city-approved trees."

"Wow." Elinor tries to share Noah's enthusiasm for the picture of the golden leaves. But suddenly the starting-over aspect of choosing a tree depresses her. How many other new things will she need in the coming months? "I may not even stay in this house," she says to the hot pink flowers of a jacaranda pictured in the book. If she and Ted don't get back together, she

215

won't need this big place for herself. She meant to fill it up with a husband and kids. "I've been sitting under the oak every morning because I don't know what I'm doing with my life."

"One thing at a time," Noah says. "Either way, you're going to need a new tree, and planting a nice one improves the value of your home."

"Right." Elinor tries to focus on the book. "Who knew there were so many types of trees?" Before sitting down with Noah to look at the book, she ducked into the bathroom to pee, change into a T-shirt, brush her teeth, and put on a little lip gloss. While she was in there she squirted perfume under her arms, in lieu of a shower, and now she's afraid she smells like a magazine insert.

Noah rattles on about acacias. They're pretty, but reseed easily, which isn't necessarily a good thing. "Suddenly you've got roots and branches where you don't want them . . ."

No wedding band today either, Elinor observes.

". . . A pink jacaranda really stands out against the landscape . . ."

Trees, trees, trees. "You married?" Elinor blurts.

". . . Deciduous — What?" Noah looks at his tree book as though he wishes it could help him answer. He shakes his head. "Divorced."

"Oh, I'm sorry. How long?" Elinor hopes she's not being too nosy, but she wants to know more about why people get divorced.

"Eight months. I thought my wife and I got along great. We both loved the outdoors . . . But one day she

216

said I was boring, and she needed more. I thought she was going to tell me what she needed — that it would be something I could provide or change. But she had already found it — the VP of sales at her software company. Tell me *that* isn't boring." He flips a page.

"I'm sorry," Elinor repeats, closing the tree book. Noah is unusually chatty for a man. But she doesn't want to hear any more about trees.

"This guy makes a ton of money," Noah continues. "They got married like that." He snaps his fingers. "I guess you could say money isn't boring. They went mountain climbing in Tibet on their honeymoon." He flips the tree book back open to a random page on root rot. "But she fell, and had to be flown home in a body cast. Turns out Money Bags was a shitty Sherpa. I visited her in the hospital once when he wasn't there. I was trying to help her eat dinner and I accidentally dropped a pea down inside her body cast. She started screaming at me. 'This is a metaphor for everything!' " He turns to Elinor in disbelief. "One pea summed it all up for her."

Elinor bursts into laughter at the thought of the pea sliding inside the body cast. "I'm sorry," she says. "That's got to tickle or itch. Can you imagine?" She covers her mouth, unable to stop laughing.

Noah frowns. "It was an *accident*."

"I know," Elinor says. "That's what's so ironic and funny about it."

Noah looks hurt. The more hurt he looks, the more Elinor can't quit laughing. She has to cover her face with her hands and turn away. When she finally turns back to him, he has that same blank, hurt look, a look she finds irresistible. She takes his face in her hands.

"I'm sorry, I'm sorry. I know that must have been hard." She moves closer and rubs her finger against his bristly mustache.

To Elinor's surprise, Noah bites her finger, closes one eye, and smiles, a broad, mischievous pirate grin that makes her think maybe there's another side to him beyond the mind-numbing details of acacia trees. In one deliberate motion Noah scoops Elinor out of her chair, twirls her into the family room, and lays her on the carpet.

"All I wanted was a tree!" she shouts.

"I'll get you one," Noah shouts back.

He kneels beside her, studying her for a moment. They look at each other the way you might examine a painting in a museum, taking in all the details. Elinor reaches to cup her hands behind his neck, pulling him down to kiss her.

When you're married, you don't get to roll around on the living room floor at ten thirty in the morning making out with the city tree surgeon. Ah, but Elinor *is* married. So this is what an affair feels like? Lying dizzy on your back, seeing the unfinished underside of your coffee table for the first time? How can it be that she's never kissed a man with a mustache before? It's thick and bristly against her mouth, like a vegetable brush. She likes the heat and weight of Noah's body hovering over hers. Noah sweeps her hair out of her eyes and kisses each of her brows, the mustache tickling her forehead. Then he pushes her T-shirt up over her belly and plants kisses between her ribs. Elinor sighs and closes her eyes.

"You're lovely," Noah whispers, lifting his head to kiss her on the mouth. This kiss is deeper and warmer and saltier. But the word *lovely* spins in Elinor's head. Isn't lovely just short of pretty? Three rungs below beautiful? Grandmothers are lovely. She should just relax and *ulp* — Noah's hand, large and pleasingly rough, massages her breasts. *This* is better than coffee under a tree.

Noah's cell phone rings. He groans and rolls over to check his watch. "Damn," he whispers. "I was supposed to be at another house twenty minutes ago."

"That's okay." Elinor is relieved. This will do for now. She needs to take a shower, for one thing.

She stands and readjusts her bra and shirt. "That was fun."

"Then I take it it's all right if I call you?"

"You have the number."

"Don't worry about the tree for now," Noah tells her, rushing to put on his boots, which he'd unlaced and kicked aside. "I'll help you." He kisses her on the cheek. Elinor likes the raw feeling left behind by the mustache.

As he jogs down the driveway toward his truck, she thinks: *Down one tree, up one tree surgeon.*

Ted and Gina have settled into a routine. Every Tuesday afternoon Ted picks up Toby at the club and takes him to Barnes & Noble, where they study. Afterward, Gina fixes them dinner at her house. Then Ted and Toby finish up homework or play a game. After

Gina convinces Toby to go to bed, she and Ted drink coffee or wine then go upstairs to her room and have sex as quietly as possible, a challenge Ted finds exciting. They are cautious of the bed, afraid it might bump or squeak. Instead, they lie on the floor, or Ted lifts Gina up onto the edge of her dresser. Once, he pressed her against the wall as she wrapped her legs around his waist. As Ted gets more excited, Gina covers his mouth with her hand, which smells like onions and garlic and lemons from cooking dinner. He traces circles on her palm with the tip of his tongue, looking into her clear green eyes. Afterward, they usually crawl into Gina's bed and fall asleep, legs entwined. Ted always leaves before dawn. He sets the alarm on his watch for five AM before even arriving at Gina's place for dinner, fearful that one morning he'll wake up in Gina's arms with the sun blazing into the room and Toby standing beside the bed.

When Ted leaves on Wednesday mornings, it's still dark and the grass is soaked with dew. An old white Ford station wagon rattles slowly through the neighborhood, a Vietnamese man tossing newspapers thumping into the driveways. The previous hours of homework, dinner, Risk, sex, and short-but-sound sleep leave Ted feeling blissful. He wishes every day were Tuesday.

The sex isn't even Ted's favorite part. He particularly likes sitting down to dinner with Gina and Toby. Sometimes they play twenty questions. Toby prides himself in continually stumping Gina and Ted. One evening he bamboozles them twice in a row, with "Howard Johnson" and "manhole cover."

"Howard Johnson was a real guy?" Gina asks.

"Yep," Toby says. "He invented premium ice cream by making it all fatty and stuff. Hey, and you know Man Hole was a real guy, too. He was German and he was called Mann Hool. But in English it's Man Hole."

"Really?" Gina's eyebrows arch with disbelief.

"*Mom!*" Toby laughs, irritated and delighted at the same time. "Mann Hooooooool!" he crows.

Gina is easy to tease, because she doesn't do ironic humor. This earnestness charms Ted. It's not in her nature to be sarcastic. She always gives people the benefit of the doubt and looks for the silver lining in everything. By contrast, silver linings are Elinor's pet peeve. "No kids! You can go to Europe whenever you want to!" well-meaning acquaintances would say to Elinor at parties, feigning envy. El would force a smile and gulp her drink. On the way home, she'd rant: "Does the EU shut the doors as soon as you procreate? I know it's heinous to take a child on a transcontinental flight and convince him that the *Mona Lisa* is worth it. I *get* it!"

"I know," Ted would say, "I know." But Elinor's anger felt directed at him. As she ranted, he found himself ducking and holding his head to the side. Still, while Ted appreciates Gina's optimism and cheerfulness, he misses Elinor's dark wit. He'd like to think that his worldview includes both of these outlooks. The truth is, he doesn't find himself thinking broadly enough to *have* a worldview. He's too myopic — that's what Elinor says. Maybe it's from looking at people's feet all day. There's nothing more myopic than a corn on a big toe. The big toe is essential, though. You can barely *walk* without your big toe. You can't stand properly, let alone navigate your way through life.

"You're so quiet," Gina says, spooning more salad onto his plate. Her silver bracelets tinkle down her tanned wrists.

Ted smiles and bites into his chicken, which is spicy and juicy, complemented by the cool lettuce, buttery avocado, and tangy mustard dressing in his salad. He washes it all down with a sip of the Zinfandel he's brought. It occurs to him, in the moment that he swallows and closes his eyes, that he is in love with *two women* at the same time. He can't imagine ever *not* loving Elinor, and the fact that he doesn't want to be anywhere on the planet right now except in this room with Gina must mean that he loves her. As he opens his eyes, the room seems to tilt sideways. He clutches the edge of the table. He sips water, then more wine. It warms his chest and makes him yearn for an unattainable world: a parallel Zinfandel universe where every combination of desire is possible — marriage with Elinor, and life with Gina, and homework with Toby.

"Oh, my gosh!" Gina laughs at Toby, who's doing an imitation of his math teacher's nasal twang. A bit of carrot flies out of her mouth.

"Gross!" Toby howls.

Gina covers her mouth with her napkin, embarrassed. She coughs, sips water, tears shining in her eyes

222

from laughing. Ted looks from Gina to Toby. They are having a *moment* — a moment without him. He feels like he should leave — sneak out of the house while these two finally share peace.

But Ted stays, and after supper, he helps Toby with the poem he's convinced him to memorize — "Paul Revere's Ride." He heard a story on the radio about how habits can't just be taken away; they have to be replaced with new ones. Ted thinks memorizing the poem might help Toby ward off the urge to count and tap. He's told Toby that whenever he wants to count, he should go over the poem in his head.

"'One if by land, and two if by sea; and I on the opposite shore shall be,'" Toby says now, standing and rocking. He seems to like the building excitement in the poem, all those exclamation points calling for a holler. "'And lo! as he looks, on the belfry's height, a glimmer, and then a gleam of light!'

"Mom!" Toby shouts proudly to Gina in the kitchen. "I totally memorized five stanzas!"

After Toby goes to bed that night, Ted and Gina sit at the kitchen table sipping port. Gina gets up to retrieve a box of chocolates from the cupboard.

"I was thinking maybe Toby and I could study together Tuesdays *and* Thursdays," Ted says. Gina's back stiffens. She holds her hand in the air for a moment before grabbing the gold foil box. She turns, slides it onto the table, but doesn't take her seat.

"Have you contacted a lawyer yet?" she asks.

"Why?"

"For a legal separation?" She lowers her voice: "A *divorce?*"

"Oh." Ted knows it's problematic that he hasn't even *thought* of this. Problematic that he's living in limbo. "No." He wants to be able to say *Not yet*, but this would be misleading. The truth is, he's waiting for Elinor to make that move. He should be able to shed this passivity. To *know* what he wants and go for it. Suddenly he hopes Gina is about to issue an ultimatum.

But she doesn't say anything.

"Monday and Wednesday would work, too," Ted says, feeling like a jackass.

Gina sits down, pushes her port glass away, and folds her hands in her lap. "If you break my kid's heart . . ." She looks up at Ted. There's a calm sternness in her voice and in her eyes that he's never seen before — a hardwired protectiveness that almost frightens him. "Elinor might want you back, and if she does you might reconcile with her. If that happens, you're not going to be able to see Toby anymore. So the more time you spend with him now, the more you're going to break his heart later." She looks away from Ted. "I'll cook dinner for you one night a week because my kid adores you, and I'll sleep with you because you make me happy and I'm an idiot, but I will *not* let you . . ." She throws back her head and presses the heels of her palms to the edges of her eyes, blotting back tears. "What am I saying?" She kicks the table leg — a Toby-like gesture. "You already *are.*"

"Tuesday," Ted says. "For now, let's stick to Tuesdays." He tries to choose his words carefully. He *wants* to be compassionate. "I'm sorry I haven't resolved things in my life. I want to. I hope to come on Thursdays, too. At some point." If this isn't a vague, half-baked, euphemistic bullshit promise, Ted doesn't know what is.

CHAPTER
TWELVE

When Elinor opens the front door, Roger is standing on the porch beside his bucket of cleaning supplies holding out a small package for her. It's wrapped in newspaper comics with a crumpled bow.

"I know you like to read." He pushes the present toward her. Charlie Brown is trying to kick a football on the front. Roger bows his head and blushes, his pale cheeks turning crimson along his sideburns and up to the edges of his reddish blond hair. He blushes easily, as though life's just too embarrassing.

Elinor takes the gift. "Thank you." Maybe Roger has a crush on her. Or maybe he only feels comfortable when he's hiding behind a camera.

As he fumbles with his vacuum, his sponge mop falls with a loud *smack* on the porch.

Elinor crouches to help him. "I have most of this stuff," she tells him. "If you don't want to bring so many supplies." Once inside, Elinor tears open the gift, newsprint smudging her fingertips. It's a book, a novel, called *Cal*. "Oh, Roger. I love novels. And I probably should read something *contemporary*. But you shouldn't have." She touches Roger's arm. His skin is sticky, like a boy's. She wishes she had a son — a sloppy

226

boy. Thanks to Ted, she'd know how to throw him a softball.

She reads the book jacket. Set in Ireland, the story is about a young man who gets involved with the IRA, then falls in love with an older woman. They end up hiding out together. Uh-oh.

"We read it in my college Irish lit class." Roger follows Elinor into the kitchen as she reads.

"Well, I've always wanted to go to Ireland." Elinor tries to assume a breezy tone. She sets the book on the counter in the kitchen. "Did you remember to bring your résumé or your portfolio?"

Roger snaps his fingers. "Forgot."

"Next time." She grabs her purse. "Thanks for the book, really. I have to run. I'm meeting my husband."

"Oh," Roger says, the color in his face deepening. "Okay, good luck."

"Thanks. I think I need it."

On his way to meet Elinor for coffee, Ted practices what he plans on saying to her.

"Life's too short to go on living in limbo," he tells the car radio. "Let's reach a decision on how we want to move forward." God, he sounds so formal, like he's negotiating a business transaction. But what *should* they do? If Elinor wants to fight to save the marriage, he will. Otherwise, they should get legally separated. Then he can stop feeling like a sneaky adulterer, poised to let Gina and Toby down.

Getting dressed this morning, Ted had hoped Elinor would want a legal separation. But now that he's driving to the coffee shop, he looks forward to just *seeing* her, to talking with her. He has the inappropriate longing to tell her about Gina. Of course, he would never hurt El by doing this. But Elinor knows him better than anyone, even though they've only been together five years. *She's* the one he wants to ask for advice on how to fix his love life. In the past, she was always so empathetic and supportive of Ted. When he went through a period when he hated work, Elinor encouraged and helped him to find a partner and open his own practice. She never made him feel pressured or trapped. She always saw a way out of things. It was as though they were hiking together in a cave and she held the flashlight. Then why the hell should they get separated? An impatient driver honks at Ted as he lingers at a green light.

"Jesus!" he barks, fighting the compulsion to give the guy the finger. "It's Sunday, for God's sake. Take it easy!" He punches the accelerator and his tires screech.

Elinor waits for Ted outside the mom-and-pop coffee shop downtown. It's cool out, and she looks pretty in jeans and a light-blue turtleneck sweater that matches her eyes. Inside, Ted pulls out a chair for her at a tiny marble table. She sits and dunks her Darjeeling tea bag in and out of her cup, pensive about something.

"I miss —" Ted starts.

"I'm kind of seeing —"

Ted laughs; Elinor doesn't.

They often do this — start speaking at the same time. While they used to say things remarkably similar, giggling at the uncanniness of their timing, now they

228

seem to utter the exact opposite of what the other is thinking.

"*You*," Ted says. "I was going to say that I miss you." He pushes aside his coffee, which he doesn't feel like drinking. For the first time that he can recall, he's sick of coffee and milk and foam.

"Oh." Elinor frowns. "I miss you, too." She says this as though it goes without saying. All of the thoughts Ted thinks of as epiphanies are already givens for Elinor — starting points. He's always five steps behind her. Finally, she removes the bag from her cup and sips at the tea.

"I still love you," Ted says. Although this was *not* in his rehearsed speech, it's certainly true. Confusion clogs his head like cotton. The shriek of an espresso machine saws at his nerves.

"I love you, too, Ted." Elinor lowers her head to meet Ted's gaze. "I'll always *love* you. You know that. But don't you think this is good for us?"

Ted shrugs. "*What* this? What are we doing? That's what I want to know. Where is this going?"

"Taking a break, I guess. I'm kind of seeing someone." Elinor looks away as she utters these words.

"Seeing someone," Ted repeats flatly. "What exactly does that mean?" He rubs his hand under the table and is disgusted when he feels a clump of hardened gum.

"Dating. Hiking."

"Sleeping together?"

"Not one hundred percent. You know, yet. But that's not the point."

"What does he do?"

"He's a tree surgeon. He's the guy who came to assess our tree."

"Tree surgeon? Sounds like he assessed more than the tree. Did he file down your burls?"

"C'mon." Elinor sighs, frustrated. "Let me get this straight. You had an affair, and now you've got a grudge because I'm dating while we're separated?"

"In all those Greek tragedies the guys are severely flawed, right?"

Elinor's lips curl up in a half smile. She looks out the window at the cars jockeying for parking spaces, people clamoring for their caffeine. "Do you suppose we have control over any of this? Maybe it's like a Greek tragedy. You know, like Dido and Aeneas. She loves him and he loves her, but he's like, see ya! Gotta go to the office because the gods said so."

"Then the gods are assholes."

"No kidding."

"That book club of yours is a little hard-core. Don't you guys ever read mysteries or anything?"

"That's what the group wants to read. But I chose *The Iliad*, and Kat chose *The Aeneid*. We're trying to mix it up with the classics. Frankly, we don't fit in. We actually want to talk about the *books*. Big faux pas. You're supposed to talk about the book for six and a half minutes, then complain about your husband and kids."

For once, Elinor doesn't seem mad at Ted. A little tree surgeon romance and she's a new person. Fine, but Paul Bunyan can go away now. What does Tarzan know about *his* wife? He doesn't know that she hates to lick envelopes and prefers bras that clasp in front and eats her moo shu pork without the pancakes and her favorite comic strip is *The Quigmans*, and her favorite Rolling Stones song is "Can't You Hear Me Knocking?" He doesn't know that she once won a camping trip talent contest by dancing the hula with a frying pan balanced on her head. Tree Guy does not know these things!

"Well, you still *look* like a Greek god," Elinor says to Ted. "You been working out?"

"Playing soccer with a group of guys."

"And sleeping with Gina?"

Ted nods, bowing his head. While he's not sure what he and Elinor should do, he knows the one thing he *must* do and that's be honest with her. "You going to sleep with your tree man? Tarzan?"

"How's work?" Elinor changes the subject.

Ted looks out the window. Everyone he sees on the sidewalk seems so filled with purpose. They all seem to have a plan for the day. "Fine," he finally answers. "How's the sabbatical going?"

"Fine. Unnerving. It's like a holiday — you feel like it should be optimally spent. Like everything should be great."

"Yeah."

They sit quietly. If it had been a year or so ago, they'd both be reading. Elinor would have her *New Yorker* and Ted would have his sports section and they would stop to read things aloud to each other and trade bites of whatever they were eating with their coffee.

231

"Maybe we should get, you know, legally separated," Elinor says. "I know a lawyer who we could work with together. We could do mediation." She gently touches Ted's chin, turns his face toward hers. Her expression is kind, questioning. "The same lawyer represents both sides. The goal is to stay out of court and negotiate a noncombative settlement agreement." Now her words sound rehearsed. As though she practiced in the car on the way over, too. Still, she sounds tentative, uncertain, as though she's as doubtful as Ted.

"If we do it, that would be the way to go," Ted says. "I don't want to shell out a bunch of money to lawyers who will just make things ugly." He isn't interested in fighting over their stuff — over money or property. He and Elinor never fought over the things that they *had*. They fought over the things they couldn't have, or lost — children, sex, passion.

"Okay," Elinor says softly. "I can call the guy."

What a bizarrely civilized conversation. It makes Ted want to tip over the little marble table. Here they are, creating clear-cut boundaries. Exactly what Ted wanted, or *thought* he wanted, when he was at Gina's house. Now he's not sure what he wants. He wants to have his cake and eat it, too. He wants Gina to bake the cake and Elinor to frost it, and he wants to eat it somewhere over the rainbow, where ice cream never melts. What a numskull.

Elinor reaches across the table and touches his hand. The pads of her small fingers are soft. "What do you think?" she asks.

232

"I don't know. Whatever you think. Whatever you want to do."

Elinor takes her hand away. "Don't make me decide."

"Okay," Ted agrees. But he can't think of anything else to say.

"I'll call him." Elinor pushes her chair away from the table. "I'll set up a meeting for us."

Jesus. They're always having a meeting with somebody. Doctors, specialists, the marriage counselor, now a lawyer. Maybe their marriage *is* beyond hope.

Elinor crushes her empty paper cup in her hands.

"You don't want to put a hundred-dollar tree in a ten-dollar hole," Noah says, standing on the edge of his shovel to dig deeper into the ground to plant the new ginkgo in Elinor's yard. "That's what I always tell my guys." He explains that the ginkgo should be planted at least six feet from where Warren's stump was ground and dug out. "Any of the oak's remaining roots will eat away at the nitrogen in the soil here, so we want to give this guy a fresh start. I'll add a fertilizer."

"Thanks," Elinor says. It's Saturday, Noah's day off, and they're supposedly planting the tree together, but really she's just standing around admiring Noah's back. His shoulders are wide and straight across, unlike Ted's, which slope downward from his neck. It's not that one physique is better looking than the other; they're just different, and different is nice. Noah goes on about how ginkgoes are originally from China and you can find them at Buddhist temples all over Asia.

They were introduced to the West when some Dutch traveling guy fell in love with the trees and brought the seeds back to the Netherlands.

"Wow." Elinor feels a little too pressured to like this ginkgo. While she loves being outside, she doesn't love all trees and shrubbery, just the way you don't love all people.

After Noah finishes the hole, Elinor helps him amend the soil, digging in Clay Buster with a rake. Finally, they tip the ginkgo from its bucket and drop it into the ground. After Noah covers the roots with dirt, he kneels and uses three fingers to make a circular trough around the tree to catch water. Elinor likes how he doesn't mind running his bare fingers through the earth.

When they're finished, they drive up to Skyline Boulevard and go for a long hike. Panting from the incline, slippery with sweat, Elinor gets a rush of first-date arousal when they stop for a break and Noah pins her against a tree for a long kiss. Everything about Noah is different from Ted — his height and build, his mustache, his baldness. Touching him gives her the same rush of energy she gets while traveling in a foreign country.

She finds the hiking trails sexy, sort of like in high school, when she and Tim Currington used to cut French class and sneak down to the reservoir to drink Colt 45 out of cans and skinny-dip. "Soup du jour!" they'd scream as they leapt from a high rock into the cold water below. After swimming, they'd wrap themselves in towels they'd swiped from the gym and practice French-kissing as their "homework."

On their fourth date — dinner fixed by Noah at his house — Elinor hopes they'll sleep together. Getting ready at home, she takes a long shower and smooths on lotion, relieved by the fact that a stomach flu has flattened her belly. She's not sure if it's nerves or a bug, but she's been nauseated and throwing up for three days. She hopes she isn't contagious, and Noah doesn't cook anything too spicy.

As Noah chops onions, Elinor sits at the island in his kitchen and watches. She offers to help, but he insists that she relax and drink a glass of wine.

"You know the ginkgo species is believed to be at least two hundred million years old," he says, peeling open a box of mushrooms. "One of its nicknames is the survivor. The Chinese have used the leaves for thousands of years for all kinds of ailments."

"Really?" Elinor wishes she enjoyed her conversations with Noah as much as she likes making out with him. His love of nature is endearing, and, she hates to admit it, a little dull. He's never heard of any of the books she's read, and he thinks Monty Python is a guy. Does Ted have more in common with Gina? For the first time, she suspects that Ted has something deeper with Gina. She pushes her wine aside, sipping at her water, which is easier on the stomach.

Noah slices the mushrooms while ranting about Silicon Valley people who buy houses and rip out the landscaping just because they can afford to. "It's like *I live here now, so I've got to spray and mark my territory.*" He pounds his chest and bellows, then shakes his head with disbelief as he continues chopping. "This one couple tore out these beautiful ceanothus bushes, which take a *long* time to get established. You know the ones with the really vibrant blue flowers in spring?" He throws onions and mushrooms sizzling into a frying pan.

"I think so." Elinor's not sure about the blue flowers. The smell of the cooking food repels her.

After dinner, they sink into the sofa in front of Noah's fireplace. His house smells earthy and masculine — like leather and saddle soap and coffee grounds.

"Nothing that's fun is good for you anymore," Noah says, sulking at the Duraflame log on the grate. "I love a real roaring, crackling wood fire, but, man, are they bad for the environment."

The bitterness in Noah's voice reminds Elinor of herself. This might be what she and Noah have most in common: glumness. They're the sort of people who could let a Duraflame log get them down. And if they ever wound up as a couple, they'd spiral into a glass-half-empty state of perpetual gloom and doom.

"There are a *few* fun things left," Elinor murmurs, scooting closer to Noah and reaching for his belt loops. She licks the bristly underside of his mustache, surprised when the narcotic high of kissing a new person still hits her. She tries to remember when this euphoria wore off with Ted. According to how she's come to understand marriage, it doesn't *wear off*; it becomes something better, deeper, more meaningful.

236

But really, it feels like a drug that stops working with time. Then you find yourself actually *reading* those magazine articles in line at the supermarket on how to spice up your sex life, grateful that the person in front of you has a cart piled high so you can make your way through the ten tips, even though you already know what they are.

"Woman," Noah growls. "In my cave. Garrrrr. Good." One thing he isn't glum about is fooling around. He has a cheerful aggressiveness that Elinor welcomes. He hauls her off the couch and carries her to his bedroom, flopping her onto her back on the bed. As he pins her arms over her head, he burrows his face under her shirt, his rough mustache scratching her belly like a loofah.

The sex is all different and all good and leaves Elinor somehow energized and exhausted at the same time. Afterward, as Noah rolls over to curl his arm around Elinor's waist, the TV clicks on.

"I rolled over on the remote!" Noah laughs.

Bugs Bunny tiptoes through a dark and stormy night toward a haunted castle. Elinor sits up. "Oh, leave it!" It's her favorite cartoon — the one with the Peter Lorre mad scientist and the heart-shaped red-haired monster in high-top sneakers. She leans back against the pillows, resting against Noah's bare shoulder. Noah cocks his head and smiles down at her, his scalp shining in the blue light from the TV. He looks at her as though she's a rare species of tree he's delighted to see, but doesn't quite understand.

"Don't you love this one?" Elinor asks him.

Noah isn't laughing. "You're a kid at heart," he says, bemused.

"Not really." Elinor points to the TV. "This is a classic." Bugs Bunny distracts the shag-carpet monster by chatting him up over a manicure, dunking his claws into soapy water, which just *kills* Elinor.

Noah nods and smiles mildly. "If you say so."

He doesn't love this cartoon? Can you be physically attracted to someone who doesn't love Bugs Bunny and the red-haired monster? Is it easier for men to sleep with women with whom they have nothing in common?

Suddenly Elinor can't debate the topic any longer. Mushrooms, onions, and risotto are boiling up into the back of her throat, and she has to leap out of bed into the bathroom to throw up.

On his way into work in the morning, Ted calls Gina. It's only Thursday and he doesn't want to wait until Tuesday to spend the evening with her and Toby. He misses them — particularly Gina's brightness. Somehow she always says things that are helpful to him. She's as smart as any therapist. Even the sound of her voice is soothing. Ted's relieved that he misses more than just sex with Gina. He misses her smile and smell and *everything*.

"Hi," he says when she picks up.

"What's the matter?" she asks. He must sound urgent, desperate.

"Nothing." Ted hates to talk on the phone while driving. It's a carelessness he rarely succumbs to. But he's got to get to the office and he wants to know when he can see Gina.

"Listen, about Thursdays. I'd like to see you guys then." He lifts his foot off the gas, realizing that he's driving too fast as he approaches an intersection. "I want to see more of you. I'm not reconciling with Elinor. She's calling a lawyer. We're getting . . ." The words stick in his throat. "Legally separated."

"Okay," Gina says with hesitation.

"Can I take you guys out for dinner tonight?"

"No. I have a . . . I have plans tonight. How about tomorrow, Friday?"

"Plans? With who?" Ted clears his throat, trying to keep calm. "Whom?"

"Barry, he's taking me to a show."

Of course. Slick, Daddy Warbucks. "Friday, then." A weekend night. That's when *real* couples go out. "You pick the restaurant."

"I can get a sitter," Gina offers.

"Great! A real date." Tuesdays, and Thursdays and Fridays. Soon Barry's Jaguar-driving ass will be out of the picture. "Great," Ted repeats. "Hey, I miss you. Heck, I *need* you."

"Plenty of people need me," Gina says flatly. "My clients need me. My son needs me. *Shane* needs me."

Ted is surprised by her tone. But of course the last thing she probably wants is another person who needs her. She wants someone who *loves* her. Yet Ted can't utter these words. "Okay, then," he says. "See you Friday."

A painful silence buzzes on the phone line.

CHAPTER
THIRTEEN

The second pink line. For two years Elinor hoped for it, wished for it on every shooting star in the sky and dandelion seed blown into the wind. Now the line stares up at her from a home pregnancy test stick balanced on a square of toilet paper at the edge of the bathroom sink. Of course. She doesn't have the stomach flu. Her period is ten days late, but she supposed that could be perimenopause. Your cycles become irregular. She attributed the overwhelming urge for afternoon naps to depression. Meanwhile, she was afraid her period would come just in time for her date with Noah. Typical. Always worrying about the exact wrong thing.

She washes her hands and dries them on her pajama bottoms, never taking her eyes off the little window on the stick. The second pink line is fainter than the first, which always appears as soon as you pee, to show that you've hit your target or have a pulse or something — Elinor's not sure what. For two years, the window taunted her: empty, empty, empty. She thought of the second pink line as the ultimate symbol of femininity. The lack of it as the ultimate sign of failure. Sometimes she'd root through the garbage an hour after the test, to check again. Other months she'd sit in the bedroom and make Ted look.

Elinor flips down the lid on the toilet and sits, giddy and dizzy. This couldn't have come at a worse time and she couldn't care less. A son or daughter is in the room with her. A baby! *Ted's* baby. She's certainly not pregnant from sleeping with Noah for the first time last night. (God, she's a terrible mother already. Climbing into bed with a strange man before she's even separated from her baby's father.) She thinks backward and arrives at the night she and Ted last had sex — after he found her sleeping under the oak tree. It was crazy to sleep in the front yard, but she felt the need to do things differently from then on — to make a real departure from her old life. As she recalls the sweetness of their lovemaking that evening, Elinor feels a rush of tenderness for Ted. This affection is calmer than passion, saner, perhaps easier to maintain. As she stands, a wave of nausea rises from her knees up into the back of her throat again. She lifts the toilet lid and sits beside it on the floor.

She needs to talk to Ted. They have to figure out what to do, particularly about the appointment she's made for them with the mediation attorney. When Elinor first tried to call the lawyer, a spasm seized her hand, and she was unable to punch in all of the numbers. *Dee-dee-dee!* the phone scolded as she paused. She clicked the thing off to think a minute. Meeting with the lawyer didn't necessarily mean they were getting *divorced*. They would just find out what a legal separation entailed — what their options were. In law school, she'd never paid attention to the details of divorce law, which seemed so adversarial. Finally, she made the appointment. As soon as she can drag herself out of this bathroom, she'll cancel it.

Elinor hoists herself up from the toilet and turns on the shower. She and Ted could separate, and the baby could live with her. They'd have joint custody. Maybe that would be too hard for Ted. Could they just be roommates? She peels off her pajama bottoms and tank top, and climbs under the warm water. As she soaps up, her breasts are tender. She lowers her head and succumbs to an even stronger wave of nausea. Maybe she's foolish to be so optimistic — to think she and Ted can make this work. *Positive thoughts*, she tells herself, drawing in a deep, cleansing breath of steam. She'll think positive thoughts from now on. Quit swearing. Only buy organic produce. Dig out the folic acid tablets. Turn down the car stereo and switch over to Mozart.

Toweling off and brushing her teeth, Elinor looks at the stick again. The second pink line is fuzzy, but definitely there. She dresses in a skirt, T-shirt, and sandals, shaking out her wet hair. How will she tell Ted? The news is too tremendous for a phone call at work. She'll call and invite him to dinner — tell him she has good news to share. Nausea gurgles in her throat again as she contemplates grilling him a steak with hollandaise. She won't try to fix a fancy dinner. Thanks to Gina, queen of the homemade meals, Elinor has developed an irrational fear of cooking for her husband. Instead she'll grab cold salads from the deli and they'll have a picnic in the park — just like the old days when they used to meet after work.

The smell of an overripe banana in the kitchen brings back the watery sick feeling. Elinor vomits into the sink, rinses everything away with water from the tap, and collapses on a counter stool. She dials Kat's cell phone.

"You sound out of breath," Kat says.

"I'm pregnant."

"Wha — ? Oh my God!" She pauses. "Who?"

"Ted." Elinor's surprised by the realization that she would be happy either way. It always seemed important to marry her true love and have a baby at the right time. But now she'd be happy if she were pregnant with the UPS guy's baby.

"Oh, *El*."

"I can't stop barfing." Panic seizes her. The baby needs nutrients. What if she miscarries again?

"You need to eat."

"Then I'll throw up."

"No, you need to eat light carbohydrates all day — toast and crackers and cereal. Keep something in your purse, and eat the crackers before you even get out of bed in the morning. Put them on the nightstand before you go to — oh my *God!*" Kat hoots.

"The nightstand," Elinor repeats, reaching wearily for the bread and sliding a piece into the toaster. She should know about crackers! The feeling of inadequacy she always had while trying to conceive returns, a little voice telling her she's not qualified.

"Does Ted know?" Kat asks.

"Nope. Called you first." The warm toast tastes good. She tries not to eat it too fast.

"I'm flattered, but you've got to call him . . ."

"I know," she says through a mouthful of bread. "Toast, then Ted." She doesn't have the energy to tell Kat about her plan to deliver the news over a picnic.

"I have so much stuff you can use!" Kat cheers. Elinor is in the sorority now. She tries to push the fear of miscarriage away.

Back in the bedroom, Elinor calls to cancel the appointment with the mediation lawyer. They can reschedule later. One thing at a time. Next she calls the fertility clinic.

"The second line is kind of dotted, is that okay?" she asks the nurse.

The nurse laughs. "Yes. You're pregnant."

Elinor sits on the edge of her unmade bed. Hearing someone else say this — a professional — makes her cry.

"Sometimes this happens soon after a patient stops treatments," the nurse says. "Your system is still a bit juiced up from the drugs. You just lucked out — one of those good eggs finally came down the chute."

When the nurse asks for the date of Elinor's last period, Elinor has to study the calendar. She used to obsess over her cycles. Now that she's given up, she hasn't paid attention. The nurse does the math and tells Elinor that she should come in for a blood test tomorrow, so they can measure her hormone levels. They'll also prescribe progesterone, as a precaution, and more prenatal vitamins. Since she's already ten days late, Elinor can come in four days from now for a vaginal ultrasound to see if there's a heartbeat. Then two weeks later, she'll have a second ultrasound. If everything's okay, they'll release her to her regular OB.

Release. Elinor has felt like she's been sentenced to the clinic. She wishes she could skip the stark examination rooms and all the tests, and ride the elevator at the hospital straight up to the maternity ward and just wait there.

"So many hoops," she says, worry burning up the toast in her stomach. She leans back into the covers on the bed and discovers a maple leaf in the sheets. What the heck? She picks it up. It's deep red, perfectly formed, and feels leathery between her fingers. She places it on the nightstand, distracted by the nurse's complicated schedule of appointments. Elinor searches for a piece of paper. The only thing she finds handy is the mediation lawyer's business card. She copies down her appointments on the back.

"It's your wife on the line," the office receptionist tells Ted as he heads toward the next examination room to check Mrs. Carson's ingrown nails. He steps into his office to take the call. Other than Larry, he hasn't told anyone that he and El are separated.

"Hi," Elinor says breathlessly when he picks up. "I've got news." She seems to be trying to contain her excitement. "Can you meet me after work at Watson Creek Park at the picnic table by the stream?"

"What kind of news?" Ted hates surprises.

Elinor pauses. "*Special* news. I'll tell you all about it. We'll talk. We'll have a nice picnic. See you then? By the stream?"

Ted leans into his desk for support. What news could be bigger than *let's get legally separated? Let's not get separated?* He looks at the black-and-white photograph on his desk of Elinor on their wedding day. She peers over her bare shoulder and smiles a huge grin at him, a sweep of blond hair dipping sexily over one eye. They had fun at their wedding. Everyone said they wouldn't, that they'd be too nervous and stressed. But they danced with their friends until midnight, then moved with the party into the hotel bar.

"Okay," Ted agrees.

As Ted leaves the office later that afternoon, he's hit with a wall of heat. It's one of those smoggy fall days when the gritty air is hard to breathe. This is when he dreams about leaving Silicon Valley. Maybe moving up to Calistoga into an old Victorian and starting a small practice. Lately, this fantasy has come to include Gina. Gina doing her yoga in the mornings on wood floors gleaming in the sun. Ted and Toby on a back screened-in porch in the evenings playing Risk by the light of a lantern.

He climbs into his car and blasts the air conditioner, comforted by the white noise, and heads for the park. *Special* isn't an Elinor word. It's an ambiguity she'd typically shun for being vague and overused. It could refer to anything from a learning-disabled kid to a wedding reception. *Wedding reception.* Ted smacks the edge of the steering wheel with his palm. That's it:

Elinor's going to marry her tree surgeon. *Special* is just spin for softening this news. Ted pounds the steering wheel with his fist. Why the hell didn't Elinor call *him* when the tree got sick? It was his house, too. *His* tree. He knows how to operate a chain saw! Who is this guy to kill his tree and take his wife?

While he knows it's irrational and selfish and childish, Ted is jealous of the other men in both Elinor's and Gina's lives. Shane, Barry, Tarzan. Whatever the tree asshole's name is. They should all hike off the edge of a cliff together.

He pulls into the lot at the reservoir. He and El used to walk here on weekends — back when they would talk for hours, about work and life and the books they were reading and how they wanted to fix up their house. Before all of their conversations focused on their problems, their *issues*. He finds a shady parking spot, climbs out, and crunches through the leaves down the hill. He stops when he sees El, standing in light filtered through the trees, looking like an impressionist painting in her sundress. Her short hair is pulled up, wisps sticking to the back of her neck. Ted closes his eyes and imagines the moist, sweet apple spot on her skin. He takes a deep breath, his nose and throat burning with pollen.

"Hi!" he calls out, trying to sound cheerful. Elinor looks up from the picnic table, which is spread with a plastic red-and-white-checked tablecloth, a bottle of wine, a bottle of fizzy water, a box of fried chicken, and a bunch of cartons from the deli, melon slices, cheese, bread, figs.

"Supper." She smiles and sits down, dabbing her brow with a paper napkin. "Whew."

He gives her a quick hug. "You look pretty. And what's all this?" Ted points to the table.

"I just want to talk in a peaceful setting. Wine?" Elinor pours him a glass of Pinot Grigio before he can answer. She sips bubbly water out of a plastic cup, then cuts him a hunk of bread and spreads it with soft cheese.

Ted chews. When they were dating, Elinor often made picnics like this. Bread and cheeses and meats from the deli. Grapes and wine. Although she hates to cook, she's always good at pulling things together from the store.

Elinor sits at the picnic table across from Ted. She seems to be having trouble gathering her words for their talk. Her face is alarmingly red from the heat, and perspiration dots her nose and brow.

"You okay?" Ted asks.

"Great." She stands up, swallows hard, then sits again. "The heat." She smiles, nibbles at the end of a grape. Then she bolts up, stumbling to unhook her legs from the bench, and lunges down the hill toward the stream. At the base of a tree, she doubles over and vomits.

"You have heatstroke!" Ted starts toward her, sticks and brambles snapping under his feet.

Elinor lifts her head and looks up at him. Suddenly she's pale and waxy looking. "Unh-unh." She laughs and wipes a tear from her cheek. "I'm pregnant."

248

"You? What?" Ted stops, spits out his bread. "*Pregnant?*" This is the moment he always wished for and this is just how he hoped it would be — Elinor blurting the news when he least expected it. *Pregnant.* His wife is going to have a baby. He's going to be a father. "*Really?* I mean . . ." He hears the disbelief in his voice and hopes it doesn't hurt El's feelings. But what crazy timing.

He swallows, feeling as though the clump of dry bread is still in his throat. Wait. What if Elinor's pregnant with the *tree guy's* baby? Maybe it was Ted who was infertile all the while. *Low motility.* He takes a step toward Elinor.

"You . . . and the tree surgeon —"

"Ted! No. *You.*" She wipes her mouth with the back of her hand. "*Us.*" Sentences longer than one word seem to require too much energy for her. "Our last night — after you found me sleeping under the tree? The nurse said I'm almost six weeks."

Ted feels dizzy. He feels hot and tired and old and happy and confused. He takes El's hand and gently leads her toward the picnic table. That's it, then: He and Elinor are getting back together. If she's going to have a baby, *their* baby, they have to stay married. His knees wobble as they walk along the uneven ground. He looks out for roots, so Elinor won't trip. Maybe the Greek guys in those stories were lucky, when you get right down to it: Their difficult decisions were made *for* them. Free will can be a burden. Just ask all those philosophers.

"I've had a blood test and my HCG is one-fifty-one." Elinor chatters with nervous energy as they walk. "That's a *good* thing. So you know, I'm probably not going to . . ." She trails off.

Miscarry, Ted thinks. But her nausea and hormone levels are encouraging factors.

Elinor stops suddenly, looks up at Ted. Her bangs stick in clumps to her forehead. She pulls her hand away from him. "Don't worry. This doesn't mean we have to get back together." She seems to have mistaken his silence for trepidation or disappointment. "I want you to be part of the baby's life, of course, but I don't want you to feel pressured to — *do* anything." She looks glumly at the ground. "I'm not sure what we should do. Something . . . peaceful."

"Sweetheart." Ted takes her hand back and squeezes it as he nudges her toward the table. "I'm processing." He means this as a joke — emphasizing one of the marriage counselor's overused words — but Elinor is still frowning.

"I'll move back in," Ted says. "If you want me to," he adds quickly. He sits Elinor on the picnic bench, grabs a few paper napkins, and wets them with soda water, dabbing at her forehead.

Elinor shakes her head. "We have to talk."

Ted considers for a moment that he and Elinor could raise the baby *without* getting back together. It could work. But then he imagines Tarzan the tree man moving into his house and holding his baby.

"No more talking," he tells her. "Let's just decide. I'm coming home. You're pregnant, I'm coming home."

250

Ted hands her the bottle of soda water. "Rinse your mouth, but spit it out. The carbonation will make you more nauseated. I'll get you some flat water." Ted looks around the park. All he sees are trees closing in on him. "Let's get the hell out of here."

Elinor swishes, spits, nods. "On top of the morning sickness, I have to take the progesterone again, which makes it ten times worse."

"You didn't have to do all this. I mean . . ." Ted motions to the picnic. "This is sweet." He lightly kisses her forehead, the bridge of her nose, and each of her cheeks. "Thanks."

Elinor nods halfheartedly. She bends her head toward her knees. Clearly she's dehydrated, and she's probably not getting enough protein. Her electrolytes might be out of whack. Ted gathers the picnic items quickly, jamming them into the brown paper bags from the store. He'll take her back to the house and put her to bed and keep an eye on her. If she can't keep liquids down, they may need to go to the hospital for IV fluids.

"Let's get you *home*." Ted likes the feeling of the word *home* in his mouth. The single syllable pleasingly definitive. The o and the m like the *om* of meditation. His wife *needs* him. They are going home.

"I'm so sorry," Ted tells Gina. He's taken her out for dinner as planned, only now he has to break up with her.

"God, I *knew* this would happen." Gina pushes her salad away. She swallows hard and looks around the restaurant at the other couples holding hands across crisp white tablecloths in the glow of candlelight. Jesus, what could be more cruelly ironic than breaking up with someone at a romantic French restaurant? It occurs to Ted now. What an ass. *Cowards* break up with lovers at restaurants. You can't show anger or dismay while you're eating foie gras in public.

"I made a promise and I broke that promise to you and to Toby. I couldn't be more sorry." Ted reaches to pour Gina more wine. She covers the glass with her hand. "You're a fantastic woman and Toby's a great kid and I know you are going to find —"

"Oh, spare me." Gina flips her hair over her shoulders. Her back straightens with tension and pride. "*I* couldn't be more sorry for being so stupid. I knew as soon as Elinor wanted you back you'd run to her. Toby and I were your rent-a-family."

"That's not fair —"

"Then why . . ." Gina draws in her breath, picks up her purse, composes herself.

"Just for right now, maybe —" Ted begins. "Elinor and I aren't really sure what we're going to do. We just need some time to figure things out." What on *earth* is he saying and how does he possibly expect Gina to reply to this?

Gina looks at him with disbelief. "Excuse me," she says, slipping on her brown velvet blazer over her skirt and pivoting to leave.

"I'll talk to Toby," Ted calls after her quietly.

She turns back to face him and presses her index finger firmly into the table. "No, you won't. *That* much is certain."

CHAPTER
FOURTEEN

"My husband wants to do this with me," Elinor explains to Noah. She figures it's not the best form to break up with someone over the telephone, but she and Noah haven't been seeing each other for long, and her energy is so sparse, she doesn't want to expend any getting together with him. "We're going for the ultrasound tomorrow."

"I understand." The disappointment in Noah's voice surprises Elinor. "You know what your problem is?" He asks this so nicely that she doesn't feel defensive.

"Which one?"

"You expect everything to happen at the right time."

"I like to think that *used* to be my problem."

"You want to be with me, but you can't because the timing isn't right."

"Noah, a baby is a lot more than timing." *And I don't want to be with you*, Elinor thinks. *I like you, but we're not meant for each other. Can't you see that?* She sighs. "You're really a nice guy."

"*Nice*. That's a curse. To my wife, nice meant boring. Besides, I don't feel so nice. I feel like kicking your husband's ass."

"Nice isn't a curse. It meant a lot to me that you came over when they cut down the oak and then you helped me plant a new tree."

"I thought you were cute."

"Thank you," Elinor says.

"No problem. It's my job to take care of sick trees."

"No, I mean thank you for spending time with me." Elinor pauses, searching for the right words. "Thank you for making me feel sexy."

"Glad I could be of service." Noah's tone lightens. "You *are* sexy."

"You're a good catch, Noah." Not for Elinor, but for someone else. "Don't let anything your wife ever said keep you from believing that."

Four days after the second pink line, Elinor and Ted get to see the heartbeat. Frankly, Elinor pretends she sees it, lying on her back with her feet in the stirrups, the white paper on the examining table crunching beneath her as she strains to examine the fuzzy image on the TV screen in the darkened room. At first Dr. Weston is quiet, studying the screen with troubled seriousness. Ted doesn't move. Elinor swallows a bubble of nervous laughter.

"There. Right there." The doctor's face brightens as she points to a teeny fuzz ball within the gray mass. "There's the heartbeat."

Elinor closes her eyes, opens them again, hoping to see something pulsate.

"Wow." Ted moves closer. *You don't see it, either!* Elinor thinks.

"That little thing makes me want to nap at red lights and barf into the gutter?" Elinor claps her hand over her mouth. Oh, dear. Critical from the start. Like a mother who doesn't approve of her daughter's outfit choice on the first day of school. "I mean, gosh. So small."

At home, Ted posts the ultrasound photo on the refrigerator. The pie-slice image of Elinor's womb looks gray and staticky — like bad reception on a black-and-white TV.

"Hello, there," Elinor says to their baby, who is a vaguely peanut-shaped white spot barely larger than the other white spots in the image. She sings a song to the tune of "Ta-Ra-Ra Boom-De-Ay":

I love you, embryo!
Please grow some fingers and toes.
I want to buy you clothes,
My little embryo!

Singing wards off her anxiety about everything that could hurt the baby. Chlorine in the pool, prescription face cream, ant spray in the garage, *soft cheese*, God knows why. The world is full of toxins. How are you supposed to stay informed without becoming paranoid?

Few foods appeal to Elinor, and Ted goes out of his way to find recipes and prepare dishes she can manage to keep down.

"Do you know about the origin of fettuccine Alfredo?" he asks, lining up cheese, milk, and butter on the counter.

Elinor does not. She should be more of a foodie.

"This Roman chef in the 1900s couldn't get his wife to eat during her pregnancy. She was growing weaker and he was frustrated that he couldn't feed her, which was the *one* thing he was supposed to be able to do. So he cooked up some fresh egg noodles, added melted butter, mixed in Parmesan, cream, a little nutmeg and pepper, and voilà." Ted switches on a pot of water to boil.

"That does sound good." Elinor is touched by Ted's thoughtfulness. He's trying so hard. She loves him for this. Who could ask for a better father? She palms her belly. Ever since Ted's moved back in, he's been so attentive and kind. So . . . *reverent*. That's the word she's looking for. He has such awe for her and this pregnancy that she feels like *more* than a wife or mother-to-be. She feels like a national monument or endangered species. Her new status has injected a formality into their relationship. A politeness toward each other that's unnerving — as though they're in an arranged marriage. If they bump into each other in the kitchen or bathroom, they jump, then apologize, giving each other quick little kisses.

"How *is* everything?" her mother asks when she calls, meaning not just the pregnancy, but the marriage.

"Fine, just fine." Elinor tells her. While this is not the glossed-over-for-Mom answer, somehow *fine* doesn't feel quite right.

Elinor recalls with astonishment how her co-workers seemed to power through their pregnancies, working long hours, traveling for business — all with astonishing capability. She can barely open a can of soup!

"That's the second trimester," Kat promises. "You'll be energized."

Elinor waits for this energy, wishing the hormones didn't make her so emotional in the meantime. When the baby elephant at the Oakland Zoo dies, she feels inconsolable. She peers at the baby elephant's photo in the paper, cupping her hand over her mouth. His bristly ears are too big for his head, flopping forward, waiting for him to grow into them. But he'll never get the chance. Below him, there's a shot of the mother elephant in her pen looking forlorn.

"Elephant!" Elinor wails to Kat on the phone.

"What?"

"He died!"

"Who?" Kat sounds ready to hang up and run across their lawns to Elinor's house.

"At the zoo. The elephant *died*. Look in the paper!"

"Oh." Rustling in the background. "Poor thing. But it's okay," Kat promises.

Elinor can't stop crying.

"Oh, honey," Kat says sympathetically. "An elephant shot you in your pajamas this morning."

"Gunk." Elinor chokes out a sob.

"It's supposed to be a twist on that joke . . ." Kat assumes a Groucho Marx voice. "I shot an elephant in my pajamas —"

"I *know*." Elinor has lost her sense of humor. It vanished with her energy. They're holed up together in a motel somewhere, drinking caffeinated beverages without her.

"Hormones," Kat says.

"I know," Elinor repeats. The answer for everything. She should calm down. Hysteria will just freak out the baby. "I'm terrible at this," she confesses.

"Oh, El. You're going to be a wonderful mother. I promise you. Try not to worry."

"Okay."

"And don't read the paper. The world is a mess."

"Okay," Elinor agrees. She'll only read about pregnancy. She showers and dresses. On the top bathroom shelf, she finds the one pregnancy book she let herself buy while struggling to conceive: *What to Expect When You're Expecting*.

At Starbucks, Elinor sips a low-fat steamed milk with a dash of cinnamon and scans *What to Expect*. For starters, she's a derelict for eating a white-flour English muffin this morning instead of whole wheat toast. And what a loser for even *thinking* about caffeine — a dirty little habit akin to crack cocaine. That hot shower last night? It probably scorched her baby's IQ. This book confirms what Elinor has known all along: She is incapable and unworthy of being a mother. "Screw you," she whispers to the pages. She gets up, grabs her milk, which is creating a sour taste in her mouth, and pushes through the double glass doors out into the parking lot. Near her car, she spies a Dumpster. She hurries up to it and tosses *What to Expect* clunking in. "Screw you," she repeats, tossing the tepid milk in after the book. As she starts her car, guilt gnaws at her gut.

258

No wonder it took her so long to conceive. She can't even read a pregnancy book. There must be others out there — nicer ones. She will ask Kat. Without Kat, Elinor would be lost.

She ditches Starbucks and heads for the In-N-Out for a cheeseburger and french fries, lusting after the iced tea on the menu, but choosing the low-fat milk. She misses caffeine as though it's a lost lover. She'd kill for tea, coffee, or Coke. Anything other than her cinnamon orange herbal brew, which smells like the potpourri at the wash.

As she sits in her car in a shady parking spot, shoveling french fries into her mouth and cursing the *What to Expect* book, Elinor thinks of Gina and her healthy recipes and her whole ground flax. In the past few days she has not been able to get Gina out of her mind. Staying home from work allows too much time to think — hundreds of solitary moments throughout the day to contemplate all the attributes that must have drawn Ted to Gina. Qualities Elinor will never possess: pep-squad cheerfulness, athleticism, a sexy, flowing litheness, like the birch trees in their neighbors' yard.

That night, Ted is too exhausted to cook and he agrees to bring Elinor home a cheese pizza with pepperoni.

"This is good," Elinor moans, cheese hanging from her chin as they sit at the coffee table in the living room in front of the TV.

Ted sips ginger ale. He's declared solidarity by also giving up wine, beer, and coffee. He leans over to push a pillow between Elinor's back and the sofa. Suddenly

Elinor recognizes her husband's kindness. It is the same compassion he has for his patients. After all, that's what Elinor *is* now — a patient.

"Can I get you anything?" Ted polishes off his ginger ale, nods toward the kitchen.

"A new brain. I'm so emotional." She balls up her napkin. "It can't be good for the baby."

"It's normal." He shrugs. "Hormones."

Elinor looks down at the pizza box, stained with grease. She wonders if Ted longs for Gina's healthy home-cooked meals.

"Do you miss her sometimes?" she asks.

"Who?" Ted asks.

"Gina."

"Not really." A good way of answering without lying. Ted is an honest man. *Always tell the truth unless it's cruel*, Elinor's mother would advise. But Ted's expression betrays him. There's woefulness about his eyebrows that says that he does in fact miss her. Elinor is sure of it. But he will give her up for this — to stay with his wife and have a baby.

"I only think about Noah a little bit," Elinor says. *In a horizontal way*, she thinks.

"*Great.*" Jealousy flares in Ted's voice.

"You're the one who —"

"Are we going there tonight? Are we getting on the Rehash Bus?" Ted tosses his pizza crust into the box.

"No." Elinor hugs her knees to her belly, which has just started to swell. But she goes there every day. Into the petty world of obsession. Talking about the affair, instead of pretending that it never happened, helps her escape these dark thoughts. When she talks to Ted, she isn't as angry. She can keep an analytical, lawyer's distance — just trying to figure out the whole mess.

"Sorry," she murmurs. She moves closer to her husband, pushing away the coffee table so she can rest her head on his thigh. He strokes her hair. She has always liked the way his hands smell of antibacterial hospital soap — a smell that fills her with a sense of safety.

"Whew!" Dr. Weston sighs with relief. "There it is." She points to the ultrasound screen. "Your baby."

Elinor and Ted have made it through the next hoop: the second, eight-week ultrasound.

Baby. This is the first time Elinor has heard anyone at the infertility clinic use this word. Follicle, egg, zygote, embryo, heartbeat, *baby.* Instead of trying to see the screen, she lifts her head to find Ted's face in the dark examining room.

His eyes are locked on the fuzzy gray picture. "Wow," he says with wonder. "So many steps just to get to where most people start off."

"You are outta here," the doctor says, flipping on the bright overhead lights. "Don't take it personally, but I love it when I don't have to see a couple again." Elinor is touched that Dr. Weston seems as nervous and hopeful as she and Ted are.

Ted helps Elinor sit up. His eyes are filled with tears, but they don't spill over.

"Call your OB," Dr. Weston says, "and make an appointment for your first prenatal exam." She stands touching each of them on the arm. "You be sure to bring that baby back to see me." She winks, then hurries out of the room for her next patient.

"Thank you," Ted calls after her.

Elinor slides off the examining table and pulls on her underwear and pants. "*Baby*," she says softly. A word she never thought would be hers.

"Want to renew our vows?" Ted asks as they lie in bed that night. "Is that too corny?"

"No." Elinor scoots backward to spoon him, comforted by the heat of his body.

"We could go to Hawaii," he muses.

"I don't think I'm supposed to fly."

"After the baby's born. About six months after. We'll go to Maui. Get a condo." He rolls toward her, lying on his side, his head propped in one hand. "Would you marry me again?"

"You know I would."

"I mean, not go back and marry me again. But after everything that's happened. Would you marry me *right now*?" Ted peers around to look at her. She smooths over his hair, stalling for time. She hears: *Even though I was unfaithful, do you forgive me?*

"Yes," she answers. "I would." *But I would want to know more about why you cheated on your wife*, she thinks. *How you came to justify it. Whether you'd ever do it again.*

Ted tightens his arms around her. She relaxes into him as he massages her breasts. She closes her eyes and sighs, feeling his erection against the small of her back.

262

For once she feels shapely, sexy, instead of like The Vessel.

"Sex won't hurt the baby," she whispers.

Ted buries his face in her hair, kissing her neck.

As she stretches her legs and arches her back, her toes touch something soft and moist toward the bottom of the bed. She sits up and peels back the covers to find a handful of yellow rose petals from the garden strewn between the sheets. They're moist and tacky between her fingers.

"How romantic." She turns to Ted, closing her eyes and lifting a velvety petal to her nose to inhale the sweet smell.

Ted says, "Um, yeah."

"How does Dublin at Christmas sound? Like something out of a James Joyce novel?" Elinor immediately recognizes the voice of her boss, Phil, on the line, even though he hasn't identified himself or said *hello*. He often catapults into a phone conversation like this when he's excited.

"Phil?" she asks. "Or is this the Irish Tourist Board?"

"How'd you like to be the lead on an acquisition team in Dublin?" Phil continues. "I'd love to send Ted with you for part of the time, if he can get away."

"I'm fine, and how are *you*?" Elinor teases, cradling the phone against her shoulder as she continues making a shopping list of foods high in folic acid. No more greasy french fries!

"We're acquiring a dynamic little networking company in Dublin — great engineering team — and

263

you're the best international employee relations person I've got. How'd you feel about working over there for six weeks? I thought it would speak to your inner English major."

Elinor has always liked international work — learning about foreign labor laws and unions, putting together decent benefits and exit packages for overseas employees. But now she's grounded.

"I'd love to, but I'm going to have to pass. I'm . . ." Elinor hadn't planned on telling anyone at the office about the pregnancy until she started to show in the second trimester. But she's been up front with Phil about the in-vitro treatments. There was no other way to explain her disappearances for doctor's appointments. Otherwise he might have suspected she'd developed a drug habit. "I'm pregnant."

"Oh." Elinor hears disappointment in his voice. "Great. Wow. Congratulations!"

"Don't worry," she assures him. "I'm going stir crazy at home. I'm coming back to work November first, as planned."

"That's what I like to hear."

That's what they always like to hear.

It's not necessary to hold the hose while deep watering the ginkgo tree. Noah said to turn on the water to a trickle and go back inside for twenty minutes. But Elinor likes feeling the sun warm her back and watching the water seep into the mulch, making a dark brown circle that smells like a redwood forest. Suddenly the image of Noah's green eyes, thick mustache and

264

two dimples flashes in her mind. She recalls his easy laugh. A drunken lightness passes over her as she imagines the roughness of his mustache against her lips and breasts.

She shudders and reaches to touch one of the bright green leaves on the tree. Instead of Noah, she allows herself to think about the baby's nursery. At first she worried this might jinx the pregnancy, but it's comforting to imagine how she'll arrange the sunny room. She'll put a sofa against one wall where she'll breast-feed and perhaps rest in the afternoons while the baby sleeps. She pictures a built-in bookshelf lined with children's classics: *Stuart Little* and *Blueberries for Sal*. One of the things Elinor loves about being pregnant is that now she can imagine the future. A future with a *real* job — a safe haven to create.

Yet she has the odd fear that she'll love this child *too* fiercely. Once, when she and Ted were at the hospital clinic for an in-vitro appointment, she spotted a row of tiny wheelchairs in a hallway. Wheelchairs for *children*. Of course. The realization hit her like a punch to the gut. You could have a child and then something could *happen* to him. Elinor knew this was a form of heartbreak she couldn't endure.

She jumps and gasps when Ted taps her on the shoulder.

"Personally," Ted says, knocking the tree with his fist as though kicking the tires on a car, "I wouldn't have chosen a deciduous shade tree for the street. Anybody who parks under this thing in the fall is going to have leaves caked to their car."

Elinor is amused by the disdain in Ted's voice. "Have you noticed those?" She points down the street to a row of brilliant green ginkgos in the distance. "They're gorgeous."

Ted shrugs. "If you say so."

Elinor laughs. "I say so."

"Mrs. Mackey?" a small voice asks when Elinor answers the phone.

"This is she." Elinor smooths over the duvet cover, satisfied at having made the bed, a task she's lacked the energy for until recently.

"Um, I was calling to see if I could babysit. You know . . . sometime."

"Who is —"

"We had this class at school today? Family Ties? I know, stupid name. But we learned how to take care of babies. We each got our own doll and they showed us how to hold the baby. You have to hold her head in the back, like make a cup out of your hand, because when they're really little they can't hold up their heads . . ."

"Toby?" Elinor recognizes the breathlessness of Gina's kid. His frantic asthmatic way of talking, as though he's running out of air. She sits on the bed.

"Oh, right! I forgot to say, this is Toby."

"Would you like to speak to Dr. Mackey?" Elinor tries to contain her irritation.

"Actually? Um, I wanted to talk to you." His voice brightens. "To ask you if I could babysit."

266

"Honey, we don't even have a baby yet." She tries to keep her cool. She certainly doesn't want Toby telling his mother, *That lady's mean!*

"I always wanted to have a brother, but you know my mom won't have one, because you know, she can't even get a *husband.* She's such a loser."

"Well, I . . ." This kid is a piece of work. Gina isn't a loser, exactly, Elinor thinks. *Whore. Adulterer.* But not a loser.

"I would totally help around the house and stop playing my Game Boy so much and babysit and help you in the yard, like plant your bulbs and stuff. My mom got mad because I wouldn't help her. She wants us to do things together. She thinks of the most *boring* stuff, though. But if I lived at your house —"

"Live?" Elinor's pregnancy furnace clicks on, heat and nausea rushing up her body. She stands, pulls off her sweater, and tosses it on the floor.

Toby gasps, finally taking in some air.

"Toby, I'm going to get Dr. Mackey."

"But —"

"Toby, I think I have to vomit now." She drops the phone on the bed and lunges toward the bathroom. "Ted!" The watery bile burns its way up the back of her throat.

"What?"

"*Phone!*" She hears Ted clamber for the phone as she leans her head into the toilet and throws up her breakfast of soft-boiled eggs, one more food she's going to have to cross off the list. She wants to eavesdrop, but it's difficult to barf and listen in at the same time. If it weren't for the damn progesterone, which is supposed to help her uterine lining, she's sure she'd be done with this morning sickness. She flushes the toilet and reaches for her toothbrush.

Standing in the hallway brushing her teeth, she listens to Ted listen to Toby.

"I know," he says soothingly. "I know. Failed? Oh, well, but you have to study, Toby. You can do it, champ, I know you can. No, Toby, I'm sorry. I know your mom put up lots of signs at the community college. I'm sure you'll get a smart new tutor soon. You mustn't call here, okay? Mrs. Mackey isn't feeling well and it might upset her. I know. I know. I have to go. Toby? I don't want to hang up until you say good-bye. Okay? Good-bye."

Elinor drops her hands at her sides. Suddenly she's as sad for this boy as she was for the baby elephant at the zoo.

Roger is remarkably thorough and meticulous when it comes to cleaning, especially for a guy in his twenties. He doesn't balk when Elinor asks him to do the picture window looking from the kitchen into the backyard. She watches from the sink as he stands on a stool working away streaks with Windex and paper towels. His plaid pants look like they once belonged to a men's suit circa 1975. His T-shirt says SQUIRREL NUT ZIPPERS. Although he's thin, his shoulders and arms are muscular. He's a nice-looking guy, Elinor concludes, loading the dishwasher and turning it on. Any young woman would be attracted to him, wouldn't she? The blue eyes and lean build and sweet demeanor?

268

The hip goatee? Gina would be attracted to him, wouldn't she? Toby would like him. This thought comes to Elinor suddenly, just as the waves of nausea have for weeks. Only now she feels a wave of *energy*. She welcomes the familiar feeling of an idea spinning in her head, albeit a maniacal one. Roger would make a nice boyfriend for Gina, a fun companion for Toby. There might be a seven- or eight-year age difference between Roger and Gina, but Roger is rather mature and he seems to like older women. How old is Gina, anyway? Elinor bristles, not wanting to consider this question too thoroughly.

Ever since Toby called their house, Elinor has sensed him and Gina hovering at the periphery of her life with Ted, like the swirling doughnut shape of a hurricane offshore on a weather map. Brewing out of anyone's control. She shouldn't have to worry about Gina and Toby! She already misses the days when she let everything go and sprawled under the oak tree staring at the sky. Life is much less intimidating when you ditch your ambitions and stop wishing for things. But you can't be so cavalier when you're pregnant. Which is why she can't afford to have Toby and Gina looming over her any longer.

"Hey, how 'bout breakfast?" she asks Roger as she puts away the last mug from the dishwasher.

"No thanks."

"Already ate?"

Roger shakes his head.

"It's the most important meal of the day." She grabs bacon, English muffins, eggs, cheese, an onion, and

269

mushrooms from the refrigerator. Finally, Elinor has discovered something she can cook — a hearty breakfast. Toast, marmalade, big wedges of peach from the farmer's market drenched in honey yogurt. She cracks eggs into a bowl, whisking them so vigorously, yolk slops onto the counter. Here she is: in suburbia, in the kitchen, barefoot, pregnant, and cooking. Back in college, these were all the things she thought she didn't want. Yet she is content.

Roger steps back from the window to check his work. "If I take a break I'll fall behind. I have another house today."

There you go: conscientious. Another great attribute. Roger will be perfect for Toby and Gina.

Elinor peels the bacon into a frying pan. "It'll take you ten minutes to eat, tops." While he eats, they'll talk about how Roger is going to ask Gina out. *How, how, how?* She chops onions, slices leftover baked potatoes, frying them in olive oil with a bit of rosemary. "You have to keep up your energy level!"

"Okay." Roger laughs, his ears turning red.

They sit together at the table, and Elinor watches Roger eat. He closes his eyes as he takes a bite of egg yolk and brown potato. "Oh, awesome." He opens his eyes, chews on his toast. Elinor beams. Roger swallows, wipes his mouth. His cheeks begin to color again.

"Um, I was wondering . . . ," Roger begins.

Elinor slides more fresh sliced tomatoes onto his plate.

"Would you like to go with me to the Avedon opening in San Francisco?" he asks.

270

"Oh, Roger." Elinor hopes she doesn't sound condescending. "I'd love to. But you know I'm not single anymore." She claps her forehead. "What a boob. I forgot to tell you — Dr. Mackey moved back in. That means extra work for you to clean up after another person, I know. But he's very neat and we'd be happy to pay you more." She doesn't want to linger over the fact that Roger sort of just asked her on a date. If he gets any more embarrassed, his face might actually catch fire.

She gets up to fetch more coffee. "Hey, so you're single?" She fills his cup, trying to sound nonchalant.

"I have a girlfriend." Roger doesn't say this with much conviction. "I did. We broke up." He pushes his bacon around. "She broke up with me."

"Oh, I'm sorry." Elinor folds a napkin. "That's hard. Breakups are the worst. I know."

"But I'm dating," Roger adds quickly. He picks up his toast.

"Really? Because I know a girl who would *love* you. There's this woman who works at my gym who's very cute. What a figure. Wow." Elinor feels a pained expression creasing her brow.

"Um. A blind date?" Roger asks with dread.

"Are you good at math?"

"Is she a mathematician?"

"No, but, I must tell you: She has a son."

"Cool."

"And he needs help with his math homework. I know that would mean a lot to her, if you could help her son." Elinor slaps her thigh. "He is such a great kid. In fact . . ." She gets up from the table, goes to her purse, and takes out her wallet to retrieve her gym membership card. ". . . you can call her at work." Elinor copies the number for Roger and tucks it under his plate. "Give her a call at the club and offer to tutor her son."

Roger frowns at the scrap of paper.

Elinor sits, covering Roger's hand with hers. "It would be sort of a personal favor to me. I really want her to meet somebody great. I think you'd be perfect. Hey, but do *not* tell her that I suggested all this. It's kind of mortifying when somebody sets you up, you know?"

"Uh, tell me about it."

"Oh! I mean for women. Sometimes." Elinor is faltering. "Anyway, she's really cute and athletic. Besides, what do you have to lose? Worst case, you get a little extra work, tutoring."

"Right," Roger says. "What does a *loser* have to lose?"

"Roger! You, my friend, are not a loser."

"Cleaning houses? Going on blind dates?" Roger tosses his napkin on the table in disgust. "I need to finish my graduate school application."

"You can. You will. Try not to worry so much. You're young."

Roger stands, carrying his plate to the sink. "Okay. I'll call her." His tone brightens. "She sounds cool. Thanks. But I gotta get back to work now, okay?"

"Okay." Elinor feels giddy. Is it crazy to imagine this plan actually working? Now she's like one of those meddling Greek gods, who always have something mischievous up their sleeves for the hapless mortals in *The Iliad* and *The Aeneid* — a pie in the face at every turn.

CHAPTER
FIFTEEN

Screw Ted. Gina is tired of thinking about him all the time. She hasn't been able to stop herself, but she will. Somehow. Whenever she thinks of Ted she'll think of something else. That's how you break bad habits — with replacements. Instead of missing Ted, she'll brainstorm how she might start her own business as a personal trainer and dietitian consultant, going into people's homes. What about health insurance? She'll carry a little pad and write down ideas and questions such as this.

She leans in the doorway to Toby's room, exasperated. When Ted was in the picture, Toby kept the place neat — for a boy — and did his homework and chores. Now he has let everything go. The room looks like it's been blown to bits by a hurricane. Dirty clothes, belts, and sneakers are strewn with all kinds of other junk — CDs, books, comic books, a half-built LEGO spaceship, the inner workings of a dismembered computer, a half-strung guitar (where'd *that* come from?). The Styrofoam solar system that used to hang from the ceiling lies tangled on the floor, with one planet crushed. The desk is piled with dirty dishes —

274

bowls caked with cereal and milk, glasses with gunk glued to the bottoms.

Gina can't do anything to persuade Toby to clean up this room. She has asked, nagged, and yelled. She tried a motivational approach, clapping her hands as though at a pep rally. "Let's work on it together for just thirty minutes," she cheered, setting the kitchen timer and placing it on Toby's dresser. "Then we'll order pizza." Toby rolled his eyes. He worked with her, but he was so cranky and slow they made little progress.

Last week Gina took away Toby's "screen time," telling him he couldn't watch TV, use the computer, or play with his Game Boy until he cleaned for half an hour. Toby shrugged and retreated to his room, burying his head in his book on medieval knights.

When Gina was in elementary school, her class took a bus to the Metropolitan Museum of Art in New York City. Her favorite section had been the Egyptian collection — the majestic sphinxes and scarabs. But all the boys loved the giant towering atrium crammed with life-size knights and horses clad in armor. Remembering the museum exhibit at work one day, Gina came up with a plan: She and Toby could go to New York City. They didn't need Ted. They'd fly east and stay for a weekend and go see the armor and eat giant slabs of cheesecake at the Carnegie Deli. When she told Toby her idea at dinner that night, his eyes widened and he clicked his tongue in his mouth, clearly growing excited. But finally he frowned and shunned the trip. "Boring," he said, rolling his eyes and kicking the table.

"No, *not* boring," Gina replied. "The real thing is much better than pictures in a book. But if you want to turn down a fun adventure just to spite me, fine."

Just chip away at it, she tells herself now, peering into her son's room. She's determined to get the disaster cleaned up before Toby gets home from school. As she steps over the threshold, she immediately slips on a CD and twists her knee. A startling cracking noise is followed by a burning pain. She rights herself, picks up the CD, limps to the desk, and begins a stack. The pain in her knee makes her eyes water until the room is blurry. "To heck with you!" she shouts at the room. She's tired of always trying to make Toby happy. "To heck with Ted!" Forever trying to convince him to love her. It's like running for office. Like she's got one of those dumb little signs in her front yard: VOTE FOR GINA! I CAN BE YOUR MOTHER! I CAN BE YOUR LOVER! CHOOSE ME! LOVE ME! "*Fuck them*," she shouts, stomping on Jupiter. The Styrofoam pops and crunches under her sneaker. Ha. There, she swore. Just like all the other grown-ups. Maybe her Goody Two-shoes, clean-language cheerfulness is a curse. *Hi! I'm Gina! Walk all over me!*

She shovels dirty clothes into the hamper, not caring when a few CDs tumble in. The room has a rank sour-milk, dirty-sock smell that makes her gag slightly. On some days, she can't even persuade Toby to take a shower.

"Do you want to be the smelly kid?" she asked him one morning as he was leaving for school. It was mean to say this, but she could *not* get through to him.

"Yeah! I want to be the smelly kid with no dad!" he screamed.

"One, you have a father," she told him, trying to be firm and upbeat at the same time. "Two, lots of kids in your class have divorced parents. I'm sorry that's the way it is. It doesn't mean you have to be miserable and make us both miserable."

But they are both miserable. And Gina is at a loss. She drags the hamper through the debris out into the hall. She gazes up at the white ceiling in the hall, which she often does when she needs to collect her energy. Sometimes you just need a blank slate for a moment. But when Gina looks back into the room, she doesn't feel any more prepared to tackle it. If she could just get everything into one pile. Yes: *one* pile. She heads for the garage.

She still owns paraphernalia from country life in Maine, where she met Toby's father: a shop vac, a small tool chest, and a leaf blower. She's always been fairly handy. Her father, who died of lung cancer when she was twenty, had been a general contractor, and he took her to work with him on Saturdays when she was a kid, letting her hand him tools and even squeeze caulk out of the gun. In high school, Gina still went on jobs with her dad, and he paid her. They ate lunch sitting at a slab of plywood between two sawhorses in someone's garage, peeling oranges and eggs and reading their horoscopes from the newspaper. To this day, Gina loves the smell of hardware stores and the tool department at Sears — the metallic odors of copper, aluminum, and stainless steel, the muskiness of wood floors. Hardware stores smell like Saturday, like her father. Like everything she loves about men.

She locates the Yard Pro super turbo blower/shredder/vacuum and drags it from a bottom shelf. It didn't seem like a strange thing to buy back in Maine. She was more independent there, relying mostly on herself for happiness. Or maybe she'd just never really been in love before she met Ted. She grabs the tube attachment for the blower and an orange extension cord and heads back to Toby's room. It would take hours to pick through all of his junk, so she'll just blow it into one corner and make him sort through it all.

Clumps of dust under the desk make Gina sneeze as she reaches to plug in the extension cord. The machine is heavier than she remembers. She should have found her headphones. As soon as she switches it on, her ears crackle from the shriek and her arms shake from the vibration. She nudges the speed control button down to 125 miles an hour, the lowest setting, and works in sweeping motions from the door of the room toward the opposite corner. Papers fly up and smack against the window screens as though trying to escape. When she lifts the blower to push down the papers (stupid!), a screen pops out and falls into the bushes outside. Gina's stomach cramps with laughter and she has to bend her knees not to drop the blower. This isn't funny, but it *is* funny. She should blow Toby's junk out the dang window!

When is the last time she *laughed*? When she was with Ted. But it wasn't Ted that made her laugh, it was Toby. Ted made Toby laugh and Toby made her laugh.

It wasn't her imagination, things *were* better when Ted was with them.

A significant pile is gathering in one corner of the room. Sweatpants, swim trunks, computer game boxes, candy wrappers, school papers, dirty socks, clean socks — who can tell the difference? The heavier things, like books and sneakers, are resistant to the blower, so she kicks them along, pleased with her progress. But Ted was never really *with* them, she thinks. That was the problem. How foolish of her to believe that he was, that he would stay. A half glass of Coke tips over, brown syrupy soda drizzling into the carpet. Gina changes directions and points the blower at a spiral notebook. A flurry of pages flaps by. As she moves the blower away she sees the words *Dear Dad* in Toby's small square handwriting. She turns off the blower and picks up the notebook. *Dear Dad, It's not so bad living with Mom now. Did you know, she is really pretty and popular? I mean popular with guys and popular at her work. Everybody wants her to be there trainer.* Gina presses the notebook to her chest, wondering exactly what Toby's agenda is here — to get his father to reconcile with her even though he's already married? *I like California because September is still like summer. It's hot enough to swim in the pool still and . . .* And nothing. The letter ends there. Gina tears out the page, folds it, and pushes it into her pocket. She looks down at the blower. There's an 800 number for customer assistance on a big yellow sticker. She'd like to call and ask how she's supposed to raise this boy of hers.

"Hey! What the hell?" Gina looks up to see Toby standing in the doorway. He's wearing his big surfer shorts, a black T-shirt, and orange Converse high-tops without socks. "What are you *doing*?" His breath is shallow and quick.

"Making a pile for you, that's what. You can go through it after you finish your homework." Gina tries to remain calm. "What would you like for a snack?"

Toby throws his backpack against his desk. "I have no screens! Get out of my room!"

"Toby, I've asked you nicely a dozen times to clean up this —"

"I don't want to clean up my room because I *hate* it. I hate it here!"

Gina crosses her arms over her chest. "Right, it's so awful here, where you have your own room and your own TV and a swimming pool practically to yourself and we eat out at least once a week." Gina digs her hand into her pocket. "You wrote to your *dad* that you like it here." She pulls out the page of notepaper, unfolds it, and points to Toby's letter.

"That's when Dr. Mackey was my tutor. Hey! You read my stuff."

Gina drops the page on Toby's desk. "You hate it here? You *hate* me? Fine. I'm calling your father and Cruella and telling them you're on your way." That's it. She gives up. She pushes aside a pair of jeans on the chair at Toby's desk, so she can sit at his computer. The keyboard keys are coated with dust and crumbs and sesame seeds from a bagel. She types in *expedia.com* and then *Bangor, Maine.*

280

"What are you doing?" Toby asks.

"I'm buying you a plane ticket." *Don't threaten your child with consequences you have no intention of following through on*, she hears her parenting book chide. *Children will call your bluff*. But maybe Gina *should* buy Toby a ticket to Maine.

"Don't." Gina is surprised by the panic in Toby's voice as she skims through flights. "Don't *touch* my computer," he hollers. "Get your own computer! Dad bought that for me." He storms at her in a whirl, swatting his arms.

Gina lifts her hands from the keyboard and folds them in her lap. "Fine. I'll buy the ticket on the telephone." There's no harm in making a reservation, she figures. You have twenty-four hours before you actually have to purchase the ticket.

She leaves the room, slamming the door behind her. Once again, she has sunken to Toby's level. The letter, the fear in Toby's voice. She doesn't understand. When you get right down to it, people don't *want just* love. They want tough love, complicated love, messy love. *Clean up your room! Do ten more reps! Meet me behind the gym*. She doesn't get it. Why do people make life so much harder than it needs to be? Suddenly the roar of the leaf blower fills the house, followed by the sound of breaking glass and Toby's laughter. Gina turns back to her son's room.

CHAPTER
SIXTEEN

The waiting room at the ob-gyn's office is Elinor and Ted's Ellis Island. They've crossed over from the land of infertility to the land of pregnancy. Elinor squeezes her clipboard of updated information in one hand and Ted's fingers in the other.

"Ow!" Ted yelps.

"Sorry!" She'd been nervously rolling and kneading his fingers in her palm. She loosens her grip, taking comfort in the warm dryness of his hand.

Women in various stages of pregnancy fan themselves in the too-warm room. A toddler wails and his mother roots through a diaper bag, producing string cheese. Ted is the only husband. Elinor feels wimpy for bringing him. For everyone here, pregnancy is routine. A woman yawns. Boring even. But Ted wanted to come. He's never met Elinor's OB, Dr. Kolcheck, and, since Elinor's nearly through her first trimester, today they're going to discuss the amnio. Ted flips through *Parenthood* magazine, pausing over a shaded box showing the merits of whole apples versus apple juice versus apple cider. Elinor touches her stomach. She feels better since she's gone off the progesterone. Now it's just her and the baby along with folic acid and

Mother Nature. When she wakes in the morning, she's no longer crushed by nausea and fatigue.

A door beside the front desk opens. "Elinor Mackey?" a nurse calls. Ted squeezes Elinor's hand as they stand.

Dr. Kolcheck is younger than Ted and Elinor. She's kind and smart, and talks quickly — maintaining an energy level Elinor can't imagine having, even without pregnancy and with caffeine. She describes the pros and cons of an amnio versus another, earlier test called CVS, which many women Elinor's age are doing. The upside of CVS is that you find out sooner if the baby has any chromosomal abnormalities. Elinor could have the test as soon as next week, and they would know the results in a matter of days. Whereas she wouldn't have the amnio until week sixteen and would have to wait two weeks for those results. For some women this results in a later termination, which of course is very traumatic. There is only a slightly higher risk of miscarriage with the CVS. The benefits of an earlier diagnosis have to be weighed with the slightly increased risk.

Acronyms, percentages, pros and cons spin in a blender-whirl in Elinor's brain. At work, she's perfectly able to absorb complex technical information and evaluate risks. But the word *termination* halts her ability to think now. She wants to keep her baby no matter what's wrong with him. Ted strokes her leg. It's a relief to have him here. He's calm in situations like this, retaining information and coming up with intelligent questions. Dr. Kolcheck pauses. She and Ted look to Elinor, who hasn't said a word. Her mouth is dry.

"If the results are bad, maybe our baby could just go to vocational school?" Elinor tries to muster a laugh. *You can't take him, no matter what's wrong with him!*

Dr. Kolcheck smiles sympathetically and reaches across her desk to squeeze Elinor's arm. "I'm sorry. I'm overwhelming you. You can go home and think about this. Read up and discuss it privately. Call me with any questions."

Next comes Elinor's physical examination, for which Ted returns to the waiting room.

"I'm so happy for you." Dr. K slips her stethoscope into her ears to listen to Elinor's heartbeat and breathing. "I'm sorry you had such trouble."

"We've been on a very expensive trip to hell and back," Elinor agrees, lying on the table. "But the worst is over. I go back to work in a week." Elinor actually looks forward to returning to the office now, with its structured days, bustle of people, and welcome distractions. There will be less time to worry there.

Dr. K frowns a little as she examines Elinor's cervix and uterus. "Let's hope you don't have a big baby." She smiles. "Your hips are tiny." This is meant as a compliment — Elinor's petite. But it brings on that familiar feeling of being unqualified. Elinor had just been gaining confidence. In the waiting room, she even imagined returning to the office for her second pregnancy, baby in tow, baby on the way.

284

"Let's have a look at this baby in the ultrasound room," Dr. Kolcheck says. "Go grab your husband."

Elinor peers into the waiting room at Ted, who is smiling and staring into space. She winks and curls her finger for him to follow.

They trail behind the doctor to a dark examining room at the end of the hall. Elinor is used to the vaginal ultrasound by now, which is painless and somehow comforting. During all those months when they couldn't conceive, Elinor felt betrayed by her body, wondering, *What's going on in there?* At least the ultrasound reveals part of the mystery.

Ted leans against the wall, giving Elinor and Dr. Kolcheck plenty of space. Elinor sighs and closes her eyes. The room is warm and quiet — womb-like. She inhales deeply to relax. Yes, there are thousands of genetic markers in the CVS test, but she is pregnant. *Positive thoughts*. The ultrasound machine clicks as Dr. Kolcheck scans the screen. Elinor rolls her head to see the cone of fuzzy light. Some of the dots on the screen are larger than others, and one of them is her baby. *Hello there.*

"*Oh,*" Dr. Kolcheck says. Her voice is different somehow, tinged with disbelief. Her fingertips touch Elinor's thigh. "Oh, I'm so sorry."

Sorry?

"There's no heartbeat. I'm so sorry." The fingertips stroke Elinor's leg.

Elinor laughs. "It's *there.*" That linty fuzz ball is so *small*. It always took Dr. Weston several minutes to find the heartbeat.

"You've lost the baby." Dr. Kolcheck points to the screen. Elinor strains to look. The image seems the same as always — gray and murky and primordial.

She rolls her head toward Ted. He flattens his back and arms against the wall, as though someone has shot him.

"It's there," Elinor repeats. Dr. Kolcheck's hand gently rubs Elinor's leg. This is not an exploratory touch. It is a gesture of sympathy.

Tell her, Ted! It's there! The baby. It's there! Ted slides all the way down the wall until he disappears below Elinor's line of vision. She peers over to see him sitting cross-legged on the floor. She feels as though the examining table is a ship and he's overboard. What is going on here? She turns back to face Dr. Kolcheck.

"I'm so sorry," the doctor repeats.

It's okay, Elinor wants to tell her. *It's there. It was just there at our last appointment. It's hard to see, that's all. Merely a polka dot of a little buddy. These machines are crazy. Ted! Tell her.* She looks to Ted again. He is shaking his head.

Dr. Kolcheck stands and looks over the examining table at him. She lowers her voice. "I'm so sorry. There's no heartbeat. There aren't any limb buds." She says this apologetically, seeming to hope that because Ted's a fellow doctor, he'll be able to register this information.

Elinor didn't know there were *supposed* to be limb buds. Was that in her book? The book she threw into the damn Dumpster! If she had *known* this — she

286

could have been thinking about them, visualizing limb buds, instead of lusting after Earl Grey.

"But . . ." Elinor cannot sit up.

Dr. Kolcheck removes the ultrasound wand and switches off the machine. "I'm going to give you guys a minute, okay?" she says.

Ted stands. His face is drained of color. Is he going to pass out?

"But . . ." Elinor snaps her knees shut, suddenly feeling exposed and ridiculous.

Ted looks at her, shakes his head.

She curls up, rolls onto her side, and manages to sit on the edge of the table. Ted stands in front of her, wrapping her in his arms. His shirt buttons are cold against her cheek. She lowers her head and buries her face against his stomach.

"Do *not* turn on the light," she begs him. She feels Ted nod. "Please. Don't turn it on."

He runs his fingers over and over her hair. "I won't, sweetie, I won't."

Ted starts the car and begins driving them away from Dr. Kolcheck's office, but he can't imagine where they should go. Home? To do what?

Dr. Kolcheck recommended that Elinor have a D&C in the morning. El should fast after midnight, and they should return first thing. While Dr. K is 100 percent positive that they've lost the baby, she doesn't think Elinor and Ted will really believe it unless they see the ultrasound again. So they'll go to the office and take one more look, then Ted will take El over to the hospital, where she'll be admitted as a day patient. At least Dr. Kolcheck has a nice bedside manner. It's about all they can hope for at this point.

"Where should we go?" he asks Elinor. He just wants to hold his wife and think for a while. No. He just wants to just hold her and *not* think. He wants it to be yesterday, last week, four and a half years ago, when they first married. Why didn't he throw her birth control pills off the balcony at their honeymoon hotel on Kauai into the fountain and fishtail palms and get her pregnant right there, like a real man? He should have convinced her to quit that blood-sucking job. Instead Elinor got a big promotion, and the company claimed more and *more* of his wife's time and energy. A slice of her soul. He should have talked her out of that promotion. But that wouldn't have been supportive.

"You can go," Elinor says, pointing to the green light above them.

"Right." Ted accelerates too quickly and they lurch forward. "Sorry. *Where?*"

"Yeah, I don't know." Elinor squints and shields the side of her face from the sun coming through her window.

The town is too busy and bright and crowded, mothers flocking out to retrieve their children as school lets out. At the next light, a traffic guard blows a whistle and glares at the stopped cars accusingly as he marches into a crosswalk to let the kids pass.

"There." Elinor points at the Chevron station. "Into the car wash. Look, no line."

The car is already clean. Ted pulls into the station. He fills the tank and presses the YES button for the wash. He's convinced that the deluxe wash and the luxury wash are the same bubbly concoction, but this time he chooses the luxury, which he hopes takes longer.

"*That's* why I feel better," Elinor says as Ted climbs back into the car. "I thought it was because I'm almost in my second trimester. But it's because we lost the baby, so my HCG levels are dropping." She rubs her hand over her stomach tentatively — a gesture that breaks Ted's heart. "No hormones, so no nausea." She leans a palm against the dashboard. "Plus, I took a really hot shower. You're not supposed to."

"No, Ellie. It's the increased chromosomal risk at our age. It's statistics. It's not you, it's life."

"Try *death*."

Ted closes his eyes and squeezes the bridge of his nose. He opens them, starts the car, and pulls around to the wash, rolling down the window and punching in the code from his receipt on a keypad.

"I shouldn't have gone off the progesterone." Elinor looks at him beseechingly.

"Honey." He rubs her shoulder, kisses her cheek. "Dr. Weston wouldn't have taken you off it if there was any danger. She errs on the cautious side."

Elinor nods and looks at her hands in her lap. "Thanks for trying to make me feel better," she says quietly. "I'm sorry. I'm not doing anything to make you feel better."

A car waiting behind them honks.

"You still want to go through?" Ted asks.

Elinor covers her face with her hands.

"I know." He puts the car in drive and pulls the car into the wash, braking and turning off the engine when the red lights flash. After a clank and a whir, the spinning blue brushes descend upon them, enveloping them, blocking out the light and heat and chaos outside. Ted unbuckles his seat belt and scoots over to wrap his arms around Elinor. She presses her forehead to his sternum. Water drums the roof and the windows. Ted's eyes and throat burn. Suddenly the car wash emits a low howl, like a tomcat about to get into a fight. Ted lifts his head, surprised to discover that the sound is coming from deep within his chest.

Everyone at the hospital either smiles and touches Elinor or gives her drugs. They don't know that *she* killed her baby. They don't know about all of the mistakes she made — those two cups of Darjeeling she finally drank, steeped as dark as caramel, the tannic acid tingling in her mouth, the caffeine clearing the cobwebs from her brain. Twice she drank tea! She finally removed the polish from her toes, looping a paper mask over her face to block out the fumes. Acetone! She did the bow pose in yoga class. Wasn't *that* the pose you weren't supposed to do if you were pregnant or menstruating? She rode her bicycle to the drugstore. The air and exercise pushed away the nausea, but surely her pulse raced to over the allowed 147 beats per minute as she pumped home with her ChapStick and shampoo. She killed her baby, and now everyone is being so nice to her and telling her it wasn't anything she did. If this is the case, why do they keep bringing it up? Clearly they're humoring her — trying to make her feel better. *You killed your baby. It happens. We're so sorry.*

Ceiling tiles sail by overhead as they wheel her down a hallway to the operating room. A face appears over her, smiling and handsome and close as a lover's. He introduces himself — Dr. Goodlooking, the anesthesiologist.

"I'm starving," Elinor blurts, embarrassed to be thinking about food.

"What I have is *better* than food," he coos. "Mind if I get your IV going?" She feels the prick of the needle, followed by warmth in her arm, and then she is floating into the operating room. This would be scary if it was *really* happening. If she wasn't flying and falling in love with everyone around her. "Count backward," Handsome says. "Ten, ni . . ."

There is a difference between sadness and insanity. Elinor thinks this as she sits on the toilet clutching her soiled, rolled-up sanitary pad. She can't let go of it. She does not want to throw it away. She should put it somewhere safe.

"God!" she hollers, finally tossing the thing in the trash.

"You okay?" Ted calls from the kitchen. He's been hovering since they got home, keeping an eye on her after the general anesthesia.

"Just jolly!" she calls out. Here she is again: being a bitch to her husband. *Crazy, stupid, shit!* The water burns her hands as she turns it on. She shakes her fingers and steps out of the bathroom.

She wraps her arms around Ted's waist and holds her ear to his chest. Yesterday she carried something that was part of both of them and now it's gone, but at least she still has him. Half of the whole.

Ted doesn't say anything. He squeezes her.

She used to love standing like this, listening to his inner workings, listening to the gurgling, beating, breathing life inside him. He rocks her, patting and kissing the top of her head. Ted might be the kindest man she's ever known. Did she forget this along the way?

All that week Elinor and Ted don't hug in bed at night; they cling. Their arms and legs intertwine into one sweaty octopus that sinks into the center of the bed, curling and squeezing and shutting out the world.

When Elinor wakes in the morning, the fact that the baby is gone hits her like a slap. "Oh!" she gasps, startling Ted. "*Right.*"

Funny, for the D&C she went to sleep counting from ten to one, and after the surgery she woke up to the nurse asking her to rate her pain level on a scale of one to ten. *Physical or psychological*, Elinor wondered. The morphine said *five*, and that's what she told the nurse. The woman patted her arm and smiled. Elinor liked how everyone touched her. Now she's still cramping and bleeding, and she wishes people would touch her.

She wants the Safeway clerk to inquire about her pain on a scale of one to ten. "Did you find everything you were looking for today? And how is your pain on a scale of one to ten?" She wants to switch on the radio in the car and hear: *In other news today, Elinor and Ted Mackey lost their baby.* "*They were already separated, anyway,*" *a neighbor of the Mackeys commented.* "*We don't know what the deal is with those two,*" *another added. The S&P is up five points . . .*

The blues hit her hardest in the afternoons. They press down on her shoulders and upper back, making her wonder if she's walking like Groucho Marx. When she's home, all she wants to do is *get out* of the house; as soon as she's out, she can't wait to get home. Now that she can have all the caffeine she wants, she dreads going to their neighborhood coffee shop, where she used to enjoy reading in the sun. In the mornings, the place buzzes with Mommy-and-Me groups, women gathering their monstrous strollers in a circle. They sip and munch and coo and commiserate. They're exhausted. They're in this miserable mommy martyrdom thing together.

Elinor's afraid she might holler at them. *Fine! Give me the damn kid!* She tries to focus on her *Aeneid*, but she can't block out the cackling women. Her thoughts race and her pulse thrums, as though she's a jack-in-the-box about to pop. She dashes to her car for cover. She tries visiting the coffeehouse in the afternoons instead, on her way to the grocery store, but then there are the mothers with schoolchildren stopping for a drink and a treat.

The whole world hurts her feelings. An *ice cream truck* hurts her feelings. One afternoon it occurs to her that the ice cream truck speeds up when it passes their house. The driver seems to think there aren't any children in this little pocket of retirees and childless Mackeys. The distorted nursery rhyme chimes maniacally faster as the truck whooshes by. *There are grandchildren!* Elinor hollers at the closed living room window. *The Aldersons have grandchildren! Kat has children! Slow down! I might want a toasted almond bar!* She should call the police to report the driver for speeding. How loony. She needs some of those drugs from the hospital, which made her believe everything would be all right. What *was* that stuff? she asks Ted. Fentanyl. Can't he write her a prescription? No. Can she drive to Mexico and cop some? No. It's anesthesia. Well, she needs to be anesthetized.

The only people she feels comfortable around are Kat and Ted. The afternoon after her D&C, Kat stood in her living room with brownies, vanilla ice cream, caramel sauce, Chardonnay, and new pajamas. "I washed the PJs," she told Elinor. "So they'd be soft and clean and ready to wear tonight."

"*I love you!*" Elinor wailed.

"I love you, too," Kat said. "And I hate it that I can't do anything for you."

Elinor buried her face in the warm, soft cotton pajamas, breathing in the comforting smell of a dryer sheet, and cried.

"I guess they make a good hanky, too." Kat laughed.

Finally, Elinor gives up on the coffee shop and the grocery store, with its diaper aisles and lurking babies. She stays home and sticks to minor tasks, such as bringing in and sorting the mail. But she's easily paralyzed. When an envelope arrives from the OB's office, she knows it's only a bill, but she imagines a letter: *We regret to inform you that you are ineligible for motherhood. Please return the fringed overalls and dispense with any fantasies of attending your daughter's college graduation.*

Ted shops and cooks. Roger keeps the place clean. For some reason, Ted doesn't like Roger.

"Maybe he's stealing from us," he gripes.

"What? Don't be ridiculous," Elinor replies.

"Why's he so flinchy? There's an aura of guilt around him like bad aftershave."

Elinor considers this. Roger *is* nervous around Ted. When Elinor first introduced the two, Roger got so flustered he dropped a bottle of lemon oil, shattering it in the driveway.

He just has a little crush on me, Elinor thinks. *Is that so hard to imagine? I might be attractive to a young stranger, too!*

Elinor is relieved when it's time to go back to work the following Monday morning. There are no babies or strollers at the office. Before leaving home, she calls her CEO and asks that he please not tell anyone other than her assistant about her miscarriage. He gives her his word. When she arrives, there's a huge bouquet of

white roses from him on her desk with a simple card —
Welcome back.

People stream into her office all morning to say hello.
"How was your sabbatical?" they ask with envy.

"Great!" Elinor barks.

"What did you do?"

"I . . ." She should have thought of a story. "Read,
slept, nothing very interesting. Yard work. You know
how time flies." *Got separated, reconciled, miscarried.*
Slept with a tree surgeon. Elinor hopes her smile isn't
too forced, hopes her hands aren't visibly shaking. It
was such a minor detail, but she had really looked
forward to shopping for maternity clothes for her
second and third trimesters at work.

Midmorning her boss stops by, sitting on the edge of
her desk and hiking up a pant leg. "It's great to have
you back."

"Thanks. Thank you so much for the flowers." She
reaches into her desk for ibuprofen. Her perma-grin
has given her a headache. "It's good to *be* back."

"Like I said," he tells her, "you are the best
international employee relations lawyer in the Valley, as
far as I can tell. I'd *love* to get you over to Ireland to
handle this acquisition. Believe me, I'd sleep better at
night." He stands and looks at her kindly. "Ted like
Guinness?"

Elinor wishes she was the best in the Valley at
something else — at being a wife, at being a mother. At
being a *woman* — a woman who can conceive and
carry a baby to term. "Let me think about it," she says,

296

managing one last smile. "Let me talk to Ted. It sounds great. It does."

By Wednesday, Elinor can't wait for the first week back at work to end; she's afraid she'll burst into tears in the middle of a meeting. Yet when Saturday finally comes, it seems weekends will be the most difficult time to get through. All those families strolling down the street and playing in their yards. Elinor tries to keep her spirits up as Ted fixes them buckwheat pancakes and turkey bacon for breakfast on Sunday. After cleaning up the kitchen, she starts a to-do list. *Get*, she writes. *Get what?* She was sure she had thought of something a moment before.

"I'm not so sure about this," Elinor says when Kat stops by to pick her up for their book group. "I don't think I should go."

"Maybe it'll be good for you to get out of the house?" Kat holds up a bottle of Chardonnay and a plate of little quiches.

This month they've finished *The Aeneid*, which Elinor does want to discuss. "Okay." She grabs her jean jacket. She has a thing or two to say about Aeneas, whom she thinks is a wuss.

As with all suburban gatherings among women, the conversation begins with children, husbands, teachers, and soccer, always circling back to children. Elinor sips her tea. "Can we go?" she asks Kat through clenched teeth.

"Ten minutes," Kat whispers. "Ladies," she says to the group. "Shall we get started on our book?"

"I gotta tell ya," Janice Meads says, swiping a hand through her cropped brown hair, "I don't love it any more than I did in college. Maybe it's me, but I find it . . ." She looks at the ceiling, grasping for a word. "Inaccessible."

"Nice way of saying boring," Doreen Whiting chimes in.

"It's so sad," Fran says. "I mean the part with Dido and Aeneas. That just gets me."

"I know," Kat says.

"Me, too," Elinor agrees. "And this time I felt angry with Aeneas." The women look at her with interest. "I mean, when you get right down to it, it's a very Silicon Valley story. They're in love, but he puts work ahead of love."

"He's duty-bound," Kat says.

"Exactly," Elinor agrees. "But it's duty to the company instead of duty to his family. He loves Dido. But then he gets called by the gods to go to Rome and he ditches her."

"Yeah," Cathy says. "I mean I didn't get that far, but right on." Cathy's husband is a VP of marketing who's never home in time for dinner or the kids' baths. While she rarely finishes the books, Elinor likes her because she drinks wine and laughs easily.

"Why can't Dido go with him?" Kat muses.

Janice says, "She has to stay and take care of her kingdom." Janice is serious about everything, even spinach dip. Once she debated the merits of green onions versus chopped red onion for a full five minutes.

298

"Why, though?" Elinor likes Kat's idea. "She's so heartbroken; she's not going to be any use to the kingdom. Why can't she give it all up for love? Aeneas gets a job transfer, she goes with him." Elinor slaps her thigh. "Screw the kingdom."

Doreen cringes. Once again, Elinor's a little too rough around the edges for suburbia. She switches from tea to wine. Now that she can have all the caffeine and alcohol she wants, she can veer between beverages. She even made an Irish coffee one afternoon.

"Duty schmoodie," Kat agrees.

"What *does* she have to lose by going?" Fran asks. Elinor likes how Fran is a sensitive, hopeless romantic. "Except she can't really go because he doesn't ask her," she adds sadly.

"Bottom line, he has no free will," Janice says. "It's the same in all these Greek stories. Which is why I find them *so* inaccessible."

Quit saying inaccessible, Elinor thinks. *It's so pompous.*

"Coffee anyone?" Sharon the hostess asks.

"Love some," Doreen says. "I am exhausted. These brownies are soooooo good." She turns to Sharon. "Where'd you get the recipe?"

"From Matty's class cookbook. They did it as a fund-raiser. It was such a cute idea. The teacher got each mom to contribute a recipe and the kids made illustrations for them and wrote a sentence about what they liked and then they had it copied and bound at Kinko's and they sold them. They raised like nine hundred bucks!"

"Did you try the oatmeal raisin? Yum." Elinor swallows a chunk of cookie, trying to push aside her grumpiness.

"Well, I can't bake *anything*, because my kitchen's being remodeled," Doreen says with exhaustion, as though this is a horrific imposition. "Does Matty have Mrs. Matson this year?" she asks Cathy.

"Oh, my gosh. Taylor *loved* her," Sharon chimes in.

"Just listen to how mad Dido is!" Fran says to Elinor. She reads from her book. "'If divine justice counts for anything, I hope and pray that on some grinding reef midway at sea you'll drink your punishment . . .'"

"She is definitely going to slash his tires," Elinor agrees.

"Oh, my gosh, you are such a nut," Cathy says to Elinor with affection.

Elinor turns to Fran, the only one who seems interested in actually discussing the book. "But you know, I think Aeneas chooses to have no free will. He *knows* what's right but he won't do it because he's pussy-whipped by the gods." She wishes she hadn't said this so resentfully.

"Okaaaaaay," Janice says.

Kat laughs at Elinor's interpretation — a hyena chuckle that is too loud and too late. Janice scowls. The others clear their throats and look to each other uncomfortably. They seem to sense that this is really about Elinor's marriage.

It's a warm evening, and Elinor imagines diving out the open living room window to escape. No one gets her. Doesn't anyone get her? Why should they? She's a barren, bitter, self-pitying grouch. And she hates this book club. She smiles and loosens the grip on the stem of her wineglass, afraid she might snap it in half.

Cathy and Doreen sit on either side of Elinor and Kat, leaning over them as they return to their chatter about their children's teachers and after-school activities.

Kat flips through her book, reading the little notes she's written in the margins. Earlier, Elinor balked when she saw that Kat had written in her book. "Why not?" Kat argued. "It's *my* book. I like to look back at my impressions." Good point, Elinor decided. She started writing in her book, too. This is what she likes about being forty. You stop sweating the little stuff. Maybe because the big stuff threatens to crush you.

"Kat, does Jason have Bill Swanson as his soccer coach?" Doreen asks.

Kat looks up, smiling mildly.

"Elinor," Cathy says, lowering her voice and leaning close. "Here we are going on and on about kids. I'm so sorry you miscarried."

"Thank you. It's been hard. Thanks." Elinor nods, willing back tears. She wishes now that she hadn't told every neighbor and checkout clerk that she was pregnant. But she and Ted saw the heartbeat, *twice*. Dr. Weston had asked them to bring back the baby for a visit.

"You know," Doreen says, "I think everything happens for a reason."

Elinor empties her wineglass and puts it on the coffee table. "Thanks, but I don't. I don't think everything happens for a reason. I don't think the Holocaust happened for a reason. I don't think Joanna Fried found a lump in her breast for a reason." Joanna is their mutual neighbor. She's too sick from her chemo to come to today's meeting. Who came up with this simplistic catchall silver lining? And its twin: *If it didn't happen, it wasn't meant to be!*

Elinor smiles at Doreen. "Thanks, though," she repeats. She slides off her chair, quietly retrieving her jacket and purse from the corner.

She tiptoes toward the front door, leaning into the kitchen to thank Sharon on her way out. "I'm not feeling well. Everything was great, though."

"Oh, I'm sorry —"

"Migraine." Elinor hears Kat's voice from behind her.

Elinor darts for the door. Kat hurries behind her. They stumble onto the porch, quietly pulling the door shut after them.

"Okay, sorry." Kat loops her arm through Elinor's. "Bad idea. I think my book-club days are numbered."

"I shouldn't have been such a crank."

"We'll start our own two-person book club," Kat says.

As they make their way down the front walk, there's a snapping sound followed by the sharp spray of a sprinkler head shooting up and drenching their pants. Kat shrieks with laughter, tugging Elinor down the sidewalk.

302

"Where to?" Elinor asks, trying to catch up.

"Ray and Eddie's? Game of pool?"

Elinor runs faster. "Yes! Game of pool." If she were Dido, that's what she would have done when Aeneas left town: gone to the bar for a pitcher of beer and a game of pool.

It seems that almost every day now, Elinor has to add something to her things-to-avoid list. Her latest nemesis is the "Baby Back Ribs" jingle from Chili's restaurant — a relentless ditty that goes: "I want my *baby back, baby back, baby back!* I want my *baby back, baby back, baby back!*" A chorus of voices joins the a cappella doo-wop frenzy, sending Elinor diving to shut it off the radio or TV. Apparently Chili's has carved out a big budget for the ad, which plays constantly. And no matter how quickly Elinor axes the song, it burrows into her psyche like a splinter under her fingernail.

One morning she's in the shower when the ad comes on her bathroom radio. She leaps over the edge of the tub, sloshing soap and water, and frantically presses the POWER button on her boom box, but the electronic keypad is shot. You press VOLUME and the stations change, and you press POWER and nothing happens.

"I waaaaaaaaant my *baby — back . . .*"

"*Shut up!*" Elinor can't pull the plug from the wall, since she's wet, so she hammers at the POWER button with her clog. The CD compartment pops open, and the CD inside cracks in half. She's huddled over the mess, dripping and cursing, when she sees Ted's bare

303

foot in the doorway. She peers up at him. He's holding out a towel for her.

"What's wrong?" he asks.

"Off," she begs, pointing and backing away.

He pushes the buttons, then yanks the plug from the wall.

"It's that damn *baby-back-rib* ad." Elinor clutches the towel to her chest and points at the radio.

"The what?"

How could Ted *not* know this song? Why isn't the world crashing down around him, too? "The rib ad. You know, *I want my baby back . . .*" Elinor looks at Ted. He seems so calm. The circles under his eyes are gone. He can sleep again.

"Oh! Well, this thing's a piece of junk." Ted jams the boom box on top of the trash can, as if to show it who's boss. "Let's get you a new one."

"Okay. Thanks." Elinor dresses, towels off her hair, and smears on some lipstick. She remembers that her sweater is in the dryer and pads to the back of the house, pulled by the warm allure of the laundry room. The load of clothes is still tumbling. She stands and listens to the *click-click* of buttons and snaps. She imagines Ted's jeans tossing with hers, their pant legs intertwined. She imagines their strings of DNA tangled into one little person pulling at the suede fringe on a pair of cowboy overalls. The heat emanating from the dryer is like a heating pad for her lingering cramps. She moves closer, folding herself over it, pressing her belly to the front and her chest and cheek to the top. She clutches the sides as though giving it a hug.

People think you only need to separate laundry by color. But it's good to separate it by texture, too — by the heaviness of the fabrics. You don't want to mix towels with T-shirts. The towels end up soggy, while the T-shirts shrink. Meanwhile, you've wasted energy.

Heat soothes Elinor's abdomen. She squeezes the dryer, pleased by its solidness.

"El, you okay?" Ted asks with concern.

Elinor lifts her cheek from the dryer, sets it back down. "It's warm," she says.

"Oh." Understanding and relief fill Ted's voice. Elinor's surprised when his waist presses against the small of her back, his crotch against her bottom. He bends so that his chest covers her back and his arms and hands hang over hers. Turning his head the other way, he rests his cheek on her ear. Elinor tenses at first, thinking she'll feel crushed. But Ted is careful with his weight. She feels draped by his body, even warmer, safer, consoled. Do they really need the rest of this big house? Couldn't they just live in the laundry room from now on? Hunker down with the Bold and Cheer? It takes Elinor a moment to realize that the tears on her cheeks aren't hers.

CHAPTER
SEVENTEEN

Gina's at work when she gets a call from the school principal, who wants her to meet with him and Toby.

"I can come Tuesday or Thursday morning," she says, pulling her appointment book from behind the fitness counter.

"I'm afraid I need you to come in right now, Ms. Ellison," the principal says. "There's been an incident and Toby is in the office with me. He's been here three times already this week."

"An incident? Three times?" Gina's stomach tightens. She hopes Toby hasn't hurt anyone or himself. Maybe he's damaged property — something expensive she won't be able to pay for.

The *incident*, Gina learns when she gets to the school, is really just a prank. Toby sneaked through the nurse's office, into the teachers' lounge, and into the women's restroom, where he put ketchup packets under the toilet seats. Mrs. Fritz's linen skirt was completely stained with ketchup.

"You have to stick them *right* under those two rubber things at the front of the seat," Toby explains, bouncing in his seat, "or it won't work!"

The principal glares at Toby incredulously.

Gina sighs, relieved that no one has been hurt. Of course, this is *not* the reaction the principal is looking for.

"Toby!" she scolds. "I'm sorry," she tells the principal. "I'm just relieved that no one was injured."

"*Yet*," the principal says. Gina suspects that he's a bit misplaced, this principal. Maybe he should be in the army. She was in the middle of a session when she left the gym, leaving a client to do most of her workout on her own. Something tells Gina that if she were a man, the principal wouldn't have insisted she leave work immediately.

"Please give Mrs. Fritz my apologies. Certainly I, we, *Toby* will pay for her dry-cleaning bill."

"That would be appropriate." The principal looks at Toby. "Clearly, there's been no discipline at home, Ms. Ellison."

"That's not true —"

The principal isn't interested in what Gina has to say. "Now, Toby," he says. "What do *you* think we should do about your behavior?"

"Kick me out of school." Toby looks at the floor.

"Is that what you're aiming for?" the principal asks.

Toby shrugs.

"Why don't we have you visit with the school psychologist, Dr. Chambers? He's a nice man."

Gina coughs. She had to go to her school psychologist once, after Tina Taylor cut off Gina's ponytail during art class. The boys called Tina "Tiny Titty Tina Taylor," so she in turn was mean to girls in the class. Her mean streak culminated the day she cut off Gina's hair. After that, Tina was sent to a sort of reform school. Gina was traumatized by the event — by the loss of her hair and the humiliation of crying in front of the entire class. Other than root beer Dum-Dums, the psychologist had little to offer. She couldn't replace Gina's hair, just as Dr. Chambers can't make Toby's father call more often. Toby looks at Gina and rolls his eyes. Gina wrinkles her nose, suppressing a smile. For a moment, they are in something together.

In the car on the way home, Gina is at a loss for what to say to her son. Lectures, pep talks. She's tried it all. "Toby, I'm tired of trying to make you happy and convince you to be good," she says, looking across the seat at him. He's twisted away from her, looking out the passenger's window. She has the urge to hug him, to squeeze his small chest and rub his sharp shoulder blades. "What do you want? Do you even know what you want?"

Toby nods. "To go and live with Dr. and Mrs. Mackey and their new baby."

Gina slams on the brakes when the traffic in front of them suddenly slows. She hasn't been keeping her eye on the road. Toby's backpack thumps to the floor in the back. *Funny*, she thinks, gripping the steering wheel, *me, too. You think we should start a commune? I don't even hate Ted's wife. I want to, but when I met her she was funny and nice.* The traffic speeds up. Gina keeps a safe distance from the Land Rover ahead of them.

308

"Toby, let me tell you something. For the rest of your life, you're going to want things you can't have. This will make you very unhappy. It may seem to you that the solution is to do everything you can to *get* those things. But the real solution is to figure out how to want the things you *do* have. I know that sounds corny. But you must do this. You don't have to want or like *all* the things you have, but at least some of them. Do you know what I mean?"

Toby makes that disapproving clucking sound.

"Well, just think about that."

Heavy sigh.

"Because you have some homework to do for *me*. I'm handing out an assignment." Gina pokes herself in the chest so firmly it hurts a little.

"Oh, *great*."

"That's right. It's going on your chore list along with taking out the trash and you'll need to do it to get your allowance." Earlier, Gina considered making Toby's room part of the deal for him to get his allowance, but she worried he might not clean up the room *or* take out the garbage and he'd forfeit the allowance, which he didn't seem to spend anyway. He had all the books and games he wanted for now, thanks to his father and Ted. Besides, he doesn't really lust after material things. People are what he really wants. She and her son have that much in common.

"All you have to do is make a list of three things you want," she continues. "One of the things can cost money. The other two can't. After you make your list, we're going to look at it together and we're going to talk about whether those are things you can have or we can make happen for you. If they're not, we're going to think of the next best thing."

There is a long silence. The woman who's driving the Land Rover ahead of them looks in her rearview mirror and laughs, talking to a child in a car seat behind her.

"Like if you wanted french fries, but there weren't any on the menu, so you'd have potato chips," Toby finally says.

Gina's relieved by this shift in his attitude. "Exactly. It might not seem easy . . . but after we do that —"

"Oh, brother."

"Just listen for a minute. We are *going* to New York City to the Metropolitan Museum and you're going to see the armor. Trust me: When you see it, you're going to put it on the list of things you want. You're going to wish you were a billionaire and you lived in a house with a suit of armor in the front hall, like Mick Jagger or somebody. The good news is that as long as you live, the exhibit will be there and you can always go and see it. So, in a way, it's yours. It's for everybody to enjoy."

Toby's posture straightens with enthusiasm. "Can I miss school to go to New York City?"

"Yes. Two days. I'll get your homework from your teacher and you'll miss two days of school and I'll miss two days of work. We'll take a four-day weekend. If you don't have fun, you'll get a full refund."

Toby frowns out the car window.

"That was a joke," Gina tells him.

"Yeah, it was so funny I forgot to laugh."

"And —"

310

"Did you drink a lot of coffee today or something?"

"For your next essay for school you're going to write about chivalry. I looked at your knight book while I was trying to clean up your room, and there's a lot of stuff in there about chivalry. It's not just about axes and swords, you know. Knights were fierce fighters, but they were also courteous and civil and they *always* practiced courtly manners toward women, particularly their mothers."

"What's courtly?"

Gina isn't sure, exactly. "Ah," she says. "That is for you to find out. You're going to write a report on chivalry and try to be more chivalrous, like a true knight."

Toby keeps his head turned away from her as he studies the passing scenery. The sun flickers through the sun roof, illuminating his matted curls. "I might be a knight for Halloween," he says, more to himself than to Gina.

Gina's counting out her client Suzanne's lunges with the medicine ball when she gets another phone call at work. She hopes it isn't the principal again.

"Ten more on each side," she tells her client, stepping away to the back office.

"Is this Gina?" The caller sounds like Shane doing an impression of a sober, polite person.

"Shane?"

"No. My name is Roger. I'm calling in reference to your son needing a tutor?"

"Oh!" Gina fumbles and retrieves her purse from her cubby and finds her list of questions. *Student? What year at the college? Math major? Hours available?* Gina thinks, *Child molester? Thief?* She should have called the learning center she saw advertised on TV, with its special after-school facility. But Brenda at work said those places charge too much and Ted seemed to think a sign at the community college would be a good idea. But what does he know? He doesn't have children!

Gina asks Roger her list of questions and as many others as she can think of. She learns that he's not a student at all, but a graduate of an arts college with a degree in photography. He was a math minor.

"I took a lot of math classes because they're easy for me, and they help with photography," Roger explains. "But maybe you'd rather wait and get a real math major. That's cool." He sounds young, yet smart and friendly. Maybe someone Toby would look up to. A serious math student might not relate to Toby's offbeat humor.

Roger agrees to meet Gina for an interview at the coffee cart outside the movie theater at the mall. Gina has already scoped out the area. It's easy to find, and in a wide-open public area, yet it's fairly quiet in the afternoons, after the lunch rush and before the movie rush.

"Great," Gina says. "See you Thursday, then, at two."

"I think I found a potential new math tutor for you," Gina tells Toby that night over a supper of organic macaroni and cheese. "He sounds really nice."

"I don't want another tutor."

"I know."

"So I'm not going to meet him. Or her. Or whoever!"

"No, I am. His name is Roger. He's a photographer."

"Is he coming here?"

"No, I'm going to meet him on Thursday at two o'clock, while you're at school. At the mall by the new theaters. He sounds like a really nice guy, Toby. A younger fellow. We'll see. I need to talk to him first."

"Right, like *you're* going to ask him questions about math. You're probably going to *date* him."

Gina ignores Toby's jab. "You're going to ask him the math questions. I'm going to find out if he's sure he wants to work with the world's crankiest ten-year-old."

As Gina approaches Toby's room later that evening — tiptoeing by to see if he's started his homework — she hears him talking to someone. She pauses in the hallway.

"You should beat it, jackass. My mom *has* a boyfriend. She has three boyfriends."

Barefoot and light on her feet, Gina moves closer to the door.

"Yeah. Barry, Dr. Mackey, and this new guy, Roger."

What on earth? Who is he talking to? She peeks into the room and sees that Toby is bent over his desk, conversing through his window to someone on the front porch. She ducks back and tiptoes to the front door to look through the peephole. Shane! He stands at the edge of the porch on crutches leaning over the jasmine toward Toby's window. His right leg curls up

313

behind him in a cast. When Gina called the hospital after Shane jumped off the roof, she wasn't able to get any information. Patient privacy, the nurse said. They told Gina she should come down and see Shane to find out how he was doing. She certainly wasn't going to do that. Two days later, she read the police report in the paper and learned that Shane was treated and eventually released. *Altercation on Lone Pine Lane*. It sounded to Gina like the name of a bad movie. *No charges pressed. Thirty-five-year-old male. Satisfactory condition*. She decided to go down to the police station and file that restraining order.

Now Gina grabs the phone from the kitchen and returns to Toby's doorway.

"*And* she's getting married," Toby continues defiantly.

"Married?" Instead of anger, Gina hears disbelief in Shane's voice. Sadness and remorse. Gina closes her eyes.

"Yeah, to Dr. Mackey."

"*Toby!*" she hisses, trying to whisper. She doesn't want Shane to know she's home. Then she'll have to call the cops and there will be another *altercation*. She doesn't want her address to appear in the police beat in the newspaper more than once, thank you. With any luck, Toby's heckling will drive Shane away.

"Who the hell is Dr. Mackey?" Shane's voice gets louder. He's been drinking.

Gina squeezes the telephone.

"He's a doctor, that's all," Toby says.

"Cool." Shane seems to be struggling to keep calm.

314

"Yeah, so she's going to have to break it to these other guys that she's marrying Dr. Mackey. But this Roger guy, he might give her a ring, too, and I don't know *what* she's gonna do then. He asked her out to the mall on Thursday and I'll bet you anything he's going to propose."

"That's cool. I'm cool with that. Which mall, bro?"

"Oakmont at two o'clock —"

Gina leaps into Toby's room, stumbling when she steps on a pencil. She tackles Toby, grabbing him around his small waist and pulling him to the floor.

"I told you I don't want another tutor," he whispers into her face.

"Point taken," Gina whispers back. "*What* is the matter with you?" The bottom of her foot burns from the pencil point. She checks to make sure the skin isn't broken.

Toby rolls out of her grasp and lies on the floor on his back, his arms and legs outstretched. "What's the matter with *you*?"

Gina waits for Shane to yell or pound on the door or God knows what. She'll have to call the police. But then she hears Shane scrabble off the porch and the *squish-slap* of his crutches, then his sneaker hitting the walkway to the street. The sound fades and then a car door clicks shut and an engine turns over. Thank God: A cab or friend or someone is taking him away.

CHAPTER
EIGHTEEN

I'm really outside the Zone now, Ted thinks as he wolfs down biscuits with butter and honey at Kentucky Fried Chicken on his lunch hour. He's come here two days in a row, skipping the chicken and coleslaw and just ordering biscuits — three of them and a carton of milk lined up on his little red plastic tray. Lately he craves carbohydrates: bagels and Frosted Flakes and Eskimo Pies. Certainly not flax. And not alcohol, thankfully. While he enjoys a nice Cabernet, he's never been one to take comfort in booze. Instead he gets up in the middle of the night to eat cereal. He stands in the kitchen, which is dark except for the yellow glow of a night-light, and eats Cheerios with bananas and sugar. As he imagines folic acid and vitamin B_{12} seeping into his bloodstream, serotonin returning to his brain, he feels calm.

Now he splits and butters the second biscuit. It seems that he and Elinor are broken in a new way, with Elinor experiencing yet another variety of pain he can't alleviate. Instead of collapsing on the floor at the OB's office, he wishes he'd stood beside Elinor and held her hand. He's a doctor, for chrissakes. He should be able to handle a poor prognosis. But there isn't a whole lot of bad news in podiatry: ingrown toenails, a foot fungus, maybe a neuroma or hammertoes. The worst-case scenario is having to amputate a diabetic's toe or toes. Nothing like the loss of a baby.

That's why he chose podiatry. It seemed to have high odds for helping patients, with low odds for losing them. He didn't know how oncologists did it, frankly. He'd freak if he lost a patient. Both Elinor and Gina tell him he's sensitive. A nice way of saying *wimp*. If he were really sensitive, he never would have had an affair and hurt his wife.

Ted licks the insides of the last honey wrapper, not caring if anyone sees this slovenly act. He's packing on the weight that Gina helped him lose. Eating to stave off the intense urge to crawl into her bed. This morning in line at the coffee shop, he found himself daydreaming about her. He recalled waking up in Gina's room at five in the morning, the alarm on his cell phone chirping, her body curled in a fetal position, her butt pushed up and back against Ted's waist, her long hair fanned across the pillow and sometimes in his face. He'd sit up and peek through the curtains by her bed at the predawn navy sky, still flecked with stars. Then he would lean over to watch Gina sleep. She always looked so peaceful; her brow never furrowed from troublesome dreams. He breathed in her China Rain perfume, remembering the day he learned the name of the stuff. He was in her bathroom after they'd had a glass of wine but before they'd made love and he was rifling through the little shelf hanging on the wall, looking for the bottle. He had to see and touch the container, to know what it was *called*. "What are you *doing* in there?" Gina had giggled outside the door. Ted let her in and confessed: He had to know about her perfume. She laughed and showed him the bottle, a little glass tube with a tiny roller ball, like deodorant, that she rubbed behind her ears and between her breasts and onto her wrists. In the mornings as he watched Gina sleep, he'd breathe in that sweet earthy smell. Finally, before getting up, he'd brush aside her hair and kiss her cheek and temple — two gentle kisses that felt like something he did for good luck, like throwing coins into a fountain.

At work, Ted starts making mistakes. Nothing major, but it isn't like him. He forgets to phone in prescriptions, addresses an elderly gentleman as *Mrs. Dawson*. He shows up at the office one morning when he's supposed to be at the hospital scrubbing up for surgery. As he's whistling and shaking off his umbrella, the out-of-breath receptionist reports that his patient has been waiting in pre-op for forty-five minutes.

"Need some time off?" his partner Larry asks hopefully.

"Maybe," Ted replies. "Think I should take Elinor somewhere nice?"

"Yeah. Go to Venice! It's so romantic. You have to go before it sinks!" The urgency in Larry's voice startles Ted, as though the water is rising right there in the office.

On his way home that night, Ted buys a travel book on Venice. He has it gift-wrapped, then picks up two steaks, potatoes, sugar snap peas, and bouquet of yellow roses. At home, he fixes Elinor dinner and puts the flowers and the book by her place setting.

Elinor unwraps the book, smoothing her hands over the cover, obviously trying to muster enthusiasm. "Oh, Venice, wow."

"Let's go," Ted says. "That's supposed to be the good part about not having kids. We get to travel."

Elinor looks shyly at her plate. "Maybe we should save the money for a trip to a country where we can *adopt* a baby."

"Oh. Okay." Ted sets down his fork and knife. "Maybe."

"You know," she continues, "most complications are with domestic adoptions — when the birth mothers can legally change their minds. Maybe we just need to choose a foreign country."

Most likely this would be a country with generations of people who have suffered from malnutrition and received poor medical care, Ted thinks. He doesn't want to dampen Elinor's spirits, but he's not ready to transfer from the infertility treatment roller coaster to the international adoption roller coaster. He wants to stay on the ground for a while. But Elinor has already started clipping and collecting articles on adoption in a manila folder. Her manila folders make him nervous. They're a sign that she wants to embark on something big.

"It won't be a *real* vacation if we go to research adoption," he argues. "It won't be much of a break."

Elinor cuts a chunk of potato. "I don't really want to take any more breaks," she says softly. "I never feel like I'm getting anywhere when I'm taking a break."

"Okay." Ted tries to sound cheerful. "Let's talk about it, okay?"

"Okay." Elinor pats the book. "This is sweet. Thanks for the book." She doesn't seem to want to argue, either. In the past few days, they've gone out of their way to be kind to each other. Yet somehow they seem to be drifting apart, all the while maintaining a politeness you'd bestow on a co-worker or houseguest.

"You're welcome," Ted says. He has lost his appetite for the dinner.

G ELLISON, the caller ID says. Ted lurches across the desk in his study to grab the phone, afraid Elinor might pick it up.

"Um, hi," Toby's nasally voice croaks.

"Toby!" Ted feels a twinge of disappointment that it's not Gina, followed by a rush of guilt. He grinds his knuckles into his desk, the pain clearing his head. "You can't call —"

"My new tutor wondered if he could meet you and talk about my math."

"You know I can't do that. You can tell him what you're working on."

"See, I *know*, but he wants to talk to you. He said he can help me better if he talks to you."

"Toby, I'm sorry, but Mrs. Mackey and I are going through a very difficult time right now and I can't cause her any additional stress."

320

"How does my math cause her stress?"

Ted hears the whine of the vacuum cleaner hitting the wood floors downstairs as Elinor moves through the house, cleaning. Carpet, then wood floor, then carpet again. Since she's been feeling better, she's been doing housework daily, even though they have that weird photographer kid coming in every other week to clean.

"Toby, your mother and I were dating and now we're not." The vacuum stops and Ted quickly lowers his voice. "So I can't be involved with you guys. I'm sorry. I know it's hard when kids get caught in the middle of stuff like this." Ted looks at the stack of medical journals on his desk. He'd been trying to read an article called "The Anti-Inflammatory Debate," but he couldn't concentrate.

"No, you don't. You don't know. That's what everybody says. But what matters most is what makes *grown-ups* feel better. They get to decide everything. Like where I live, and who might be my stepdad. How come *I* don't get to decide anything?"

"Toby, I know your mother includes you in her decisions. She can't influence your father's decisions, unfortunately, buddy. It's a bum rap. I'm not going to tell you otherwise." Ted remains standing, his way of not committing to a lengthy talk. Toby has an unnerving knack for drawing you into a conversation and holding you there. "What are you working on in math now, sport?"

"We're computing the volume and areas of objects."

"That sounds fun." Ted gazes out his office window. It's Sunday, and a stream of dog walkers and runners and families parades down the street. The days are getting shorter. The weak, watery light depresses him.

"I'm flunking!" Toby snaps. Then his tone softens. "Hey, I think this tutor guy has a crush on my mom. I mean, she makes guys so crazy. She had to file a restraining order on Shane. And you know that guy Barry keeps buying her jewelry. He got her a really fancy diamond ring."

Ted feels a spark of jealousy as he imagines Barry presenting Gina with a ring in a velvet box. He's alarmed by the realization that perhaps Toby *knows* that jealousy is a weakness of Ted's. Maybe he knows that Ted's weakness is jealousy and Gina's weakness is a big heart and each of them has a lingering weakness for the other. Maybe Toby is smarter than any of them, even though he's only ten years old. Ted collapses into his chair. This kid should respect people's privacy, damn it.

"Well, you know your mom's a great lady and she's going to find somebody wonderful who you'll really like."

"Yeah, Barry got me tickets to see the White Stripes. Hey, you want to go with me?"

Ted laughs. "Toby, even if I could go with you, I don't even know who the White Stripes are."

"Me neither. Kids in my class like them. Barry said I could invite someone from my class. I want to ask this girl, Melanie? But I don't think she knows who the White Stripes are, either. She plays the violin."

"Well, that's good, buddy. Maybe you could invite her to something else."

"Yeah. I'm going to marry somebody totally smart. Not a dumb girl, like my mom."

Ted lowers his voice again. "Toby, listen to me, your mother is not dumb. And you're not being nice to her or giving her a fair shake. She's doing everything she can for you. I'll bet you can think of five nice things she did for you this week alone right off the top of your head."

"Like blowing my room to pieces with a leaf blower?"

"What?"

"Yeah, her new way of clean —"

Ted stands. He's getting sucked down by Toby's undertow again. "Toby, I have to go."

"Okay. Are you going shopping for your baby?"

The question makes Ted stop breathing until he's dizzy. He inhales deeply, smelling artificial pine in the cleaner Elinor's using. He slumps in his chair again. "Mrs. Mackey and I aren't going to have a baby after all, Toby, I'm sad to say."

"What do you mean?"

"She had a miscarriage."

"A what?"

"We lost the baby."

"Where?"

"Well, at the doctor's office, sort of. We found out that the baby was no longer alive."

"Oh." The enthusiasm drains out of Toby's voice. "You mean the baby died *inside* of Mrs. Mackey? How come?"

"Well, sport. We don't know. Sometimes nature takes a different course. Like when you plant tomatoes or flowers, not all of them make it, right? Usually this happens with a baby because something wasn't right to begin with. Something chromosomal. So it's kind of a blessing." Ted hasn't really been able to convince himself of this.

"What *are* chromosomes, anyways?"

"They're a string of genes inside the nucleus of a cell. They're very small. You can't even see them without a microscope. And Mrs. Mackey is very sad. We have to be considerate of her, which is why I have to ask you not to call anymore."

"Okay." Toby sniffles.

"Toby, you're a great kid. You know all about history, and you make people laugh. Everything is going to work out for you. You can't see that now, but I really believe things will." Ted wishes he could help make things work out for Toby. He feels guilty that he wishes he hadn't lost this opportunity.

"Yeah, that's what my mom says. Like, *You can't do anything you want to, but everything will work out!* You guys need to believe that so *you* feel better."

"Tobe, I have to go now, okay? Be nice to your mother. And invite that violinist to the movies."

Ted hears the click of the telephone on the other end. He looks back out the window. A young couple pull a child in a red wagon down the sidewalk. Their heads are bowed as they discuss something. The kid — a boy or a girl, Ted can't tell which — throws bits of food from a Baggie out behind the wagon, shrieking with glee. Suddenly Ted understands why Elinor retreated to the laundry room. Not that it wasn't understandable before — the need to hide in a warm, dark place. But for the first time he experiences pain at seeing a couple with a child. He was going to be a *father*. He focuses on the window, instead of the street. He notices that the muntins between the two thick panes of weatherproof glass are made of aluminum. They're expensive windows, designed to keep out cold and rain and burglars. Yet Ted wishes he lived in an old house with windows that had real panes and muntins. He wonders if he and Elinor should move. Get away from this place.

Elinor takes a long sip from her cup of Darjeeling, closing her eyes and savoring the warmth and sweet honey. She slides a basket full of folded laundry off the kitchen counter and balances it on her hip on the way to the bedroom.

As she passes Ted's study, she sees him standing at his desk holding up the phone, staring into space. He turns to her. He looks stunned, as though he just received bad news. Maybe the doctor called with the results of the pathology report. But what could be worse than *you've lost the baby*?

"What?"

"Nothing." Ted puts the phone back on its charger and smooths over his khakis with his palms.

"Who called?" She shifts the laundry basket to her other hip.

"Toby." He rubs his face. "Sorry. I think this time I convinced him not to call again."

Elinor drops the basket on the floor and leans in the doorway. "He still wants to babysit?" She's irritated, yet touched by Toby's attachment to Ted.

"Nah. I told him we lost the baby."

It's comforting to hear Ted say *we*. The late-afternoon sun filtering through the window makes his hair shine like mahogany. He takes after his father in that he doesn't have a single gray hair yet. Elinor married a man who has aged beautifully. How lucky. No matter how tired or despondent he is, no matter how mad she might be at him, Ted is always handsome to Elinor. Yet her love for him seems altered somehow. It's more like the love she feels for Kat, and for her mother. Maybe this is how marriage is supposed to be — how it evolves. She wishes she were certain about this.

Ted rubs the back of his neck and studies the floor. Elinor should cook for him. Filet mignon, maybe. She should take cooking lessons. It would be much smarter to focus on food than laundry.

"Toby wants me to meet his new tutor to talk about his math." Ted looks out the window. "I told him I couldn't."

What difference would it make at this point? Elinor wonders. She can't shake the feeling that she's already lost everything there is to lose. Every morning when she wakes up, she tells herself *no*, this isn't so: They could lose their house; Ted could lose his practice (patients sue sometimes!); one of them could have cancer.

Thoughts of these dire scenarios propel her out of bed, fueled by a manic gratefulness that deteriorates into sadness as the day wears on. "You know what?" Elinor hugs her waist, bracing herself for what she's about to propose.

Ted looks at her.

"Go. Meet the tutor. See the kid. One time won't hurt. Talk about math with the tutor and take Toby out for an ice cream cone."

"I don't know," Ted says. "It's a slippery slope."

A slippery slope careening into what? Toby's heart or Gina's bed? Elinor shrugs. "He's going to keep calling here."

"We could get an unlisted number."

Elinor shakes her head. "Something tells me you really make a difference in this kid's life. I mean, our hearts are broken, but maybe we don't have to break his heart, too."

Ted rubs his eyes. "He'll be okay."

Elinor knows Ted won't call Toby. But she also knows that he wants to. Toby must seem to Ted like the only thing that he might be able to fix right now. She doesn't want to be the one to take this away from him. She crosses the room, grabs the phone from Ted's desk, and punches *69. Her pulse speeds up as she realizes she may be calling her husband's ex-lover's house. Then she thrusts the phone at Ted and steps out of the room, leaving the laundry behind. "Just promise to tell me if you're fucking her," she calls out over her shoulder. The words shock her as they echo in the hallway. Really, it's all she wants to know. She pivots in her stocking feet and turns back to Ted's office. Standing just outside the door, she listens.

"You sure I shouldn't call this fella?" Ted asks. "The *mall*? Okay." She can hear Ted writing on one of the little drug company pads from his desk. "By the movies. Okay. Okay. His name's Stan? Got it. Tell him I'll be there."

Elinor hurries down the hall toward the kitchen. She's going to make a real dinner tonight for her husband. Chicken cordon bleu and steamed asparagus with hollandaise. It's pretty easy. Kat showed her how once — pounding out chicken breasts between waxed paper with a rolling pin, then layering on ham and cheese and rolling it all up. She remembers how. You just have to wrap up the pieces tightly.

In the marriage counselor's office, Ted squeezes Elinor's hand in his. While he's known his wife for five years, he's still astonished by how small her fingers are — like a child's.

"An important part of recovering from the loss of your baby is to allow yourself time to mourn," Dr. Brewster says. "It doesn't happen overnight."

They both nod. *Tell me something I don't know*, Ted thinks.

"Right now it may feel as though all hope is lost," Dr. Brewster continues. "But once you've allowed yourself time to grieve, I'd like for us to discuss other options you have."

"Right," Elinor says wearily. "Adoption. Donor eggs. Stealing a baby from the mall."

328

Dr. Brewster smiles. "And the concept of living child-*free* versus child*less*," she adds.

"Yeah, I don't love that term," Elinor says. "It sounds like living money-free or food-free or air-free. I just don't feel so free."

Ted's not big on pop psychology, but he finds the turn of phrase positive. A sort of resolution that allows you to move forward. When they first decided to take a break from in vitro, he bought a book called *Sweet Grapes: How to Stop Being Infertile and Start Living Again*. He thought he could read a few pages to Elinor each night before bed. But the book just made her cry.

Ted's surprised when Elinor stands and begins to speak to Dr. Brewster firmly, as though she's trying a case in court. "I want *grandchildren*. Do you understand that? It's not about having a *baby*, it's about having a *family*."

"Absolutely," Dr. Brewster concurs. "Let's discuss this in future weeks."

Future weeks. The words sound like a prison sentence to Ted. Why are he and Elinor in a hole again, and why can't he dig them out? And why isn't Elinor bringing up the fact that he's going to meet Toby's new tutor? It troubles Ted how much he's looking forward to this — to the opportunity to find out how Gina's doing. He's promised himself he won't press the guy for too much information about her.

"I'm going to meet Toby's tutor," Ted blurts. He rubs his knees, relieved by this confession.

"Toby?" Dr. Brewster looks perplexed.

329

"You missed that chapter," Elinor tells her. "Ted's ex-lover had a kid. *Has* a kid. Anyway. The boy's got a real thing for Ted. I told Ted he should go see him."

"Do you think it's healthy to maintain this relationship?" Dr. Brewster asks Ted.

"What *is* healthy," Elinor interrupts, "when you get right down to it? What, other than green tea, is healthy?"

"I asked Ted," Dr. Brewster says.

Elinor sits down, bites her lip.

Ted coughs, chooses his words carefully. "I care a lot about this boy. I want him to succeed in life. For some reason, I seem to have a positive influence on him. And I'm just going to meet his tutor for now."

"How does this make you feel?" Dr. Brewster asks Elinor.

"I don't think it's possible to feel any worse than I already do," El says. "I can't see how it'll make a difference."

Ted reaches out to rub the back of her neck. She doesn't relax at his touch.

"He's going to keep calling the house either way," Elinor adds bitterly.

"You have every right to be angry about this," Dr. Brewster says.

Elinor gets up again and paces the room. "I'm *sick* of having every right to be angry!"

Dr. Brewster slides forward, perched on the edge of her chair.

"I'm sick of having every right to be sad," Elinor continues. "I want to have every right to be happy!"

She runs a hand through her hair over and over, tugging at the cropped ends. "For the past two years everything's been a mess, and I'm always angry."

Ted grabs Elinor's hand as she passes him, giving it a squeeze and gently tugging her back into her chair. In the past, Elinor has told Ted that she thinks the marriage counselor encourages her to maintain her feelings, instead of getting over them. "My anger pays the mortgage on her house in the mountains," she complained. "Oh, now," Ted had said. "She's doing her job. We're not paying her to just sit on the sidelines." But he'd agreed. Sometimes at Dr. Brewster's office — maybe it was that slick, scooped leather chair — he had the distinct sensation of sinking or sliding backward, of their problems being insurmountable.

"And you know what?" Elinor continues now. "Maybe talking *doesn't* help. Maybe it just exacerbates the present by trapping us in the past. By constantly reminding us of all that's gone wrong, and what we could have done differently, and why we're mad at each other. Oh, yeah! I remember now why I'm mad at you!" She lowers her voice, regaining her composure. "Maybe you don't have to talk *everything* through." She looks to Dr. Brewster, then imploringly at Ted.

Ted nods in awe, reaching out to stroke her hair. She's doing that thing she used to do all the time, where she'd say *exactly* what he was thinking. Only she always had a funnier, more articulate way of vocalizing his sentiments. "What *she* said!" he'd joke.

"I'm sorry," Ted says.

"I know," Elinor says. "Me, too."

"You didn't do anything," he tells her.

"Let's not start," she replies.

"Okay," Ted agrees.

"Listen," the therapist says after another long silence. "You're right. It's not good to always feel like you're in crisis mode. You two have been through a lot. You have to give yourselves more credit for how hard you've worked and how well you're doing."

"Thank you," Elinor says. "Really, I mean it. I didn't mean to attack you personally. I think you're very good at your job." She looks at her watch. "But you know what? Our time is up."

CHAPTER
NINETEEN

The overwhelming smells of the food court at the mall remind Roger that he hasn't eaten lunch. Bombarded by the aromas of cookies and waffle cones baking, popcorn burning in fake butter, and something greasy frying on a grill, he feels hungry and nauseated at the same time. He checks the paper in the palm of his hand: *Gina Ellison, 2:00, food court*. It's two ten. So where is this lady? Jesus, he'd do anything Mrs. Mackey asked. Good thing she's not running a cult. Roger paces by the movie ticket windows, where Gina said they should meet. He didn't even know they had movies at the mall now. A nearby escalator churns up to a second level with multiplexes, and the box office is surrounded by a huge seating area of tables and chairs, circled by fast-food places offering everything from sugar to fat to caffeine.

"Roger?" He turns to see a thin woman with long hair approaching some other guy — a scraggly-looking dude wearing a woolen cap pulled over his ears and baggy pants with a chain dangling from them.

"No," the kid mumbles.

Damn, she must be glad. Roger looks like Clark Kent compared with that derelict.

"Are you Toby's mom?" he asks. She looks young for a mom. "Mrs. Ellison?"

She turns and nods, relieved. "Gina."

Roger feels more comfortable calling his clients Mr. and Mrs.

She extends a hand. Everything about her is kind of long. Long arms and long fingers and long hair that sweeps down to her waist. Guys probably dig this. But she's not really his type. He's, like, the *least* athletic person on the planet, for one thing.

She's wearing a light blue sweat suit and flip-flops with sparkles on them. The sweatshirt is short and her stomach shows. It's pretty and flat, but Roger tries not to look at it. Maybe he'll tutor the kid, but he's not going to ask her out.

"Hi." He tries to make his handshake seem businesslike — quick and firm.

Gina clutches a notebook to her chest. "Let's sit down." She surveys the rows and rows of tables.

He follows Gina to a spot by the corn dog stand and they sit beside a giant fake palm thing. Roger's curious to know if there's fake dirt in the pot. He tries to peer in and see.

Gina opens her notebook on the table and digs in her bag for a pen. She seems stressed. "My son Toby is a very bright boy, but he has trouble focusing and he really needs help with his math. We've found that a tutor has helped in the past." She tosses her hair over her shoulder and studies the notebook. If Roger were to shoot her portrait he'd ask her to hang upside down from the jungle gym bars at the playground by his house. Her hair would fall straight down, maybe grazing the tan sand below, and more of her belly would show. She'd probably laugh, and a vein in her forehead would come to the surface.

"Okay." He hoped they'd get coffee so he could at least have a scone or something to soak up the acid in his stomach.

"So." Gina looks at her notes. "You've never tutored before?" She sounds confused, verging on suspicious.

"No, but it's something I want to start doing." Why the hell is he saying this? Why isn't he home working on his portfolio and grad school application essay? He *did* student-teach elementary school art in college, and considered being a teacher. He liked the kids, but you had to take so many classes to get certified and it seemed like the pay would always be junk. There were easier ways to make money while he built his portfolio.

"Oh, okay." Gina nods. "I work at a fitness club. Three afternoons a week I'd like somebody to tutor Toby. You'd meet him at the Barnes and Noble café, help him get a snack, and work with him for about an hour and a half. Then I'll pick him up. Would that be okay?" She raises her voice over the mall's din. It's weird: The place is really noisy, with people talking, lame pseudo-jazz Muzak playing, spatulas clanging on grills, ATM machines beeping, but all the noises kind of cancel each other out, making a hum in your brain. Roger could probably sleep here.

"What's he working on in math class now?" Roger asks. Who knows, maybe he could start a tutoring business. Clean houses in the mornings and tutor kids in the afternoons. That would break up the monotony of scrubbing toilets and mopping floors. His ex-girlfriend Elissa said he doesn't strive for things to happen, he waits for things to happen. So what? But now he's going to get his shit together. Start tutoring, continue cleaning, finish his portfolio, and finally apply to graduate school. Suddenly he realizes why he hasn't done this yet: What if he doesn't get in? Then what? He'll choose a few crappy programs, that's all.

". . . Fractions and long division," Gina is saying. "It's starting to get hard. All that pre-algebra stuff." She waves a hand in the air. "I was a terrible math student. It gave me ulcers."

"Don't worry," Roger tells her. "Algebra's a pain, but it's not so bad if you break it down." He feels the need to reassure Gina, who seems totally worried.

"Do you have references?" Gina asks. "I'd like to call three people."

"Okay." This is like a real job application! He can give her the number of his adviser from school and a couple of his clients. Maybe Mrs. Mackey.

"Great." Gina smiles for the first time.

She's not so bad, this lady. She seems sweet. Hopefully the kid isn't a nightmare. He's lucky to have a hot mom.

"I think my son would like to have a young, hip tutor."

People are always telling Roger he's hip. He's not sure why. He doesn't feel hip.

"When would you be able to start? If the references check out?"

336

"Soon, I guess."

Roger looks around. With its marble floors, brass railings, and towering walls, the inside of the mall feels like a temple. The Church of Capitalism. Maybe before grad school he should travel to Tibet or Bali. Hike in the Himalayas. Find himself. Except he doesn't want to find himself. He wants to find someone else. He did: Mrs. Mackey. But she's married, and now she's going to have a baby.

The cloying smell of cookies baking overpowers him. It feels like there's eggy dough stuck in the back of his throat. He gazes out at the glass case of cookies. The disks are way too big and underdone looking, like all the patrons at this mall. He gags and nearly dry-heaves, as though he's hung over. Out of the corners of his eyes he sees fuzzy white stars. Shit, is he going to pass out? He puts his head down for a minute. Maybe he's diabetic. He doesn't even have health insurance! What kind of loser doesn't have health insurance? What the hell is he *doing* with his life?

"Are you okay?" Gina stands and bends toward Roger. Some of her hair falls onto his shirt.

"Yeah. I think I just need to eat."

"Let me get you something." The maternal tone of Gina's voice soothes him. "I'll be right back."

Roger keeps his head lowered, flinching at the screech of her chair moving across the floor. He focuses on the sound of her feet — *flip-flop, flip-flop* — glad to be alone for a minute.

★　★　★

Ted hasn't been to the mall since it's been refurbished. It used to be seedy — with B-grade stores and too-dark parking lots and little to offer in the way of restaurants. Now there's a whole new wing with a giant food court and movie marquee.

Toby said to meet Stan, this tutor fellow, near the ticket counter. Ted takes a seat on a long Naugahyde booth that runs behind a row of tables. From here he can keep a lookout. It's only a little after two, but already people are lining up for the movies, buying the less expensive matinee tickets. He and Elinor should escape to a matinee for an afternoon. Or maybe for a couple of months, until after the holidays. This morning he dreamed that Elinor was waking him up with good news. "There's a baby for us," she was saying as she shook him. "Get dressed! We can go pick her up now. But we have to get there *first* or somebody else might get her!" In the dream, Ted felt a rush of excitement. He was *glad*. He had no doubt or fear. "Oh, great!" he said, waking himself up from the dream.

"What's great?" Elinor asked. She was already awake, with the covers pulled up to her chin, a cup of tea in one hand and a novel balanced on her chest. He didn't have the heart to tell her about the dream.

Ted watches people funnel through the food court, many of them young mothers pushing strollers loaded with diaper and shopping bags. Now he sees why Elinor jokes about stealing a baby from the mall. Most of the young women are heavy, with tattoos, and rolls of flesh that ooze over their low-waisted pants. He should have brought something to read. But then he couldn't keep

338

an eye out for Stan. Toby said he didn't know what Stan looked like, but the guy would be by himself, somewhere around the theaters.

Maybe Ted should look on the other side of the ticket booth. Once, he and Elinor met after work at a restaurant downtown with outdoor seating. There was a round bar with a big tropical fish tank in the center and it turned out that he was sitting at a table on one side of the bar while El sat on the other side, both of them growing irritated. Finally, Elinor strolled around and saw Ted. They laughed when they found each other. Back then, they thought a snafu in the day was funny and random, rather than another confirmation that *everything* in their lives was going wrong.

Now Ted circles to the other side of the ticket booth, systematically scanning the seating area table by table for anyone who's alone. All he sees is an elderly woman in a white raincoat working a crossword. He looks out to the horseshoe row of restaurants beyond. His heart leaps when he sees *Gina* paying for a tray of food at a Chinese joint. He's surprised by how quickly he knows it's her — *her* fan of golden-brown hair across her back, *her* perfectly round ass, *her* long, straight boy's legs. He ducks behind a planter. She glides between the tables, carrying the tray of food, which also has a carton of milk. Maybe it's lunch for Toby. But why would they be here the same time as Stan? She slides the tray onto a table and pushes it in front of a kid who's considerably older than Toby. The guy bows with appreciation, lifts a fork, and digs in. Gina sits, smiling. It makes her happy to feed people. Ted's always been charmed by that.

339

Gina finds pleasure in cooking, pleasure in sex, pleasure in loving her child, pleasure in helping people. This is what Ted loves about her. *Loves?* Yes, he still loves Gina. And right now he is hiding behind a potted palm at the mall, officially stalking her. After breaking her heart, no less. Or maybe he didn't, really. Maybe she's doing fine. She seems to be on a date right now. The guy eating the Chinese food turns to look at something and Ted gets a better view of his face. He certainly isn't Barry, the concert promoter. Yet Ted recognizes him from somewhere. The strawberry-blond hair and the goatee. It's the kid who cleans their house! What the hell? What are *these two* doing together? Where's Toby? And where's Stan? And why the hell is Gina buying the housecleaner kid lunch?

Whatever's going on, certainly Toby wouldn't have told his mom that Ted is going to meet Toby's new tutor. She wouldn't have allowed him to finagle that. Ted steps away from the leafy palm. From behind him, he hears an odd clamber of *squish-slap, squish-slap* as someone approaches. He turns to see a guy on crutches hobbling across the food court. The fellow takes long strides and big hops, his shaggy black hair bouncing above his head, his broken foot or leg dragging behind like an unwilling companion. His face is dark with anger and determination. As he passes Ted, his open flannel shirt flaps at his sides. While the mall has been refurbished, it seems that no amount of fancy marble can get rid of the shopping-center subculture of shady characters. Ted is surprised to see that this guy is making a straight line for Gina's table. Gina talks and writes in a notebook as she watches the cleaner kid eat. But as soon as she sees the character on crutches approaching, her jaw drops. She stands and pushes back her chair, balling up a napkin or something in her fist. The cleaner kid — his name is Roger, Ted remembers now — whirls around to look. He stops chewing.

Ted can't hear what Gina says to the guy on crutches. But she looks stern, shaking her head with disapproval. Crutches Guy laughs. No one else is amused. Roger's eyebrows shoot up with concern. The intruder swats Roger's leg with one crutch. Roger raises his hands in the air above his food tray as if to say *Whoa.*

It seems as though the guy has been drinking. Shane. This must be Shane, Gina's rock-star boyfriend. Of course, he's not a rock star, but from the moment Gina mentioned him Ted romanticized the fact that he played in a band for a living. Now this Shane just looks like a scary mall rat.

Roger stands, unsteady on his feet. He wipes his mouth with a napkin, tosses it on his tray, and nods at Gina, as if to say good-bye. Meanwhile Shane leans on his good leg and one crutch and swings the other crutch in the air, the arc of it crashing into Roger's chest.

"Jesus, dude!" Ted hears Roger yell. Shane hisses something. Ted doesn't catch the words, but he hears petulance. People at nearby tables freeze. Their expressions say: *Altercation. Wait and see.*

"That's enough!" Ted hears himself shout over the food court's monotonous din. Then he is charging through the rows of tables, bumping chairs and knocking drinks, propelled by an anger that seems larger than he is.

Roger spins around. "Dr. Mackey!" He looks hopeful.

"Ted?" Gina backs away from the table. She clutches her stomach and Ted knows that her stomach pains are setting in.

"It's okay," he tells her. He looks around the food court. Jesus, usually these places are crawling with cops. Where are they now? He looks at Shane squarely.

Gina shakes her head at Ted. A subtle warning: *No*.

"So *you're* the *doc-tor*," Shane says in a haughty, mocking tone. He *is* good looking in a rock-star sort of way. Startling blue eyes and a youthful face framed by shaggy black hair that shines in the light. Yet he reeks of whiskey and cigarettes.

"I'm *a* doctor. And you, my friend, are way out of line here. You need to leave these folks alone or we'll get the police over here in about ten seconds."

"My *friend*?" Shane laughs. "We don't even know each other. What do we have in common? Except that you *fucked* my girlfriend?"

"Oh, nice, Shane." Gina looks disgusted.

"I gotta go," Roger says.

"Okay, but . . ." Gina sounds disappointed. It was probably only their first date. Roger looks too young for her, anyway.

342

"Wait a second," Ted says to Roger. "We need to get the police before you leave and get this on the record."

"Nah, no problem, man." Roger looks at Ted, then Shane. "Just a misunderstanding." He holds up his hands and shuffles backward, as though afraid to turn his back on the group.

Shane takes a bounding hop toward Roger, swinging his crutch at him. When he misses, he whirls around and flails the crutch at Gina. She steps aside and it clatters to the floor. Ted lunges between them.

"Don't you *touch* her." His statement is low and guttural and comes from somewhere deep within him. He pivots to face Shane, his arms outstretched, blocking Gina.

"You're married and you fucked my girlfriend, you asshole. Now *move*."

Ted does not move. Shane jerks his arm toward him, as if to throw a punch. His hand is hidden by a curtain of flannel shirt. A burning slice of pain sears Ted's abdomen. It is small in diameter at first — a bee sting. Then the burning blossoms, as though he's been splashed with boiling water. Something is warm and sticky against his shirt. He presses a hand above his hip.

"*Knife*," he hears Roger say.

Tiles from the marble floor swim up toward Ted's hands, which are suddenly groping the air before him. As Shane moves closer, the black pupils of his marble-blue eyes dilate. Behind him the blurry image of Gina lifts a metal chair and brings it crashing down on Shane. Like in a cartoon! How did she lift it over her head? Despite her litheness, she is so strong. Ted tries

343

to take a step. A giant poster of a woman in the window at Victoria's Secret smiles down at him — red lips shimmering. Then Ted is sinking. How can he be sinking and floating at the same time? The sensation seems to defy the laws of physics and gravity. Then it's too dark to think about any of this.

A patch of bright sky overhead burns Ted's eyes as they load him into a hearse. He gurgles the word "shoes," because he feels a distinct lack of them on his feet. A person in white — an angel of some sort in a crisp uniform — speaks to him soothingly. Ted feels his lips purse, grasping for the letter *W. What?* But he knows what. He has bled to death, repeated stab wounds gutting him like a fish, but somehow failing to extract the guilty parts.

Now he's dead and they're going to bury him in a cemetery. Where's Elinor? She knows he wishes to be cremated! He wants his ashes sprinkled at the top of Mount Katahdin in Maine, where he used to hike with his father every Labor Day. They're to be sprinkled over the Knife's-Edge Trail. Ha. And Elinor says he's slow to get irony.

Ted sees a long cord running from his arm into the air above, like the string on a balloon. A face floats over him. "You're going to be all right," a voice whispers. *Gina.* He imagines his hand moving up to touch her hair but he can't lift his arm, which has been hammered into this bed or whatever it is he's lying on. Gina kisses his forehead. Warm, moist breath against his skin. Hair tickling his arm. Ted broke Gina's heart.

He betrayed his wife and broke this beautiful woman's heart. Shane was right to stab him to death. But Shane shouldn't have killed Gina, too. Now here they are — two dead lovers. Like Romeo and Juliet in the crypt. Only in that play there's no afterlife. Ted has never believed in such a thing as an afterlife but apparently there is one, because here he is. He shouldn't have been so skeptical. Someone tells Gina she has to leave. She has to get out. She can't stay in the afterlife with Ted. *Please, ma'am. Thank you.* A siren pierces the air. Of course: Ted is in an ambulance.

"Don't . . ." He pushes the word out, hoping it reaches Gina. *Don't leave me*, he wants to say. *I love you. I'm sorry. Don't leave me. Where's Elinor? Someone tell her I love her, too. And I'm sorry, too. Don't . . .*

Ted feels the lurch and speed of the ambulance. But it cannot outrun the pain, which races alongside, catching up and overtaking him. He looks up at the swinging IV cord and searches the young face of a paramedic. Where is the morphine? For some reason he can't have morphine? Maybe because he's hurt so many others. Now it's his turn.

CHAPTER
TWENTY

By the time Elinor gets to the hospital, Ted has been taken from the emergency room upstairs for an MRI. She'd been at the office when Roger called — breathless and flustered and talking too fast, The fear in his voice made Elinor's heart stop. *Gina, then this maniac out of nowhere, then Ted out of nowhere, stabbed, ambulance.* When she got to the ER, a doctor explained that Ted's stab wound was superficial — it required only a few stitches — but the blow to his head from falling is of some concern.

Now Elinor sits in a hallway in the ER, waiting for the neurologist, who will talk with her after he's read the MRI results. It worries her that a neurologist is needed. *Of some concern.* What's *that* supposed to mean? Usually she relies on Ted to interpret these vague medical explanations. To her, it's like trying to figure out the difference between a *partly cloudy* and *mostly sunny* forecast.

Roger appears from an examining room. A large Band-Aid covers one of his elbows. He looks frazzled: His eyes are bloodshot, and his reddish hair sticks up in all directions. He takes a seat beside Elinor. As he smooths his palms over his knees, his hands shake.

"How's Dr. Mackey?" he asks.

"I wish I knew. Nobody's told me anything yet. Are you okay?"

Roger touches his bandaged elbow gingerly. "Yeah. I want to leave but the cops say I have to wait until the police detective comes to interview me."

"But you didn't do anything," Elinor says.

Roger glares at her. "No kidding. To get the story about the *other* guy."

"The man who stabbed Ted? Do they know who he is?"

"Some boyfriend of Gina's. Jesus, how many boyfriends does that chick *have*?"

Not enough to keep her away from my husband, Elinor thinks. "What was Ted doing at the mall?" she asks.

Roger looks incredulous. "You know more than I do! He just showed up. First this Shane dude blows out of nowhere on crutches, then Dr. Mackey is in the middle of everything, trying to keep him away from Gina."

"Great. Ted's her knight in shining armor."

"Whatever," Roger says, irritated, rubbing the lump on his elbow. This calamity may have cured him of his crush on Elinor.

Elinor peers down the hallway. This hospital is unfamiliar to her. She wishes they were at Stage Mill General, where Ted performs his surgeries. Everyone there *knows* Ted.

Finally, a nurse emerges from the ER to tell Elinor that Ted has been admitted and she can go up to his room.

The neurologist will visit them there before too long. Roger lingers behind to make a phone call.

Elinor doesn't want to wait for the elevator, so she runs up three flights of stairs to Ted's room. He's going to be fine, she tells herself as she takes the stairs two at a time. He would be in the ICU if he were in real trouble. But when she gets to Ted's room, she freezes in the doorway. She expected to find him awake, but his eyes are closed and he's completely still. His complexion is gray, as though he's not getting enough oxygen. In fact, she can't even tell if he's *breathing*. She steadies herself on the threshold, not wanting him to sense her fear when he opens his eyes.

Elinor has never seen Ted as a patient before. He's the *doctor*. *She's* the patient. People with toe infections are the patients. *What's wrong with him?* She clutches the doorjamb and presses her lips between her teeth so she can't scream these words. She lost the baby and now she is losing Ted. Again! How can you lose a person so many times? Over and over, like a beating. Suddenly, she's glad that *she* was the one who underwent the in-vitro treatments. Before, she'd resented Ted for not having to endure any of the physical pain. But she wouldn't have been able to bear seeing him in pre-op and post-op and all the hellish scenarios in between.

"He's sedated, so he won't move too much," a nurse says, pushing past Elinor into the room.

"Oh," a voice says from *within* the room. *Gina.*

Elinor peers around the corner and sees that Gina is sitting in a chair beside Ted's bed. How did she get in here so fast? Did she go with Ted to the MRI? The fact that Elinor is the last one to arrive at the hospital seems to confirm how little influence she has over the events in her life.

"*Oh!*" Gina repeats, standing when she sees Elinor step into the room. She's wearing one of those itty-bitty sweat suits that nobody ever seems to sweat in. It's warm in the room and she's taken off the jacket and wrapped it around her waist. Her tank top shows off small, firm breasts.

"*You're* here?" Elinor says.

"The police detective asked me to wait. He wants to interview each of us individually." Gina crosses her arms around her waist and backs toward the door.

The nurse examines Ted's IV bag, then begins taking his blood pressure.

"Where *is* the police detective?" Elinor asks Gina.

"He's with . . . he's with the perpetrator . . ." She steps sideways around Elinor. "I'll be in the hall."

"No, wait," Elinor says. "I want to hear what happened." She is torn between getting the story from Gina, from *someone*, and grabbing ahold of Ted.

She moves to the side of Ted's bed and strokes the inside of his arm, alarmed by the fact that he doesn't stir. Usually when he sleeps, his lips move or his eyelids flutter. She takes his hand in hers, smoothing it over and over as though petting an animal. She realizes that all her anxiety and dread may be flowing from her body into his. She places his hand at his side and kisses his forehead, which is warm and moist. His face is expressionless, his breathing shallow. She has the urge to tuck in the loose sheets around him — to tuck him in. She clings to the metal railing of the hospital bed, feeling like a toddler with a toy. *Mine.*

Gina hovers by the door.

Her long hair is pretty, but it's too thin. You could call it stringy. Elinor's husband is lying in a hospital bed, barely conscious, and she is focusing on his lover's hair. *Ex*-lover. Elinor wishes she were the one who was unconscious.

"So?" she says to Gina.

"I was interviewing a prospective tutor for my son at the shopping center, and my ex-boyfriend, Shane, who I've filed a restraining order against, showed up and started hassling us, and then suddenly Ted was there and Shane, who'd been drinking, started to swing at Roger, then at Ted, and somehow he stabbed Ted and Ted fell."

"What was Ted *doing* there?"

"I don't know." Gina's pretty eyebrows are raised. She takes another step toward the door.

"Great. Even your *stalkers* have stalkers." No wonder Gina fell for Ted. If a homicidal maniac is her alternative.

The nurse takes Ted's pulse, scowling as she concentrates.

Elinor looks away at the panel of mysterious gadgets above Ted's bed. "First you ruin my marriage," she tells Gina, "then you nearly get my husband killed."

Gina opens her mouth to speak, then closes it. She narrows her eyes, lowers her voice, and says, "I didn't ruin your marriage. I just walked through the rubble. It was a terrible mistake. Don't think I don't realize that."

"Marriage isn't that easy, just so you know." Elinor squeezes the metal railing on the bed. It was cold at first, but now it's warm and damp in her hands. "I notice *you're* not married."

"That's not the point." Gina pushes her hair off her shoulders — a gesture that looks like she's rolling up her sleeves, ready for action.

"What *is* the point, Gina?"

"The point is" — the nurse cuts into their conversation — "this gentleman has incurred a stab wound and a potentially dangerous head injury and you ladies need to take *Days of Our Lives* out to the waiting area or I'm going to call security." The nurse is a solid barrel of a woman with a large bosom and tight ponytail revealing streaks of white scalp beneath her dark hair. She moves to Elinor's side of the bed, pushing Elinor away. As she starts a new IV bag, she clucks her tongue, as if to say, *The rubbish I have to deal with here.* "The patient can hear you, you know," she adds. "And I doubt you're making him feel better."

"This is my husband." Elinor still has one finger looped firmly around the bed's metal railing.

The nurse squints at Elinor.

Suddenly Ted turns his head away from Elinor and the nurse toward the door. His eyes flutter and open. His gaze seems to fall on Gina, who has spun around to leave the room again. While she isn't even looking at Ted, Gina seems to sense that his eyes have opened. She turns to him. Her mouth falls open.

351

"*Oh*," she says.

Elinor has never heard one syllable filled with so much tenderness and despair.

Ted's face breaks into a grin. "Hi, angel," he says. He is not speaking to Elinor or the nurse. He is speaking to Gina.

Gina's eyes well with tears. "I have to go." She steps toward the door.

Elinor clears her throat. Ted looks to her. "Oh!" He sounds surprised and relieved, as though *she* were the one who got stabbed and fell. "Hi!" he says.

"Hi. You're okay." Elinor squeezes his hand, and he squeezes back weakly.

Gina disappears out the door.

"I think so." His speech is slurred. He doesn't seem to be aware of the fact that he just joyfully greeted his mistress in front of Elinor. That he just confirmed that he is in love with Gina. It could be his head injury or the meds, but Elinor doesn't think so. She is both astonished and hurt by how happy Ted was as soon as he laid eyes on Gina. And she is surprised to find that she is not struck with anger, but instead crushed by sadness, by the truth.

The nurse leaves the room, shaking her head.

"You're okay," Elinor repeats. She might lose Ted to another woman, but not to death. Not today.

Suddenly Toby bursts into the room, dragging his mother back in with him. In the hallway behind them, Elinor sees a teenager pocketing money from Gina and giving a quick report on homework and Otter Pops. Gina thanks the girl and tries to drag Toby into the hall, but he rushes to Ted's bedside, bursting into tears when he sees the IV and the bluish circles under Ted's eyes.

"Hey, buddy," Ted says sweetly, straining to lift his head off the pillow. "I'm okay. But I couldn't find Stan." Whatever drugs they've got Ted on seem to make him believe that he can have a relaxed chat with both Elinor and Gina in the room, as though they're all just friends at a cocktail party.

"*Who* is Stan?" Gina grasps her son by the shoulders and turns him to face her.

"There is no Stan," Toby admits, kicking the hospital room floor and lowering his head to hide beneath his curls.

"No wonder I couldn't find him." Ted giggles.

"Toby!" Gina scolds. "You sent Dr. Mackey to the mall looking for some nonexistent person? What on earth?" She obviously has no control over the boy. Elinor has to admit, she probably wouldn't, either.

Toby's face reddens and his voice grows louder. "I wanted him to see you there! Dr. Mackey doesn't go to the gym anymore so you can't ever meet each other . . ."

So! Both Elinor and Toby were trying to be matchmakers.

"Dr. Mackey is seriously hurt now." Gina stares into her son's eyes.

"Yeah, thanks to your jackass boyfriend."

"He is not my — Toby! Tell Mrs. Mackey you are very, very sorry." Gina shifts her macramé purse to the other arm and turns Toby toward Elinor.

"I'm sorry." Toby looks at Elinor with genuine disappointment. His plan backfired. Elinor can't decide how she feels about this kid. He's manipulative, that's for sure. But his haplessness pulls at her heart. That hair, like bad shag carpet. And his unyielding affection for Ted. All Elinor wanted was for Roger to slip into Ted's place. But it seems that Toby and Gina don't want just *some* guy in their lives. They want Ted. It's not something you ever think you're going to have to worry about — a party of *two* falling in love with your husband. She looks at Ted, who has drifted back to sleep. He's starting to get the teeniest bit of a double chin — filling out and settling back into middle age since he moved back into their house.

Elinor nods at Toby. She can't say *It's all right*, because it isn't all right. Certainly not until she speaks to the neurologist.

"Toby, we're going to the waiting area until the police get here," Gina says, turning Toby toward the door. She looks back at Elinor. "We'll be out there."

Roger sidles into the room, nodding hello to Gina. "Hey." He waves to Elinor. "Dr. Mackey doing any better?"

"Hopefully," Elinor says. "We still don't have much information."

"My car's at the mall."

"I can give you a ride later," Elinor tells him.

"Cool," Roger says.

Gina stops just outside the room. "Wait. You two *know* each other?" She points to Roger, then Elinor.

"I work for the Mackeys," Roger says. "I clean their house. Mrs. Mackey thought I could tutor Toby."

Gina puts her hands on her hips, trying to comprehend this information. "*Why?*"

"Gee, I don't know," Elinor says. "Maybe to help you find a math tutor other than my husband? Maybe so your son would stop calling my house?"

"Toby, did you call —"

"See, it wasn't *all* my fault," Toby protests, untangling himself from his mother's arms.

"You're not off the hook, buddy," Gina says, pushing him out of sight down the hall.

"I'll be out there, too, I guess," Roger grumbles, following them.

Elinor sits in the chair beside Ted's bed, a whoosh of air shooting up around her. Although this may be the oddest day of her life, she doesn't believe anything will ever really surprise her again after her miscarriage. The first miscarriage she could comprehend — it had been quite early in the pregnancy. But the second one, after they'd seen the heartbeat, *twice*, and graduated from the IVF clinic.

Ted shifts and smiles up at her.

"Do you remember what happened?" Elinor asks him. "At the mall?"

"Unfortunately. Gina's insane boyfriend stabbed me and I fell and hit my head." He licks his lips, swallows. His voice is hoarse. "I'm sorry."

Elinor shakes her head. "The main thing is that you're okay." Ted doesn't owe her any more apologies. She sent Roger to meet Gina, and Toby sent Ted after them. Elinor reaches for a pink plastic cup with a straw in it, and holds it to Ted's mouth so he can drink. He sips water, closing his eyes and swallowing, his face relaxing with gratitude.

"You cause quite a reaction in people," she tells Ted. "A ten-year-old is in love with you, and Kid Rock is insane with the idea of your touching his woman."

"Oh, God." Ted closes his eyes.

"The neurologist should *be* here," Elinor adds. She doesn't tell Ted about the ER doctor's words: *a blow to the head of some concern.* "And a detective is coming to interview you."

"Oh." Ted sounds disappointed. "I was hoping it was all over with. Can't I go soon? How long have I been sleeping?"

"Maybe an hour," Elinor says. "Do you remember the MRI?"

"I hate that blasted thing. It's like being in your coffin." He motions for more water, and she helps him drink. "I was dreaming," he tells her. "I was dreaming that you and I were driving — on some kind of road trip — and we couldn't find our exit."

Elinor thinks, *We took the wrong exit months ago.*

Finally the neurologist arrives. Elinor watches as the doctor bends over the bed and peers into Ted's pupils with a pencil-thin light. Once again, she's astonished by the youthfulness of physicians these days. She tries to do the math in her head to figure out how many years of experience this guy could possibly have.

"You're lucky," the doctor reports. He's tall and athletic looking, with cropped hair and large hands.

"I guess so," Ted replies tentatively. He's sitting up now, and his speech is clear.

"Excuse me," the doctor says to Elinor, smiling mildly. She realizes she's hovering too close and steps away. Ted follows the neurologist's finger back and forth, then up and down. Next, he answers a series of questions about the date and time and where he is and who is president.

And do you remember that you're in love with Gina? Elinor thinks. *And do you still love your wife? You do, don't you? But not in the same way?*

"Good." The doctor pulls a stool on wheels up to the side of Ted's bed and motions for Elinor to have a seat. "We were concerned," he says, looking from Elinor to Ted, "because of your loss of consciousness, followed by your brief state of confusion. However, the MRI doesn't look too bad. You have a small hematoma, but beyond that goose egg, I don't see any significant swelling of the brain. Still, with a trauma like this, coupled with the stab wound, we'll keep you overnight. I've got you on some medication that will prevent you from having a seizure, which is a remote possibility."

"You're *okay*," Elinor says to Ted. This is meant to be a statement, but it comes out with the uncertainty of a question. She wants confirmation from Ted that this is essentially what the doctor just said. Everything is going to be all right. Medically, at least. She touches Ted's shoulder, feeling the heat of his skin through the thin hospital gown.

Ted raises his eyebrows and nods timidly, as though he doesn't feel entirely *okay* just yet.

Elinor straightens his covers. She feels the need to be touching the bed at all times.

"He passed the *who-what-where-when* test just fine," the doctor confirms. "His post-traumatic amnesia lasted less than an hour, which is a good sign."

"Thank you," she says to the doctor, feeling her voice crack with gratefulness.

"I didn't actually *do* anything." The neurologist smiles. "But you're welcome."

"A swollen head." Ted laughs weakly, reaching up to touch the protruding egg shape just above his right temple.

But it isn't true. While he's an excellent doctor, a good athlete, and a handsome man, he isn't arrogant. This is one thing Elinor has always appreciated about her husband.

A new nurse comes on duty — a younger, less terse woman with a long black braid down her back. Elinor convinces the nurse to let her stay overnight in Ted's room on the foldout chair. Soon the police detective shows up and asks Elinor to step out of the room so he can speak with Ted privately.

The hallway waiting area is decorated like a living room, with couches, chairs, and softly lit lamps. Care has been taken to transform the hospital milieu. Still, under the pretty Oriental carpet, the hospital floor gleams, glossy and institutional. Elinor takes a seat two rows of chairs behind Gina and Toby. Roger slouches in an opposite corner, reading a well-worn paperback. They are all sitting as far away from each other as possible, without actually leaving the seating area, which looks to Elinor like a set for a play or TV show. She'd like to call Kat, but a nearby sign picturing a cell phone with a slash through it glares down at her.

"Hey! I have the list of the things I want," Elinor hears Toby tell his mother. "The one you *told* me to make," he adds accusingly. He reaches to pull a notebook from the backpack leaning against the side of his chair.

"Not right now, sweetheart." Gina tips back her head, her hair tumbling over the edge of the chair, and massages her temples. "We'll talk later."

"Okay, I'll just tell you the number one thing." Toby rips out the page. "I want Dr. Mackey to go *with* us to New York City."

"New York City?" Elinor blurts, giving up on pretending to read a tattered issue of *Family Circle*.

Gina sits up straighter in her chair and looks to her son. "Toby, remember when we talked about how you can't have *everything* you want? People aren't things that you can *have*."

Elinor looks back to an article on one-bowl cupcakes. In a picture, the cupcakes are cleverly decorated for Halloween with orange icing, candy corn, and black plastic spiders.

"So quit asking me what I want, okay?" Toby whines. He throws his foot out to the side of his chair and pounds the carpet with his heel. "*Just quit asking me!*"

A tired-looking woman across a coffee table from them stuffs her knitting into a plastic bag and gets up to leave.

"Okay." Gina shushes Toby and tries to draw him to her. "We're going to talk to the police and then we're going home." She dips into her purse. "Here's two dollars. Go to the vending machines and get yourself something. Candy, whatever you want." Gina turns to point to a hallway, which is apparently where the vending machines are, and catches Elinor watching them.

Elinor looks back to her magazine. Toby launches into a full-scale fit, crying and kicking and pounding his fists.

"You probably think I'm a terrible mother," Gina says to Elinor. She raises her voice to be heard, but her tone is flat and without emotion.

Elinor is startled by this candor. She closes the magazine and looks past Gina, out the window at a patch of blue sky pierced by a palm tree. "You probably think I'm a terrible wife."

Roger snaps his book shut and rubs his eyes with the heels of his palms.

"What if Dr. Mackey *dies*?" Toby wails. He drops the money Gina gave him on the floor and doubles over, so that Elinor can no longer see his head.

"Toby!" Elinor snaps at the boy. "Look at me." The magazine slides out of her lap and smacks the floor. Toby turns slowly toward her. His face is mottled with red splotches from crying. "Dr. Mackey is going to be *fine.* The neurologist came and told us so. The MRI was fine."

"That's right," Gina agrees.

What do you know! Elinor picks up the magazine. She flips through the pages, trying to maintain her cool, searching for the goofy plastic spiders, which had soothed her nerves a moment ago.

Toby turns from his mother, crosses his arms on the opposite arm of his chair, and rests his head, crying quietly. Gina rubs circles on his back. They are silent, but connected by Gina's touch. Elinor can't blame Toby for melting down. The kid's been dealt a crappy hand — a single working mother who had an affair with a married man, an unloving father in another state. Elinor's husband is the number one thing this ten-year-old boy wants in his life. And a ten-year-old boy is probably the number one thing Elinor wants in *her* life. The truth is, she's a little afraid of having an infant. She's never admitted this to anyone. Not even Kat. She's afraid she might not be qualified to handle something so fragile, afraid of the sleep-deprivation crazies. Afraid she'll fail at breast-feeding. Afraid she'll do a bad job in Ted's eyes. Yet she can't wait to have a child in elementary school. Someone to decorate the Halloween cupcakes with. If, as Kat did, she had to make cupcakes for her kids' school, she'd try to get her kids to decorate them with her. Their cupcakes wouldn't be nearly as neat as the ones in the magazine. Theirs would be crazier, messier, more fun. She wants to be more fun. She supposes there's a difference between being funny and fun. Gina is probably fun.

Sex, weed, stir-fires, accommodating yoga poses. Elinor is funny, but lately she hasn't been much fun.

The detective emerges from Ted's hospital room. He speaks to Gina, Roger, and Elinor individually, then to all of them at once, in a semicircle around the coffee table. He has an inky black mustache, and Elinor licks her upper lip, remembering the sensation of Noah's mustache. While he's probably seen it all, the detective seems impressed by the details of the afternoon as he repeats them: Elinor encouraged Roger to contact Gina to tutor Toby, who told Ted to go to the mall to meet Stan, only there is no Stan, but there's a Shane, whom Ms. Ellison has filed a restraining order against, for previous drunken and disorderly behavior. Then the "actual altercation" occurred, including a stabbing, which led to a head injury. *Right*, everyone agrees. The officer reports that Shane has been booked without bail.

"Do we need to press charges?" Gina asks.

"No, ma'am. I automatically send the report with the assault charge to the district attorney. A prosecuting attorney is assigned on behalf of the state. Would you like to press additional charges for violation of the restraining order?"

Gina nods.

Elinor is glad she stuck to civil law. Still, she wouldn't mind pressing a few charges herself. Against Shane for stabbing Ted. Against Gina for sleeping with Ted. Against Toby for calling her house repeatedly. Against Noah for cutting down her tree. Against God for taking her baby. This is what she doesn't like about practicing law — forever trying to enforce justice, to fight life's unfairness. It takes so much energy, and somehow seems to miss the point.

"He is a threat to my son and I," Gina says.

Me, not I, Elinor thinks. *You're prettier. I'm smarter.* She wrings her hands. *I'm pettier. I'm pretty petty!* She feels exhaustion tug at her from the earth's core.

"And clearly he's a threat to society," Gina adds. "He's not the way he used to be." She sounds genuinely sad about this.

"It's not *your* fault," Roger says.

Why are men always racing to Gina's rescue?

"Well, I'm sorry anyway," Gina tells Roger. "And you seem like you would have been a good tutor."

The cop narrows his eyes. He opens his mouth to ask Roger something, then seems to decide he doesn't need to. He pats the surface of the coffee table, which is brown Formica made to look like wood. "I'll let you all go now. I know it's been a long day."

They all stand. Gina turns to leave, tugging Toby behind her by the hand. He begins to cry again. Gina bends to hoist him into her arms. He's a big boy to carry, but Gina seems strong. Elinor is surprised that they are leaving. She thought they would hang around — say good-bye to Ted, linger. She imagined she might be jockeying for position with them throughout Ted's hospital stay. Whether she likes it or not, she realizes she has gotten used to sharing her husband with these two. She watches Gina release Toby so he can walk and they amble down the hall — Toby's head resting against his mother's narrow waist, Gina's arm draped lazily across her son's back. Although they are leaving the hospital, getting smaller and smaller as they shuffle away, they are inevitably following Ted and Elinor home.

CHAPTER
TWENTY-ONE

As Elinor drives home to grab a few things for her night at the hospital, she calls Kat to let her know that Ted's going to be okay. She doesn't want to recap the soap opera while driving, so they agree to meet at the house.

By the time she turns onto their street, the sun has dipped over the hill and the ginkgo tree — bright yellow, now that fall is here — seems to hold all the remaining light of the day. Elinor parks in the driveway and climbs out of her car to water it. She unloops and drags the hose across the lawn. Probably she's been overcompensating with the watering, but she's desperate for something to take care of other than corporate mergers.

People tend to flood the surface without ever reaching the roots, she remembers Noah explaining, showing her how to adjust the hose to a slow trickle. Elinor watches the soil turn dark and moist. Maybe she shouldn't have been so dismissive of Noah and his tree trivia. A plane rumbles overhead. The neighbors' house across the street is still decorated for Halloween. Little blow-up bats flutter in the thin branches of the birch trees. Elinor is always surprised and excited by how many trick-or-treaters come to their door every year. It's a painfully good neighborhood for kids.

"Tree's looking great," Kat says from behind. "Tell me more about Ted."

Elinor relays the sordid details of the showdown at the mall, followed by the neurologist's prognosis.

Kat shakes her head. "Thank God Ted's going to be all right." She looks at Elinor. "*Roger* and *Gina?*" she asks, skeptical but non-judgmental. "Two birds with one stone?"

"Theoretically. My short-lived matchmaking career. Maybe the only thing I *can* do is work in an office."

One of the ginkgo's scalloped leaves spirals to the ground, like a tiny yellow fan. "You know those are *supposed* to fall off now," Kat says with concern.

Elinor nods. While the oak provided more shade, she has to admit that the ginkgo is prettier. The oak was gnarled and arthritic, while the ginkgo is as graceful and demure as a geisha.

"Hey!" Elinor hands Kat the hose. The calamity of the day made her forget the present she picked up for her in town this morning. "I know it's not your birthday yet, but I don't feel like waiting." She scoops a little velvet box out of her purse and passes it to Kat.

Kat hands back the hose. "What . . ." She takes the box. "Oh!" she exclaims as she opens it.

Elinor spent weeks searching for the emerald earrings. While Kat's ears are pierced, she hardly ever bothers with earrings, which she insists get in the way. Finally, Elinor asked the jeweler downtown to design something with lever-back hoops that wouldn't be too dangly, so Kat could wear them while running and wrestling with her boys.

"Wow." Kat holds up one of the small white-gold earrings, admiring the emerald on its end. She struggles a little sliding it into her earlobe. "Ouch! What's the occasion?"

"You being you. Putting up with me." Elinor turns to hug her friend, accidentally watering her leg, making them both yelp with surprise.

Sleep smothers Ted. But it isn't a restful sleep. Since his body can't toss and turn, his mind does. In his troublesome dreams, he recreates the scene at the mall with more violent outcomes. Ted stabs Shane. Shane stabs Toby. Toby is sprawled on the cream-colored marble floor, his eyes closed, his mouth open, blood everywhere. It's Toby, but it doesn't look like Toby. It is a different boy.

"I'm a doctor!" Ted shouts. The crowd of strangers parts to let him get to the boy.

"I know," a voice says.

Ted feels the familiar pinch of the blood-pressure cuff.

"What practice are you in?" A nurse hovers at his side. Mickey and Minnie Mouse are dancing on her pink scrubs.

"What?" Ted's tongue is too big for his mouth.

"You were telling me that you're a doctor. What kind?"

"Oh, a podiatrist." Usually, Ted feels sorry for hospital patients because they're always woken up. It's impossible to get any rest. But he's glad this nurse stirred him from his dreams.

"Your wife just went home to get a few things." The nurse smiles and removes the cuff. "You're doing great, but she'd like to spend the night with you."

"Oh, that's not necessary," Ted says. But he's happy that Elinor's coming back. He wishes the nurse would stay with him until El gets here — help keep him awake. The woman heads for the door. Ted says, "Would . . . ?" He almost asks the nurse to sit with him. How ridiculous. Hospitals are so understaffed as it is. And he's a grown man. A doctor!

"Can I get you anything?" the nurse asks. "A Popsicle?"

"Popsicle," Ted repeats. The word comes out clearly as he says it. He's relieved to no longer have the sensation of slurring his speech. "Popsicle," he says again, the two *P*'s making a pleasing *pop* sound. The nurse mistakes his enthusiasm for a *yes* and brings him one.

At home, Elinor showers and changes into sweats. She'll curl up in the chair beside Ted's hospital bed and read. She collects a few magazines, and her paperback of *The Moviegoer*. She and Kat have started their own two-person "greatest hits" book club, trading picks of their favorite college novels. Elinor's been pulling old paperbacks off the narrow top shelf in her study and turning through their brown, brittle pages, savoring their slightly moldy smell and the fact that the stories she loves most are still there, word for word. All is not lost. As she slides Walker Percy into a canvas bag along with a bottle of water, she looks at their bed, neatly made. At one point, she thought they should throw out the unlucky mattress and buy a new one. That's when she and Ted started checking into hotel rooms on weekends, trying to make getting pregnant fun. Once they even set up their tent in the backyard and slept outside. They zipped their sleeping bags together, made love, and fell asleep quickly. But they awoke at two thirty achy and damp, and crept back inside. Elinor had become so superstitious, she believed that if they had lain in the tent until dawn she would have conceived. You weren't supposed to be leaping up at all hours of the night.

Now, as she sits on the end of the bed to pull on her Ugg boots, something crunches under the duvet. Elinor gets up and peels back the covers to find a scrap of eggshell on her side. What the hell? Are birds laying eggs in their bed? The piece of shell is white and bumpy, with a few coffee grounds smudged on it. Maybe it traveled in from the kitchen floor, stuck on her sock. She always seems to be tracking things into the covers. She balances the shell on the nightstand, unsure of why she doesn't want to throw it away.

Leaning back on the bed, she peers into their closet. When Ted moved out, he did a big purge, dragging many of his old clothes, shoes, books, and CDs to the Salvation Army. Although he's moved back in, his clutter-free side of the closet seems temporary. *They* seem temporary — their marriage an experiment as fragile as embryos in a lab.

Ted's shoes have been winnowed to six pairs — three sets of loafers, a pair of Tevas, hiking boots, and sneakers. Elinor realizes that she can stand the notion of Ted leaving, of him moving out of the house again. Having seen him prone in a hospital bed, she knows now that what she *can't* bear is the thought of him dying.

It hurts not to follow your heart. Elinor sees this in Ted's face every day. She's not sure if he even realizes that he's in love with Gina. If you *do* follow your heart, it will likely hurt others. But she's not hurt or angry anymore. Just sad, which feels less crazy. She'll always love Ted. Even when she hated him, she loved Ted. And she believes they'll always be friends to some degree. She's pretty sure this is wisdom, and not cockiness or exhaustion. It's easy to love someone, when you get right down to it. What's really hard is to have compassion for them.

She stands up to close the folding closet doors, the slatted wood creaking shut as his sneakers and her clogs disappear.

The next time Ted awakens, he discovers that his sutures have burst and his stab wound is bleeding. A fried-egg shape stain of blood covers his gown.

"*Oh!*" The sound of his own voice startles him. Then he laughs. The Popsicle was cherry, and he fell asleep eating it. He reaches for the call button to get help with the mess, then decides against it. Everyone says how doctors are the worst pain-in-the-ass patients in the world. He doesn't want to live up to that reputation.

Besides, Gina will be here soon. No, not Gina! Elinor! *Elinor* will be here soon.

Ted chews the end of the Popsicle stick, the wood soft between his teeth. He closes his eyes and allows himself to imagine Gina's embrace — how, after they made love, she would massage the small of his back, his sacrum, then knead her fingers up either side of his spine. It was a heavenly massage that ended with her fingers vigorously rubbing his scalp until the stress of the day would tingle up and off to the ceiling.

As Elinor passes through the kitchen toward the garage, she notices the red light blinking on the answering machine. She presses the button and the voice of her OB, Dr. Kolcheck, fills the room. The pathology report from the miscarriage came back. It was a trisomy 15, which is *uniformally lethal*. "In other words," the doctor says, "there was no chance of survival for the fetus." She apologizes for leaving this information on the machine, but she wants Elinor and Ted to know that there was absolutely nothing they did wrong. Elinor's eyes fill when she hears the words *female fetus*. A girl. She won't tell Ted tonight. She'll wait until he's released from the hospital and feeling better.

They would have had a girl. You see, she imagined a boy. That was the problem. Cowboy boots and overalls and . . . *no*, she will not do this.

Dr. K is cut off by the answering machine, but then the second message is from her, too. "There's more information I'd like to share with you," she says. "So

371

please feel free to page me at this number anytime until eleven o'clock tonight. I'll be up."

Elinor writes down the number, dreading the thought of *more* information. From now on, she'd like *less* information. Fewer reality checks. Still, she dials the phone.

"Oh God," Elinor says when Dr. Kolcheck answers cheerfully. "I'm so sorry to disturb you during the evening."

Dr. K lowers her voice. Elinor hears a door close. "No, you saved me. I am at the most *boring* party. All these people talk about is wine. Vintage this and vintage that. I mean drink it and shaddup!"

Elinor laughs. It would have been great if Dr. Kolcheck had delivered their baby.

"Listen." Dr. Kolcheck is more serious now. "Because the miscarriage was due to a chromosomal anomaly, I ordered a test for a rare condition that I was pretty certain you don't have. But surprisingly, you do."

"Why am I *not* surprised?" Elinor squeezes her eyes shut.

"I know," the doctor says sympathetically. "It's called a balanced translocation and it is *completely* harmless to you. We wouldn't even know about it if it weren't for this test. You'd never sense a thing."

"Wha — ?" Elinor sits on a stool at the counter. This is just the type of information she doesn't want to have to assimilate anymore.

"It's very rare. Only one in fifty thousand people have the combination that you have. The correct number of chromosomes is there, but two pieces of chromosomal material are swapped. In your case, numbers three and fifteen. It's as though you've got one spoon in your fork slot, and one fork in your spoon slot. It's completely harmless to the patient. You're healthy. The problem is . . ."

There is always a problem. Elinor doesn't want to be a *patient*. She wants to be a *person*. A person without a medical file as thick as a phone book.

". . . it increases the odds of miscarriage and lowers the odds of conception. So, before we move forward, I'd like you and Ted to go for genetic counseling. I'm out of my league here, but I know of a great doc in town who can present you with more specific statistical odds for conception and miscarriage."

Elinor holds a pen poised over a pad of paper, but all she's managed to write is: *3, 15, swapped, silverware.* Little bits of information stick in her head: *One in fifty thousand people. Fork in your spoon slot.* And the words *move on.*

She drops the pen. She and Ted shouldn't go for genetic counseling. Not another consultation. Elinor pictures them sitting in chairs at another doctor's desk, behind another closed door, looking across another wide expanse of blotter at another well-meaning medic in a white coat. She imagines her head dropping with a *thunk* onto the genetic counselor doctor's desk, and how she might bang her forehead over and over until she's got a goose egg bigger than Ted's.

"We'll see," she tells Dr. Kolcheck.

"I know, you probably need some time to digest all this. You're a good candidate to try donor eggs. The great thing about that is, time is less of a factor. You can wait until it feels right. I've had some patients who've been very happy with this choice."

"Uh-huh," Elinor says weakly. She's learned that it can be a mistake to wait for the right time. You have to be more spontaneous. And there will never be a right time for her and Ted to continue with these treatments. She can't imagine Ted giving her another injection at their kitchen counter. She can't imagine him stressing over producing yet another sample in a plastic cup at the clinic. They should adopt.

Elinor should adopt. Ted would do it for her, but he's wary, and she doesn't want to have to convince him. It shouldn't have to be a fight anymore. A fight to save the marriage. A fight to have a family. (*Do you guys have kids? We're trying! Trying, trying, trying!*)

Elinor should take that overseas assignment for her company in Dublin. She should find Oscar Wilde's house and sit on the front stoop and drink a Guinness and wrap up the merger and then come home and adopt a baby. A flicker of fear seizes her. Will they let her adopt without a husband? Ted would go with her to Ireland, but she knows he would prefer to use his vacation time to scubadive in Australia. Still, he'd go to Ireland to try to make her happy. He'd do almost anything to try to make Elinor happy. Yet he deserves happiness, too.

Dr. Kolcheck says again how sorry she is about this news, and she'll be glad to see Ted and Elinor in her office after they visit the genetic counselor. Elinor thanks her.

374

"I'll make an appointment," she lies, not wanting Dr. Kolcheck to feel bad. They say good-bye.

Elinor looks at the telephone. Instead of calling the genetic counselor, she will call the mediation lawyer again. For a moment she isn't sad about the prospect of a divorce. She knows she'll be devastated later — probably as early as tomorrow. Perhaps even sadder than she felt about the miscarriage. But right now a clarity of vision places her outside of herself ten years from now. *Oh, my first husband. He was a really good guy.*

She's the one who has to decide they should divorce. Ted would stick it out, stick by her, no matter what. She looks at the pen and little pad on the counter. A year ago, if she were sitting in this chair at this moment, she would have started a list: *Ted follow-up doc app'ts. Sked genetic counselor. Donor eggs? Research. Timeline? Buy books to get Ted interested in adoption.*

Elinor's shoulders drop with a lowered sense of ambition that feels as liberating as a stiff drink. She'll have to phone her mom with the news. Retrieving the pen, she writes: *Dublin?* Then she gets up and turns on the light over the kitchen sink and brings in the mail from the box. Overdue medical bills. The beginning of the onslaught of holiday catalogs. She dumps it all in the empty fruit bowl.

In the bathroom, Elinor brushes her teeth, working to get the bad hospital coffee sludge off her tongue. Maybe foreign adoption would be best. Russia, perhaps. She hopes she can adopt more than one child. She already knows she's going to be one of those

375

mothers who lets the kids sleep in the bed. Kids, cats, toys, storybooks. She hopes they'll all fall asleep together every night reading.

In the meantime, if she's going to be single, she wouldn't mind sleeping with Noah again. She can imagine dating him casually. Are you allowed to do such a thing when you're forty? It's very likely that Noah has met someone else. If he has, she'll wish him well. She wishes Noah well. She wishes Ted well. She wishes Gina would gain thirty pounds and develop a mammoth zit. "An oozy carbuncle," she says to the bathroom mirror, narrowing her eyes, relishing this moment of pettiness. She does *not* have to like her husband's mistress or whatever the hell she is or was or will be in the future. She combs her hair back with her fingers and flicks out the light.

Returning to the bedroom for a sweater, she thinks about her conversation with Dr. Kolcheck. *A balanced translocation*. A fork in her spoon slot! She's a screwed-up silverware drawer. Yet there's solace in learning that something is *tangibly* wrong. A diagnosis other than *you're old*. Ted will understand the translocation thing better than she does. He might even push for the genetic counseling. He'll want to do it for her. She grabs a collection of Dave Barry essays from Ted's nightstand. She'll read them to him in the hospital. It is his favorite book. He needs to laugh. They both do.

Acknowledgments

First, thanks to my agent Laurie Fox, the most generous person I know. I am always grateful for her guidance and friendship. Thanks to my wonderfully smart editor Amy Einhorn, and to all the kind folks at Warner Books, particularly Jennifer Romanello, for always making me laugh, and to Karen Torres and Martha Otis for their unyielding support. Thanks, too, to Linda Chester for her cheerleading. Without these people I'd be eating burned microwave popcorn in a cubicle by day, and writing in a drafty garret by night.

Thanks to my San Francisco writers group — the best readers and writers I know: Rich Register, Gordon Jack, Susan Edmiston, Cheyenne Richards, Karen Roy, Laurence Howard, and Julie Knight. And much gratitude to my writing partner Vicky Mlyniec.

Thanks to Kim and Dr. Jim Ratcliff, to Julie Dunger Anderson, and to Wyatt Nelson. Without them I wouldn't know anything about hammertoes, restraining orders, or the Xbox.

Thanks to savvy readers Gail K. Baker, Eileen Bordy, Emily Griffin, Aimee Prall, Nicolle Henneuse, Cindy Walker, and copy editor Laura Jorstad. Without them this book would be filled with blunders and bloopers.

As always, thanks to Karen Eberle, and especially to Anders Wallgren for his moral and technical support.

Without him I'd still be writing with a Smith Corona and bottle of Wite-Out and living in a van down by the river.

A special thank-you to Ellen Sussman, for always offering just the right balance of encouragement and ass-kicking. Without her, I'd still be writing chapter four of this book.

Thanks to Popoki, Piglet, and Einstein, who are always willing to discuss the finer points of literature over turkey treats and tea.

And always thanks to Frank Baldwin for that very first push of encouragement. Without him I'd still be writing *Good Grief*.

Finally, thanks to the independent bookstores across the country for their support of new authors and emerging literature. Without them, reading wouldn't be such a wonderfully diverse pleasure.

Also available in ISIS Large Print:

Lucky Girl

Fiona Gibson

Everyone always told Stella Moon how lucky she was to have a famous dad.

She just wished he was more like everyone else's. And when her mum died, and he withdrew to his allotment leaving Stella and her brother alone to play in rusty cars and exist for a whole week on Black Forest gateaux, she didn't feel lucky at all.

Now in her thirties Stella has made sure her life couldn't be further from her chaotic upbringing, with a strict routine as a music teacher and a peaceful, tidy home. Until two noisy little girls move in next door.

At first, she feels besieged. The girls hound her, bearing sticky gifts of edible jewellery and firing personal questions about her mum, her dad and her love life. But it's their friendship that helps her to confront the truth about her own childhood and start living life to the full.

ISBN 978-0-7531-7778-5 (hb)
ISBN 978-0-7531-7779-2 (pb)

Plain Truth

Jodi Picoult

The discovery of a dead infant in a barn shakes the Amish community in Lancaster County to its core. But the police investigation leads to a more shocking disclosure: circumstantial evidence suggests that 18-year-old Katie Fisher, an unmarried Amish woman believed to be the newborn's mother, took the child's life.

When Ellie Hathaway, a disillusioned big city attorney, arrives to defend Katie, two cultures collide — and, for the first time in her high profile career, Ellie faces a system of justice very different from her own. Delving deep into the world of those who live "plain", Ellie must find a way to reach Katie on her terms.

As she unravels the tangled case, Ellie also looks deep within — to confront her own fears and desires when a man from her past comes back into her life.

ISBN 978-0-7531-7594-1 (hb)
ISBN 978-0-7531-7595-8 (pb)

Midnight Cactus

Bella Pollen

On the run from her claustrophobic marriage in London, Alice Coleman moves her two small children to a ghost town in the Arizona desert — and there finds an escape she hadn't thought possible.

But the mythic Southwest has room for more than one fugitive. In the dusty, alien atmosphere, it seems that everyone — from Benjamin, the town's loyal caretaker, to the laconic and mysterious Duval — has something to hide.

And as winter moves to scorching summer, what seemed idyllic turns deadly as Alice is drawn deeper into an obsessive quest for revenge, until finally she must decide how far she is willing to go.

ISBN 978-0-7531-7732-7 (hb)
ISBN 978-0-7531-7733-4 (pb)

Love & Other Impossible Pursuits

Ayelet Waldman

Is Emilia the wicked stepmother incarnate? Passionately in love with her husband, Emilia has a secret, guilty loathing for her precocious little stepson, William — a 40-year-old in a five-year-old's body, whom she picks up from nursery every Wednesday afternoon. He is lactose intolerant, she feeds him dairy products; he mustn't get cold, she pushes him — accidentally — into a pond in Central Park. How can she forgive William for living, when her own cherished child has gone?

A candid, raw, humorous and emotional novel about family in today's fractured society.

ISBN 978-0-7531-7682-5 (hb)
ISBN 978-0-7531-7683-2 (pb)

Goodnight Nobody

Jennifer Weiner

From the author of *In Her Shoes*.

Who said life in the suburbs was sleepy?

Kate Klein loved her life in New York, but when she was robbed at gunpoint on the streets of Manhattan her husband decided it was time to get out of the city.

Cue a move to the upmarket suburbia of Upchurch, Connecticut, where the immaculate supermums routinely snub her and her husband is hardly ever home. Kate's life revolves around looking after her children and trying to keep up with the other mothers, at least until the mysterious death of Kitty Cavanaugh, the neighbourhood Queen Bee.

Kate is drawn deep into the dead woman's double life when she launches her own investigation with the help of her best friend Janie, and former flame, Evan McKenna.

ISBN 978-0-7531-7636-8 (hb)
ISBN 978-0-7531-7637-5 (pb)

ISIS publish a wide range of books in large print, from fiction to biography. Any suggestions for books you would like to see in large print or audio are always welcome. Please send to the Editorial Department at:

ISIS Publishing Limited
7 Centremead
Osney Mead
Oxford OX2 0ES

A full list of titles is available free of charge from:

Ulverscroft Large Print Books Limited

(UK)
The Green
Bradgate Road, Anstey
Leicester LE7 7FU
Tel: (0116) 236 4325

(Australia)
P.O. Box 314
St Leonards
NSW 1590
Tel: (02) 9436 2622

(USA)
P.O. Box 1230
West Seneca
N.Y. 14224-1230
Tel: (716) 674 4270

(Canada)
P.O. Box 80038
Burlington
Ontario L7L 6B1
Tel: (905) 637 8734

(New Zealand)
P.O. Box 456
Feilding
Tel: (06) 323 6828

Details of **ISIS** complete and unabridged audio books are also available from these offices. Alternatively, contact your local library for details of their collection of **ISIS** large print and unabridged audio books.